GHOST CHASES THE HORIZON

MIKE MALLOW

WEST VANDALIA LLC
NORTH MANKATO, MN

A GHOST CHASES THE HORIZON
First edition: October 2025
© 2025 Mike Mallow

The characters and events portrayed in this book are fictitious, except where historically documented. Any resemblance to actual persons, living or dead, are otherwise entirely coincidental.
No artificial intelligence was used in the creation of this story.

Editing by Ashley Earley (Earley Editing, LLC)
and Jeni Conrad and Tara Wine-Queen (Second Set Author Services, LLC)
Consultant support provided by Martha Williams,
Laura Moyers Fears, Kelsea Reeves, and Brad Cook
Editorial support provided by JP Nutt, Jessica Burkhart, Joel Brigham, and Derek Krissoff
Additional support by Jason Smith, Sharon Martin, Jean Flanagan, Dana Fraedrich, and John & Michelle Connor (Full Quiver Consulting, LLC)
Cover, logo, and formatting by Mike Mallow (West Vandalia, LLC)
Printed in the U.S.A.
ISBN: 979-8-9926451-0-1 (Paperback)
ISBN: 979-8-9926451-2-5 (Hardback)
Printed by West Vandalia LLC

To those discarded and forgotten by history.
May your names be uncovered and raised high.

In 1999, off-duty law enforcement officers damaged the interior of the shuttered Weston Hospital during a series of illicit paintball games. Though this and other events from Weston's history are factual, the people portrayed in this story are not. The truth is often more outlandish than the fiction, and separating the two would be its own kind of madness.

"Belief in ghosts is not of modern origin, but reaches back to the childhood of man, and the night of time. Try as they may, skepticism, disbelief, and civilization cannot dislodge nor efface the belief in ghosts, as ghosts exist and have their origin in man. They are in him and of him, his own progeny. They follow him through age and race and, whether he does or does not believe in them, will, according to his kind, follow or precede him as do his shadows."

– H. W. PERCIVAL

From "Ghosts"

Published in *The Word*

Vol. 17, No. 4, July 1913

THE KIRKBRIDE RESTED

It was 1905 when the state of West Virginia took Henrietta Tidewater's ovaries in an experimental surgery. The twenty-year-old pleasured in assembling items from diagrams, reading, and blonde mustaches—the curlier, the better. Henrietta disliked tomatoes and language barriers.

It was 1935 when Eugene JD Spangold urinated on the floor of the Floyd Funeral Home. The forty-eight-year-old admired forged glassware, the actress Janet Gaynor, and books read aloud by his wife—the wordier, the better. Eugene disliked alcoholism and the overzealous.

It was 1999 when Brittany Jean Loughry sustained a permanent limp after falling from an unstable ladder. The eighteen-year-old enjoyed fruit juice beverages, post-grunge alternative music, and abandoned buildings—the larger, the better. Brittany disliked early mornings and vintage motorcycles.

It was 2019 when Neil Hutchence stood before a moving train in rural Minnesota. The forty-year-old appreciated manicured lawns, green tea-infused drinks, and solitude—the quieter, the better. He disliked faulty light fixtures and doors with handles.

It was 1905. It was 1935. It was 1999. It was 2019.

It was my curse to see those years all at once.

I was somewhere in the years beyond, but I had been so preoccupied with playing with shadows that I had lost track of the true year. The fact I understood numbers at all was impressive enough for a structure never meant to count, or think, or know, or remember.

I was the main administrative building on the campus of the former Weston Hospital. The Kirkbride was my unofficial moniker. In my advanced years, I developed a particular talent for knowing and remembering. Structures of a centennial age developed unexplained sentience, and stone buildings could be chatty when conscious talents matured.

It was raining now. It had rained for days, and the absence of lightning gave me the notion it was early spring. Hot and cold currents had yet to irritate the atmosphere. It may have been late autumn. *No.* The trees had been leaf-barren for a season, and snow blankets were not long removed from Weston lawns.

But what was the year? Neil was old, but still alive for now. He recently uncovered the truth about Henrietta, and the news had returned to the campus within the day. An assistant manager joked about devoting a museum section to her, though it was not the first instance Neil's discoveries warranted addition to the collected history.

Neil had been inside recently, too, finally permitted access to the property after a decades-long ban for a physical altercation with a tour guide manager. Time was kind to him in the later years. What hair resided on his head had gone glassy gray, and wrinkles distorted his features, but he still had those distinct, deep-set eyes.

But this year? It was surely past 2063. West Virginia made a big to-do about its bicentennial. I was featured in the celebrations among the most prominent structures still in use.

It was after 2063. 2071? Maybe.

That was my final guess. It felt right. It was a sorry statement that time had now eluded the timeless, but in all my battles, the clock remained undefeated.

Regardless of the year, the campus remained famous for its hauntings. Casting projections in the empty rooms and corridors had only just started to slow in this late year. People still came for the thrills, though they were less interested in learning the history with each passing year. They did not know the secret—the truth of the matter.

It was not the ghosts that haunted, but the moments.

Ghosts did not seek the living. If they did, those sheeted and shackled spirits would find whom they sought with little effort. From my perspective, spirits were indifferent to their worldly counterparts and remained confined to a particular place. A place of tragedy, a place of sentiment, or a place where stone walls could capture a memory of someone once among the living.

No better place filled those requisites than this campus. It was tragic because of the horrors that had befallen the mentally ill community at any given time in history. It was sentimental in how ingrained my existence was in the history of Weston. My Gothic megastructure cast a long shadow upon the town from the Weston Hospital campus.

Though odd for a hospital, I was also part of the social scene. There were community dances in my auditorium, and the high school football team had exhibitions on the lawn. Elementary classes took field trips to learn about mental illness, but they often devolved into gawking, zoo-like, at those society considered undesirable.

Much of the community's prosperity and economy took root on the opposite side of the river. When my doors closed in 1994, I would have stood as a mausoleum to Weston's opulence if not for a new facility constructed on the opposite side of the property.

The hospital's vast campus had gone by many names throughout its history. Although first named Trans-Allegheny Lunatic Asylum, the name was never uttered during its operating years. It was West Virginia Hospital for the Insane in 1905, Weston State Hospital in 1935, and Weston Hospital by the time it closed in 1994. It remained with the final name until 2007, when my property was auctioned to a family who honored the site for its historical value. Only then was the campus's birth name, Trans-Allegheny, restored.

By the time the new owners began hosting tours, it had become clear there was something more notable about the property than its history.

I was the oldest and largest of the dozen buildings gracing the property. Within me was where the bulk of the hauntings transpired. Paranormal events became frequent throughout the hospital grounds as the surrounding buildings came into sentience.

My nickname, Kirkbride, was derived from the pioneer behind the building's architectural design. Doctor Thomas Story Kirkbride was an advocate for mental health. He believed that all a mentally ill patient required was sunlight and peace. The hospitals he developed were intended to be like resorts—luxury spaces where someone at odds with societal norms could relax and repair the broken pieces of their psyche. It was a humane gesture that gained traction, inspiring many hospitals to adopt Kirkbride's roadmap to recovery.

The brown and tan limestone blocks of my four-story structure grayed as they withstood the seasons. My walls stretched so far from one end to the other that it was difficult to capture the panorama. Additional ground-floor wards ran perpendicular to the face of my compound, forming an inverted comb. An eggshell-white clock tower, trimmed in a flush green, stood as the centerpiece. A spire matching the color climbed above the tower and proudly viewed Weston.

Three clock faces gave the hour to the east, north, and south, leaving the rear of the property timeless. The clocks themselves were not keeping correct account when the hospital shuttered. The hands moved, but operated with a different sense of time, never keeping the correct synchronization with the rest of the world. By the end of the millennium, each was keeping their own hours of reality.

The new owners decided the clock tower was too treacherous and affixed a padlock to the entrance. Its interior was the last of my exhaustive restoration, which was being completed this late year.

A lonely era followed the 1994 closure. This was the period in which I developed most in my consciousness. The joys and horrors of past events scratched moments into the architecture, and an unknown system operated as a rudimentary recording device. When people began visiting again, I had already begun to replay many etched events.

No one ever considered the hauntings to be more than one-sided affairs. The projections, the entities on the other side of the veil, were as spooked by their encounter with someone in the present. My old Kirkbride walls would hold onto most of their secrets, save the occasional glimpse. More than a peek could lead to an existential cataclysm, and enough madness had already passed through these halls.

What I could witness once extended far beyond the current era, but I lacked the discernment to know what type of warning to broadcast from the years beyond.

Replaying projections did not come easily. I tried, failed, toiled in the practice, and got better. I often faltered and sharpened my abilities on lesser events, which were made more profound by the experiment. The era was lonely, and in the suffocating air and constant silence, I began to play back the moments I could recall. I replicated sights, sounds, and smells, then put them into reality. Shadows walked down long halls and disappeared into empty rooms. Nodes of light danced in corners of wards and sometimes took the shape of a human who tarried there or had yet to tarry. The retelling was imperfect, never verbatim, and never certain of the time stamp. Still, I tried.

I willed forth unknown things within those elements. I tried to forget the horrors, attempting to disregard the lobotomized, the electrocuted, the raped, and the murdered, but they were all there. Their tragedies had bled into the bedrock and refused to fade from memory. For all the good I tried to project, wicked moments permeated. Still, I tried.

I continued with my Trans-Allegheny birth name restored, and regular visitors began to frequent my halls again. I had been reborn and had somehow returned to the social circuit. As such, the property's reputation for hauntings grew stronger. Historians, investigators, and innocent onlookers took notice of the fragmented projections and informed the world. The benign mixed with the malignant, and the darker of the two found more success in garnering attention. Door slams, screams, and scratches persisted. The scratches were the worst because something was trying to manifest onto the physical plane. I disapproved at first, but could not resist over time. The attention resulted in more people visiting the site.

I was again full of people to remember—people who were not full of the same terror, people I did not have to dread. I hoped the new visitors could overwrite the old memories over time. I did not want to forget everything, only the horrors. I had no way of knowing my reputation beyond the grounds would not allow it. The stains of history would disappear over time, but like blood, they remained bound in the stone, only seen when held to the light of a particular spectrum. Still, I tried.

I would recount each story from the perspective of my subject to the best of my knowledge. What did not occur in my presence was assembled later with scraps of details that came to me by various means. Weston spoke to me. The town echoed what they said and did, and I listened. The same was true for the county and state, though words spread more slowly from those distant realms.

I would start in 1999 when I helped Brittany Jean Loughry experience her first haunting. Though initially terrified, she became fascinated by the occasion and even obsessed for a brief period. Despite the fleeting nature of her interest, the moment of first contact and lesser moments continued to haunt Brittany until she passed away. Her son, Joel, and daughter, Della, were present when her last ragged breath broke her spirit free from mortal moorings.

Because life moved in circles, the start and finish of Brittany's story were not aligned with her purpose. I had discovered from my craft that beginnings and ends lacked cohesion with the machinations of a universe meant to cycle eternally. Brittany's beginning and end were only crucial for setting the boundary of her life and understanding the contents within. The moments when she contributed most to humanity's cause did not always fall within those parameters. Brittany came from more and begat more, even as she considered the smallness of her life among the rippling ocean of time.

Brittany never discovered her meaning, and neither did Henrietta or Eugene. They knew their purpose was there, like a dark speck within the vastness of the universe. Their reason fluttered in dust particles around their heads at odd hours, shimmering in the light for only a moment before dissipating.

Besides, Brittany never understood how I was the cornerstone for everything her meaning represented. She and I shared a bond in our loneliness. We commiserated, loved, and moved on with the monotonous workaday trudge together. We did so with a unique ability to dwell on the past and glimpse snippets of the future. Still, the answers were broadcast on a frequency she could not fully hear.

It was the same with Henrietta in 1905, and Eugene in 1935. Neil understood his purpose, though it came late and was borne from what remained to close their story. The quartet would never know they were completing a rotation of purpose within my walls otherwise—another circular mechanism of the universe, fueled by both the energies of the living and would-be ghosts. I wished I could have told them everything—or anything—but the hour was far too late. Three were gone, and Neil was near the end. There was no way to arrange a meeting with them now.

Still, I tried.

PART I

THE GHOSTS

BRITTANY WAS ALWAYS A GHOST

TUESDAY, JUNE 15, 1999

The departing sun slurped the last drop of pigment from the clouds hanging low in the western sky, leaving only tufts of gray to linger on the edge of night. The days stretched to their furthest limit at the precipice of pure solstice. In the blackened hour, Brittany Loughry came down from her hillside home on McGary Avenue and into the municipal blocks of Weston.

The humid air carried the aroma of fresh grass clippings from front lawns and freshly tilled soil from backyard gardens. The symphony of scents built to a crescendo, already holding the nostalgia of seasons past.

In contrast to the pleasant smells, the lingering tinge of diesel exhaust sliced through the pleasant aromas as teenage boys rip-roared through tight streets. They revved and rattled their engines as a mating call to the eligible females within earshot. It played companion to the local brood of cicadas, who emerged after seventeen years underground to scream and rattle endlessly beyond the twilight.

19

Brittany did her best to ignore both the revving and trilling. She walked with purpose, nearing the social commons of town.

Dressed in all black with a matching JanSport backpack, Brittany's hair was a common shoulder-length brown with bangs already out of style near the decade's end. She'd debated dying or styling her hair, but the effort did not feel worthwhile. The slender frame she kept was out of fear it was a product of adolescence. She was much stouter in her childhood. Her mother, Glenda, warned rotundness was hereditary and would return without strict adherence to a diet—though Glenda never carried much weight, either. Brittany dismissed the warning signs for now. Walking to town provided enough exercise to offset a teenage appetite.

The curfew siren wailed at ten o'clock as it had every night for decades. The alert was as much a relic as the curfew. The repurposed World War II air raid siren blared a single tone for thirty seconds before dissipating with faint echoes. The sound was loud and long enough to garner the attention of the Weston teenagers who were to return home. They often did not, and instead, looked for ways to defy the law without outright violation. Law enforcement was indifferent anyway. They were one of the few agencies left that held the task of imposing bedtime.

It was a weeknight, but summer break was in full swing, and there was little else for youth to do once they separated from their pals to return home. Still, the town officers would make halfhearted sweeps of the shops and alleys where the teens tended to loiter, shooing them back to their respective dwellings.

Brittany didn't have to obey those rules now that she was a full-fledged adult. For five days, she strutted confidently about the evening with documentation showing she had outgrown the restriction and never hesitated to flash her driver's license as proof.

Tonight, the fewer crimes, the better. Being nabbed for an archaic scofflaw would seem trivial when trespassing was on the agenda.

The Weston Hospital sat on the far corner of town for generations and had recently marked its fifth year of abandonment. The longer the property sat empty, the more it became a symbol of urban spelunking's crown jewel.

Brittany first began exploring abandoned homes with friends during their junior year. Many of the teens caught colds from the October chill. Brittany escaped sickness but caught a bug for the illicit activity. She spent many weekends sneaking into abandoned homes. It started with a group of friends, then a few friends, until her excursions became singular affairs. She came to prefer the solitude; not having to worry about whom to trust if the police came calling.

Despite the many excursions, law enforcement only caught her scent in two incidents. The first incident involved vandalism that had occurred shortly before Brittany arrived. Fortunately, the guilty were caught before any evidence pointed to Brittany's presence on the property.

The second time occurred earlier in the year. Law enforcement had traced Brittany's tracks through light snow to the Loughry home, but they had insufficient evidence to bring charges. Her father helped her case by insisting Brittany had been in her room all night. Law enforcement had only to check the soles of her snow boots to prove guilt, but her father's claim was enough for the city police to relent.

After the close call, Brittany suspended her nocturnal hobby until the summer. During the break, she began thinking more about what it would be like to explore the empty Weston Hospital. The buildings making up the campus would have been the obvious choice for Brittany to hone her exploratory abilities if not for a catch. Unlike the forgotten properties dotting the Lewis County countryside, the hospital grounds were neither forgotten nor condemned.

She made plans to explore the hospital in late spring and began sizing up the security by seeking out classmates who had accomplished the feat.

According to Brittany's sources, it was effortless to sneak past the guards. The security detail was a contract job by the state of West Virginia and left the guards little supervision or direction other than to keep the building standing. The entire property spanned almost seven hundred acres, with a significant portion of the acreage located within the Kirkbride. It was too comprehensive a sweep for three guards, but they managed to keep rabble-rousers at bay—or at least those who left an imprint.

Brittany's first attempt to enter the asylum was a failure. It was on May 22, 1999. She only committed the date to memory a decade later after stumbling upon an archived story on the *Pittsburgh Post-Gazette* website. The article referenced the night. Looking back, Brittany was surprised her first and second attempts to enter the building were so close together.

"Where you going on this fine evening?" Jennifer Sampson called from the corner of the convenience store. Jennifer had a three-month head start over Brittany on being an adult and displayed the badge in the form of a lit cigarette. She held a large convenience store cup in the other hand and took intermittent sips from its curled straw.

Brittany's lip pulled up in response. She could not deny a smirk, but molded the expression into something sheepish. "It's a nice evening. Figured I'd wander around the town for a bit."

Jennifer had been in the group during Brittany's inaugural expedition. Jennifer was also one who caught the cold.

The young woman whipped her head back to force her dark hair behind her shoulder. She flicked the ash off the receding cigarette with one hand, and the other rattled the ice in the white Styrofoam cup. She took a last noisy sip of her drink, followed by a long drag from the smoke. The ritual lasted for some time, and Brittany wondered if she should move on from the rite. But Jennifer looked out of place. She wore flip-flops and frayed shorts that rode high on her pale thighs, and Brittany took the time to marvel.

"I see which direction you're going," Jennifer finally said, nodding toward downtown. "I call bullshit on your wanderings."

Brittany turned her eyes in the same direction. Two blocks of downtown were still obscuring the view of the hospital, but Brittany knew she was already busted.

"You're going to have a hard time getting inside," Jennifer continued without receiving an answer. "Didn't you hear about the paintball incident?"

She had, but feigned ignorance to gather more information. "No. What happened?"

Jennifer took a final puff before letting the butt drop to the ground.

"Bunch of police officers—local and state guys—all broke into the hospital and had a paintball war. This apparently happened two weekends in a row. They completely wrecked the inside. We're talking thousands of dollars' worth of damage."

Brittany found her first failed attempt to enter the Kirkbride odd. She had not been turned away by the normal security guards, but by a town officer cloaked in tactical gear. Stuart Prince, or Officer S. K. Prince, as he preferred, seemed nervous.

She stammered to explain that she was passing through. Some shortcuts intersected the property, but not so close to the building. Still, Officer Prince allowed her to continue without incident.

Brittany released a frustrated exhale. "I reckon security is going to be tight then?"

"Maybe." Jennifer swaggered a bit and approached Brittany. Her leaning posture indicated Jennifer had secret information to pass. When she spoke, it was with a whispered rasp, yet she maintained an average volume.

"If you're trying to get into the main building, the inside of the closest wing to Second Street has a broken door in the back. It's a white wooden door, and the hinges are rusted. Turn the latch and lift. It should slip off the lock and open. There are extra guards on patrol, but no one goes inside. They're too chickenshit. Guards don't watch the street from that side, either. It's supposed to be the town police's job."

Brittany snickered. "You mean, the ones who caused the problem to start with?"

Jennifer backed up and tapped on the side of her nose. "They would love for someone else to cause trouble in there. Take the heat off them, you know? If you make it inside, just tell me how bad they fucked up the place."

"Thanks for the tip. I owe you a pack of smokes," Brittany said. "That's a thing I can buy now."

Jennifer gave a nod. Brittany returned it with a halfhearted salute and rounded the corner to the front of the store. She had intended to buy a bottle of SoBe fruit juice, but Jennifer held her for too long. Brittany did not want to be drawn into the herd of teens who were being wrangled from social pasture.

As she passed the large window, Brittany caught sight of Samuel Beck at the magazine rack. He held the fruit drink she craved. She liked

Sam, finding him pleasant in humor and temperament. He was also present during her first spelunking trip. She was unsure whether he engaged in similar activities before or after that night. Brittany did know that he maintained a humorous outlook throughout the entire event, which added to the enjoyment of the group activity.

Sam had charm, though Brittany did not find his round face and heavier frame attractive. The young man's personality and physicality made him average, but he excelled in every other way. She stared through the glowing window a moment more before declining to enter. She craved a quip from his keen insight, but there were more pressing matters. She waved goodbye to no one and disappeared into the night.

Brittany was never a lonely girl but reveled in lonely places. Her status as an only child accustomed her to introversion. She made it a skill to adjust her social dial as needed, keeping her default setting low. Shyness was not a factor in her choice to interact, nor was it a reason to remain in solitude. Brittany simply preferred silence to a loud, blustering world.

She connected with Second Street two blocks down and traversed the short bridge across the river. Though trees blocked most of the view, the outline of the Kirkbride took shape in the night. Light from Weston illuminated the front, but the far-reaching facade stretched into the dark. The northern end of the building stretched close to the street, save some trees and several yards of turf.

A joyous tingle jolted through Brittany's core, but focus returned when she remembered the most treacherous part. After crossing the short bridge, Weston City Hall sat on the opposite side of the roadway. It was once a rail depot that was later converted into offices for town officials and the Weston Police Department. The police department was what worried Brittany the most. She kept an eye on the empty lot as she passed. The parking lot was clear except for personal vehicles and a retired cruiser. The officers were likely in the thick of the teenage wilderness, nudging high schoolers home.

Lewis County Emergency Services was the last hurdle along the path. The squad bay sat another block away behind the Kirkbride. She did not fret about them as much as she had about the town police. Someone was likely on call inside the facility. Only an active call or a scheduled smoke break would bring someone outside. Brittany cut a path between the rescue squad building and the rear of the Kirkbride, keeping watch on the squad bay doors.

The squad's fluorescent lights emitted a loud hum. A collection of insects danced around the blue glow, providing the area's only movement.

The buzzing of the lights faded behind her as she continued. Brittany made one last turn toward the space between the wards jutting east to west. Though it was dark, the residual glow of the squad bay produced enough illumination for Brittany to discern a white door along the limestone exterior.

The splintered and rotting door left Brittany wondering if it had been as damaged while the hospital was still open. The nightmare of maintaining security in such a large and decrepit place had to be as exhausting as it was impossible.

The doorhandle had a bike pedal shape but with a hollowed center for a hand to grip. She grabbed and twisted. Flecks of rust scraped free from the mechanism, but the door allowed nothing. Brittany tried again, taking Jennifer's advice by pressing upward on the handle as she rotated. Then she placed her free hand under the torquing wrist to provide extra pressure. The handle still did not turn, but the combination of pressing and twisting caused the latch to slip from its groove.

Brittany sighed in amazement. She pulled the door open enough to spin inside. She gave one last scan outside before pulling the trick door firmly to the frame behind her.

A corridor bejeweled with glazed tile spirited Brittany from the dark rear of the Kirkbride into friendlier halls lit by the red glow of EXIT signs.

She made minimal use of her flashlight, shining it only when she detected an obstruction—an old wheelchair left to deteriorate, a bedframe partially pulled from a room, folding chairs, both open and closed. The obstacles were few compared to the vast stretch of halls that reached inward, but Brittany took time to marvel at every item as if they had been relics.

Each burst of her flashlight revealed thick motes of floating dust; they bobbed away, giving the appearance that they were leading her inward.

There was already abundant evidence of the paintball war. Sporadic specks of red, white, blue, pink, and green appeared throughout the first floor corridor, leaving color spots and splintered plastic casings caked on the walls. They were too interspersed to suggest the site of a great battle. A minor skirmish may have occurred en route to the frontline.

Brittany heaved through a final metal door and spotted a perpendicular hallway ahead. She reached the center of the Kirkbride, the hall where patients would enter on their way to admittance—captivity. They either exited the front when they achieved acceptable wellness or were removed through the back to a waiting hearse.

Brittany took a chill while studying objects illuminated by the outside light. A sense of despair still lingered in the corridor. The night watchmen would be canvassing nearby, and she couldn't risk using the flashlight here. Brittany padded slowly, keeping close to the wall. She listened for the possibility of a guard, but all was quiet inside the building. There did not seem to be any sound within the surrounding corridors and rooms. Even the usual sounds of creaking and settling were absent. It was unusual, especially for a cool night after a simmering June day. The quiet felt more startling than that of door slams or footsteps. It gave Brittany the sudden desire to leave the main hall. Two staircases sat on opposite sides, twisting upward. Brittany stepped softly as she climbed. The oak and mahogany groaned as it shouldered her weight.

Brittany took her time, continuing past the second floor. If a watchman decided to enter the building, they would hear her footsteps on the floor above. Moving to the third floor would create a buffer and give Brittany more opportunity to flee should she hear someone climb the staircase.

The third floor also allowed many escape possibilities. The center section had an exit to a balcony at the front of the building. To the rear was a large room Brittany could not examine without shining a light. Her movements echoed from the entrance, suggesting a large room. She had heard stories of school dances being held in the hospital, including her father's prom. She dismissed the claim as a tall tale until other parents corroborated the story.

A closed door on the far side led to the southern wing, prompting Brittany to go north.

The entrance of the northern wing led to an incline opening to the first ward. Brittany felt it safe to shine her flashlight.

Brittany assumed it was a women's ward based on the pink trim and flower patterns painted on the white walls. A closer inspection revealed the flower pattern interspersed with sprigs of olive branches; an emblem of peace likely lost on the patients. Brittany ran a finger over the flowers to feel their raised surface. She looked at the next flower design and realized they were not identical. *Painted?* Brittany wondered.

The third bouquet Brittany found only had a partial replication. What remained was eroded by chipped plaster and paintball splotches.

Brittany gasped and pointed her light down the corridor. The rows of doors were opened outward and marked with oily red, blue, and green paint.

Battlefront found. The Kirkbride was already in disrepair, and the remains of the war zone further deteriorated its condition. Brittany's stomach turned at the carnage, and she closed her eyes to dispel raw emotion and sigh. "Cops did this." The people who arrested such offenders were now the vandals who levied careless destruction upon another's property.

Remembering Jennifer's request, Brittany removed her backpack to extract a disposable camera. As she did, metal clanking rippled throughout the hall. She waited for the reverberation to cease. The building was waking. It seemed to yawn. A guttural groan roared from deep in its bowels. Brittany was unsure if she was the one who had roused it. She moved faster and wound the camera for the first snap.

The first pictures were of the patterns. The pristine replication, followed by the one damaged by police. She moved three doors down and pointed the camera into the void of the deep hall. After two snaps, Brittany realized the camera's flash was not up to the challenge and focused on the paintball-damaged doors.

Brittany stepped into the center of the hall and snapped pictures of the room's interior. The number 668 was on a black label above the door. The number immediately prompted Brittany to check the neighboring doors, curious if there had been a room 666. The number was not there. A blackboard with patients' names still scrawled in pink chalk hung where the portal of the damned would have been. The next room from there was 664.

Brittany returned to 668 after checking. Something odd caught her attention. Splatters of paint and plastic were so thick they bled together and mixed into new colors. The damage was the best example of the vandalism Brittany could condense into a single snapshot. She began documenting the room, snapping first the barred windows and then the walls.

A flash of white lit the room as Brittany snapped a picture. She knew immediately the light had not come from her flash. More disheartening, it did not subside after the flash. Brittany lowered the camera to see the glowing image of a human floating before her.

Brittany first screamed in a low pitch, but her voice intensified to a screech as she jerked toward the door. She reached the center of the hall and screamed again, this time in a shrill voice at peak volume. The building felt like it was tightening, the endless walls forming an esophagus to swallow her into some hellish pit. Panic overcame her, and she cut toward the center rather than seeking an exit in the northern wards.

Brittany opened her mouth to exhale but screamed again. She could not help it. Fear expelled from her with every curdle. Back in the center hall, she rounded the stairs and lumbered downward, not caring for the sounds she was making.

In the lobby, she considered bursting through the exits and running like hell, but the idea shattered when something grabbed her.

Brittany screamed once more, the loudest she could muster.

"Ah! Geez, my ear," a male voice groaned. "You did that right in my ear!"

Brittany shook loose from the man but grew faint and toppled to the floor. The jingle of keys and authoritative stride confirmed he was a night watchman. The door to the front of the building was ajar, and another shadow spilled inside.

"I told you I thought I saw a flash of light upstairs," a second guard boasted.

The first watchman ignored his colleague. "Are you in here by yourself?"

Brittany said nothing. She thought she had been alone, but the encounter made her question everything.

2

NEIL WAS JUST THE GUY FROM THE END

The temperature tumbled into the negatives, as it often did on winter nights in the upper Midwest. The town of Murdock, Minnesota, was not spared the extreme chill. The night brought a self-imposed lockdown to the three hundred residents who wanted to avoid the bite of a vicious climate.

At 2:00 a.m., the town was calm, leaving Neil Hutchence free to wander the neighborhood and contemplate the execution of the ghastly deed.

A rail line for Burlington Northern Santa Fe skirted the western edge of Murdock. Neil avoided the well-lit areas and walked along the tracks by the city limits.

The constant isolation of Murdock was what he had prescribed, but self-medication had flaws. He came to favor being away from everyone in the months beyond his divorce. With friends far away, he never needed to explain what went wrong, why promises of lifelong love had become unsustainable between him and Caitlyn, or how his apathy and neglect of their two daughters had led to the final straw.

They had met in college at West Virginia University. She was a marketing major from Saint Paul, and he was an English major out of Moundsville, a small city in West Virginia. Neil had first laid eyes on her at a college party, drunk and brawling with another woman in a bottle-littered parking area outside his house. She left her opponent a bloodied mess, lying on the asphalt long enough to compose herself before hobbling into the night. Afterward, a proud Caitlyn brushed aside her blonde, disheveled hair, and strutted into the house. She was a vision of battle-hardened beauty, and Neil chose to pursue her. The pair hit it off and remained compatible when sober heads returned. The first stage of their relationship ended with the school year. Caitlyn's graduation sent her back to Minnesota with a bachelor's in marketing and a job offer.

Three years after college, Neil moved to Minneapolis at the request of a college friend, Demetry Oswald. Demetry was also an English major, but later returned to school to pad his resumé with a journalism degree. His promise landed him a job at the *Minneapolis Star Tribune*, and his invitation for Neil to move with him served a dual purpose. Demetry would not be alone in the cities, and Neil could resume his romance with Caitlyn.

The ploy was successful. Demetry better integrated into big city life, and Neil and Caitlyn wed in 2006. Their first child, Madeline, was born on their sixth anniversary. Five years later, Madeline welcomed her sister, Meriwether.

By the time Meriwether was born, Caitlyn had advanced to Senior Vice President of Marketing at Birch Financial. The position was all-consuming, and Neil spent very few hours a day with his wife. To compound the frustration, Neil lost his job while Caitlyn was on her final week of maternity leave. Rather than find another, Caitlyn tasked her husband with watching their children. Her new salary was enough to support them, removing the hassle of running kids to daycare between shifts.

Neil was a failure as a parent, a verdict agreed on in whispers by everyone who knew him. Diapers remained dirty longer than they should have, bottles stayed empty longer than they should have, and Neil slept longer than he should have. Caitlyn took a running tally of the shortcomings, and resentment built. She spoke to him less, and intimacy evaporated from their marriage.

The breaking point came in April 2018, during one of Neil's marathon naps. Madeline was now in school and unavailable to play hall monitor to Meriwether's escalating movements. She crawled fast, bordering on walking, but had not mastered the skill. She could stand if she pulled herself up on objects and scooted where the edges took her. On that day, the front door did the trick. With a determined stretch, the door handle took little effort to reach. Because it was a handle and not a knob, a mighty pull was all it took to release the latch from the frame. Meriwether crawled down the front steps into the yard.

The story would have had a tragic ending if not for Meriwether catching the eye of a patrolman from a perpendicular road. The officer woke Neil with Meriwether in his arms. A stern lecture was given, but no charges were filed; therefore, Neil decided to keep the incident a secret from Caitlyn. Such an omission came at a cost with nosy neighbors. They saw the flashing lights from the street and were quick to message Caitlyn, quick to tell her toddler was in the road, and quick to say an officer returned Meriwether to her father. Knowing her child was safe, Caitlyn decided not to broach the topic with Neil. Instead, she waited to see if he would confess to the incident on his own.

Nothing came. The days turned into a week, and Caitlyn had divorce papers composed after the second week. The time for an explanation was over. There was nothing left to do but say goodbye.

Neil did not fight the divorce or custody. The weight of his failures kept him too down to care. Depression was constant, even before. The death of his brother served as a forerunner to the misery, but he refused to place those events in his mind's eye. He was killed in a Chicago terrorist attack, which was the only footnote Neil would allow.

He left Minneapolis with a small assortment of belongings, and made a hideaway in Murdock.

*****

THERE was always a train around 2:00 a.m. The whistle shrieked each night as the locomotive huffed toward town, hauling crude oil and lumber to places beyond. It often roused Neil, who was not a light sleeper. Lately, he was not a sleeper at all. Insomnia reigned when depression had a foothold.

Down the track, a single yellow circle of light grew larger. Neil centered himself between the rails and stared at the beam—the only thing flashing before his eyes. His breath quickened and formed icicles on the edges of his unkempt facial hair. He wanted to reflect on his happy past with Caitlyn. The infusion of joy might give him enough reason to exit the tracks; however, his recent history suppressed better memories.

The train had reached the edge of town. It sounded its horn. Neil took it as a signal and raised his arms outward as if to embrace the engine when the two met. The nylon of his puffy jacket groaned as it extended, and Neil shivered and exhaled through his mouth; the brief burst of steam clouded his vision.

Turning away from the fog, Neil's eye caught sight of the Catholic cemetery across the road that ran parallel to the tracks. *Perhaps I could be interred there,* he thought. He had been a Catholic once, but self-excommunicated. *Perhaps past attendance would be enough to rate a plot.* He considered it, though it was certainly too late to dictate his wishes to anyone.

There was a bone-white statue depicting the crucifixion of Jesus Christ standing tall above the cemetery, which had attracted him to the town in the first place. There wasn't anything particularly remarkable about the sculpture. Similar portrayals adorned cemeteries across prairie towns and beyond, but Neil had spotted this one first. It was a statue as bright as light with a cross as dark as death. The Marys of the Gospels knelt below the sagging body, frozen in various stations of anguish. What made it stand out was its stark contrast to everything around it. Only the cylindrical grain bins along the railway loomed more prominent. Maybe the water tower, perhaps the church steeples, but none felt as displaced in the middle of nowhere as the crucifixion depiction. Even among the stubborn snowpack, its brilliance overpowered the landscape as Christ watched over the graves.

The train horn wailed again, and Neil considered the irony of his pose. Christ knew he was going to die. Knowing you were going to die and doing so to redeem others seemed noble. Neil could not erase the sins of others, but he could erase the sins of his existence for his children. They would know nothing of him beyond his name and genetic ticks.

Whether Neil lost his nerve or gained it, a visualization of how the train would mangle his body prompted Neil to lower his arms. A sickness settled in his stomach. He remained facing the engine but stumbled off the track and fell rigid into the snow. The train chugged past, each car delivering a *thump-thump, thump-thump* as it passed. Neil kept still on the jagged snowbank. The yellow light of the train left an aura in his vision.

Hard snow crunched under his weight, and he considered letting it take him under. Take him further than under. Take him straight to Hell. Any place warmer would be preferable, but the snow held. Neil collected himself and returned to the heat of his rental.

*****

IT was the first day of June when he first heard Silkie's name. Neil was in better spirits, though he spent much of his free time lying in bed and considering the failures he had accumulated in his past, present, and those to come.

His current failure was choosing Murdock as his home. At the time, he knew nothing about the hamlet other than the statue of Christ. Upon moving, he soon discovered no jobs were available in the immediate area.

Twelve miles north of Murdock was the larger city of Benson. Neil was hired there as part of the park maintenance crew. He came to enjoy Benson much more than Murdock. If not shackled to a lease, he would have moved there right away.

The 700-square-foot domicile in Murdock was suitable for sleeping and a standing lunch, and that was about all. The canary yellow building stood in a quiet corner of Murdock out of sight from everyone. A thick row of pine trees fenced the property line, leaving Neil with a view of his path to the road. He often saw his neighbor's Confederate flag flapping in the breeze, which always caught his eye for how out of place it seemed to be in the north country.

Neil had worked at the park for eight months and had become familiar with the wide perimeter. He walked the trail daily and could list every fracture in the asphalt, every lap of patching tar, and every ant hill that routed an exit along the track.

The light poles lining the path were like a flock of sheep he tended. Lamp thirty-eight had a noticeable lean. Shrubs engulfed lights ten and twelve, and vegetation left green stains on their bases. Lamp thirty-five had a bulb that frequently burned out despite being an LED filament with a ten-year warranty.

The park bordered the town cemetery. Days past Memorial Day, the rich scent of flowers had been drifting in from the monuments, creating a collective aroma that sweetened the air. Neil wasn't sure how all the varieties of flowers could merge to form a singular smell indistinct from any other flower. After a few days, the scent turned sour. It gave Neil a moment to ponder the metaphor that all sweet things begin to rot over time. He appreciated the sentiment.

With the lease ending, Neil began calling every apartment and townhouse he could find in Benson. After the third unsuccessful call, there was a knock at the door.

"Demetry?" Neil said, upon seeing his friend standing behind the screen door. It was a surprise, but one welcome enough for Neil to crack a smile.

Demetry gave a joyful shrug and brandished his infectious grin. "Hutch! How's my friend?"

Neil pushed open the flimsy screen barrier, and the two embraced.

"Come in and sit down." Neil directed a hand toward the couch. "How did you even know where to find me?"

Demetry sat. "Remember you gave me your address so I could get you a complimentary edition of *The Star Tribune*? I kept the address."

"I never did get a paper," Neil mentioned. "Good thing it didn't cost me nothing."

"Yeah … Turns out they don't mail papers this far out anymore. Everything is digital. Everything is changing. Newsrooms are shrinking.

Evolving, they call it. Dying feels more like the operative word. Either way, the end result is that it's harder for subscribers to consume."

"Sounds like a winning business model," Neil said, voice dripping with sarcasm.

Demetry slapped his hands on his thighs. "Listen. I know it's getting close to the anniversary of your divorce, and I know you've sworn off people. Regardless, I think it's important for you to have some sort of social interaction around this time."

Neil shrugged. "I've gotten along just fine so far."

"Have you?" Demetry asked with a judgmental tilt of his head.

Neil scanned the look to try to understand what his friend was discerning. "Yeah. Peachy."

"You've been drinking?"

Neil scoffed. "Who doesn't drink after a divorce?"

"Is that your pickup outside with whiskey tags?"

"It was a lot of drinking, and then it stopped."

"Stopped … by the Minnesota State Patrol?"

Neil sputtered, growing tired of defending himself.

"Have you been suicidal?" Demetry continued.

Neil huffed. "Why would you think that?"

Demetry stood. "You have always praised artists whose work became popular after their untimely and self-inflicted deaths. Van Gough, Cobain, John Kennedy Toole …"

"I don't have a work … any creative works," Neil responded, his voice reaching a new pitch. "I have grass clippings and stubborn light fixtures. There is nothing there to weave into a tapestry of timeless works."

"Man, are you suicidal?" Demetry repeated.

"Was."

"What?"

"Was. I *was* suicidal."

"What changed?"

"I tried suicide. Was a failure at it, too."

"Shit." Demetry pursed his lips and paced.

Neil slumped. His eye darted from object to object before he would finally look to his friend.

"You need to think in the long-term," Demetry offered with a firm gesture. "Everything gets better down the line, but you cannot see it."

"Why? Why can't I see it? I was a failure at writing, I was a failure at marriage, I was a failure at parenthood."

"You can't see it 'cause you ain't looking. You've spoken of death and suicide and all the loose threads of glory associated with the transaction of life and death and pain and legacy. That's where your eyes are."

A heavy sense of shame came over Neil, and he looked to the floor. Demetry took the opportunity to place a hand on Neil's shoulder and met him forehead to forehead. Demetry spoke softly and with emotion. "Look away, brother. Look away. There are no gains from looking down that path."

The mention of "brother" made Neil wince. "I'm sorry." He looked straight down. A tear dropped from the corner of his eye to the dingy white linoleum. "I miss my wife and kids. I miss them, but I also have no desire to see them. It's fucked up, I know, but I don't have it in me."

"You've lost yourself." Demetry detached from the awkward posture of their embrace. "We'll find you again. Let's go look together. Maybe if you come along on my journey, you can find yourself along the way."

"Journey?" Neil questioned. He was now the one to sit on the couch while Demetry stood.

"I received a writing grant from the Woodrow G. Gunderson Foundation," Demetry said, beaming with pride. "It's an arts grant that gives money to various types of arts—paintings, sculptures, mixed media type things, but also fiction and non-fiction story writing."

"And which did you get?" Neil asked. "Have you become a talented sculptor without my knowing?"

"No, man, shit," Demetry laughed. "It's for writing, as you may have seriously guessed. I was awarded $50,000 in the non-fiction section. The grant is backed by the Frances Indra Foundation out of New York, which gets my foot in the door with the literary world there."

Neil's eyes widened, but his reply emerged listless. "That's fantastic. I'm happy for you."

Demetry seemed unfazed by the lack of enthusiasm. "It's an unrestricted grant, which I plan to use for food, board, travel, and two research assistants."

"Research," Neil repeated before realizing what it meant. "Do you want me to be a research assistant?"

"Miguel has already agreed to do it for a couple of trips. I just need to fill that final slot. It can be more permanent for you if you want."

Neil grabbed the single pillow on the couch and squeezed it like a plush toy. "Do you have any ideas about what you will write?"

Demetry clasped his hands together. "Yes, sir. I already know what I'm going to write about. Or who, I should say."

"Who?" Neil smiled. His friend's happiness was a viral contagion.

"Her name was Silkie Le Margaux. She was a young, enslaved person in Louisiana when the Civil War erupted. She witnessed many horrors during her short time on the plantation. It's believed her time there caused her to develop some serial killer tendencies. Either way, she decided to take vengeance after the war. She dedicated her life to hunting down and killing former slave owners, particularly ones known to be notoriously cruel."

"Vengeance stories do sell well."

"They do! As do true crime novels. And this has both elements. There were at least twelve unsolved murders with plantation connections between 1872 and 1903. Between 1903 and 1905, she was institutionalized and moved three times before landing in a West Virginia asylum. That was where she spent the rest of her days."

With his interest piqued, Neil stood and moved to the kitchen to remove a can of soda from the fridge.

"So, what do you need me and Miguel for?" The can cracked and hissed when Neil pressed the tab. "You seem like you have a pretty good lid on things."

"Mainly, you get paid just to be my traveling companions." Demetry chuckled. "Plus, Miguel has an interest in being a writer, and I figure this would be a good entry point for him. You could get back into writing, too. Plus, we need you for white credibility. Black and Puerto Rican men poking around West Virginia may be deemed suspicious." Demetry laughed, but they both knew the remark contained too much truth.

"I can do the white thing. But I'll never write again," Neil stated in a glum tone. "All the best stories have already been told, and to counter that, all my ideas become overblown. I tried once to write my memoir, but completely in Latin. I don't know a lick about Latin. Phrases, maybe, like Carpe Diem and Memento Mori, but that's it. Then I started writing it with only Latin chapter titles before giving up entirely."

"Memento Mori? I don't know that one."

"It means, 'remember you will die,' or 'remember to die.'"

"Oh, yeah." Demetry scuffed the linoleum floor with his foot. "I've only seen it written. It's weird to hear it. Also, what a depressing phrase to carry through the ages."

Neil took a sip and sat the can aside. "All that is to say, I doubt I'll ever stumble onto a long-lost post-abolitionist antihero to write about. What's even in West Virginia to research? I haven't been there in almost a decade."

Demetry washed his hands in the kitchen sink and dried them with a towel hanging on the front of the stove. "No one ever caught Silkie or even suspected her of the murders. She confessed to the crimes in a diary she kept on her, even in captivity. It was recovered after her death, but they put it in storage since you can't prosecute a dead woman. The victims' families were informed. Some of their stories made the paper, but most did not. The article I found was from a 1906 edition of the *Cleveland Daily Banner*. Cleveland, Tennessee, that is. It mentions a diary found in West Virginia left behind by one Silkie Le Margaux. She describes the planning and murder of twelve men, but also only mentions one by name: Leeman Saint Cloud, a former enslaver from a cotton plantation outside of Charleston, South Carolina."

"And the diary is still in West Virginia?" Neil guessed. The two men were now standing face-to-face in a kitchen meant for one.

"There's a museum in an old mental hospital where she spent the last years of her life. It's called the Trans-Allegheny Lunatic Asylum. You'll like the place. They do overnight ghost tours, so we can scratch our paranormal explorer itch while we're at it."

Neil smiled. "I like this assignment more and more."

"Great!" Demetry slapped his friend on the shoulder and scooted passed him. "Silkie is supposedly buried there, too, so there's a chance you could see *her* ghost."

HENRIETTA WAS STILL A LONG WAY FROM JUSTICE

Sunday, May 21, 1905

Henrietta wished she had something more than a mortal frame to stand and strut about the earth. The boys of her upbringing called her athletic, but she never utilized her body for speed or sport, even when the family genes gave her the gift freely. She had squandered the gift of her youth, utilized only to highlight her beauty to the male population of Monongalia County.

It was a brother to one of those men who had her institutionalized. He, too, wasted the potential of her coil. He wasted everything about Henrietta. Hindsight brought her the desire to have done more with her time and youth. She used what would be her only turn at marriage to wed a passionate miner who dealt in love and death. The latter stuck with stubborn permanence. Henrietta did not want to think of him as a waste of time. Time was the villain here. It gave in months what should have lasted for decades.

Henrietta and Strickland Cedric were newlyweds for no more than a month. The romantic build-up to their marriage lasted many times longer. Still, he had spent those premarital months in the safer coal mines of northern Monongalia County before the newlyweds sojourned south to the town of Monongah.

Henrietta knew that Strickland's career as a coal miner was a lit fuse. Conditions in the mine were fraught, and the Monongah Mine was two years away from becoming a tomb for more than three hundred souls. Strickland was not mourned as part of a mass casualty. Doing so may have equated to more funeral attendees. However, when he died in a rockfall in December of 1903, there was only Henrietta to grieve. Strickland had no family other than a brother who arrived a month later and presented himself as indifferent to his sibling's demise.

Donovan Cedric had the same angular looks as his younger brother. A square jaw, deep-set eyes, and a torso that looked as if it were chiseled from pure obsidian. He was taller and more muscular and gained the extra girth from years of driving railroad ties between Utah and California. What Donovan gained in strength, he lacked tenfold in passion. He seemed almost devoid of joy and personality altogether. But grief was a curious fish that listed about in uneven tides, and Henrietta thought it was his way of listing beyond the waves of sadness. In Henrietta's mourning, she began to believe a relationship with the elder Cedric could be a suitable replacement for what she lost in Strickland. Perhaps Henrietta could rekindle some lost yearning deep in the brother's soul. Donovan often paid her no mind, ignored her advances, and seemed only mindful of the property Strickland had left behind.

It was not long before Donovan showed his true intention. To acquire what remained of Strickland's estate, Donovan petitioned the county to commit Henrietta for psychiatric observation, citing erotomania, and grief that caused her to act out in ways unbecoming of a new widow.

The county court was quick to approve cases where someone claimed insanity against another. Even so, Henrietta was still an exception as a young Black woman. It was forty years beyond the American Civil War. Four decades in which a Black person held full rights as a human being, fractions more than what the country had allocated. Still, they were

not treated as such. The South had yet to adjust to the idea. Southern
mental institutions contained little of the Black population, stuck on
the wrongheaded belief that insanity was not much different from the
supposed inherent ignorance of Black people. West Virginia, a state created
as a direct result of the war, seemed to waver on the concept, even in their
liberation from it.

Was West Virginia part of the South? The state never committed
to a direction, though it contained one within its name. It was too north
to be south, too south to be north; the East wouldn't have it, and it was
otherwise west of nothing, save its namesake. Even though it was borne
out of sympathies with the North, it still held a Southern mentality toward
African descendants.

The verdict in Henrietta's case was that grief came in any color.
She was, therefore, committed to the West Virginia Hospital for the
Insane. Donovan's plan to remedy his sister-in-law and obtain his brother's
property was flawless. Donovan sold their remaining belongings before
making his way westward, a little more change jingling in his pocket.
Henrietta never heard from him again, but she would be better for it when
the fog of her plight finally cleared.

It was mid-May, but Henrietta did not know it when she awoke
groggy. Pain radiated from her abdomen when she tried to shift on a lumpy
mattress. Her displeasured groans matched those of the metal frame that
strained underneath her. Consciousness slowly returned, along with the
weight of reality in which Henrietta found herself.

The woman, all of twenty, was neither in the operating room,
nor the quarters she shared with the other Black patients in the hospital.
Henrietta was alone, inside a realm of existence she had not occupied since
being first committed to the hospital.

Henrietta was not sure if it had been a year yet. A year felt much
different in captivity. In her mind-space, it felt like thousands of years had
slogged past since the stormy morning the public health officer led her
to the hospital door. She had nothing more than the clothes on her back,
and a necklace once given by her mother, Malkia. She had pierced a hole
through an Indian Head cent and strung it with a thin chain. The year of
the bronze piece was 1885, Henrietta's birth year. She was most distraught

seeing the cherished item vanish into a box of her effects, impounded until she resolved her grief.

Henrietta never saw the letter passed to the admitting attendant. Based on the interviews in the following months, she gathered that it had something to do with promiscuity. A word on a doctor's notepad next to her name once read "nymphomania derived from grief." "Nymphomania" was a word Henrietta was not familiar with, but she assumed that if it was a mania, she indeed possessed some brand of situational madness. It must have been bad if it granted an endless stay within the thick walls of the institution.

Henrietta was sure it had been more than eleven months. June was when she arrived, and it was getting hot again after months of shivering in the colored ward. Their quarters were separate from the main building, tucked behind the hospital, where the clock tower had no face. No year and no time could be known there.

The Black wards were not granted the same allotment of heat from the industrious boiler. Though state of the art at the turn of the century, the furnace was not without its flaws. The hot currents circled the facility, but by the time the back building received its heat, it was already spent through most of its circuit around the main compound.

Henrietta was not in the derelict back building. These walls were a muted pink color, a hue she had not seen in their white-tiled quarters. The evening light struck the room differently, and the hallway had much more chatter. *A hallway?* Their wards were three compartments in a two-story building with five rooms on the back wall. Nothing resembled a hallway on either floor. The voices outside did not echo the way they usually had.

Breathing deep, Henrietta stopped short of sucking in so much air it would further irritate the pain in her stomach. Whatever cocktail of anesthetics and painkillers the doctors had her ingest worked wonders. They were beginning to wear thin. Henrietta had lost herself in the haze of delirium and painlessness and wished she could remain in that domain longer. She wanted to shun the agony and forget where she was and what she was, a young widow abandoned by her family.

Her father, Henry, was still living, and kept a house in a ramshackle town built from the bones of an abandoned coal camp. With it being a

Black community, the tract did not have an official name. Locals in nearby population centers referred to it by a number of derogatory names, though none had stuck by the time a zip code finally designated the community as Mandersville.

Malkia died three years earlier from a disease that swelled within her abdomen and took little time to reduce her to nothing. That was the event for which Henrietta was most grief-stricken. Her mother was kind and cautious, taught her the world's ways, and educated Henrietta beyond her own understanding.

Malkia and Henry had been slaves on a tobacco plantation near Yorktown when the Civil War erupted. Barely teenagers when set free, they fled north together and remained close while a romance percolated.

The couple received the surname Tidewater from the judge who married them. Both claimed not to have a last name, determined to shun their slave roots. They disavowed Graham, their owner's name. Tidewater was not much better. It was taken from the area of Virginia they had left, those horrors still fresh in memory. However, it was also the place where they met, so they decided the name was good enough. It had to be.

The Tidewaters settled in Maryland for a time, where they had their first three children, Pauline, Jules, and Wilma. Wilma unexpectedly died from an unknown illness at age eight. The tragedy and subsequent reminders of the horror prompted the family to disassociate from their Hagerstown home and move westward. They lived in the Allegheny Mountains for a time before establishing a homestead in the Morgantown area. Henrietta was born the following year and viewed by her older sisters as a replacement for their lost sibling.

Malkia's death weighed on Henrietta—a tragedy compounded by Pauline and Jules's absence at any of the funeral proceedings that followed. Pauline traversed north to New York and became consumed by the nightlife, while Jules took an opposite approach and headed to Virginia Beach to become a schoolteacher. Henrietta never kept up with her sisters, but until the funeral, she was unaware of how little they kept up with her or her parents.

Henrietta accepted Strickland's death almost immediately in comparison, but Henrietta let the grief flow over her. She wanted sympathy; she wanted the community to pour out to her. And they did. Monongah had kind characters from all stripes who were generous enough to provide subsistence for another struggling person. Henrietta would return to the town to repay the favor two years later when the worst mining disaster in American history occurred in the same mine.

She had a knack for showing up at disasters. Monongah was the first. Weston's turn would come decades later.

It had been an hour since Henrietta woke. The haze of the drugs was clearing. She wanted to rise but feared doing so would worsen the abdominal wound. From her vantage, it looked well bandaged

The doctor entered the room after another half hour. Doctor Felix Koenig was someone with whom Henrietta had an intimate familiarity. He was a tall man with a thick chest and tall, slender legs. Felix kept his blond hair gelled into a point above his widow's peak, and the matching handlebars of his blonde mustache twisted around his face. A German immigrant, his accent had eroded from his time studying and working in America, but there were rough edges to his native tongue he was still unwilling to purge.

"I figured you might be awake," the doctor said.

"Have been for a bit," Henrietta confirmed in a groggy voice. "Where am I?"

Felix turned and shuffled items on a metal shelf at the corner nearest to the door. "Oh, you are in die main building. Die Kirkbride. I vanted to keep an eye on you vile you recovered from surgery."

"What was my surgery?" Henrietta asked, but suddenly remembered a key detail. "The baby? Where is the baby?"

The doctor was quick to turn and motion for her to calm down. "Dem baby is fine. You ver awake when you birthed him. Do you not remember?"

"Him? Where is he?"

"Ya, it was a boy," Felix answered. "A little over three kilograms. Seems quite healthy. He is down on the first floor being nursed by a voman who lost her baby at birth. Ve did not vant her milk to dry."

"I should have milk, too," Henrietta stated, and looked to her covered chest.

The doctor matched her gaze. "I am sure you vill, but we had concerns das morphine und other tonics ve gave you vould spread to die breast milk. Tomorrow, it vill be out of your system."

Felix returned to the metal table and continued to clank items around. Henrietta relaxed and breathed a sigh of relief. *My son. How could I have laid there for an hour and not remember his birth?* Henrietta wanted to search for the moment longer, except a more aching question emerged.

"What is wrong with my stomach? Why was I given morphine after the birth?"

"It vas morphine und a cocktail of some other drugs," Doctor Felix corrected. "Some are being tested for das first time here. Even die surgery technique is somewhat new."

"What did you do?" Henrietta grew upset. "What was done to me?"

Felix sighed and pulled a short wooden stool from the edge of the wall. He sat down, but his knees elevated past his waist. The humorous display dampened the serious effect. Still, the doctor spoke with the grimmest tone he could muster.

"A patient who becomes pregnant vile committed to die hospital has to be mandatorily sterilized." He threw his arms outward as if he were helpless. "It is simply policy. You had already come to us with a history of promiscuity and nymphomania. There vas no appeal you could make to satisfy those who made die decision."

"Nymphomania?" *There was that word again.* Henrietta believed she knew what it meant, but if it were a word to alter her body so significantly, then she wanted to hear a clear definition.

Doctor Felix cleared his throat. "It means you make a practice of lying with men. Letting them impregnate you."

"No," Henrietta said in horror. She raised her head as far as the pain would allow. "No. I'm not promiscuous. I do not lie with many men. I lay with my husband until he died, and then I lay with you. You were the only one. The only one who could impregnate me."

Doctor Felix's back grew rigid in the chair. "Only me? It cannot be."

Henrietta hummed a confirmation.

Doctor Felix closed his eyes. "Das wird ein …" He paused as if his reversion to the Deutsche tongue surprised him.

Henrietta glared at him with suspicious eyes. She spent enough time with Felix to know the doctor only slipped into full Deutsche when his emotions heightened.

Felix took several deep breaths, then stood to pace the room. He seemed to be collecting himself. "Let me change your bandages," he finally said. Felix knelt in front of the metal desk to remove clean linen from a shelf out of view.

"What did you say in Deutsche just now? You know I don't speak it."

"Darüber freue ich mich."

Henrietta tilted her head in silent scolding. Felix kept his eyes trained on his work and began undoing the spent dressing.

"Ve made two incisions. Vun on each side of your abdomen. If you refrain from using those muscles, you should be healed und moving normally in about a month."

"What did you say in Deutsche? German?" Henrietta insisted.

The doctor sighed. "I simply stated surprise at how you have not picked up more Deutsche vords. The shift from English to Deutsche is not hard, or umgekehrt."

Henrietta was not taken for a fool. "I know enough to tell you had more to say before that last sentence."

Felix rubbed a thin potion against her stitches that simultaneously chilled and burned. Henrietta believed Felix had done this to suspend an answer further, but the doctor instead winced while he queued a whopper.

"I said that I could get into much trouble if the administrator found out I had ein tryst vith you. Perhaps ven you leave this place ve can have ein official romance vare ve do not have to hide our lives. But vithin these valls—ehm, walls—it is something that ve must do. It is forbidden."

For all the obfuscation, the answer was acceptable to Henrietta. "If we must, then we will."

She had fallen for the doctor's charms and foreign intrigue early in her stay. Hundreds of patients resided on the campus, and women well outnumbered the men. Despite the multitude, the doctor seemed to have his eye on her since the beginning. He returned her Indian Head Penny necklace as a gesture of affection and allowed her to wear it out of view of the kleptomaniacs among the wards. His constant visits and sweet words swooned her into a love beyond Strickland.

The doctor often interviewed her in private offices or walked with her in the back lots where Black patients were allowed to roam. The Kirkbride plan did not allow for the intermingling of colors, and the rule remained in place in 1905. The doctor looked for any excuse to whisk Henrietta away, and it was in one of those secret outings they conceived the child. He never questioned his parentage until now. Henrietta had assumed he knew he was the father, and Felix must have assumed her false diagnoses gave him cover to do as he pleased. There were plenty of studs in the Black ward who could cover his unethical insemination.

Once Henrietta informed Felix of her pregnancy, the doctor's interest appeared to wane. He continued to spend time with her, even though the nature of their intimacy had changed. He ceased discussing his plans, which involved relocating to more prestigious medical institutions in Baltimore and New York City. Instead, he began to talk more about his past. He expressed his disdain for Kaiser Wilhelm II, whose new vision for world order included more xenophobia than Felix could tolerate. It was the Kaiser's 1900 speech during the Boxer Rebellion that drove Felix to the new world. The Kaiser had spoken with contempt toward the Chinese, calling for their slaughter. Shortly after the speech, Felix had fled to medical school in America, pledging not to return to Germany while the Kaiser remained in power.

"I hate it when people judge others on vare they are from, vat color they are," the doctor expressed, reliving the memories. "Black or vite does not matter. Ve are all red on the inside. Our hearts are all built the same. Skin color is bedeutungslos. Um. How do you say … vithout meaning. I vant you to know that. Die treatment of people your color in this country is abhorrent. It was not so bad in New York City, vare they seem to hate die Irish more. They seem to despise those who come hungry. They don't realize hunger is nature's most keen trigger for motivation. America needs to learn this about die Irish, Deutschland needs to learn this about die Chinese. Because man is separated by country, I don't think there is a need to be separated any other way. I am against black und vite und red und yellow persons being separated in this same facility. How can there ever be unity within der human race if ve do not first physically unite?" Doctor Felix finished wrapping the bandages and rose to shift Henrietta back into a sleeping position. "Vat I am trying to say is that I'm going to see to it that you stay in die main building for as long as possible. I vant you to be united with der rest des country."

Henrietta was still digesting her situation but could only muster saying, "That's right nice of you."

The doctor nodded. "I vill see if a nurse can bring you a late dinner."

"When do you think I can leave here?" Henrietta questioned, trying to suppress her eagerness. Her stomach was still raw from the drug cocktail, and she had no craving for nourishment.

Felix bristled at the question. "You are still grieving …"

"But I want to be with you," Henrietta said in a whine.

"Und I vould like to be with you as vell, but I need to know your love und lust for me is not related to die grief you feel."

Henrietta leaned back and propped herself up on her forearms. "When will you know?"

Felix scratched his brow. "Das mind is a tricky thing to cure. Men und vomen get crushed by life's events. Something terrible happens und it breaks them to bits und die bits scatter everywhere. Fragments of their psyche are verstreut all over der ground und it is our job to put them back together again. Ve can do that; it is our job. Das problem is ve do not know vat der whole body of ein man or eine voman looked like before. Ve simply have shards of das whole that ve are trying to reassemble."

"When do you think that will be for me?"

Doctor Felix's hands formed fists and bobbed them three times before releasing them back to his sides. He looked directly at her, brandishing another friendly smile.

"I am still to figure out vat you vere like before your husband's death. Maybe soon. Ven you are settled, maybe we vill get your son up here und you can nurse him. Babies have a good vay of cancelling grief."

"Wallace," Henrietta called firmly.

"Vat?"

"I want to name the baby Wallace. Wallace Felix Tidewater."

Felix groaned and rubbed his face. "If ve are trying to hide my parentage, I suggest concealing den middle name. You could name him after your father."

Henrietta nodded. "Wallace Henry Tidewater."

Felix paused and forced his lips into an unnatural smile.

"Tell me, Doctor Felix, do they sterilize the men who have this nymphomania?"

The doctor writhed. He kept his hand on his face and twisted the edge of his mustache. "We have done so under certain circumstances. You see, it is much harder to prove a man's parentage. For you, there vas clear evidence. Ve observed the birth of Vallace …" He gyrated his jaw as if it reconfigured his diction. "Wallace."

Henrietta nodded happily in confirmation.

"Das ist gut. Bis bald," Felix ended before disappearing through the door. He was almost followed instantly by a nurse who entered with fresh linens for the room.

"Good evening, Mrs. Cedric," the nurse greeted.

"Tidewater."

The nurse cocked her head. "What?"

"I prefer to go by Miss Tidewater. My maiden name."

"Oh?" The nurse said as she hunched to the bottom shelf. "Sure."

Henrietta debated whether she wanted to elaborate, to tell her that she had disavowed her married name. It was now a name that led her to ruin, held only by a man who sought to steal and confine her to a bondage only her parents had known in the unforgiving South. They shunned the name of their incarcerator and so would she.

The nurse finished unpacking the supplies, stood, and flattened out the creases in her white dress. She was a petite woman with a round face and flat nose. Her eyes were deep, and the nurse's bonnet exposed a scar across her forehead.

"I am Nurse Gail Showalter. I will be looking after you during the times of day that Doctor Koenig is not available."

"I appreciate it," Henrietta said. As much as she craved interaction, she was ready to be alone again.

"Congratulations on your new child. I'm sorry your time with him will be so short."

Henrietta shifted into a comfortable position. The stitches in her abdomen were aflame at the speed, but she paid it no mind. "What do you mean by short?"

The eyes of Nurse Showalter enlarged. Her chest made a single heave before letting the air flow outward. "The doctor didn't tell you?"

Henrietta shook her head in the negative.

"Any child born while the mother is in state custody becomes custody of the state. You get to keep your baby until he is weaned and ready for adoption."

A lump formed in Henrietta's throat, but a complementary surge of rage held it in place. "I haven't even met my baby yet, and you're telling me I can't keep him?"

The nurse nodded. "'Fraid so."

The hospital was going to take her child away. They already stripped her of her ability to conceive again. The pain in her abdomen revealed something empty within her, and the hole was growing cavernous as she dwelt on the reality of her situation.

"The grief don't stop once it starts, does it?" Henrietta commented through a clenched jaw.

The young nurse stood frozen in place. She could feel the waves of anger radiating from Henrietta and sighed. "Figuring that out is why you are here."

EUGENE IS STILL OUT THERE, SOMEWHERE

Friday, May 30, 1935

Drought depression, delinquency. The twentieth century had begun with such promise. Man, always saddled with a sense of greatness, often looked for the proper units to measure such worth. Who could be the richest? Who could climb the highest? Who could reach the top? Who could touch the bottom? Who could find the center? Man sought challenges as much out of necessity as a need for conquest, and commanding the elements continued in place of purpose. It was only the measurement that mattered.

God was never one to suffer man's hubris, and in step with nature, rendered a correction upon the populous. Large ships sank, peaceful nations declared war, the healthy fell victim to plague, and the rich fell victim to greed. A poisonous cocktail of these brought depression to the United States. The plight forced people to once again rely on the land to provide food and provisions, which also began to falter.

In 1935, the farmlands of the heartland gave way to erosion, and black blizzards of dust formed in the sky and intensified as the year continued into the next. They signaled to the seaboard that something from far away had died, and the cremated remains fluttered toward a burial at sea. Along the way, the dry, stormy clouds signaled to the eastern onlookers something worth a requiem was passing.

The first dark clouds wafted above Weston in late May 1935. Eugene James David Spangold watched the plumes brush along the sky as he stepped onto the campus of Weston State Hospital.

Eugene's name was overloaded in the middle with both his grandfathers' names. Each patriarch was a drunkard in his own right with a similar brand of cruelty when soused. Neither was worthy of a namesake. Eugene often denied he had a middle name. It was not worth speaking on kin who would sooner suck down their family income and replace hunger pangs with the pain of a swift backhand across the jaw.

Eugene's father also held the James middle moniker, going by Jacob James Spangold. A kick in the head from an uncooperative bull cut his life short on the farm. Eugene was too small to remember his father, but held him in high regard for the things he did not know. Jacob was a good father as far as the family could attest. His mother, Ruby, never spoke ill of him, at least. She was not one to mince words about the poor humanity of his grandfathers. This led Eugene to believe Jacob had to be of noble character.

After Jacob's death, Ruby took Eugene to live with her father, David. She opted to endure his abuses rather than stay on the Spangold farm with James. It was the devil she knew, and a beast she knew how to leave sleeping. Eugene was not as mastered in the skill and took regular beatings from Grandfather David. It was never in the presence of Ruby, but she knew and turned a blind eye. In her calculations, it was worth sacrificing her son's wellbeing for a roof overhead. Eugene toughened and developed the sense to avoid activating David's ire. Eugene made light use of childish noises or leaving playthings out.

Ruby remarried when Eugene was fifteen. Rather than join his mother in West Virginia's northern panhandle, the boy lied about his age to join the army.

The horrors of battle never affected Eugene, not during skirmishes in Panama while still coming of age or later during World War I, when he witnessed dozens of deaths firsthand in the trenches of Germany. He had no taste for the atrocities, but also lacked empathy in his youth. His outlook was not sociopathic, but a desensitization from his upbringing. He cared about the people he cared about, but remained indifferent to the plight of those he did not know.

For all his underlying mania and raving outbursts, Eugene came to the Weston State Hospital of his own accord. He hoisted along a black steamer trunk edged with silver buckles and scuffed corners. In the center of the lid was a single travel sticker from Toronto, Canada. It was the only place Eugene traveled abroad not dictated by the United States Army. Ethel, Eugene's wife, had insisted on the trip. She desired to visit someplace outside of the United States but with the caveat not to travel across open water. The restriction limited their options to Canada or Mexico.

The sticker was nearly a decade old. Time had left it faded, abraded, and worn around the edges. Eugene dared not remove it. He treated the decal with the same care as his longtime luggage. After all, it reminded him of Ethel.

The hospital reminded him of Ethel, too. They had met there during a social event in the auditorium, where a mutual enamoring blossomed. It was Ethel's bright spirit that showed him what true compassion and love could be. There was someone to care about. Her patience with him buffed the hard edge of his outlook on life, and their daughter, Opal, solidified his feelings.

Upon entering Weston State Hospital, he left his baggage at the nurse station for inspection, and the attendants led him to a side room to wait for the admitting doctor. The room was not as ornate as the main hall. The entryway contained rounded plaster archways, beautiful rugs, and two handcrafted staircases that spiraled up the height of the four floors. The room Eugene found himself in was plain, white, and with a loose collection of books and ledgers scattered in unorganized piles. The only trait the space shared with the corridor was the dark, ornate woodwork framing the bland walls.

It was an older doctor by the name of Samuel Timmons who entered the room. He removed a tweed jacket to rest it on a wooden peg by the door. The removal left the doctor in all white with a matching bowtie. By Eugene's standard, he was old, even though Eugene himself was nearing fifty. The decrepit doctor had white hair that rimmed his head much in the same manner as Eugene's gray hair, but lacked any semblance of facial hair. A full beard normally sported Eugene's face, but he shaved all but his chin, leaving the remaining stalk shorn down to an inch of its former height. That was days ago, leaving time for a grove of stubble to return to his jaw's edge.

"Criminy, you're decrepit," Eugene told Doctor Timmons at the onset.

"Oh?" The doctor seemed surprised by the comment.

"I'm no yearling, but you've taken the appearance of jerky by comparison. What are you? Seventy-Five? Eighty? Ninety?"

"I'm sixty-six," the doctor huffed. "Do you greet most people in such a fashion?"

Eugene waved off the question. "You probably take ear of a lot of rudeness, being gatekeeper to the loony bin and all. I personally mean it to ease the tension. You don't have to act a sissy."

Doctor Timmons ignored the response by shuffling papers. "Well, let me ask you a series of questions then, and we'll see if your steadfast demeanor holds."

Eugene shimmied in the hard metal chair. "I'm ready, Doc."

"Your name is Eugene Spangold?"

"Yes, sir."

"And you live at Rural Route 6 in Gad, West Virginia?"

"It's a Gad damn wonderful place."

His quip prompted the doctor to look up from the paper and purse his lips before continuing. "You are admitting yourself voluntarily. Why?"

Scratching his chin strands with three inner fingers, Eugene queued an elaborate yarn. "I suspected it would be only a matter of time before your dog-catchers came calling for me with their chain leashes and capacious butterfly nets. Gad is a small-town, and there are only so many places to cache myself from view. I submit myself willfully because I know of your administrator, and he knows of me. Willard C. Crane. He was my superior officer during our time as West Virginia's tribute to the Great War. He thinks himself a hometown hero in all of this, but he was no Louis Bennett. He was no flying ace. A joker among the cards whom I seem to recollect possessed a fantastic fear of flying besides. His name will be plastered nowhere among the heroes of the day. As feckless of an individual as he may be, Willard C. Crane has a talent for inadequate leadership and inflating his role in anything; but greatest is his ability to leverage discomfort against a large population at his bidding and prompt disposal. Crane is an appropriate surname because I, like Ichabod, feel as if I am pursued by an entity without head."

The doctor looked away from the notes he was scrawling. "Those are some complex words for a farmer from Gad. Where did you come up with that?"

Indeed, Eugene had rehearsed the spiel, but he often took to oral evisceration against members of society who inflated their importance. It was something of a hobby, darting dictionary entries at unsuspecting victims who were lured into ignorance by Eugene's folksy composition.

"My wife held employment as a schoolteacher. She provided me with the best words from which I could temper into insults of my own branding."

Doctor Timmons did not seem impressed. "You believe our administrator has a grudge against you, and that's why you think you would have been committed?"

"Crane's tendrils of influence curl deep into West Virginia. Yes, sir. Gad is a bit of a hike from here, but I allowed myself to take a social respite in Weston recently, and that was when predator encircled a long arm around prey."

Doctor Timmons set down his pencil and retrieved the stack of paper he'd brought with him. "But you're submitting yourself voluntarily? How did the administrator come to influence your personal choice?"

"You can believe me when I say he will come knocking at a time of his choosing. I'd rather get this over with and find out what devouring my freedom has to do with his nefarious appetite."

With an eye affixed to the paperwork, the doctor continued speaking with an even tone. "But what did you do that makes you think you would be committed?"

Eugene scoffed at the stack of notes. "You have the transcribed orders right there, don't you? Don't you dare cite paranoia among my hysterias. It has proven well justified. You were already building your case for commitment. You already know of what I am accused."

"The sheriff felt you warranted an evaluation, it's true, and you were likely to be brought in for an evaluation in the coming days. But"—Doctor Timmons straightened his bow tie—"I digress. There are two sides to every story, Mr. Spangold. What I have here are the police and the funeral home's side of the story. I would like to hear your side."

Eugene whirled his tongue across his gums and forced the answer. "I … urinated on the floor of the funeral home."

Doctor Timmons paused, which encouraged Eugene to elaborate at a normal cadence. He flailed his arms. "I—it was in an area of t-their hallway that didn't often see use. I had been in there a time or two before and had t-taken a reprieve to observe the comings and goings of corpse gawkers. I am most assured in my assessment. No one traveled the route. No one would have dipped a toe in my puddle. No one would have heard the drippings over all the chatter, but there was a moment of silence the second I began. As poor luck would have it, urine is extra loud when it hits worn carpet. Yes, sir, it turned out to be an assault on every ear within range."

"Don't you think getting urine out of the carpet would be difficult?" Doctor Timmons questioned and shuffled his body in his padded wooden chair. The frame groaning was the only sound while Eugene considered an answer.

"With modern technology, I'm sure the mortician has some brand of fancy liquid sucker." He made a slurping sound with his lips. "Lots of regular tears and puking probably occur at the parlor. Yes, sir. They may have a contraption like that in their broom closet already. Little perfume afterward and it'll be good as new, I tell ya."

The doctor laid the papers on the table and scratched each of his clean-shaven cheeks simultaneously with a thumb and forefinger. "That well could be, but I'm not here to diagnose their problem. I'm here to diagnose yours."

"I already compensated Floyd Funeral Home for my transgressions against their drugget."

The doctor overpowered him. "You are missing the point. This is a mental institution, not a jail. I don't care how you resolved the problem. I am trying to determine why there was a problem to begin with."

Gulping hard, Eugene beat on his knees like a drum as he focused on the truth. "I … was at my wife's funeral."

The doctor nodded. "And?"

"And my bladder was full, and I lost my wits about the time and the direction of the powder room. I made a poor calculation between sound and liquid and foot traffic."

"You later told the officer that you were considering lighting the funeral home on fire."

Eugene shot forward in his seat. "They wrote that down? Sonuva bitch!"

"It's all right here. That is a big leap—from public urination to arson. Why would you want to set the funeral home on fire?"

"To get the piss smell out."

A sigh burst from the doctor, which Eugene first thought to be a chuckle.

"You've told a lie somewhere along the line," the doctor continued. "Fire is a big leap from perfume. Now, you've been spinning your yarn long enough that you've tied yourself in knots. Let's try the truth."

"I'll tell you, Doc. That is, I want to tell you, but I don't think you'll take heed of my account as that of a sane person. I think you'll believe I belong here for an extended stay. Yes, sir, after the things I've seen, perhaps I do deserve a loon's vacation within your fold."

The seasoned doctor smirked. Eugene took notice and realized the doctor had him exactly where he wanted.

"Let me tell you something, Mr. Spangold. You don't get to be a thousand-year-old shaman without learning a few things about patients. I understand your situation perfectly. You believe if you commit yourself voluntarily, you may leave voluntarily anytime you wish. Well, that is not the case. I have the police report, which is more than enough to prove your erratic behavior is threatening to society. I also took it upon myself to investigate further, and people close to you tell me you go into frequent periods of belligerence where you rattle off long and meaningless rants."

Eugene smiled. "Did anyone tell you I've always done that?"

The doctor looked from his papers while keeping his head lowered. "Did you … always do that?"

Eugene sighed. "No, I don't reckon."

Doctor Timmons grunted in satisfaction. "When did it start?"

"Honestly? It was just after the accident."

"Can you tell me about the accident?"

Eugene clawed the top of his thighs. "No! I was not present for the accident. If you don't possess the paperwork, I am certain it exists. You can eye it over when you obtain it. If you haven't by now, you have not truly been doing your due diligence."

"Are you sure I didn't?" Doctor Timmons held up a single, earmarked paper from the end of the table.

Eugene's eyes narrowed. He crossed his arms and stamped the floor with his left foot. "Fine. Just fine. I will cooperate and give you the bona fide truth when you ask about the funeral home again."

"Why did you want to burn it down?"

Eugene straightened and cleared his throat. "I put eyes on something from beyond, Doc! It was a vision." Eugene locked his gaze with the doctor so he could prove sincerity in his farfetched truth. "A banshee, like from the moors of old, appeared in the middle of the parlor. It was detached from everyone and soon manifested into a human shape. It was … a man … the President of the United States."

"Roosevelt?" the doctor questioned as he leaned forward, placing both elbows on the table.

"No, this particular individual was confined to a wheelchair," Eugene responded with increased vigor. "He spoke to me, but I couldn't hear the words. All I could do was see his mouth move. In my heart, though, and deep in the contours of my mind and caverns of my soul, I could discern his words. They were being delivered to me from beyond time and space. Yes, sir, Mister President, somewhere from outside existence. He said 'As your president, I need you to help me. There is a great evil threatening my existence, and I need you to go forth to find and destroy it with fire!'"

The doctor's eyes widened as the story trundled to its conclusion. "Well …" The doctor filled his cheeks with air and slowly let it spurt through puckered lips.

"You can see now why I wanted to keep my vision under wraps, Doc. Yes, sir, mister, you're going to make me a pin cushion for Crane's machinations."

Doctor Timmons cleared his throat and erected his posture. "Mr. Spangold, do you ever consume alcohol?"

Eugene shook his head. "No. Never."

"Did you consume alcohol that night at the funeral home?"

"Oh, yes. Plenty of it." Eugene nodded. "But never any other time. My grandfathers were both elbow-deep in moonshine and spirits, and I never forgave them for the state in which they left my family."

Doctor Timmons returned to his even demeanor. "Do you think your outbursts and visions may have to do with consuming alcohol that you normally wouldn't?" the doctor further pressed. "Folks who don't often consume alcohol are more susceptible to its effects."

Eugene leaned his head back and sighed, a drop of spittle rode the air current and landed on his manicured chin. He further emptied his lungs and returned to normal posture.

"Alcohol may have been a factor in my conduct. I do not wish to speak to the effects of those spirits on my person. I see no reason to believe the liquid spirits manifested the ghostly spirit."

The doctor hummed. "Someone else from Gad reported that you are obsessed with a Hollywood actress. Claimed to be dating her …"

"Janet Gaynor! A real bona fide Hollywood type. Yes, sir, I tell ya I was able to see her in *High Society Blues*. Eleanor Divine was her name in the movie, and I'll tell ya, it is a fine name. We were going to name our daughter Eleanor, but me and Ethel decided we could name ten people on one finger with the same name, so we assigned her Opal Lee. We know exactly zero people with that moniker. Yes, sir, mister, it also went with the precious stone motif the women in my family had. You see, my mother's name was Ruby."

Eugene paused to sniffle. Gravity had found him, and emotions suspended in the air began to fall upon his heart. The doctor leaned forward as if he knew drastic change was taking place and was ready to observe.

"My mom died … years ago, but she died. Ethel LeeAnn died, too. She died! She died young, yes, sir. And I got drunk and took a leak on the carpet of Floyd Funeral Home. You want to know why, Doc? It's because I didn't know where the bathroom was, and I was too far gone to care. But then everyone was staring, and the president came to me with marching orders. Oh. I said I couldn't make out what he said, but I did hear him say one thing clear as a bell, 'Those damn trees get in the way sometimes.' I'm not sure he was talking to me because it didn't make a great deal of sense. He wasn't looking at me, but there was no one else there. He was sitting in the pee-saturated hallway at that point."

Doctor Timmons observed the mania and scribbled quick notes, taking glee in witnessing the outburst. "But why did you want to burn down the funeral home?" he said over the rambling.

"The president didn't allow much intelligence on where to find the spirits threatening him. I considered the parlor the best place to start. Indeed, if the funeral home was where those evil spirits were, yes, sir, Mister President, then it was my duty to consign them to hellfire. Don't you understand my plight, Doc?" Eugene stopped, scanning the room to find it quiet, still, and occupied by the two men. "So that's why I'm wishing to commit myself," Eugene continued. The belligerence had vanished, leaving an even-keeled individual in his place. "Yes, sir."

The doctor scribbled something onto his notepad, grunted in satisfaction, then laid the pen beside the paper. "We would certainly like to have you for treatment and observation, and then maybe we can get you on your way after a few weeks. Let's go have a look at the fourth floor."

The doctor stood and twisted his body in a way that suggested an attempt at loosening a vertebra within his ancient spine. Eugene nodded in the assurance of the doctor's geriatric nature, but a pop from his own back leveled the reality of his own age. He grumbled and followed Doctor Timmons from the receiving area.

"You keep your flight risks on the fourth floor," Eugene noted while the two began up the oak stairs spanning the levels.

"That is generally correct," Doctor Timmons replied. "How do you know that?"

With chest puffed, Eugene explained, "I have some reputable knowledge about your workplace. I first met my wife in these walls."

"Oh?" Doctor Timmons nearly missed a step as they rounded to the second floor.

Eugene picked up on the tone. "Oh. Not how you are thinking. Not as a patient. I first caught wind of her elegance at one of Weston's socials held in your auditorium."

"Oh." The doctor's voice deflated the second time. He waited until they climbed the flight to the third floor before he continued. The floor led straight to the assembly hall's entrance. "This is where it all began for your family?"

The two paused on the level to allow Eugene to reminisce. He stared at the door to the assembly hall and observed denim-clad maintenance workers carrying out large paper decorations.

Doctor Timmons placed an ushering hand on Eugene's shoulder. "They just had a dance this weekend. I guess they're arranging for whatever comes next."

Eugene tensed and kept his feet planted. "She was wearing a light pink dress. Her hair was curled in a fanciful way that suggested effort. I cannot begin to describe it, Doc. Yes, sir, she was a creature of pure splendor."

"How does that make you feel?"

A well of emotion was building in Eugene's chest, but a deep sigh managed to ward much of it off. "Tired, Doc," he finally allowed. "Let's go view these quarters."

The two made the ascent up the final flight, and Eugene considered how easy it would be in the moment to flee. The doctor was above him with no orderlies or guards. It would take nothing to wrap hands around the man's grandfatherly neck and yank him down the flight. A more mentally deranged man would have done so with no hesitation, but it was not in Eugene's nature to inflict direct harm on another. War had snuffed such a flame, if there were ever a spark for violence to begin with. Maybe it was his grandfathers who squelched it.

They arrived on the top floor and turned to the south wing to follow a long corridor of human misery. The overcrowded ward left little room for passage. Any space of the wall not reserved for a door held a mattress with no frame. Along the corridor, men slept, confined within the building and their illnesses. Existence was a cage with no key, nor even a lock to place it. The faces of the men along the hall were somber, disconnected. One man hooped and hollered, but another irritable man shushed him. One individual wept and wailed from a room near the hall's end.

Eugene took a chill in the presence of the downtrodden. The empathy he had lacked in his youth had bloomed late and flourished when he had a wife and child to call his own. Now, he saw his family in the faces of everyone, save those he despised.

The ward came to an end and cut to a short, perpendicular hall that connected to the next vertical corridor.

"This ward is where you will be staying," Doctor Timmons revealed after he pulled open a heavy metal door.

While the doctor did not communicate with any of the patients in the previous ward, his sociability awakened the second he stepped into the new area.

"Emmet, how are you today? You look great, Peter. How's your temperament today, Morris? What are you petting, Larry? A puppy? That's nice." The latter man, Larry, was standing in the middle of a larger room lined with beds. He bent to stroke the air with a flat palm.

The ward was hazy with cigarette smoke intensified by the different arrangement of lighting. Being on the top floor, a skylight allowed the sun to beam downward, diffusing the cloudy corridor.

The men on the floor were much livelier than the previous ward, with howling of a more jubilant nature. Men played poker in the middle of the floor, and adolescent boys ran about in a furious game of tag.

Doctor Timmons gave a light cough. "How many cigarettes have they had today?" he asked the attendant when they approached.

"They've already burned through the day's allotment," a nearby nurse responded. "We prefer the smokers all go at once, so individuals won't feel pressured into sharing their ration."

The doctor nodded and continued to the end of the hall, which was the southernmost corner of the building.

"This will be your room for the time being," the doctor announced, pointing to a smaller space two doors from the end.

Eugene stepped onto the precipice and came to view two empty beds and a third occupied by a young man reading *The Bridge of San Luis Rey*. After reaching the terminus of a paragraph, the boy glanced up from the tome at Eugene and Timmons in the doorway.

"Vernon, this is Eugene. He's going to be your new roommate." Doctor Timmons turned to Eugene. "This is Vernon, but most of his friends call him Flip."

Vernon's face contorted into a look of horror, and it became clear that Eugene was to be an unwelcome addition to the menagerie. Vernon's first squealing response pressed further salt into the wound.

"Ah, damn. Not another geezer."

BRITTANY AT THE END OF THE MILLENNIUM

WEDNESDAY, JUNE 16, 1999

The leather seats of the Crown Victoria were sticky. The residue clung to Brittany's shorts, binding her to the upholstery. She wanted to lay flat across the bench, but feared adhering more of her body to the surface than could be easily released. *Maybe many a shoplifter once sat here*, she thought. Their sticky fingers were quite literal.

Across the screened divider, Officer S.K. Prince sat in the driver's seat of the large police car, remaining silent since they had left the police station. Brittany was quiet, too, exercising her right. A fresh revelation, given freely by the officer, stunned her into silence. It was the answer to a question she had never intended to ask, but was grateful for the answer.

Brittany was familiar with the officer and had seen him plenty during her last high school days. In April, a mass shooting at Columbine High School sparked a generation of similar events. The tragedy was uncommon for the time, and the massacre inspired communities to overprotect. In an abundance of caution, the nation spared no expense to pour in resources to keep students safe for the short stretch remaining in the school year, unaware the floodgates for future massacres had opened.

Officer Prince was the law enforcement officer assigned to patrol the school during those waning days. He was not long removed from his own high school career, which allowed him to connect easily with the senior class. A fortunate few were allowed to call him Stuart without consequence. Brittany was not among them, but she often mingled with those who were.

On Brittany's first attempt to enter the hospital, she was not turned away by the normal security guards, but by Officer Prince. Cloaked in tactical gear, the officer seemed nervous as he gleaned her intentions near the Kirkbride.

Brittany stammered that she was just passing through. Shortcuts crossed the property but were not as close in proximity to the building. Still, Officer Prince allowed her to go on without incident, which felt both fortunate and suspicious. As Brittany walked away from the encounter, questions began to burn in her mind. *What was Stuart doing on the hospital grounds? Why didn't I think to ask?* In that first moment, he seemed eager to send her away with minimal suspicion.

He was not one to let incidents slide, and there was no reason to believe he would have then, either. He could have at least written her up for trespassing. Her excuse was flimsy, and she had practically admitted to the crime. The burning questions from that night were still ablaze, but the answers were now coming in fast. Brittany's thoughts stopped when the officer broke the silence.

"You were lucky they didn't turn you over to the state police. They wouldn't have gone as easy on you."

"Weren't they at your paintball party?" Brittany commented, holding back from outright mocking the officer.

His response was heavy with exhaustion but truthful. "Some of them were." Officer Prince cut the wheel sharply onto Brown Avenue. It was a different route than Brittany had traversed earlier in the night, one less friendly to pedestrians. The officer straightened his wheels before continuing. "State police don't operate with the same awareness of their hypocrisy that we do."

The comment made Brittany realize the reason for their leniency. The officers were going easy on her because they were in the same predicament as the hospital's security guards. At the station, the other officer on-duty, J.K. Mixon, told Brittany that law enforcement likely would not face consequences for trespassing. When Brittany took a soapbox to protest the unfairness, Officer Mixon clarified the reason. Security had allowed them to enter the Kirkbride on those nights. It all made sense then. The watchmen were in trouble, the city officers were in trouble, and Brittany was in trouble. It seemed their camaraderie in wrongdoing had forged an alliance among the guilty parties. She smirked at this realization. It was quite convenient the consequences of her trespassing were being overlooked along with the officers' more significant crime of vandalizing a historic landmark.

Confident her deductions were correct, Brittany shelved the revelation and changed topics. "Does your police car have a nickname?"

"No," Officer Prince grumbled.

Brittany peeled a hand from the seat. "You should consider calling it Sticky Vicky."

The porch light was still on when they pulled into the driveway. Moths and millers too lazy to flutter downtown took residence around the bulb's radius, casting mini shadows across the powder-blue porch.

Brittany expected the fragility of their alliance to shatter the second Officer Prince rapped the door of 723 McGary Avenue. Brittany did not announce her departure to her parents, but she did not sneak out, either. She was an adult now, and they held a tepid respect on the matter … *for the moment.*

There was a light on in the kitchen, but the sudden illumination of the stairwell indicated her parents were both upstairs. Through the small window at the top of the door, Brittany watched her mother stagger down the staircase. Brittany inhaled and waited for the locks on the door to rattle and the knob to turn.

"Brittany?" Mom, Glenda, queried without further context. She was in a light pink nightgown with her blonde and gray hair pulled into a sloppy ponytail.

A sudden wave of shame washed over Brittany. She squeezed passed Glenda, darting down the side hallway and into her first floor bedroom. She closed the door and turned the lock, even though the latch never fully secured it. A simple push would grant access.

Brittany flung herself face down on the bed, and silence surrounded her again. Distant words from Officer Prince began to seep through the insulation, but they reached Brittany as mumbles. Only a few full sentences reached her ears.

"Because of recent events involving the hospital, we are going to keep a lid on this and not file charges at this time. We don't believe we can rightly carry out our duties in this matter, and we and the hospital guards agree we will just pass this off as kids being kids."

"I'm an adult," Brittany corrected to the cobwebs in the corner. She lost interest in the officer's spiel after the raging error. Brittany rolled onto her back to retrieve headphones and the attached CD player. A band called Orbit was in the disc tray and she made little effort with the buttons to select track five, "Medicine."

Bass and drums filled her ears, and she closed her eyes to meditate on the song. It was a bouncy rock ballad with lyrics about a girl alone in a small-town.

Brittany was still captivated by the grunge era—a time of rock that had faded away before she realized good music existed. However, many suitable songs were released in its aftermath, and she developed a hobby for collecting albums from more obscure artists. Radish, Tonic, The Flys, and I Mother Earth were the four bands she loved, aside from Orbit. While the world was enthralled with Britney Spears, Brittany Loughry couldn't find it in herself to support her name twin. Posters of major rock acts from the 1990s adorned the walls. A Pearl Jam poster was the centerpiece of her private gallery, and it was the first to fade and fray along the edges. A stereo she had purchased with her allowance rested on a dresser but, aside from the radio, was no longer functional.

Before the tape deck quit working, Brittany recorded as much music as she could from distant rock stations. Because her kind of music was not available in the heart of West Virginia, Brittany would tap into her father's genetic resourcefulness. Using unraveled notebook wire, one end spliced to the stereo's antenna, and one connected to the cable box outlet, she generated a signal boost that tapped into an alternative rock station from State College, Pennsylvania.

She reflected on the haunting presence of her last words. "I'm an adult." The statement was true, and it seemed the youthful items she utilized to get past the threshold would not continue the journey onward to maturity. *Childish things put away, indeed. Everything is temporary. Everything is left behind.*

Brittany continued to listen to the song. She would soon tire of the tune and forget it for good in a few years. But "Medicine" was in her ears for the moment, and she let the feeling consume her. She mouthed the lyrics and caressed the empty CD case, scratching a nail over the rows of plastic grooves along the bottom.

Her father, John Rocco, interrupted the sacrament when he pushed through the faulty latch. "What did you do?" he shouted over the speaker, pointing back through the hallway toward the front door.

Officer Prince had delivered his news and returned to the night. She pressed pause, removed the headphones, and tossed them on the bed. "It was a mess in there, Dad. They … The cops—they absolutely wrecked the place."

"You shouldn't have been in there to begin with."

"The cops shouldn't have been, either!" Brittany's pitch rose to match John Rocco's. "At least I'm not a fucking vandal!"

"Language!" John Rocco shouted and placed both hands on his high hips.

He was still in khakis and a button-up shirt despite being past midnight. The man refurbished and sold computers as a hobby in addition to his day job managing a RadioShack. The second bedroom upstairs consisted of a labyrinth of CPU towers and monitors with pitfalls of keyboards and mice. Brittany's lawless action roused John Rocco from his late-night liturgy and was now interrupting hers.

"I wanted to see it for myself … how bad it was," Brittany explained.

John Rocco sighed. "I expect we'll see pictures in the newspaper soon enough. Ray tells me a reporter from Pittsburgh has already been there with the sheriff. The local folks will be covering it soon, too. We're all going to see without having to commit crimes."

Her dad was calm again. John Rocco had a slow fuse. He would explode in a grandiose way and return to calm in the next breath. He made a motion to sit on her bed, and Brittany shuffled to accommodate him. She stretched and lay face down on the edge, propping up her head with her arms.

"You snuck out in the winter, too, didn't you?" John Rocco asked, recollecting Brittany's last close call. "Those were your footprints in the snow?"

"I like exploring old places." There was no point in denial. "It's … it's a hobby."

John Rocco sighed through his nose and brushed a hand through long strands of platinum hair he usually kept neatly combed but was now disheveled. The computer he was reviving in his lair must have been vexing for John Rocco's hair to become so unkempt.

"IBM?" Brittany guessed. She saw an opportunity to evade a hard conversation by pivoting to John Rocco's hobbies.

"Aptiva. 1995. It's trying to run Windows '98 and doing a crummy job."

Brittany hoped there would be more. A technical schematic of how each internal component connected to the motherboard would have been something, anything, to further detract from the matter at hand. But there was nothing, and the conversation returned.

"Your escapades tonight aren't making me feel too great about your going off to college." John Rocco leaned forward, staring at the posters on the wall. "Maybe I should take back that nice new computer I got you."

On her desk in the far corner of the room was an Apple iMac G3, which John Rocco bought Brittany as a dual graduation and birthday gift. Recognizing the need for college students to stay up on modern technology, Brittany's father sprung for a full-price model rather than refurbishing his own. He even picked a unique color. A translucent pink allowed all the moving parts within to be visible. Brittany speculated that with the opaque plastic, her father could point out all the components inside the all-in-one device without prying open the case.

Brittany had no interest in computers, but the major step to becoming a college student was an exciting prospect. She even left its box along the wall, ready to pack when August arrived.

"I'm sorry," Brittany said, waving the white flag of her defiance.

"You got lucky tonight, honey. I reckon for the second time. You could have served time, or paid a fine."

"They confiscated my backpack. I had taken some interesting pictures, too."

"Well, let that be a lesson. If losing a few snapshots was all you got for trespassing on government property, I'd count those blessings once more." John Rocco patted Brittany's back and stood. "I think I'm going to hit the sack." He shuffled to the door and turned. "I guess I'll talk with your mom and find out if any further punishment is needed. She was too mad to talk with you just now."

Brittany's dad left, latching the door as best he could. She breathed a sigh of relief. Trouble had eluded her once again. The feeling was short-lived when commotion between Mom and Dad rumbled in the hallway.

"Well, I'll tell her!" Glenda spoke loudly, like she was in the room already. Brittany pushed to her knees and braced herself, holding her posture against the bed with both arms.

"What the hell were you thinking?" Glenda started before even entering the room. She tripped as she pushed through the door, but caught herself. Though embarrassed, Glenda kept her forward motion and the anger rode along.

"Brittany Jean, you think you're going to go breaking into other people's property like a little hoodlum? This is why you're never going to amount to nothing! How can you hope to accomplish anything if you're too busy running amok about this town? We ought to take everything away from you."

"I am an adult!" Brittany shouted in defense. She had fought the urge to engage, but her mother had used the same line for years. "You're never going to amount to nothing."

The phrase had lost its meaning. In fact, the double negative evoked the opposite meaning, but Brittany knew not to correct the statement. They were empty words and losing everything seemed to be an empty threat now, too. Glenda Loughry's problem and answer to every equation was to reduce it to zero. There was no sum between the problem and the solution. Therefore, the problem and the solution had no meaning. Brittany could not form the idea into such profound words; all she could aggregate was a vulgar variation of her previous phrase.

"I am a fucking adult. Deal with it."

Glenda snapped back, "You're still under this roof, and when you're gone from here, you're still under a roof that we're paying oodles of dollars for. You're going to be under our thumb for several more years, so you're going to need to deal with it."

"Great!" Brittany said almost in a scream. "I can't wait to be away from you. You made growing up so, so hard."

Glenda chuckled in a threatening way. "If you think growing up was so hard, then maybe you're not grown enough, Miss Brittany."

Signing off with a "Miss Brittany" usually meant she was about to levy a punishment. Brittany cringed and braced for the sentence. "You're grounded for a week. No going out after five p.m. No talking to friends on the phone. For saying the F-word earlier, you get to come with me to clean Miss Mabel's house on Saturday."

Brittany groaned. Glenda cleaned houses on the weekend for different women within their church. The punishment was not a penance Brittany had any interest in paying, particularly because Glenda always gave her the jobs she did not enjoy doing. Scrubbing toilets seemed to be the most common task assigned to Brittany.

"I'm doing Great-Aunt Gail's house that day, too," Glenda said. "I can bring you along to that one if you're gonna whine about it."

"Ugh, Mom, she has four bathrooms!"

"Yeah, she does. I doubt she uses them all, but you're sure as heck gonna clean them all."

Brittany lay back in and huffed. "I accept my punishment."

"Good." Glenda snorted with satisfaction. "See you don't pull shenanigans like that again."

"Uh-huh," Brittany croaked.

Glenda stepped backward through the door and closed it softly. She did not leave departing words. Brittany soon heard two sets of footsteps clop to the second floor.

Quiet had returned. Like the dark, only operating in the absence of something else. Sound and light rushed into spaces to take away silence and shade. It was in the presence of both that Brittany could finally review the night's top story.

"I saw a ghost," Brittany blurted. Such a unique event was forgotten so easily when the world closed around her. In the stillness, she remembered, and alternating thoughts grappled for dominance.

A week of home confinement. It could have been real confinement— real jail. I did get lucky … No! You saw a ghost. Don't let the world take away what happened. It was a glowing creature. Human, I think. It was blinding white light. I could almost make out features. Features! It had clothes on. It had something on its belt. It had jeans! What did I see?

But it wasn't just Brittany who witnessed something. At the police station, while Officer Mixon spoke with the hospital security guards in his office, Officer Prince sat with his arms crossed against a desk in the lobby. He appeared uncomfortable at the mention of Weston Hospital.

"You were in the paintball game, weren't you?" she asked him. "I spoke to you beforehand that night. You were in tactical gear. It was paintball gear, wasn't it?"

Officer Prince did not respond, growing more pensive instead. He perspired more than usual for the air-conditioned room.

"What did you see in there? Were you on the third floor? It was a woman's ward because it had pink walls."

"I can't speak about the event," the officer mumbled, barely opening his mouth.

"The event?" Brittany pressed. "Do you mean the paintball or the ghost?"

The question caused Officer Prince to jolt as if a shock of electricity had gone through him. "How did you know about the ghost? Was it room 668?"

It was very unbecoming to see a hardened law enforcement officer melt into a reduced state. Brittany almost pitied him as he nodded in the affirmative.

"It was a dark spirit. A phantom black as night. Me and another teammate could see the movement, thought it was one of our opponents, and began firing. Once we started, we realized that the black figure was levitating in the center of the room. It began flailing when we started firing. When we realized what it was, we couldn't stop. We were joined by another office … er … teammate, and he began firing, too. When we were done, we shined a light into the room, but there was nothing there. It was just our paint. No evidence of anything else."

Brittany thought about the officer's account. It was a dark ghost. Her ghost was a luminous white. Did the paint attack activate some sort of bioluminescence?

The night required answers. Brittany craved them, coveted them, and demanded them. Being grounded like a common teenager was a terrible setback. She elected not to think about what she had done, but what she would do when the sentence expired.

She returned to music, grabbing the next closest jewel case to change discs. It was a band called Hum. Brittany pressed the buttons to reach the third track.

The disc began spinning, playing an angsty ballad of another girl, waiting.

NEIL AT THE CLOSE
OF THE DECADE

SATURDAY, JUNE 15, 2019

The statue of Christ saved Neil in a much more literal way. Although it was not enough to make him consider returning to organized worship, he was beginning to feel better about the prospect of living.

In a sort of spiritual ritual, Neil spent many fair-weather days standing among the tombstones. He admired the towering depiction of Christ in his final moments before the world broke free from sin. The accumulated spirits fled their tombs in a violent quake that shook the very core of existence. A lot of time has passed since then. The fabric of time, space, and earth healed from the celestial rupture, tethering more spirits to a terrestrial eternity. Or so Neil understood it.

Neil and his friends had taken an interest in these trapped places. Places where spooks may roam. Trapped spirits, fallen angels, or something else still lurked in places long-standing. Stories, occurrences, and coincidences were too common for outright dismissal of logic. The unknown element was what made it exciting to Neil and his companions.

There wasn't much paranormal activity in the Midwest that could be experienced firsthand. The history had yet to establish a solid foundation for ghost stories. The Twin Cities offered haunted tours, but most featured anecdotal tales narrated by guides with indirect experience. Too often, these stories were secondhand accounts. These hauntings were rarely verified or replicated, making them somewhat underwhelming for thrill-seekers.

The best experience was one that Neil and his friends created for themselves when they traveled to Yellow Medicine County, in southwest Minnesota, to search for Eddie Swan. Swan was a stranded motorist who went missing on a farm road in 2010 while returning home from a college party. He was on the phone with his parents late that May night as he walked to the nearest town. Suddenly, he shouted, and the call ended. There had been no sign of the student in the nine years since.

Stories about what happened ranged from falling into a nearby river to being abducted by a cult roaming the rural fields at night. The rumors sparked public interest and transformed the event into a new legend. Neil and his friends decided to take a shot at solving the cold case. In 2017, Neil, Demetry, and Miguel spent the seventh anniversary of Swan's disappearance on the same dirt road where he went missing.

Demetry was the friend most passionate about chasing thrills. After building his career at the *Star Tribune*, he embraced adventurous activities like skydiving and bungee jumping. He organized their trips, and the pursuit of Swan was no exception. He showed remarkable fearlessness when he vanished into a field of sugar beet sprouts on a pitch-black night. Neil and Miguel Seymour-Leone also entered the field, yet neither had the wits to match Demetry's endurance.

After hours of walking around the field, Neil and Miguel's minds began playing wicked tricks on them. They returned to the road, spooked. Demetry mocked them upon his return an hour later. They drove around and explored the desolate farmlands some more before starting back to the city as light rimmed the eastern sky.

On the return trip, Neil first laid eyes upon Murdock and the statue of Christ. There was a certain hopefulness to it. A night full of thrills for them and terror for the Swans could end with a notion of comfort—a comfort represented by the violent depiction of a mutilated god. Overcoming death was the message, but it was always the preamble to death displayed in the iconography.

Crossing the Ohio River into West Virginia, Neil stared at a picture of the statue. Taking the photo was his last order of business before leaving Murdock for good. Neil had a habit of fixating on inanimate objects, and the statue was his current obsession. The sculpture prompted him to select Murdock as his new home once his divorce was final.

A series of exits and bridges brought the sedan to a large cantilever bridge, which suspended the WILD WONDERFUL WEST VIRGINIA signage in its trusses. The last leg of their fifteen-hour journey across the Midwest brought the trio into the heart of Appalachia.

"Two more hours, counting a stop for gas," Demetry stated with glee. He had driven the entire route himself and was shaking off the signs of fatigue until the moment they crossed the state line.

"Are we still going to do the ghost tour?" Neil asked from his nest in the back seat. They had planned to start on Friday and split the trip into two days, but Demetry's final day before the sabbatical took longer than expected. The group decided to start the trip early the next morning.

Demetry yawned and tapped the clock on the dashboard, still set for the central time zone. "You see that? It's actually six-thirty here. If we keep to our schedule, we will arrive in Weston at eight-thirty, which will only give us a half hour to get our shit in the hotel room and get to the asylum."

"So, you're chickening out?" Neil said with a more offensive lilt than intended.

"No," Demetry defended, "I am not chickening out. I am slothing out. It's been a long day, and I don't think I can muster another eight hours of being conscious."

"I napped. And me and Miguel both offered to take over driving duties so you could rest. Admit it. You are afraid."

"I was afraid of you and Miguel dinging up my Honda with your dank-ass driving skills."

"That does make sense," Miguel agreed. "To be honest, I'm kinda tired, too. Maybe we can do it next weekend."

"We're already paid up for tonight, so there's no sense in wasting it," Neil argued. "I'll go if no one else will. I didn't leave my job and travel a thousand miles just to rest."

"No, you're describing a vacation," Demetry joked. He did not inspire any humor.

"Regardless, I'd like to try to go on the tour tonight. You can drop me off at the asylum and leave my stuff in the car. Come get me at four in the morning."

Demetry acted as if he wanted to argue more but remembered the reason why he brought forlorn Neil. "Very well. If it's anything like Eddie Swan, you'll call me crying by midnight."

*****

"This was the violent women's ward. Some would argue that it was more dangerous than the violent men's ward. Men tend to be blunter with their attacks, whereas women would plan out an assault. Nurses often had to walk down this hallway back-to-back with arms linked," Greg, a younger male guide with a pierced lip, told the flock of visitors huddled together in an unlit passage.

Each of the dozen in the group held flashlights and flipped them in all directions. Neil thought it was no wonder shadows appeared to move in the halls of the asylum with so many beams of light being cast.

It was nearing midnight, and the tour already had time to explore the fourth floor. The northern end felt grimy and claustrophobic. The wooden floors on the southern side could have been enough to creep anyone out, but it was early enough that light still seeped in through the room windows and skylights unique to the top floor of the Trans-Allegheny Lunatic Asylum.

The third floor felt different. The ceilings were higher, allowing more space for the ghost hunters to stand apart.

"On this side of the hall were the solitary confinement cells," Greg continued. "They would sometimes perform electroshock therapy in those rooms, and some recent visitors have said they have heard the sound of electricity in this hall."

Whispers from the patrons scurried across the room; anything louder would cast a thunderous echo, demonstrated anytime the guide delivered his spiel.

"On this side, we have two interesting rooms." Greg walked to an open room two doors from the main hall. "This room once had a woman who spent two decades at the asylum in the early 1900s. She would spend her days walking in the same pattern in the communal area." He pointed further down the hall. "Down there. By the time she died, she had etched the word 'love' into the tile with her feet. Now, the reason I didn't show you is because the word is no longer there. The tiles were all removed years ago because they were made with asbestos."

More whispers passed as the guide walked to the next room. Its closed door looked as if it did not serve as much of a barrier. Like most doors in the area, this one had oily spots pocked across it. The guide said the marks came from an illegal paintball match held in the late 1990s. One visitor refused to believe law enforcement agencies were the perpetrators.

"It's all on record," Greg responded with confidence. "*The Weston Democrat* article is in our museum if you want to come back during the day to see it for yourself."

Neil also found the story hard to believe, but he knew the museum archive would confirm the truth.

"This room is interesting for a more recent and haunted reason. Back in September of 2012, a group of ghost hunters were in this hallway, asking questions to potential spirits. They asked the question, 'Can we talk?' Suddenly, this door slammed shut. They were not able to open it again, nor was anyone else on staff or otherwise. To this day, it remains sealed shut, though visitors have reported the sound of a door slamming in this hall around the same time every September."

An older male visitor studied the small numbers above the door. "668," he said in a deep baritone. "It's close to being 666."

Greg snickered. "We hear that a lot. It looks like they purposely avoided using the number."

The tour moved to the next ward, which once housed the violent men of the hospital. Stories of the section were more robust. Tales of angry spirits refusing to speak, slamming barred doors, manifesting to blow in ears and scratch on backs. The bedpost room—a large room at the end of the hall—provided the grimmest story of murder. Two patients killed their snoring roommate by placing his head under a bedpost and jumping on the bed until the snoring ceased for good.

The morbid tale piqued the interest of the professional ghost hunters among them. They remained in the area to set up recording devices and equipment. The more novice paranormal investigators remained in the ward to observe the spectacle. When a grid of green lights began projecting on the bedpost room wall, Neil decided it better to strike out on his own. The walk from the ward was long, but he recognized the violent male ward was tough to escape by design.

The violent female ward cast an eerie glow from the streetlights of Weston. The window frames created a shadow grid along the pink corridor and inside the front-facing rooms.

As Neil entered the ward, he thought he detected movement near the end of the hall. All he had for light was his phone, still clipped to his belt.

"Hello?" Neil shouted, startling himself with the volume. He repeated the word at a reduced decibel.

The shadow had entered a room near the end of the hall. He believed it to be the third one from the end, next to the chalkboard.

Room 668. The door sealed shut by a supposed supernatural event? He felt certain that was where he had seen the body go. He placed a wary hand on the doorknob and felt his body quiver. *Excitement, fear, or both?*

"Hello?" he whispered one last time. Movies and television taught him this was the part where the phantom leaped from the shadows to attack. His depression still dulled his receptors for extreme emotion. Paired with not wanting Demetry to clown him about being a coward later, Neil suppressed his fears, and turned the handle to room 668. To his surprise, it opened.

Neil exhaled and peeked into the room. Empty. He entered, feeling emboldened by the lack of paranormal activity and the door opening only for him. *Had it just been a tale? Was this something the tour guides told that was never verified by a simple turn of a handle? No.* He had watched his fellow guests try their luck. *Maybe there was a trick to turning the knob?*

Nevertheless, Neil found himself to be the accidental savant. He was inside the sealed room on turf that no one had tread for years.

The room appeared as pink and empty as the corridor, but it was coated with stains of several different colors. A plethora of round splatters left tails as the residue trickled down the wall and dried.

The historic paintball event left its influence most in this room. The view from the window overlooked the front campus, where mature trees once produced swaths of shade. One tree immediately in front of the room had seen better days. It was a birch whose trunk had been cleft in two by what must have been a lightning strike. The white bark appeared burned on one side, leaving half the branches bare. The other half bloomed as usual. Its full plight was hard to make out in the dim glow of Weston.

A flash of light interrupted the observation. It was like lightning inside the room, with none of the thunder. As Neil turned to seek the source, another flash bleached the room. It fell dark again, and before Neil floated the apparition of a young woman.

Neil bellowed and recoiled against the outer wall. He watched as the ghostly form also jumped back and streaked from the room.

Neil backed into the corner and slid to the floor. His heart accelerated. He could not make sense of what he saw but knew he had found definitive proof the stories of the haunted insane asylum were real.

More momentous to the occasion was excitement returning to Neil's body for the first time in more than a year. The electricity of his fright hit like pleasure. The adrenaline pumps were working, and he remained sitting in the dusty corner to let his heart race. The circumstances of the event did not matter in the present. He was simply happy to feel something again.

7
HENRIETTA AT THE TURN OF THE CENTURY

The door was open. A searing light cast yellow beams across the pink room. The illumination roused Henrietta from a light slumber, still addled by opioids. She pulled herself upright with her elbows.

Never had she observed such a brilliant light after sundown. The hospital had electricity even though the rest of Weston remained without. The light was not from the night bulbs. The hall light burned orange and dim. The rays pouring into the room were brilliant and cast a different glow.

Henrietta shielded her eyes and attempted to look beyond the source of the light, but no other object manifested. Instead, a muffled male voice cried out in fear.

"What the hell is that!"

The voice startled Henrietta more than the sound of *pops* and *pings* around her.

"Shoot it!" another voice shouted as the rhythmic snaps intensified in a crackling stream. Henrietta failed her arms and screamed at the highest pitch as the torrent of noise erupted around her.

The clamor ceased, and the male voices continued but grew distant and unintelligible.

Henrietta felt as if she were being pinched across her body, but rubbing her skin revealed no injury.

While she investigated, another form arrived at the entrance. Henrietta was still focused on her skin when she heard what sounded like the hinges of a door. She snapped her head upward to look, but the ethereal light had disappeared. In the doorway was the night watch, Nurse Hatfield. The warm aura of hall lights behind her cast a shadow, but Henrietta could see in the dim glow that the nurse was just as startled.

"Oh, my!" the night nurse exclaimed to herself before hurrying away.

Silence and darkness returned to the room. Henrietta could hear her heart pounding in her ears and nothing else. She cupped her hands to her face and eased back to lie down.

Several minutes later, Nurse Hatfield returned with two other nurses and a half-dressed Doctor Koenig. The four huddled in the doorway, whispered, and periodically glanced at Henrietta.

Doctor Koenig was the first to speak. "I do not see anything." He struggled to pull a suspender strap over his shoulders in his freshly awakened state.

A stupefied Nurse Hatfield tried to settle herself. "I-I swear that is what I saw just a moment ago."

Henrietta, unwilling to be a thing to gawk at, grew frustrated with the mystery. "What did you see?" she asked.

The four medical professionals reacted in a startled way, as if they had, indeed, forgotten about her sentience.

"You ..." Nurse Hatfield began shakily. "You ... you were covered in blood."

"Are you sure it was blood?" Doctor Koenig asked, taking a step into the room while he scanned the space for anomalies.

"It's possible it wasn't," Nurse Hatfield admitted in a calmer tone. "It could have been paint. There appeared to be blue and green colors, too, but it was difficult to make out in the low light."

Doctor Koenig finished his visual assessment and extended back to his full posture. "Either vay, that could not explain how it appeared und vanished so quickly."

"Felix? Um. Doctor Koenig?" Henrietta was seeking reassurance, but the doctor cut off her words before they could escape her mouth.

"Vat did you experience, meine Patienten?"

Henrietta stared back at the doorway. "Bright light. Loud popping sounds that grew faster as they continued. I felt bites against my skin … like … like I was being hit by something hard and small like gravel or corn kernels. My skin felt greasy for a moment afterward. Now it feels normal."

The doctor stroked the left blonde handlebar with his thumb. "Peculiar. Mutual psychosis."

"Do you have orders for us?" one of the unidentified nurses asked. She had slipped back into the hallways and was cast in silhouette by the exterior light.

Doctor Koenig pulled the string that ignited the single bulb in the room. The coils burned intensely for a moment before settling into a dull glow. The doctor scanned the room once more and then pressed his face close to Henrietta's body, canvassing it as the nurses waited patiently behind him.

"Show me one of der places vere you felt you had been struck," the doctor asked after stopping close to her face.

Henrietta raised the inside of her right arm and pointed to a spot above her elbow. Doctor Koenig stared at it briefly and hummed to himself.

"Take Miss Tidewater to the bath und give her a scrub. Once she is clean, check for lactation und bring her child if you find her milk production adequate."

"I thought her baby died," Nurse Hatfield said without the slightest register of empathy.

"What?" Henrietta cried. If it had been rationally measured, she may have seen the freedom from parenthood as a relief. The burden of caring for a child she would have to give up in a few months would take on a greater emotional toll. And once they separated, any shade of dark skin would make his adoption difficult. He would grow up a child of the system, passed around on the conveyors of an unloving mechanism until he was, at last, dropped into the wilderness of adulthood. Henrietta internalized it all with a seething anger. The brain chemicals associated with early motherhood had blotted out any rational thought. There was only a wolf and an endangered cub.

"Nien!" Doctor Koenig shouted the correction to freeze the room. "Sie verwirren Ihre Patienten erneut." The doctor pumped his hands into fists to find calm. "You are confusing your patients again. Poor Mrs. Johnston on der first floor is the one who lost her child. She is acting as a surrogate to Henrietta."

"But you said—"

"Aber nichts!" Doctor Koenig took a breath before proceeding. "Her child is safe. Ve vill discuss this privately tomorrow. Now, nurse, please do as instructed."

The nurses began to swarm Henrietta when the doctor raised a finger. The signal paused their actions.

"Ah, also be sure to have her secured back in this room before the rest of the vard rouses in the morning."

*****

WHEN Henrietta dipped her toe into the tub, it became apparent the hastily heated bathwater was not yet above room temperature. A metal stool in the center of the bath kept her abdomen above the water level. The cold seat generated goose bumps that started at Henrietta's tailbone and rippled outward across her legs.

"You were covered in paint, weren't you?" Nurse Hatfield questioned from the back of the room. She watched a second nurse wrap a piece of pumice in cloth and dip it in the water. "You were covered in something?"

"Something happened," Henrietta said. "I didn't see paint, but I felt something, and I heard something."

"What did you hear?" An unidentified nurse asked from a desk in the corner. She was etching a report onto a large notepad.

"Male voices."

"Oh, dear," Nurse Hatfield gasped.

"What did they say?" the other nurse quizzed further.

"'What's that? Shoot it.'" Henrietta paraphrased.

The nurse dropped the writing tool on the desk and shuffled in her seat so she could view Henrietta and Nurse Hatfield squarely.

"Did you see any men on the ward, Nurse Hatfield?"

The nurse let the washcloth sink into the tub of water. Staring at the ceiling, Nurse Hatfield took much more time calculating an answer.

"Um, no. There is sometimes a male night watch, but he's not on the grounds tonight."

"Hooligans came for her then," the nurse decided and shuffled back to the desk. "Make sure we keep Mrs. Cedric's door always locked. If they know she's on the floor, they will come back. If they can get to her, they will surely try to string her up by the pipes."

Henrietta wanted to correct her surname, but Nurse Hatfield posed a follow-up question as she retrieved the rag from its sunken location.

"There's a whole ward of coloreds out back. Why wouldn't they do their terrorizing there?"

Remaining hunched over her notes, the other nurse gave a dour reply. "Reckon they view the building out back as their place. A Black woman in a white woman's ward, now that is a crime in some people's minds. Grounds for punishment, even though the crime isn't hers."

The abrasive cloth delivered a harsh exfoliation that diverted pain sensors from Henrietta's abdomen. She could not see the patchwork of her operation. A bandage extended below her navel from left to right, held in place by a yellow adhesive.

"I just don't know what I saw," Nurse Hatfield continued a beat later. Her thoughts had drifted back to that haunting moment, and she was shaken by what she had seen. She paused and placed a damp hand on her cheek as she replayed the memory.

"There was nothing there," the other nurse said, growing irritable. "Maybe you need to have a mental evaluation of your own?"

"Don't say that," Nurse Hatfield scoffed, but her demeanor did not change.

"Check her milk," the writing nurse said in change of subject.

Nurse Hatfield stopped to grab a nipple and pressed toward her breast before pulling outward. A spray of pressurized milk blasted a thin line across the water and dissipated.

Nurse Hatfield turned toward the exit and saw another nurse approaching. "I'll send for the child if you want to take over."

Immediately after Nurse Hatfield exited, a muffled exchange took place beyond the door. When it finally ceased, Nurse Showalter entered and gazed upon Henrietta's nude body just long enough to become disquieted.

"You don't look covered in paint."

Henrietta stared down at her own body as if to confirm. "I don't feel covered in paint, either."

The nurse groaned and took note of the nurse washing Henrietta. "Careful not to get her bandages wet."

"That Judy is always seeing strange things that no one else does," the washing nurse griped as she extended Henrietta's left arm for scrubbing. "Don't get me wrong, I've seen some queer stuff about. But we mostly keep our traps shut and go about our job. Nurse Hatfield has got to speak about every single happenstance."

"Hatfield gets jumpy when she's the night watch, but this tale seems even stranger than usual," Nurse Showalter said. "She has never fabricated a story this bizarre. I'll report it to Doctor Koenig in the morning. He was angered to be roused as it were."

The nurses dried Henrietta, changed her into fresh dressings, and returned her to the room. Henrietta's skin burned from the scrub. She felt more scuffed than cleansed. Soon after, Nurse Showalter arrived with a basket wrapped in linens. The nurse handed it to Henrietta, who saw a jolt of movement under the sheet.

"He's waking up," Nurse Showalter said as she reached for the light cord.

When she first saw the baby, Henrietta's wide smile eased. Nurse Showalter quickly noted the diminished joy and turned to the other two nurses.

"Ladies, you're dismissed. Return to the station for further instruction." The demure nurses nodded and disappeared from the entrance. Nurse Showalter pulled the door shut and sat by Henrietta.

"This isn't my child," Henrietta said, her voice broken but not upset. Nurse Showalter leaned inward. "Oh, but it is."

"He's so white." The second the words left her mouth, Henrietta let out a gasp, suddenly becoming aware of the implication.

"Takes after his father, I'm sure." Nurse Showalter placed a hand on Henrietta's knee and brandished a warm smile. "Doctor Koenig made me aware of his parentage, and I must assure you your secret will be kept."

"How can it be?" Henrietta's mood was finally beginning to turn. "All anyone has to do is look at him. A fool could figure out that his father didn't come from the Black ward."

"He'll darken up." Nurse Showalter stood. "At least enough that he'll be taken for a light-skinned Black boy. The doctor believes he will, at least."

Henrietta scoffed. "'Darken up?' The doctor acts tolerant toward all colors until his own skin is on the line. Are you for certain this one is mine?"

"I am." Nurse Showalter reached to pull down the front of the child's linens, revealing the upper part of his chest. "I was there when he was delivered. The child that came from you had a heart-shaped birthmark just below his neck."

Henrietta sobbed. "How can I trust you? Nurse Hatfield was wrong about which baby died. You could be wrong, too. You could be … deceiving me."

Nurse Showalter placed her hands on her hips and tilted forward in a scolding manner. "The doctor has a lot to lose by being exposed as the father. We wouldn't give you someone else's white baby just for nothing."

The nurse retreated to a rolling crib at the edge of the room. The baby's bed was full of linens and bedclothes, which the nurse made short work of sorting. Nurse Showalter's aggressive movements suggested there was something she wanted to say.

Henrietta hesitated to speak. "Is anything the matter?"

"I expect Nurse Hatfield will be without work in a matter of days. Truthfully, there was a consideration to let Mrs. Johnston keep your baby and tell the story that your baby had died. But Mrs. Johnston is an upstanding citizen of Clarksburg, and this hospital is only a temporary stay. If she returns to society and your baby does show signs of your … heritage, then there will surely be a scandal. We abandoned the ploy, but Judy Hatfield was ill-informed or incapable of understanding the change of plan."

Henrietta gasped. Anger was now returning to the cocktail of her emotions. "Why would you tell me this?"

The nurse finished sorting and returned to the seat next to the bed. "I am telling you to earn your trust. This hospital is a difficult place to remain if you cannot trust the others around you. Can I have your trust?"

Henrietta took a deep breath and felt calmer with the exhale. "Was that the doctor's idea? To lie about my son? His son?"

The nurse bit her lip and gave a reluctant nod. "I don't believe skin color matters to him in terms of culture, but in the matter of pigmentation, there is a lot at stake."

The boy's chest was still exposed, and Henrietta looked down upon the rudimentary pink heart tattooed by life. A tear splashed onto the skin near it, followed by another before the nurse returned the linen.

"He's beautiful. Perfect. No matter the color." Henrietta sobbed as she smiled.

The nurse stood. "You named him Wallace, according to the papers. Why Wallace?"

The smile tried to leave Henrietta, but she forced it to stay, even though doing so taxed every muscle on her face. The exercise diminished her remaining emotional barriers, and the tears began to stream in full force.

"My husband. Strick … Strickland. It was the name he had picked if we'd ever had children. I shunned his last name because of his snake of a brother. I wanted some way to honor him. This is enough. It has to be."

"No middle name?"

"I don't have one, and it's never bothered me. As far as I know, we're the only Tidewaters about. My mother is gone, and I'm sure my sisters have married out of the name by now. That leaves me, my father, and Wallace. There are no more Henrietta Tidewaters out there, and I don't expect there to be any Wallace Tidewaters either."

Nurse Showalter looked down at the mother and child and could not help but smile at the cloying sight. "Well, it's a good name."

Henrietta tightened her arms around the child in a loving but careful embrace. "No. It's a perfect name."

8

EUGENE AT THE LAST LIGHT OF DAY

Tuesday, June 4, 1935

Eugene would have been a good candidate for lobotomy had fortune not been on his side.

The fortune was it was the middle of 1935, and the first lobotomy was still four months away from its debut overseas. It would take time to perfect and carry across the Atlantic. By the time the method arrived stateside, it had evolved from something helpful into something sinister. It went from an operation to a procedure, and from surgical tools to an appliance meant for drink preparation.

It was the icepick that became the popular tool for doctors at the mental asylums in the 1940s. Especially at Weston, where the architect of the icepick lobotomy, Doctor Walter Freeman, set up shop for a time. During his reign of terror, Freeman inflicted countless patients with brain damage disguised as helpful treatment. Freeman lost his license in the end, but the damage he caused was irrevocable. In his last days, Freeman was more interested in performing speed runs—seeing how many people he could lobotomize in a single day. It was second nature for the pioneer, and he had streamlined the process down to the basics. Insert an icepick in the corner of the eye socket, hammer, jiggle to and fro, remove the pick, and turn the patient over to the nurses for observation. He often picked patients at random to meet his goal. Once, he crossed the centennial mark for the number of victims lobotomized in a single day.

For all the effort, Freeman's own account declared only a third of the procedures successful, leaving the rest vegetative, dead, or worse.

It was too early for Eugene, and he was therefore spared the pick. His condition in those early days would have warranted a disconnection from his senses. The worst of his mania came and went in 1935. Regardless, his guilt-flushed mind kept Eugene at the hospital until 1951 when he contracted a bout of tuberculosis. In an ironic and erroneous fashion, tuberculosis was one of the diseases Doctor Freeman claimed to be curable through lobotomy.

Eugene would spend his last days at Weston Hospital in the building constructed to house tuberculosis patients. That was sixteen years later. In 1935, Eugene observed the preliminary phases of the building's construction from his fourth floor window. The window was small and only useful in allowing light to enter the space. A platform elevating the radiator provided extra height for a decent snapshot of the landscape.

It had been four days since Eugene's arrival in the bright, teal room, where he concealed himself. In true nature as a farmer, he would still awaken at the crack of dawn and dress in a white button-up shirt and navy slacks with matching suspenders. The nurses let him keep three similar outfits, but only one pair of suspenders. It was a worn set too threadbare to suspend the weight of a human body by the neck.

Uncertain about how his laundry would be cared for and returned, he chose to wear the same outfit for as long as possible. Today marked the first day in fresh clothes. There were no sheep to tend to, but that fact wouldn't have changed had he remained at home in Gad, West Virginia. Eugene sold the remaining flock to pay back taxes on the farm. If he had stayed in Gad, Eugene would have retained a similar occupation of gazing through windows. He spent his time looking through the hospital window

at Weston across the West Fork River. The view was grander than the
rocky hills and hollows of Gad, but far less quaint.

He could almost make out the activities of townsfolk across the
West Fork. He could see his father-in-law's business and could read ER
BLOOM GLASSWARE COMPANY in white block letters on the
side of the brick building. Eugene's wife, Ethel, would have inherited the
business had she outlived her father. She was the youngest of five, but her
brother died in World War I, and two of her sisters fell to influenza the
following year. Hazel, the last surviving member of the Bloom children,
went west, leaving no prospect of a return trip. With no children available
to pass on the family business, Edgar Bloom's last will and testament
demanded the business be sold upon his demise and the remaining revenue
forwarded to Hazel.

By design, the distribution of wealth did not consider
grandchildren. The Bloom family detested Ethel taking on the role of
farmer's wife and made it a point to shun any aspect of her life involving
Eugene, including children.

The white lettering reminded Eugene of that resentment, and he
focused on the building only in short bursts. Instead, he concentrated on
the various activities on the hospital's front lawn. Able-bodied women
played with red paper streamers, swirling them around in the breeze. On
Eugene's side of the grounds, a sizable group of boys played baseball on a
makeshift diamond. Four of the boys brought pillows from their rooms to
use as bases. Eugene found amusement in their cleverness until he realized
that his own pillow was among the plates.

"You have a visitor, Eugene," a male voice called from the door.

Eugene turned, expecting an orderly, but found no one waiting.
Discarded patients littered the hall and shuffled about in episodes of their
respective manias. Shrieks, cries, and angry rants carried in long voices
down the corridor. It was likely the orderly had already turned his attention
to a commotion among the hall dwellers.

Eugene stepped down from the radiator platform and waited. After
an extended moment, a young woman appeared in the doorway. She was in
her midtwenties, with short brown hair and a stern, familiar face. She wore
a tight black dress with white trim suitable for formal business affairs. An

angular leather clutch mimicking the aesthetic of an attaché completed the look.

"Hello, Dad," the young woman said as a hesitant greeting.

Eugene craned his neck and peered, unblinking. "Opal Lee? I didn't recognize you. You have certainly ripened."

"I've been working in publishing in New York City. Things may be down in these economic times, but people still like to read."

"You're a writer?" Eugene asked. He stepped to the side and took a seat on his pillowless bed.

"Oh. No, I'm not a writer. I just make sure people who are writers use the right kind of sentences."

Eugene croaked. "Not too shabby for a farm girl from Gad."

Opal gave a polite smile and nodded. The beat gave her respite enough to scan the room. She noticed a second bed on the opposite side. "You have a roommate?"

Eugene nodded. "His name is Vernon, but he prefers the moniker of Flip. It's a bastardization of his middle name, Philip. His grandfather wasn't too precise in oratory accuracy and just called him Flip, and the Flip adhered." There was a pause. "We had more than one roommate, but for the moment, it is just Flip and me. He's down in the field playing with his little friends."

Opal furrowed her brow at the comment, and Eugene struggled little to understand why. "Oh. He's only fourteen."

"Do they make it a practice to put grown men in the same room as juveniles?" Opal asked with veiled disgust.

"He protested. As did I. Seems he lived with an uncle who made a habit of doing unsavory things within the … zone … of Flip's private area. Having shared more violent afflictions in my youth, I can tell you that he'll never live that down. Especially if he keeps reliving it with a similarly aged creature in the room."

Opal stepped inward while Eugene stood and returned to the window. "They put me in here because it was the only lodging available upon my arrival. You journeyed those crowded hallways. Some of the larger wards are packed in so tight that you couldn't fit a frog's ass hair between mattresses. A third gentleman named Daniel was also held here until yesterday. He split mine and Flip's ages, so it felt less unwholesome for a time, but he wasn't a short-timer and was desperate for escape. He loosened the bars in the sitting room enough to jump out while harnessed to a cluster of bedsheets. For his efforts, he shattered one leg and broke another. They have him laid up a little closer to the ground. I suspect it will be a short order before they pile us into a trio again. Until then, I suppose I lucked out on this much space, even if Flip didn't."

"At least you're not a pedophile?" Opal's statement sounded more like a question.

Eugene shook his head. "Probably better me in here than a lot of the kids they cage here. They're either arsonists or masturbators. Maybe both, on occasion. Boys of an adolescent age shouldn't be huddled together when the urges fly. I can't blame them much; my youthful mind could have avoided such carnal things. But in the absence of female interaction, what else are they to do? Flip is not like that—hates to be touched altogether. Not sure he even enjoys the self-gratification. I don't expect he does."

Opal didn't seem to want to continue the line of conversation and entered the space to sit on Flip's bed. Eugene suspected she now believed his quarters to be free of bodily fluids.

The silence gave Eugene time to realize the spiel he was delivering was to his daughter. Boy parts and their uses were not a topic that would ever breach the Spangold homestead. He clenched his jaw at the realization, but Opal had already strayed to another topic.

"So, tell me why you're in here." Her tone matched the sharp angles of her face. The outside corners of her eyes puckered, and the space between pressed into two parallel wrinkles.

"I committed myself if you're thinking I was inserted against my will," Eugene defended. "I, for one, am a fan of crowds, despite my rural upbringing. Must run in our family if you enjoy living among the walls of people in New York."

Opal seemed unimpressed. "The fact that you're here at all means you've sinned against society's norms. So, what was it?"

Eugene sighed and folded his chest against his thighs to grab his ankles. "I got mixed up at Floyd Funeral Home. Told them I wanted to burn the place down. May have soiled a desolate corner of their parlor."

He rocked back and forth in his compact position, expecting excitability or a lecture from his daughter. But she did not say anything. Eugene looked up and saw her staring at a photograph affixed to his wall.

"That's Janet Gaynor! She's an actress. A real bona fide Hollywood type …"

"I know who she is. Why did you want to burn down the funeral home? A nurse told me about it."

Eugene ignored the question. "They didn't let me keep the frame I had the picture in. Something about sharp corners. I brought my nice black steamer trunk with the silver buckles. They didn't let me keep that either. Wish they'd communicated its location, at least. It's priceless to me. Remember when we took that sojourn to Canada?"

"Why did you want to burn down the funeral home?" Opal repeated. "Are you taking to a rambling fit?"

"You know nothing of my fits," Eugene fired back, standing. "I never had those fits while you were around. You've been gone for years, my dear, sweet, Opal Lee. Why did you stop writing to us?"

Opal answered in a whisper. "Mom."

Eugene's head twitched in confusion.

"Don't you know what happened?"

"She said you wanted to visit friends for Christmas instead of celebrating with us."

Opal sighed and assumed a similar posture to Eugene. "I don't wish to talk about it."

"Your mom didn't, either." He had a feeling some hard truths were coming and unwound from his twisted position.

"Where is Mom? Has she visited you here yet?"

"It was your mom's funeral that I was attending when things went awry."

"Oh." Opal opened her mouth to say more, but her vigor shifted. "I know."

Eugene squinted at his daughter. *Something wasn't adding up.* "You got here awful fast. To West Virginia from New York, that is. It would take this many days just to send word to you that I was confined here."

"I was already on my way," Opal amended from her previous statement. "Word got to me that Mom had passed. Four days ago, in fact. I was poking around the area when I was informed you had been committed here."

"She's buried in the Bloom family cemetery on the hill above your Grandpa Edgar's estate." Eugene extended a hand. "You should go visit her. Since it's private property, Edgar maliciously bars me from entry. Ethel LeeAnn was curated as part of a backyard installation I can never view. I don't expect he'll allow me to be deposited into the ground next to her when that date arrives. Even as I lie in a state he would most prefer."

"I'll go," Opal said after Eugene helped her up. "And then I'll go to the farm and see what affairs of yours need to be settled there."

"I have a hand there, keeping watch in my stead," Eugene reassured.

"Farmhand? You've never had one before."

"I have never been mortared to the walls of a loony bin either."

Opal started for the door. "I'm going to check it out anyway. It's been a while since I've been there."

"More than four years," Eugene calculated.

"That long?"

"Too long." Eugene blustered under his breath as if the words he had dissipated before they could reach his lips. "If you must know, I lost the farm," Eugene stated with suppressed shame. "It had been underwater for some time. Even when your great-grandpa James had it, he took on debts to support his drinking interests. I could never recover it from that, and the state finally up and reclaimed it."

"Hmm. I guess I won't go then."

"I'm sorry to tell you like this, here, in this paradise for the psychotic."

Opal slinked to the doorframe. "There's just a lot to take in. My mom is gone. My childhood home is gone. I'm going to head back and do some reflecting."

"It was good to see you—" Before Eugene could finish, she had already spilled into the sea of hallway hecklers.

A moment later, Flip arrived back at the room. Eugene had yet to sit and watch the young man plop down on his cot. Flip pressed his face as deep into the mattress as the springs would allow.

"Hey, Flip, my daughter was just here, yes, sir. Didja see her? You would have passed her in the hall."

"I didn't see anyone that looked like a woman," Flip murmured.

"Hey, now. That was my Opal Lee in the hallway. Love her with all my heart, only sharing the cavity with my sweet, departed Ethel. Oh, I don't know what became of my sweet darling Opal Lee. She seemed so disconnected from the world. New York City must be so full of the indifferent. Like a wasteland full of cactus people, prickly and sour. Yes, sir, that shining, golden land warped my sweet Opal Lee into a wraith set to wander the Earth with all purpose and no drive. How could America ever achieve its utopian predestination with such wayward influence?"

"You're rambling again," Flip said, but his voice remained muted.

"That's correct," Eugene continued aimlessly. "America can never achieve utopia. Ironically, the amount of freedom granted is at issue. Yes, sir. Our system of governance tries to tailor utopia to specifications that suit everyone. But no fit can suit the whole of the population. Everyone has a different sense of liberty. Utopia must be a patchwork of varying measures …"

Flip raised his head. "What's that have to do with Opal?"

Opal's name coming from someone else struck a harsh note in his mind. *Opal Lee was here, but we did not reconcile.* Eugene realized he had been acting disconnected from his daughter as well.

"You know, I had not set eyes upon the lovely Opal Lee in four years. She ran off Christmas Eve after fighting with her mother, and I hadn't seen her until this day. I did not treat it as such. Yes, sir, I downright played it like we had conversed every day in the intermediary. How did I let our interaction slip past so casually? There was so much more I wanted to disburse and wanted to learn for myself. My dear wife Ethel and I had once wondered why she did not take a husband. Perhaps she has in the meantime. I am no ring trawler. If she were betrothed, I wouldn't have known it any other way besides asking. Yes, sir, I assumed not and let it be. She had long plotted the forbearance of being a spinster."

Flip lowered his book, having concocted a way to stop the monologue. "We lost our pillow privileges. The ward doesn't get any new pillows."

Eugene did, in fact, stop his address. "And mine did not return?"

Flip shook his head. "Not unless you enjoy having your face against mud and grass."

"You cad," Eugene cursed, but pivoted from rage to reminiscing. "Well, I do enjoy the smell of grass stains. When you're in the army, you sleep assigned to the softest available place. Never mind the composition of the mattress, if there even were one. Often, it's a mound of dirt. I can do without a pillow better than any of our neighbors within our confines save Sergeant Rust."

Flip scuffed the mattress with his knuckles. "I've never been much for nature. Never camped. Never even hunted. I'll miss my pillow."

"Boy, you should try to be one with nature on occasion. Sniff the apple blossoms and kiss the dirt. It tempers you and allows insight into the depravity man has brought against the base things. We are as much like nature as the trees." Eugene spread his arms.

Flip sighed. "Trees?"

"We are trees if you think about it for a moment. As our seasons change, the leaves on our crown change color and fall to the floor." Eugene brushed the bald part of his head to illustrate his meaning, allowing flurries of dandruff to precipitate from the edges of his hairline.

Flip allowed a tentative nod. The gesture gave Eugene the confidence to continue his reasoning. "And this place. Oh, this place is like a scrap pile for wood of poor stock. We cannot be lumber of any use. Too full of burls and knots. Too splintered to be anything worth salvaging. It wouldn't be so much injustice for me, but they did not bother to count the rings before scrapping you. You're young, with fruit still hanging from the tree, in fact. Yes, sir, mister, young men don't belong in such places. I am not beyond repurpose, and neither are you by a greater degree."

Flip watched the vivid presentation and grew despondent. "I should be able to go back out there before too long. But what would be the point?"

Eugene stopped his flailing about and sat on his cot across from Flip. He was careful not to invade the boy's space in such a moment of vulnerability.

"You're a good kid, though. You're not one of these fire-starting miscreants who scurry among us. I am elated not to host them as roommates. I would remain in constant fear of being struck with errant strands of adolescent seed."

"They don't do that too much," Flip defended.

Eugene huffed. "I don't need to know that they do it at all. The fact that I do means it's too much."

The two sighed that the topic had swung to pubescent ejections. Eugene took another deep breath and tried to recall the point he set out to make.

"Like I said, you're a good kid. Bad memories heal, like every other wound. It just takes time and perhaps a good salve. A Brogan's Liniment for the soul."

The boy cringed at the name. "That was my uncle's brand. The smell alone makes my stomach churn."

"Ooh. I'm sorry." Eugene leaped forward and patted the boy on the head. "Just time, then. It just takes time."

*****

THE next morning began with the clamor of metal screeching against the asbestos tile. Eugene cranked one eye open enough to see two orderlies reassembling a third bed.

"A new tenant?" Eugene asked in a croaking morning voice.

Neither of the men replied immediately. After clipping a latch into place, one orderly turned to lock eyes with Eugene. The man answered the question with a slight nod.

"What do you know about him?" Eugene hoisted himself to the edge of his bed. "Is he deep in his psychosis?"

The other orderly turned and raised an eyebrow at the phrasing. "You eva hear of the Crabbottom Believer's Church?" He spoke with an Appalachian dialect that fringed on Southern drawl.

"Can't say that I have."

"They a group a religious nuts about the Virginia and West Virginia border. Snake handlers, Bible-thumpers—they try tah carry out God's judgment on His behalf."

Eugene groaned. "And this poor soul is one of them?"

"The last of 'em," the attendant stated. "The law was coming to arrest the leader for stringing up a local whore. 'Stead of fightin', he up and commanded his congregation to kill 'emselves. Each member drank a juice made from the pokeweed."

Eugene scratched his head. "And this gentleman, the one to be encamped with us, he didn't drink the juice?"

"No-sir-e."

"And what's so crazy about that?"

The orderly slapped the completed bed to confirm its sturdiness. "All 'em nuts woulda been in here if the law had gotten to 'em quick enough."

Eugene folded his arms. "And where would you have put them?"

The man scanned the room as he moved to the door with his associate. "We coulda fit at least two more in with y'all." He gave a wave and disappeared into the quiet corridor.

Eugene considered returning to sleep, but he noticed Flip resting with his eyes open. "You didn't scream last night."

Flip huffed with approval and filled his lungs with morning air. "One step closer to recovery, I reckon."

"You heard we have a new companion inbound?"

A stretch overcame Flip, impeding his response. "I heard part of it. Did you catch his age?"

"Didn't. I expect he's a youngin' like you. Yes, sir. Older men who see the inevitability of their demise tend not to shy away from it. This individual had. I suspect he concluded there to be more life yet to absorb."

Eugene was not excited about a new roommate. Gaining Flip's trust was going to take time and patience. Introducing a new element to the formula would throw off the result Eugene tried so hard to build.

But Eugene needed to speak with the doctor who would be admitting their new roommate. If the protocols were common to his case, the medical officer would march him to the room. If it were Doctor Timmons, Eugene could inquire about his delay in evaluation.

"Why would a preacher kill his congregation?" Flip asked as his mind awakened. "He seems like the insane one."

"Yes, sir, Flip," Eugene agreed. "Some people are so desperate to be cast in the Bible that they'll take any role. I suspect the parson was trying out for a few roles at once."

Several minutes later, a younger man entered the room. Following was a doctor Eugene did not know. The man in the white coat had a more youthful appearance than Doctor Timmons.

"Gentlemen, this is Archibald Clump. He will be residing with you while his mental condition is being evaluated. Please treat him as civilly as you would anyone else here."

Archibald did not acknowledge those in the room. He instead walked straight to the empty bed and sat with a posture as upright as the wall.

Eugene was the first to give a greeting. "Good to meet you. Can I call you Archie?"

"No," Archibald was terse in his reply.

"Arch?"

"No," Archibald repeated with added irritation.

"Bald?" Flip included but could not hide his smirk when Archibald's eyes darted to him.

"How old are you?" Flip changed the subject.

"Twenty."

Eugene returned his eyes to the doctor's location to find him no longer present. He leaped from his bed and skidded into the hallway. "Doc!" he shouted to attract the man's attention successfully. "I was hoping to see Doctor Timmons today. Is he around?"

The new doctor's jaw tensed. "I am afraid he is not."

"It's just …" Eugene laughed nervously. "It's just that he was supposed to render a new evaluation upon me … days ago. I cannot prove my sanity the longer I am absorbing the ambiance of your addled archways."

"Um." The doctor looked around the hall. The ward had not yet awakened in full, keeping the traffic in the corridor light. One man at the end of the hall was demanding it to be "cigarette time." Sergeant Rust, a geriatric soldier always ready for battle, did pushups in his olive fatigues in a far corner. Aside from the notables, there was no one taking mind of Eugene and the doctor.

"Doctor Timmons died two days ago," the doctor whispered.

Eugene's face scrunched into a tight ball, revealing every crease on his scruffy visage. "I knew that bastard would keel over in the imminent. Old age. Was it old age?"

"One of his patients brained him with a rusty fire axe. He likely died on the first impact."

Eugene stroked his beard. "Indeed, his demise was a wager I could have won had there been a bookie on the level. Though the method was a fiction I would not have anticipated." He wanted to know more and shifted to his usual tactics. "Where did this barbarous character acquire such a weapon, Doc?"

"It's Doctor Brinx, sir. The fire axe was buried on the front lawn somewhere around the front gate. It had a Maltese etched on the head, so it must have belonged to a fire department. There was wording on the handle that was no longer readable. It had been buried there for some time … I … ah … I really shouldn't be telling patients this."

"It is quite fine," Eugene reassured. "Yes, sir, mister, I'm one of the sane ones."

Doctor Brinx gazed into the patient's eyes as if he were using some metric to gauge honesty within Eugene's pupils.

Eugene ignored the scan and continued. "I'm sure a younger man could have weathered at least that initial blow. Time surely softened the integrity of his skeleton."

The doctor dismissed the remaining details. "In brief, Doctor Timmons has passed. We have found ourselves short on qualified professionals. It will take us time to find and reconcile your records. If you sit tight for a few days, I'm sure we will get all this righted."

Eugene gave a nod and grunted. "You tell Willard C. Crane that I wish not to remain in his institutionalized squalor for much longer."

The doctor rolled his eyes, though he was quick to close his lids as he did so. "I will see what I can do. In the meantime, please exert some of that energy on Mr. Clump. He believes himself to be living in the biblical times of tribulation."

Eugene took a step backward, toward his room. "I can't speak to biblical times, but I can tell from my own observations this establishment makes for a good practice tribulation."

BRITTANY AND THE ZEITGEIST

The air-conditioning unit in Brittany's window had rumbled through the night. The accumulated condensation sloshed and gurgled inside the machine before taking passage on the projected air. The droplets connected with Brittany's face, waking her on the third volley. She grasped for the dial, but it was beyond reach from the edge of the bed. She attempted a deep stretch, which only resulted in Brittany spilling onto the floor. She landed on her knees, avoiding a complete face plant, but the mishap did not fail to leave her embarrassed.

Sunlight attempted to cast beams through creases in the closed blinds. However, the house and the sun's angle at the summer solstice were not in proper alignment to illuminate the room.

It must have been early for the daylight to seep through the blinds in such a way. Brittany despised her alarm clock and was giddy to yank its plug upon finishing her last day of high school. It remained a brown box with a blank face.

After massaging cucumber melon lotion into her hands and bare shoulders, Brittany adjusted a white tank top and stumbled into the day. Her legs were not yet cursed with the same consciousness. She made it to the kitchen doorway before the tingling in her extremities became too painful.

A bottle of riesling was already uncorked and breathing on the counter. There was often some local variety of wine sitting around the kitchen, but never that early. Brittany expected to see her mother at the kitchen counter or dining room table, sipping from a long-stemmed goblet. There was a specific glass her mom preferred, given to her as a door prize at her twenty-fifth class reunion.

Glenda was absent from view, but Brittany—not her mother's keeper—fixed her attention on the stove clock.

"Seven oh-eight," Brittany said aloud, followed by an extended groan.

Her comment prompted movement in her periphery, and she turned to see her mother at the edge of the dining room. Glenda had pushed a chair to the large dining room window and occupied a seat in a white bathrobe. Her hair, usually a puffy dusty-brown, was slick and darkened from the dampness of a fresh shower. Her hands cradled a glass of riesling and a green Gideon's Bible.

"Morning routine?" Brittany remarked.

Glenda started hot. "Did you know the world is going to end at the end of the year? Y2K. Computers control everything, Brittany Jean."

Brittany was familiar with the term. It had been circulating in the news and as a joke for months. Brittany erred on the side of humor because of one specific metric.

"Dad don't seem too concerned about it."

Glenda tapped on the book with her index finger. "That's because your father deals in computer code. What I'm dealing with is Bible code. Betty Wesmith says the Lord spoke to her and told her the programmers would miss something critical, and the world's nuclear missiles would be able to be launched by anyone. As a sign that this is going to happen, she said to look for two senators and a member of the president's family to die before then."

Brittany closed her eyes so that her mother could not see her roll them. "And who is Betty Wesmith?"

"She has a program on channel ten at four in the morning."

"You've been awake since four?"

Glenda glanced down at the small green book. "I'd been watching TV since four in the morning. Been awake a might longer than that."

It was the fifth prophecy Glenda had shared that year. The dates of the first four had already come to pass with no communication from God. Brittany wondered at what point a person who claimed to be so versed in foretelling would admit defeat. Greater still, what was the threshold for a faithful listener to lose faith after so many busted attempts at discerning God's intentions? Brittany decided to let it go for now. It was not a death cult dealing in suicide pacts and plague parties. That was enough to stay out of an argument for now.

"I wasn't talking about that stuff, anyway," Brittany finally said. She clinked her fingernails along the nearby wine bottle. "That's what I was meaning."

"You don't need to worry with that, Brittany Jean." Glenda crossed her legs and returned a gaze to the outer world.

Brittany worried about it. She didn't recall her mother having wine at any point before sophomore year. Consumption seemed to increase as time fumbled forward. Glenda lost her job as a housekeeping manager at a nearby resort in 1996. Details of her departure ground through the rumor mill. Classmates with kin close to the situation murmured speculations of an affair, but Brittany found the claims dubious. Even in his preoccupations, John Rocco would not have tolerated such an egregious violation of their vows. It was possible he didn't know the truth, either, and had accepted whatever reason Glenda fed him without further verification.

Regardless, in the three years that followed, Glenda had not sought further employment. She cleaned the homes of older ladies from their church for side cash; otherwise, the family lived off her husband's wages. An inheritance left by John Rocco's father, Rocco George Loughry, provided additional support. The elder Loughry began a farm supply company at a young age, eventually expanding to fifteen stores across three states over thirty years. A conglomerate absorbed the company in the late

1980s, providing Rocco Loughry with a sizable retirement package. Upon his death in 1996, what remained of the fortune was split between his three children. John Rocco had enough to pay his debts and fund Brittany's post-secondary education. What was left would cover any losses from Glenda's lack of employment and stimulate the local vineyards.

Brittany retrieved orange juice from the refrigerator and poured it into a waiting glass. She sipped while her mother did the same and contemplated the unknown. Outside the window was a small patch of dirt used for a garden. For all the effort, the plot only kept three tomato plants to maturity. The neighbor's motorboat took up the other half of the lot, skirting the property line with the starboard side.

Brittany broke the morning serenity to ask, "Where's Dad? He usually makes breakfast around this time."

"Your father always goes in early to do inventory on Wednesdays. You would know that if you bothered to wake up at a reasonable hour, Brittany Jean," Glenda scolded.

"Oh, it's Wednesday." Brittany then remembered why it was important. "So, my punishment is over?"

Glenda sighed. "Yeah, I guess. Don't be breaking no laws from now on, you hear? That's the easiest you're ever going to get off."

"Yes, ma'am," Brittany said before swigging the last of her juice. She then made for the door, grabbing a wrinkled cardigan from a hamper near the basement door.

"Where are you going?" Glenda called from her perch.

"Police station," Brittany shouted back. "I'm going to see if I can get my backpack back."

*****

BRITTANY was thankful that she had awoken early. The summer sun was already heating the air, and the clouds had all but disappeared. She kept the same attire that she had slept in but added necessary undergarments for public presentation. Still, a tank top and blue flannel pajama pants were a violation of tasteful attire.

A Wednesday morning in Weston was much quainter than a Tuesday night. The cicadas had completed their mating cycle and returned to the earth for another seventeen years. Their juvenile skins were left behind, crispy and fused to neighborhood trees. The seventeen-year-old boys were also silent, apathetic to the morning in the same manner as Brittany.

But Brittany was on the march in the early hour. Like her last stroll across Weston, she focused on a single mission.

"Hey, Brittany!" a voice called from the town office parking lot after Brittany crossed the Second Street Bridge.

"Officer Prince?" Brittany answered when she caught sight of the man jogging her way.

"I've been fixin' to come see you," Officer Prince said.

"I'm coming to get my backpack. Can I have it back?"

"Yeah, I just put it in my car." Prince nodded toward the cluster of vehicles in the lot.

"Sticky Vicky? Can I have a ride back home then? I walked all this way, and the sun is starting to beat down."

Officer Prince winked. "Sure. You can even ride shotgun this time. Wouldn't want people to think I arrested you for dress code violations."

"Weston has a dress code?"

"No, but we have a curfew, so we're not all that removed from the possibility."

The Ford Crown Victoria sat at the opposite end of the lot, but the two made a quick pace of crossing the expanse.

"I got your pictures developed," Officer Prince said as they reached the car.

"Ah, man, but I still had exposures left! I only used about half."

The officer cracked the door. "Eight by my count." He paused so they could sit. "Besides, it was police evidence."

"On a case that didn't happen," Brittany reminded. "I would have shared my findings with you if you'd asked."

Officer Prince handed her a resealed yellow envelope containing a bulge of pictures. "I had duplicates made, so there are forty-eight in that package, including the blanks."

"Half of these are blank?" Brittany concluded as she pulled open the sticky flap. "You could've just thrown those out."

Officer Prince was reversing the car and began making a circular motion with his right arm. "You're focusing on the wrong things here. Have a look."

Brittany removed the stack and began flipping through them, separating the blank pictures from the successful exposures on top.

"Did you take all of those that night last week?" the officer questioned.

"Yeah. Why don't you just get to the point?" Brittany chided as she reviewed her photos of the hand-painted wallpaper.

"The last picture. Look at the last picture before the blanks."

Brittany flipped to the final image of her good stack to see the white light that had purged her from the Kirkbride. Goose bumps formed at the sight, and Brittany had to look away for a moment, turning her head to the driver.

"Is that your ghost?" Prince asked.

Brittany pursed her lips and nodded. "Yep. Room 668 on the third floor."

"Yeah ..."

Forcing herself to look again, Brittany studied the features. The entity was close enough to the camera that its full body didn't fit in the frame. An arm was visible. *A torso. Pants!* A belt and zipper were evident, along with a device clipped to the belt.

"You see the features, don't you?" Officer Prince asked.

Dread left Brittany at the sight of the device. "Is it a ghost?"

"I couldn't see a face, but it looks like someone as modern as me and you. Are you sure there wasn't someone in there with you?"

"Why would someone glow like that?" Brittany dismissed. "It was made of light."

"Did you see the device?" Officer Prince asked.

"I did." When Brittany looked closer again, a familiar detail emerged.

"That device has an Apple logo on it." She pressed the glossy photo toward the officer's face. "See?

"I see it," Officer Prince said, but his eyes only darted to the image for a blip before returning to the road.

"I got one of their computers for college," Brittany continued. "Not sure what this little thing is. It's only the size of a pocket notebook."

Officer Prince scratched his shoulder near his radio. "I reckon if you can find out what kind of Apple device it is, then you should have a lead on finding out who your ghost is."

"Yes! Can you run me up to RadioShack? My dad will know what it is."

The store was in a shopping plaza far from Weston's residential center. A highway coming from the east suddenly ended at Weston's doorstep, where the corridor of Interstate 79 ran north to south. The strip mall was an effort for Weston to reach motorists before they branched off on adventures beyond the town's ability to collect commerce. The grasping hand did not go unfilled. The pull of chain restaurants and retail opportunities kept the area busy and the surrounding businesses fed.

Officer Prince did not stick around after delivering Brittany to her dad's store, and she was fine with that. There was enough within a casual stroll to keep her occupied until John Rocco's lunch break, which he often returned home to take.

Business hours had just begun, but she found the front of the shop unoccupied.

"Hello?" Brittany called. Her voice carried through the rows of electronic doodads and gadgets wrapped in hard plastic and dangling from long pegs.

The call prompted the shuffling of cardboard from a back room, followed by a *thud* and hastened footsteps.

"Oh, Britt. I was hoping it was my help," a bewildered John Rocco said.

Preoccupied, the man hurried to the front counter, retrieved a cordless phone, and began scanning a scrap of paper taped to the glass display case.

"How did you get here? Did your mom drop you off?"

"Um, no. Officer Prince gave me a ride."

John Rocco began punching numbers on the phone, each of the seven making its own robotic tone.

"I hope you're not in trouble again," John Rocco said.

"Not at all. In fact, I'm helping with an investigation," Brittany stated with a strange pride.

John Rocco looked up after the sixth beep. "You're still in your pajamas. That's not very professional."

Brittany scoffed at the comment and took a step away.

An eighth beep came when John Rocco glanced to see someone else approaching the door. "Ah, there's my guy."

Brittany spun to see Samuel Beck yank on the door, the suction of the air creating a light breeze within the cavernous space. She hadn't seen Sam since the ghost night when she declined to enter the convenience store. Brittany smiled and was about to deliver a warm greeting when John Rocco cut in line.

"You're late, Sam!" he growled.

"I know. I know. I'm sorry. I hit the snooze button on my alarm too many times." Sam pressed his hands together and bowed. "It won't happen again."

John Rocco appeared reluctant to accept the apology right away. "It's ten-thirty. Even Brittany got here before you, and she doesn't have a vehicle. I'm pretty sure she doesn't even have an alarm clock plugged in."

Sam looked at Brittany and cocked his head. "Did you walk here?"

"No."

Sam wiped his brow. "I was gonna say. I could have given you a ride."

Brittany looked at her dad and back at Sam. "I didn't know you worked here."

"If he'd given you a ride you would have been late, too," John Rocco interrupted. "Now Britt, what were you saying about an investigation?"

Brittany had been keeping a tight grip on her packet of photos and carefully removed the one on top—the only one that mattered to her now.

"Can you tell me what kind of device this is?"

John Rocco widened and squinted his eyes in succession as he tried to make sense of what he was seeing. "Whoa, that's one heck of an overexposure."

He laid the photograph on the counter, and Brittany pointed to the logo near the bottom of the image. "See that? What kind of Apple device is that?"

John Rocco hummed as he studied the device. "I'm not sure. I have a couple of Macworld magazines in the back room. I may take a look quick and see if this is something new that's been released. Sam, get clocked in and on the register."

Sam saluted as John Rocco disappeared into the back again. Punching a code into the register, Sam looked gleeful in his task. After checking the amount of cash in his drawer, he turned his attention to Brittany.

"Are you ready for college?"

She leaned across the glass counter. "Yep. Less than two months away. I'm ready to get out of this Podunk and onto bigger and better things."

"Are you going to WVU, too?"

"Yep." She smiled. "A big school conveniently located just an hour up the interstate. Easy to hop home on weekends, if I had a car."

"I can always give you a ride," Sam offered. He stepped away from the kiosk and ripped a sliver of paper from a notepad sitting along the wall. "I'll write down my address in Morgantown. I'm not in any of the student housing. My parents are renting a basement apartment in a house on the far end of Grant Avenue."

"Grant? Stephanie told me that's the party street," Brittany noted. Stephanie was a friend, a year their elder, and had already returned from WVU with wild college stories.

"It's a long street," Sam stated as he slid the paper to Brittany. "Basically, you look for the parties and then follow the road north until you hit my address. I'll be there after the first of August."

"Thanks." Brittany took the slip and tucked it in the picture pouch. "My dad has this old minivan that he's been keeping in working order, but he mostly drives it. He's not as good a mechanic as he is a computer guy, so he feels it isn't safe for anyone else to drive. I'm still going to see if he'll let me take it. Otherwise, he has an old motorcycle. I don't think it would help me much in the winter, even if I knew how to ride it."

Sam nodded as he sorted papers on a clipboard. "What are you up to this summer? No summer job, like me? I'm surprised you're not working here."

"Ah gee, I'd never work well with Dad. Our approach to doing things is wildly different, and we'd do nothing here but fight. We put a desk together one time and about got into a fight with the screwdrivers."

"Fair enough. What are you doing in your free time, then?"

Brittany felt comfortable enough with Sam to let him into her world, and she smiled devilishly while leaning closer to him.

"I'm doing some last-minute exploring." She winked. "You know, abandoned places."

Sam stared at her, confused for a moment. The bewilderment turned to admiration before he realized he had beheld her for too long. "Um … You sure like those old bedrooms. Er, houses. Houses!"

Brittany recognized what was happening and pulled back from the counter, remembering she was still in her loose night clothes. She gave a nervous laugh. "Yeah. I'm working on a plan to get permission to the mental hospital."

"Wow. Really?" Sam replied. "Did you hear about the paintball thing, though?"

"That's my ticket in," Brittany stated confidently. "I'll play the security for rubes; just you wait."

"Rubes." Sam, amused by the word, repeated it playfully. "Well, I hope it works out well for you."

Sam wanted to say more, but the bells above the door jingled as a customer entered. "Can I help you today, good sir?" Sam began.

Brittany wandered off to the rows, pretending to be a customer. The aisle she selected was full of cables, transistors, and components she didn't understand. Disinterested, she started toward the section with the car stereos when John Rocco reappeared from the storage area.

"The only thing I can find, like in the picture, was a gadget Apple made earlier in the decade called a Newton." John Rocco held up a picture of it in an aged magazine. "Based on the size of the person in your picture wearing it, their device seems to be smaller and designed differently."

Brittany took a hard glance at it. "Yeah, the logo isn't in the right place either."

"The other thing I noticed. There is also a component on the top of the rectangle. It almost looks like a sensor or some type of spy camera."

Brittany hadn't paid too much attention to that detail until then and studied the new clue. It did remind her of the end of a laser pointer.

"What is your professional opinion of this device?"

John Rocco crossed his arms, a sign to Brittany that she was about to get a serious reflection. "It's not something Apple makes or ever has made, as far as I can tell. My guess is this is a homemade device that someone slapped an Apple logo on as a joke. They like to give out stickers with their products, albeit not ones that small. I'd say this is probably some type of a fake."

"Oh," Brittany said, disappointedly.

John Rocco noted his daughter's distraught reaction and shrugged. "Unless they're testing out products that haven't been released yet. Now that Steve Jobs is running the company again, I imagine they have some interesting things coming in the future."

"Future?" Brittany mumbled. "Is it all right if I hang out in the back room until lunchtime?"

"Sure," John Rocco answered and held up the yellowing magazine. "There are years of these back there if you want to take a look for yourself."

Brittany shuffled through the door to the back room while her dad returned to the front to help Sam and the customer. In the back corner of the open storeroom was a tiny room where John Rocco had carved out a manager's office. She retreated to the secondary chair and closed the door without turning on the light.

She wanted the dark. The dark helped her clear her head, and, except for a strip of light sliding from under the door, she had achieved it.

Future, she thought to herself. All the world's thoughts on apparitions have only considered them inhabitants of the past. No one had uttered the word "future" in the presence of their topic. *If life is not a boundary for ghosts, why should time be either?*

"I saw a future ghost," Brittany said aloud, and the words created a chill that began at the base of her back and ran upward into her shoulder blades.

The goose bumps intensified from the sudden loss of light under the door. A shadow disappeared and reappeared as if someone had passed by. She paused as the jolt subsided and listened outside, but she heard nothing. No steps, no movement, and no reason for anyone to have followed her.

Brittany folded her arms over her chest, leaned back into the seat, and felt the muscles of her face form into a satisfied smile.

The blip of darkness was a signal—a sign she had gotten the answer right.

10

NEIL AND THE VISITANT

As agreed, Demetry was waiting for Neil in the parking lot of the Trans-Allegheny Lunatic Asylum when Neil left the ghost hunt at four o'clock in the morning. Demetry had been waiting long enough for a layer of moisture to blanket the windows. Inside, Demetry had lumbered back to sleep with his seat protracted to the furthest it could recline.

Neil rapped on the glass, causing a jolt in Demetry, who shimmied upright and quickly inspected the disruptor.

"Fuck, man," Neil heard Demetry gripe from the inside, then heard the doors click in unison.

A barrage of swearing continued once Neil entered.

"Scared the shit out of me, Hutch. We're right next to a building full of ghosts! Shit, man."

"I saw one," Neil said, pouncing on the opportunity. "I saw a ghost!"

Blearily, Demetry winked each eye, then both together. "I was joking, but clearly you are not."

121

"No. It's real." Neil bounced in the seat like an excited child. "It was a full-body apparition. And it wasn't just me! Someone had scratches on them in the violent male ward. Someone on the wood floors heard footsteps coming toward them, then heard them stop and start again behind them. Someone heard screams down an empty hallway. It's all true. All of it!"

Demetry chuckled. Whether nervously or sleepily, Neil could not tell. Feelings were hard to gauge with exhaustion in the mix. "If you weren't a true believer before, you sure are now."

Neil inhaled a deep breath and returned a "Yeah" on the exhale. "I feel … awake. Alive."

"I imagine being in a building full of dead people all night would make you appreciate the side of mortality you're on."

The car came to a red light. They held at the crossing for no one as the early morning mist diffused the crimson glow. Demetry tapped on the steering wheel as a song played at a volume heard only in idle moments.

"You need to come with me next time they do this," Neil finally said, his energy dipping, but still high in enthusiasm. "You know, prove to me those brave moments chasing Eddie Swan's ghost weren't just flukes."

The car moved again.

"Sure thing, man." Demetry's smile glowed in the light of the passing streetlights as they neared the hotel. "I prefer open spaces for ghost hunting. A lot more places to run should the phantom you're chasing start chasing you. Ya know?"

Neil shuffled in the passenger seat as they turned into the plaza that housed the hotel. The lots of the strip mall had been full during the day, but the absence of vehicles only highlighted the stores on the far side. He watched the names and logos on the marquees as the car straightened to its final approach. Subway, Peking, Shoe Show, Nail Show, an empty storefront with the outline of a RadioShack logo on the unfaded paint.

The absence of people made the property feel as lonely as the asylum had. The night brought a certain sadness. An undeniable melancholy interrupted by daybreak and repopulation by the waking world. The mediation calmed Neil's receptors further, and he expelled his first yawn of the ride.

"You're going to sleep good for what remains of the night," Demetry said. He put the car in park. "I know I am."

"When are you getting started?" Neil asked with another yawn.

Exiting the car, Demetry stretched, raising his arms over his head. "We're meeting with a guide at eight o'clock for a special tour. We're going to try and check out the cemeteries and the museum area where they keep The Haint's diary."

*****

It took Neil another two hours to settle his mind for rest. When his eyes opened again, the oversized display on the hotel alarm clock beamed 1:23 p.m.

He shuffled in the bed, his chest buzzing with the intake of conscious oxygen. His fuzzy eyes had the crust of sleep on the edges. The dust from the asylum had settled onto his body and reconstituted into excretions.

A few minutes later, there was a knock on the door. Neil rose in only boxers and was prompt to cover up with a pair of basketball shorts.

"Who is it?" he called.

"Who'd ya think?" Demetry's voice called from the outside.

Neil pulled the door open. "Geez, where'd you stuff Miguel?"

Demetry did not seem like himself. A decisive frown adorned his face and a defeated slouch lowered his height. He approached the bed and sat with his elbows on his knees.

"He walked over to Subway to get some lunch."

Neil let the door close. "What's wrong?"

"The graveyard was a bust." Demetry stared at the floor. Beads of sweat merged on his forehead and dripped to the floor.

Neil took note and adjusted the thermostat on the air-conditioner. He also took the opportunity to open the heavy curtain, revealing a bright overview of the outskirts of Weston. Neil's room faced the highway, where more stores and restaurants dotted the other side. A prominent memorial garden was plotted along the fringes of the industrial zone, driving home the moment's theme.

Demetry remained unflinching as he studied the threads of the carpet. "We didn't find The Haint. We couldn't even figure out where to look."

"There were that many bodies there?"

No answer came from Demetry. His trance deepened.

"Dude, now you're the one who looks like they've seen a ghost." Neil sat next to his friend and punched his shoulder. The action snapped Demetry from his stupor.

"Yeah. It was haunting. More than twenty thousand people died there during its operation. I mean, that's a lot of fucking people. The guide said most of the graves are double- and triple-stacked with caskets."

Neil shook his head in disbelief. "Damn! How do they handle the gravestones in that case?"

Demetry snorted. "Poorly." He opened his mouth for an expanded reply but stopped. He exhaled and changed the subject. "Why don't we go for a ride today? The asylum museum is going to let us inspect The Haint's diary on Monday, so we mostly have a free day today. I never really got to see much of West Virginia south of here. I want to see the bridge!"

"New River Gorge?" Neil joked. "You know they have more than one bridge."

"Yep. That big boy," Demetry replied, and his cheerful demeanor reemerged.

*****

THE bridge spanning the New River Gorge was as large as all the photos depicted. The three men took a path of wooden planks to the observation deck.

It was once the tallest bridge in the world, but like all things manmade, somebody built one taller. The bridge remained a popular attraction for sightseers, and a fall festival where BASE jumping was legal on it for a single day.

The men gawked at the arch structure for the appropriate length of time, climbed the endless stairs to the start of the path, and perused the gift shop. When they had their fill of the tourist trap, they started back to Weston.

Not long into the return journey, Demetry developed a hankering for a cup of coffee. After the sleepless night, the quest for caffeine was unanimous, and the men took a detour into the city of Summersville. Finding an open shop proved difficult on a late Sunday afternoon, but Demetry remained undaunted.

"There's a Starbucks on the other side of town," Demetry noted as he turned onto the surface streets.

"What about there?" Miguel asked. On the following block, a red food truck parked along the street, with a silhouette of a coffee cup painted on the lower corner.

Demetry immediately flicked on the turn signal. "I'm going to see if this is anything. I'd prefer to give a local business my dimes first."

Demetry and Miguel exited the vehicle, but Neil remained planted.

"See if they have matcha drinks," he requested.

"A what?" Demetry squinted one eye to the point of closing.

"Matcha—it's green tea powder. They put it in drinks at coffee shops now. It's a thing. I haven't had one like it in a few months."

Demetry scowled further. "Man, I ain't asking for that. Why don't you come with me to see if they're open?"

Neil groaned and exited while Demetry rounded the trailer. Before the two could reach the curb, Demetry had already returned, crestfallen. "Nobody's there."

Miguel noticed a group of yard signs secured to the front of the trailer and read it aloud. "Gad Dam Brewing."

The others looked to the sign, too, assuming the mispronunciation was from Miguel's accent.

"Gad Dam," Demetry repeated. "Ha! Funny. Wonder what that even means?"

Neil perked. "Oh, I know why. As your official West Virginia Sherpa, would you like to hear it?"

"Absolutely!" Demetry rubbed his hands together with anticipation.

"There used to be a town near here called Gad," Neil started, pointing back the way they had come through Summersville. "The government bought up the town when they built the lake back in the 1960s. Gad is now a ghost town on the bottom. Traditionally, the Army Corp of Engineers names the lake dam after the nearest town, but they refused to call it Gad Dam. They went with Summersville Dam instead."

"A whole town is underwater at that lake we passed." Demetry scratched his chin. "Do you know where it was?"

"Near the marina, wherever that is."

Demetry clapped his hands. "Let's head on to Starbucks and backtrack to the marina. I want to see this underwater town."

Back in the car, with a coffee in each hand of the trio, Neil broached the topic of the next ghost hunt.

"When is it?" Demetry asked as he entered the highway back to the lake.

"Next Saturday."

Demetry grunted. "Um. Yeah. We're not going to stay here that long. We may go back next Saturday."

"Oh?" Neil wanted to argue, but he wasn't sure how best to proceed. Demetry defended the decision, anyway.

"After we get the diary pages, I don't think we're going to have much more reason to be here. The rest is interviews and newspaper clippings, which can be found online."

A renewed sadness came over Neil, compounded by Demetry's haymaker comment.

"I also need to get back to the wife. She misses me."

Careful not to present a negative reaction, Neil wanted to see if the car's occupants could detect his disdain. The cabin remained quiet, but the subject soon returned to the book.

"I don't know, guys. I'm not sure I'm going to get anything I need for this book." Demetry's doubt cast renewed shade over the group. "Maybe I'm not qualified to write it."

"Of course, you are," Neil said. "You are the best writer I know. The only hurdle is gathering information, and we have a whole week."

"Nah, man, if we don't get enough info out of Silkie's diary, I don't think I'm going to have a way forward to write it. Maybe you can write it after I strike out. Dust off your author aspirations and give it a try."

"No, man. I'm too white to tell a Black story," Neil dismissed. He crossed his legs in the passenger seat. "It's not going to carry the right weight if I write it."

"Nonsense," Demetry spat. "Black, white, or red, if a story ends up in your head, you write it. You can't help what you are. If a story came to you, it's yours. If you don't tell it, it won't get told."

"But this is *your* story," Miguel interjected.

"And I'm bequeathing it."

"I don't want to write anything about race," Neil continued. "I don't want to write about anything at all, but especially not race. There's just no way to get it right these days. If you write a person of color unconvincingly, they'll say it's just a white character in colored skin. If you write them too convincingly, they call it a stereotype. And it's not bitterness or hatefulness or anything. There are just a lot of intricacies I'm not sure I'm equipped to handle. Like right now, if I were writing a story about our trip. Sure, we got someone Black and someone Latino, that checks some boxes for diversity, but now I have to describe you. Do I describe the color of your skin? The way you've been raised to pronounce certain words? These things should be okay to write about, right? That makes you who you are. But right off the bat, someone would complain I'm not giving Miguel enough to say even though he's naturally quiet. They'd say that you curse and say 'man' a lot. These aren't unfair ways to describe who you are, specifically. Like, I wouldn't write some weird, specifically racist trope, like munching on a watermelon or something."

"Of course not," Demetry said with a faux angry expression. "I don't munch on watermelon in the car. It would get sticky."

Neil snorted and leaned back in his seat. Demetry wasn't being serious. "They don't give A-for-effort stickers anymore. You either get it right, or you get the world's ire, and often you still receive both when you get it right. Even if you get it right, there's a whole other side of the argument that will come after you. White supremacists or conservative propagandists who will signal boost the same screed. They're violently motivated to carry out any slight—or perceived slight—to their way of life."

"But I understand your plight as a white man," Demetry said, now considering the conversation with the correct weight. "You can call it privilege or whatever you want. I'm just happy you consider it. I'll give you my own personal A-for-effort." Demetry paused and ran his tongue across his teeth. "Us Black folk have come a long way from the start. First, we were in bondage, then we were fighting to escape, then we were fighting to survive, then we were scrapping to overcome the prejudices of an unfriendly world. Those battles are still waged in various stages, and we had good times in between. There is both a zenith and a nadir to the cycle, and we've achieved measures of both. Guessing how the world works, I expect if there's ever a day where the battle is done, it'll still involve a bunch of white folks wholly and definitively acknowledging we had been a valuable part of society this whole time."

Neil wasn't sure what it was about the moment. He wasn't sure whether it was the surge of caffeine molecules tickling his synapses, the warm wind from the lowered car window assaulting his face with earthy country smells, or how every element was in its rightful place. For whatever it was, he knew he would remember this day.

*****

At the marina dock, Demetry tilted between two pontoon boats and stared deep into the water. "Man, you can't see nothing. Murky shit."

Miguel stared at a brochure he found. "Says here it is the clearest water east of the Mississippi River."

"Oof. Hate to see what constitutes as unclear." Demetry pulled away from the edge, aggravated, and started back to the shoreline. "Buncha manmade bullshit anyways. The Minnesotan in me is reeling from this nonsense."

"We never destroyed the wilderness for our lakes," Miguel added.

"Damn right," Demetry continued as he marched of the dock and rounded a vehicle to find a clear swath of bank. "I hope a mosquito bites the ass of every person who boats here. They wiped out an entire community just for people's entertainment. Colonist bullshit."

Demetry sighed and flopped onto the bank. He stared out at the water as far as he could, like he was expecting an unknown answer to surface in the distance.

A cool breeze wafted from the lake. The grave of Gad was below them, and Neil could sense its ghosts. Not the individual people who would not have died there, but the ghost of a community. An apparition locked in a watery grave, unable to pierce the surface tension. It was screaming, but there was no air to carry the sound to the top. Neil could only sense its spirit as the gases of its mournfulness rose to the top and lingered in the humidity.

The haunted feeling returned Neil's thoughts. The spirit—the ghost he had encountered the night before. *What was it? It was so real. It could not have been a dream, not a sleep-deprived hallucination, nor a mirage of kinship.* He had to know the truth.

"I want to stay here. In West Virginia," Neil said finally. It was as much an admission to himself as it was to his friends. "I need to see this asylum ghost again. Investigating it would be a surefire cure to the funk I've been in since the divorce."

There was silence for a beat, filled by the crickets warming their instruments for the night's serenades. Other critters of the evening began to lend their musical abilities.

"I figured you'd come to that conclusion, ghost or not," Demetry finally said as his lip curled. "The goal was to make you feel alive again. Figured the warm hug of the mountains would do the trick, but if that's your reason. If happiness is what this accomplishes, you need to continue to do what you can to hang onto that feeling."

Neil slapped a mosquito off his arm. "I mean, I guess I'll go back with you so I can bring back my truck and stuff, but I want to keep investigating. I want to know more about everything. The building, the ghosts, I want to know it all."

Demetry slapped Neil's shoulder and stood before turning to help Miguel upright. "I'll keep sending you research pay until the book is finished, or the money runs out. Hopefully the prior. I could use a researcher at ground zero to investigate the area, should new details emerge."

The two traded firm grips and Demetry pulled Neil to his feet. Dusting the seat of their pants in synchronization, both took a parting look at the lake. Neil stared back at the flooded valley and tried to imagine what the area would have looked like a hundred years earlier. He tried to picture those who lived there, what their lives were like, how their echoes would ring across the walls of their hollow. But Neil's imagination failed, leaving the effort fruitless. The drowned town would remain unknown. *But The Haint?*

Neil turned away from the lake to face Demetry. "I would be honored to help. Nothing would make me happier."

HENRIETTA AND THE HAINT

Henrietta met Silkie Le Margaux in the garden on the last day of spring. A vast tract of farmland enveloped within the valley produced crops to feed the entire population of the hospital. Livestock grazed on a separate parcel partitioned by an oft-breached fence. The corn recently suffered the hunger of wayward cattle, reducing the yield. A bumper crop of peas and carrots took up the slack. There would be plenty to sustain the hospital population through winter.

Henrietta remained isolated from the rest of the hospital population, unable to take part in chores or crafts. Nursing Wallace, watching him sleep, and healing were all she had to pass the hours. Nurse Showalter or one of her acolytes began leaving her books and newspapers to read. She would often read the material in a day, return it to the evening nurse, and have a new volume presented to her the next day. After a dozen books, the nurses began to have difficulty finding suitable material to keep Henrietta occupied. She found an assembly and operations manual for an autoclave one day. Staff returned hours later to reclaim it, citing a continued need to have it on hand. All the same, Henrietta devoured it within the first hour and considered it more riveting than some of the drier works of the last month.

Their substitution was a newer work called *Where Angels Fear to Tread.* Henrietta had little interest in scouring it immediately and began posing multiple requests.

"Could I do arts and crafts?"

"Could I work in the laundry?"

"Could I assemble furniture?"

"Could I assemble autoclaves? It looks like it could be fun."

All the questions returned a stern "No."

"Could I go work on the farm?"

"No." But this time, with a reason. "You can't be spotted by your wardmates. The white population can't find you here."

"Can I farm with the Black population?"

The question finally elicited a pause.

"You're still healing." Nurse Showalter fielded the answer.

"You said it yourself that I was healing faster than most," Henrietta pleaded.

Another pause. Henrietta was wearing the nurse down.

"Let me speak with Doctor Koenig about the matter," Nurse Showalter conceded. Henrietta celebrated the small victory against solitude, if only for a moment.

Two days passed, Henrietta read the book, threw it across the room when the baby in the story died, and never returned to it. The book remained in the corner when Nurse Showalter returned the next day.

"Doctor Koenig is deeply engaged in his work at the moment, so I did not ask him."

Henrietta was about to turn crestfallen until the nurse inserted a "But."

"Because he delegated a lot of the decisions about your care to me, I am making this decision on his behalf. I will allow you light duty on the farm with the other Black patients, but say nothing to the doctor, and say nothing to the other patients about your child. Tell them he's a surrogate if you must. Your permissions will be revoked if I find you disobeyed this agreement."

Henrietta had the task of weeding what remained of the corn and pruning what they called "The Suckers." It amounted to shucking unproductive branches from the base of the corn stalk.

Not wanting to risk reopening her wounds, Henrietta remained on her knees and slid about in the soft soil. She yanked the leafy green invaders with a satisfying *pop*. The work was an effort, but the effort was what she longed for.

Wallace was bound to her chest and aligned for easy access to a nipple. She would only stop and check him in the moments when his movements stilled. She always found him asleep or drunk with nourishment.

The close spacing of the leggy plants kept her out of the aim of an unforgiving sun. She never felt the need to rush, either. Though the thought of her parents being whipped for working at her slow pace never left her mind. The knotted ropes of skin on their back spoke testament to the trauma. Henrietta's father, in all the days she knew him, would not place direct body weight on his back. He always opted to lay on his side or stomach. He said it did not hurt, but he had never grown beyond the habit of avoiding pressure on the area. He would never speak anything about his time in slavery that didn't impact everyday life. He was untrusting of banks, so he hid their money; he was untrusting of grocers, so he squirreled away canned goods. He was untrusting of doctors, which Henrietta blamed for her mother's lack of care and resulting death.

He made himself trust the mortician. Henry Tidewater could dig the perfect hole for his wife, place her inside, and carve a fine marker. He could not do the same for himself. He would need to trust someone to place him in the ground. He needed the relationship to ensure the execution of his final wishes.

Henrietta missed her mother. She missed her even more while in the field. She recalled Malkia's anecdotes on those enslaved days, telling stories of farm accidents, and slights from among her large family. Brothers were always stealing food from her plate. They were often whipped or switched by an elder for their efforts. An uncle lost two toes from a hoe mishap. A brother had an arm broken by a runaway cart.

For all its horrors, Malkia allowed herself nostalgia in those moments. Henrietta could not blame her for assigning great value to meager times when the surrounding days had no worth. She would not speak about the cruelty, but their scars said more than she ever could. Malkia once mused about their farm's proximity to Yorktown. The place where the United States had won its freedom was not a win for everyone. Not Malkia's. Not Henry's. The war for their liberty postponed. A battle won, followed by more postponement. Later, and again later, and again later, then it would be someone else's turn. The battle for liberty was an eternal war. A skirmish to gain, a fight to keep. A game of King of the Hill with room at the top for everyone, but few factions sharing the summit.

Emerging from the corn cluster, Henrietta came face-to-face with an older woman. The woman's weathered face appeared startled, and she pulled her head as far back as it would allow.

"'Scuse me," Henrietta said as she skirted the woman and continued onward. Henrietta was partly aware the woman's gaze was following her.

"You just a youngin'," the woman said. She had a tired, Southern drawl. Deliberately choosing the fewest words and uttering them in the shortest way possible.

Henrietta huffed. "I'm twenty."

"Babies sucklin' on babies." The woman shook her head. She shuffled her feet and changed direction, walking toward one of the attendants who had taken respite on a barrier of baled straw.

"Who that?" Henrietta could faintly hear the woman quiz the doughy man. His coveralls were taut with the weight of his gut, taxing the straps. He responded at a low register Henrietta could not understand. Unfazed, she returned to her task.

The patchy rows of corn ravaged by the cattle were all that remained. Henrietta had saved them for last. Protection from the heat would be scarce, and the day's sizzle only grew worse.

Henrietta eased herself to her knees and began scooting to the first cabal of weeds when a shadow offered relief.

"Hadn't seen you 'round." The woman stood above her, blocking the light.

"I could say the same for you," Henrietta replied and began prying nettles from the soil.

"Been here two weeks. Met e'ryone in the ward. I thought."

Henrietta paused to look up at the woman. She wore a tan sleeveless shirt, and Henrietta immediately noticed a bandage wrapped around her left bicep.

"I've been in isolation. This child gave me an awful lot of trouble in birth, and I had an awful lot of healing after." Henrietta immediately realized she had broken the agreement with Nurse Showalter and tried to cover. "What's your story?"

The older woman scoffed. "Had me in Staunton. Western State Hospital or somethin' like that. Western, Weston, West Virginia. All sounds the same. Was in Milledgeville before. Can't remember its proper name."

It felt rude to ask what the woman had done to prompt residence in three different institutions, but Henrietta caught sight of scars on her arms. Miniature versions of her parents' scars lined her arm like a ladder. At least eight of the healed cuts appeared on each arm. The woman remained still, as if she were giving Henrietta time to admire them.

"Name is Silkie. Was named after a type of chicken."

"I am Henrietta. I have a hen in my name."

The two laughed, and Silkie sat down in the dirt and crossed her legs.

"We are like chickens to 'em, or cattle. Burdensome beasts meant for use of nothin' but farm tools. They cut us up and wear our skin and say 'Don' that look good on me' when they spent a lifetime actin' like it didn't look good on us."

Silkie beat a fist into the dirt. The wrinkles on her face tightened with either pain or anger, or both. In the weeks to come, Henrietta never detected an ounce of ignorance in Silkie, despite her simple vocabulary. An attendant insulted her speech once, to which she had replied, "Why waste time on words? Thoughts are greater in all ways." Even in practice, an intricate thought would often slip from Silkie's mouth, and her response was often heavy with shame. In truth, it was because Silkie knew the most devastating weapon white power feared was an education. Silkie went to great pains to keep her weapon sheathed, but this would be the first occasion Henrietta noticed the concealment.

"A complaint for another time," she explained with a wince. "No whips here. Much more different from how I's reared. They only fuss here if ya run."

"You were a slave?" Henrietta did not know too many former slaves outside of her parents. Even the community she had grown up in was either too young or had already achieved their freedom ahead of emancipation.

Silkie nodded. "In Louisiana. Don't remember where. Was a Shreveport nearby. Never saw it again, will never find it again. Went into Arkansas after that. It was my home. How about you? Your family slaves?"

Henrietta wanted to tell her about the Yorktown-adjacent tobacco plantation. How the town where the country earned its bloody freedom was the place where her parents stayed locked in bloody bondage. But she couldn't. Henrietta could not shake the sense Silkie had ulterior motives for speaking with her.

"Do you chat up all the negroes you meet here?" Henrietta asked with a barb of rudeness.

"True that I'd not met you. You are from the main building, and your baby is as white as the northern star." Silkie tapped her pointer finger haphazardly into the fine soil. "When slave drivers fancied a girl, they would treat them better and give them better quarters and better food. Pretty soon, they start walkin' around with a child lighter-skinned than them. Yours is the lightest I've ever saw."

She sighed and pressed her palm down to flatten the holes she'd been making in the dirt. "Is a white man's world. Reckon is somethin' that can't change. Just like how north is north, and south is south."

Henrietta shook her head in disagreement, or perhaps a refusal to believe. "A Black man put me in here, and a white man is keeping me in here. My quarrel doesn't seem to be with the color so much as with the man."

"Man had to of gotten you that little teat sucker." Silkie pointed to Wallace, who was now awake and nursing.

"It was at great cost to the man," Henrietta said, though she arched to admire the product. "Though I suspect I'll pay his due before it's all over."

Silkie nodded with a scowl. "Men with power oft forward the coin."

Henrietta considered adding more, but a man whom they knew as Wheaty climbed atop the largest stack of hay and began an impromptu sermon. No one was sure if he spoke on behalf of God through anointment, but his ravings always had a kernel of potential.

"… and lo I looked around and saw only wolves, my shepherd not among them. And so, I wandered off. I trusted more that my shepherd would leave his flock to come find me, rather than remain and stay in the care of those who seek to devour."

Silkie spoke over the sermon with a chuckle. "Wheaty is losing it. Same speech as the other day."

Henrietta matched the laugh and turned to her chores. "I need to finish up. Everyone is done but me."

Silkie reached a hand to halt Henrietta. "Who is the father?"

"I can't tell you." Henrietta lowered her head and tried to turn away, but Silkie held her shoulder.

"My knowing is good for you."

Henrietta bit her lip as she met Silkie's gaze.

Silkie peered deep into Henrieta's eyes, as if reading her life's story from her pupils. "A doctor?"

Henrietta closed her eyes tightly and nodded.

"Which one?"

"I can't say. I really can't." Henrietta stood, and Silkie followed. "Let this be enough for now."

"Why not?"

"Because I just met you," Henreitta growled. "I can't say I rightly trust you yet."

The comment gave Silkie pause, and she lowered her arms.

Henrietta didn't realize she was frightened until all she could hear was the sound of her heavy breathing. She took another step away and pointed at Silkie's bandage. "How did you get that injury? How did you get all of those scars?"

Silkie placed an arm on her wrapped bicep. "They won't let me work in the kitchen no more. I like the knife. Like the pain. That's why I'm here."

Henrietta curled her lip in disgust.

"White men took me when I was young. No better food. No better quarter. They just wanted me for nothing. Tried but got no baby out of me. I cut myself up so they couldn't take me again. They tried again and said no when they saw what I done. No pleasure there now. The only pleasure comes from the pain."

The thought of mutilation turned Henrietta's stomach. "I'm so sorry. I know there were horrors. I couldn't imagine living through those days."

But a pain reverberated from Henrietta's lower torso, one that she did not find pleasurable. Standing stressed the left incision, and she pressed a hand against it to soothe the compromised muscle. *I had been mutilated, too*, it occurred to her. Silkie had discerned as much information from the simple flinch.

"They fixed you, too." Silkie didn't ask it as a question but as a bold summation of fact.

Henrietta's inability to speak in response compelled Silkie, and she continued with more force behind her words.

"We ain't free. Negroes can be free, but they don't want us to breed freely. Only allowed it because we were livestock. We are not now. White men have no need for our chicks. They took something from you. Only one way to get it back now."

The aggressive response forced Henrietta's mood to plummet further. Silkie was not wrong in her outlook. Like beasts of burden, slaves were genetically engineered to be the finest machinery of their time. With freedom, they had the advantage of a future enhanced by the eugenics of their past. It had to be threatening to the powers. Stolen, bred, perfected, and Black folks were now superior beings, more than capable of being more than a minority.

"H-how can we get it back?"

Silkie allowed a wicked grin. "Revenge."

Another flinch came from Henrietta, a pain born now from emotional trauma rather than physical.

"I can't."

Silkie sighed. "You in love?"

The word triggered the same disgusted response that the topic of mutilation had. "Love? No. There are feelings. I would not call it love."

"Good," Silkie replied. "Think about how it ends. The end will come, whether you like it or not."

Henrietta had never considered the ending. The very thought sank her disposition to the depths.

Silkie stared at Henrietta, studying her for several breaths longer before breaking away when Wheaty's sermon ended.

"You don't need to tell me the name. Trust first, then tell. We have time before the end."

*****

Wailing permeated Ward C when Henrietta returned in the early evening. In the sparse times, Henrietta left her room, the nurses covered her head to toe with a bedsheet. Led by a firm grip on her shoulder, Henrietta heard screeches of "ghost," "spook," and "costume," but it wasn't until the current trip that she heard a new remark.

"Klansman!"

The voice came from nearby, which startled Henrietta.

"Jansy, get back in your room!" the nurse scolded. "Who let you out anyways?"

The nurse turned to Henrietta and shouted, though the sheet did little to dampen the sound. "I'm going to get Jansy back in her room. Don't move."

The nurse detached from Henrietta's shoulder and her shadowy form disappeared. Though concealed, Henrietta felt exposed to everyone. She clutched Wallace in his wraps and shielded him from any unseen threats on the other side of the sheet. Someone was looming like they were observing the stationary spirit.

"There ain't no darkies on this floor, Mr. Klansman!" Jansy shouted, her voice darting around the room. She was evading capture. "They don't

139

allow them in our building. They got their own room out back. If you can spring me from this joint, we'll go torch it together."

"Attendant!" the nurse called to the other side of the hall. "I need assistance."

An additional commotion sounded in mumbles and shouts from farther away. Then the screams of "Ghost!" began in earnest.

"Ain't no ghost," Jansy said in the belligerent hall. "It's a Klansman. Klu Klux Klan. Exterminators come to rid us of coal-faced vermin. Black rats. The peskiest of 'em all."

Another observer became curious enough to inspect the blanket and found it to be harmless. Emboldened, they gave it a single yank. The sheet skidded across Henrietta's unkempt hair with a static charge. When it stopped, she was exposed to everyone in the hall.

Henrietta had never seen the corridor occupied. Now, it bustled. White women shuffled about to the far end of the hall. A nearby woman with a goiter under her ear scraped flecks of paint off the wall with her index finger. A frail woman in the commons area slid her feet to an unheard rhythm, pacing in a predestined pattern around the floor.

Jansy was the first to take notice of Henrietta. She was a middle-aged woman with fading blonde hair, flat-faced and beady eyes, which widened as if she had seen a true ghost. Jansy raised an accusing finger and jabbed violently in Henrietta's direction.

"Ain't no Klansman! That darky is an impostor! This is heresy! Sacrilege!"

The attendant grabbed Jansy around the waist and pulled her in the direction of her room. Jansy struggled and tried to pull away as a second attendant joined. "Who let a Black bitch onto this floor? Posing as a Klansman is blasphemous! Injustice. Injustice!"

The nurse ran to Henrietta and ushered her into Room 668. Henrietta craned her neck as she left the hall. The orderlies forced Jansy into the room next door. Her shrieks were still piercing with both doors closed.

"I'm sorry," the nurse said while Henrietta secured Wallace in the makeshift bassinet. "I am going to be in such trouble with Doctor Koenig."

Henrietta eased herself back onto the bed. "Can you see if I can be moved back to the Black ward? I spent the day in the field with them, and there are several who I miss spending time with."

"I will speak with the doctor," the nurse replied hesitantly before mumbling under her breath. "Perhaps I can catch him in a less bristly mood."

The comment caught Henrietta's attention. "What do you mean? I've only known the doctor as a kind man."

The nurse looked between Henrietta and Wallace and began to blink rapidly. "I've not said anything. Please don't repeat it to anyone. I'm a little new to nursing. Training under the doctor has been …"

"I understand," Henrietta said. The nurse's hesitation gave nutrients to the doubts Henrietta had about Doctor Felix. Perhaps, his standoffish nature said more about him than his kind words. She considered the notion as she reached to pull a blanket over Wallace. Realizing the nurse's unfinished comment was still lingering in the air, Henrietta returned to her initial point. "Being a captive of this ward has been burdensome, and I miss my old wardmates."

The nurse's mind had drifted, too. She snapped back to attention and nodded. "Yes! I will speak with the doctor."

Henrietta bowed her head. "Thank you, nurse …"

"Nurse Chokio. Nancy Chokio."

The two shared a smile until Nurse Chokio noticed the book Henrietta had flung into the corner. She lifted it, read the cover, and scoffed. "I didn't care for it either."

EUGENE AND
THE MANIFESTATION

Monday, June 26, 1935

The boy reeked, though Eugene was hypocritical in turning his nose. He had also eschewed time in the showers of the Weston State Hospital, dreading nude encounters with others. He had his fill of such interactions in the army, and his distaste only grew in the veteran years. In that way, he was like Flip, but the boy's fragrance indicated a finer vintage. Eugene had not been in the hospital for a month, but who knew how long Flip had gone since bathing? His ripeness implied days beyond number, so Eugene inquired.

"Maybe three months," Flip offered. Bathing wasn't mandatory, and priority went to those who had no reservations about wallowing in excrement. Flip kept tidy, but the natural progression of stench amassed. Too many days had passed now, and it was time for Eugene to say so.

Not alone in the protest, Archibald joined in duet to the sentiment, adding that Eugene's fermentation was also becoming apparent.

"You have resided here eight months. What needle of opportunity did you thread to accomplish a cleanse at the five-month mark?" Eugene inquired.

"I worked out an agreement with a night attendant to let me shower after midnight when everyone else was locked tight in their rooms," Flip answered. "That attendant doesn't work the floor anymore, and the ones who followed felt like my request was some kind of unknown ruse."

"Ruse," Eugene repeated as if he were filing the term away in his internal dictionary for later use. "Good word."

Flip remained on topic. "What do you suggest then?"

"Guard duty. Since we both need a hygienic refresh, I propose we take turns. We'll clear the stalls, and you can shower while I mind the door. You, likewise, guard when I go in for my own dousing."

Flip showed hesitancy to involve an older man in plans that involved disrobing, albeit at separate times. He stared pensively at Eugene while weighing trust against his stench.

"I'll go first, if it makes for a better bargain," Eugene offered.

"No." Flip puffed his chest as confidence built. "I'll go ahead first."

Archibald had been eavesdropping on the bargaining, as there was no other activity available. "Good. It will give me some quiet time to commune with the Lord."

"You and the good Lord can conduct business anytime it suits you, so long as you are not audibly casting judgment on us or anyone that appears as us," Eugene chided. "Yes, sir, know that any premature verdict on my soul on behalf of your god shall be met with a swift vengeance at my hand."

"But 'vengeance is mine, says the Lord.'"

Eugene scoffed. "'Judge not less ye be judged.' It doesn't specify by whom, but I don't expect God suffers such trivial things. My boot in your keister will suffice in lieu of His."

Archibald sputtered, coughed, and struggled to reply. Eugene took the display as a good time to exit with Flip to prepare for showering.

It had been twenty days of trading barbs between Eugene and the endangered cultist. The pair began in the wrong when Archibald mocked Flip's aversion to touch as fearful.

"Fear comes from the devil," Archibald had chastised. "Don't let the devil control your life."

"Fear kept you from killing yourself with your loony pals," Eugene had rebutted. "The notion that it comes from the devil is laughable anyhow. Fear is a defense mechanism interwoven into our being by nature. A deer hears a stick crack in the forest, and you believe it took flight because the devil suddenly leaped into his hide and told him to giddy up?"

Archibald huffed, the defense offending him in dueling ways. Aside from attacking his beliefs on fear, the insinuation that he had chickened out of a suicide pact was beyond the pale. Archibald lunged toward Eugene, but the elder was able to deflect his advance. Aiding the maneuver was Archibald losing consciousness and toppling into Eugene's cot. His head and chest made a soft landing, but his back half twisted and knocked his hips against the edge of the metal frame.

Archibald regained composure minutes later. He explained his tendency to faint under sudden and undue stress, which was why he missed his turn at the pokeweed communion. He woke up after everyone else was dead on the floor around him and the sheriff at the church door.

"You come down awful hard on Archibald," Flip commented as he was about to go alone into the showers. Eugene had already scouted the room and found no one present.

Eugene scratched his beard. "How so?"

"He's a good Christian man. Believes in good. Tries to be pious in his way."

"So much of religious history is the denial of truth," Eugene said as he leaned against the doorframe. "God sends us a message of love, and man spends centuries undermining it with an agenda tailored to earthly needs. God sends His son to reintroduce that message of love, and the process begins anew. From what I gleaned from interviews with Archie about his congregation's doctrine, those folks were looking at a way to wield the political influence to topple the Roosevelt administration. Afterward, they would instate a party that would establish a single religion policy. Never mind modern politics consisting of cropped wings that are the appendages of the same wretched bird. Religion should not get into bed with politics. If they mate, it'll make for ugly children who are certain to take after their father, the senator. The point is, there is nothing in their worldview focused on love. It is all agenda. Yes, sir, no one must die in God's name to please God. It gratified the ego of their illustrious reverend and no one more. Nothing gained. Yes, sir, there was no lesson to be learned. No character. Livin' is the only thing that can build character, and anyone telling you different is just mad you don't conform to their worldview."

Flip yawned and moved to retract his opinion. "Fine. Can you cut the ramble?"

"Almost done," Eugene insisted. "My wife Ethel told me something to test my love once, and it changed my outlook from head to toe. I acted bitterly and hatefully toward the world. Not as a fragment of the whole, but the whole itself. I learned to love the things that deserve it and project consternation on the things that do not."

"What did your wife say that changed you?" Flip's interest piqued at this one nugget within the bedrock of the statement.

"What are you waiting for? Shower's empty." Eugene extended an arm to push Flip along, but the possibility of contact moved the boy faster.

Satisfied, Eugene crossed his arms and took a serious posture in his guard post. The Monday afternoon regulars lingered in the long hall. Eugene knew some by name. Frank, Reginald, Jake, Larry. The quartet often congregated around the entrance to their shared room and played rummy or poker, often with an incomplete deck. An argument would ensue that the attendant would have to moderate. The foursome then scattered across the ward, only to gradually regroup back at their room entrance.

A heavy-set man called Sly sat cross-legged near his room at the beginning of the hall. He had a cleft palate, and on the surface, it seemed to be his only sin against society. The inability to speak properly shouldn't have resulted in a hospital sentence. One of the boys said he was a simpleton, but Eugene's observations concluded he was a bright man in the interior. Always observing, always internalizing interactions based on what he saw. Sly's failure was in outward expression. He absorbed the world around him, but could not properly convey that he understood. For that failing, society abandoned Sly altogether. The man could observe the other bodies of his type, interred in these living mausoleums. Shoved in cramped spaces within the walls and forgotten. The doctors could have seen within

Sly what Eugene did. And if they did, they could release him back into a loved one's care to live out his days in a free and happy world. Short-staffed doctors, paired with overcrowding in the hospital, would allow no such outcome. Not for Sly, and Eugene was growing more fearful it was also his destiny.

It had been three weeks since he learned of Doctor Timmons's death. The new doctor, whose name he had forgotten, had yet to make another appearance. He could recognize the medical official by the perfect part in his blonde hair. The crease split down the middle of his scalp in a faultless line and came to a halt at the tips of his ears. Nobody had hair like that on the ward. Besides the attendant, those who had hair often looked as if they had recently risen from slumber. Eugene's own hair pointed in several directions and partly concealed the bald places of his crown. He often reached to straighten the strands but dubbed the task futile each time.

The follicle thoughts stopped when Louie, a man cursed with coprolalia, began screaming obscenities from his room in the center of the ward. He was louder than usual, or it could be that Eugene's room offered more sound protection than realized. Nevertheless, the sound of rapid-fire cursing filled the space. The vulgarities were often peppered with racial disparagements, which made the current burst pleasant by normal standards.

Louie was, in turn, interrupted by a flying chamber pot that flew from the room across from the quartet and crashed off the opposite wall. The pot grazed Jake, as he stood in his doorway and shuffled a half deck. The impact sent bodily waste flying in all directions, splattering across the walls and tile. Even though there were toilets in the shower room, each patient's room contained a pot in case nature called during nighttime lockdown.

Groans came from those who watched. Jake shrieked the loudest as a loose stool of feces splattered his chest. His roommates approached but then backed away when they saw his darkened white shirt and the smell took hold.

"Who was that?" the attendant asked from his post. He had seen what had happened, knew he would be responsible for the cleanup, and wasn't ready to commit to it yet.

"It was Peter!" Frank shouted, pointing to the room across from theirs.

Before the attendant could move, Frank and Reginald marched into Peter's room and threw the man into the hallway. He was a younger man in his midtwenties, who was lanky and awkward. Peter landed in the center of the hall and rolled end-over-end before coming to a halt.

"I'm sick. I don't like being sick!" Peter explained. "Had some bad eggs during lunch. They were poisoned eggs! Can't get to the bathroom. Don't like the smell."

"You peckerwood!" Jake called from where he stood. "That was an lousy thing to do!"

Before Peter could explain further, Frank and Reginald began kicking the gangly man, and he yelped in pain with each impact.

"Orderlies!" the attendant cried out as he ran toward the quarrel, more inclined to halt the commotion than clean up a soiled man.

Eugene continued to observe from his guard post. "You better wash swiftly, Flip! Another occupant will soon join you! I dare not stop him."

When Eugene's eyes returned to the fray, he caught sight beyond the scurry of a woman at the end of the hall. A woman whom he thought was Opal emerged from the ward entrance. She saw the scuffle unfolding in the vicinity and disappeared back through the door.

"Opal Lee?" Eugene said. The question pressed too hard for him to remain, so he moved toward the door to confirm his observation.

Flip emerged from the shower room, fully clothed, but his hair still dripping wet. "What's going on?"

"Return to the room," Eugene ordered. There's a right fierce brawl unfolding, and I don't want you to sully your newfound shine."

Eugene abandoned his post and started for the ward door, slipping past the melee to reach the entrance. The woman had closed the door so softly that it had not latched completely, giving Eugene the possibility to slip through. He was unsure if it was a door they kept locked. He only used it when headed to the cafeteria or during optional craft time.

Giving the handle a light jiggle revealed it was unsecured. The loud metal door was the only one of its kind on the floor and made a distinct sound when opened and closed. Eugene figured the attendants considered the noise alarm enough. But there was chaos in the ward. The screams and shouts of the brawling floormates would mask Eugene's departure.

In contrast, the adjacent ward was quiet with very few people in the hall. Eugene peered through the sprawl to see the hem of striped clothing disappear through the final metal door leading to the center of the Kirkbride.

An orderly and a nurse occupied the attendant's station near the door. Despite the jeopardy, Eugene felt attempting passage was worth the risk.

"Can I help you?" the nurse questioned when she looked up at Eugene.

Thinking fast, Eugene concocted a story. "I was here to visit my child." *Not a lie.*

The nurse noticed Eugene's civilian clothing and discerned his outfit worthy of leave. She waved him onward.

The pause cost too much time, and the stripe-clad woman had disappeared into the greater building. After pushing through the heavy door, Eugene paused to admire the cleanliness of the nexus between wings. The yellow walls were freshly painted and uncured with patient messes. Residents didn't mingle there. Meals, treatments, and recreations were the only reasons to pass through, and time was not allotted to fraternize.

Eugene had enough time now and stepped into the projector area overlooking the third floor auditorium. He leaned in the window used by the unmovable iron movie projector to shine a film into the room when requested. The auditorium floor was empty now, save a few folding chairs stowed along the edges. Eugene's view could see much more. He could pinpoint the corner of the room he was standing all those years ago when Ethel Bloom plucked him from among the wallflowers.

They had danced three times that night. Eugene remained close to her to ward off potential suitors and succeeded with her assistance. He must have done something right because she was smitten enough to follow him to the Nicholas County hollows. She cast off her role as a Lewis County socialite and took up a life as a farmer's wife, spending many years alone when Eugene returned to the army.

He laughed off any question of why she would want to be with him or want to stay with him. She was, she had been, and then she was gone. It felt like it was all in the same stroke of time, and there was nothing left to do but mourn the years and move along. Eugene had become a stranger to humanity, but maybe it was time to reintroduce himself. Maybe it was time for reinvention. He failed as a husband, as a father, and as a farmer, but there was more in the world still to be.

Eugene felt a sudden confidence. He would soon be removed from mental care. It had been weeks since his last outburst, and he was sure both the funeral home and police had forgotten about his incident by now. He only needed a doctor to sign off on his accomplishment.

For all its clear failings, the hospital did provide a curative effect.

Before he could complete the notion, Eugene heard another metal door creak behind him. He turned and arched his neck to see the door leading to the clock tower inch shut.

It was the only sound he had heard in the area. *Had Opal Lee gone into the tower?* No one had spoken of the spire or what was within. Curiosity and opportunity prompted Eugene to slide through the door before it could snap closed.

A flight of stairs—a continuation of the grand oak staircase—led to a ladder a timekeeper could climb into the clock's guts. Eugene stood at the top of the landing and stared upward at the gears and mechanisms.

It was cold, and as the man stood at the tower's precipice, the space only grew colder. It was odd on an early summer day for there to be such frigid air in the building, especially at its highest peak.

"No." Eugene spoke to the room. "Let this be no manic episode. I had been doing well enough that I could face the doctors without deceit. Whatever folly of the mind this is, please let it take leave of me!"

The machinery above became blurred with fog, and he began to hear the harmonic male vocals of a soldier's chorus. A drummer tapped in time and kept a driving beat with the vocals. Eugene covered his ears. The muffling seemed to help, at least a little.

Against his better judgment, Eugene investigated the fog once again. In the haze, he could see into eternity. It looked like the underside of a staircase creeping endlessly into the distance. As far as he peered, Eugene could only see more. The gears of the clock churned around it, representing the circle of time, never ceasing, only completing a circuit and starting anew.

The existential vision seared Eugene's soul, and he cried out. "What wicked place is this, truly? Demons! Demons reside at the peak of this timepiece. They control the rotation, the endless cycle from this perch. They will consume all if allowed to run amok about the world. Is this what the president has asked of me? Is this what I must do to declare ultimate sanity?"

The singing and fog stopped when the hallway door opened below.

A woman's voice called. "Hello? Is there someone in here?"

"Yes!" Eugene shouted. He heel-turned and stammered down the short flight. "I was looking to go down, but fed myself the wrong direction."

He reached the door and saw the same nurse from the next ward.

"Thank you, ma'am," Eugene said as he rushed past her and down the next flight of stairs.

Hoping the nurse would have moved on, Eugene walked to the third floor landing but pivoted back to the fourth story using the opposite oak stairs. He made a stealthy effort to climb those steps, but the creaks and groans of the wood still gave away his presence.

The fourth floor parlor was empty when Eugene peeked from the stairwell. The nurse was absent from the outer ward when he glanced through the small window in the door.

Eugene entered the area and walked past the attendant, acting as casually as he could. The ward remained empty, but it was not unusual. Eugene took the opportunity to cover his tracks by feigning ignorance.

"Where is everyone today?"

The orderly had been staring at him, giving him the same discerning eye as the nurse. The question caused the man to glance down at the charts on his table.

"The ward is at crafts this time of day. They all go at once."

"Ah. Mandatory amusement," Eugene said. "What is the grand creation for today?"

The attendant looked up to see Eugene standing near him and waiting for an answer. "Um. They're spinning wire to new bed frames. A lot of the frames in Bedland are falling to pieces."

"Bedland?" It was a term Eugene had not heard.

"Yes. That's what we call the first floor wards, which run this direction." The attendant made a line with his arm perpendicular to the hallway. "If you're touring the facility, check out those areas. They are packed to the gills with beds."

Eugene nodded. "Appropriate name I reckon." Feeling that it had been enough small talk, Eugene turned to his ward. "Well, you have a good evening."

*****

The nurses bandaged Peter's wounds and took him to a downstairs treatment room, where an injection of insulin calmed him.

Flip had already departed through the side stairs to play evening ball by the time Eugene returned. Even at dinner, Eugene couldn't spot his roommate amongst the meal takers.

Back in the room, Eugene elected to nap when Archibald chose to tether himself to the space. Tired and fearing a boorish rant from his more unhinged roommate, Eugene fell asleep fast and awoke well after midnight.

To his surprise, Flip was also awake and reading a book by the meager light pollution emanating from Weston.

"You must have cat eyes to see in such darkness," Eugene said. "Where have you been all evening?"

Flip had his book turned to the window and kinked his neck in an uncomfortable way to read the page. "Thinking."

"About?"

"How much I hate undressing."

"I'm sorry," Eugene offered.

Flip didn't respond, and Eugene waited until he heard the turn of a page to continue.

"Whatever happened to your uncle? The one who committed those atrocities against you?"

"A group of men found and hanged him."

"How'd they catch wind?"

Flip fidgeted on his mattress. "I told my church pastor, and he informed the men. I thought it was a thing preachers were supposed to keep secret."

"Secrets of such repulsion sometimes aren't worth keeping, even if it violates some sacred oath."

Both paused to test Archibald's consciousness. He was sleeping on the bed between them and continued a light cadence of snores.

Flip continued, setting his book down to focus. "The law knew. The sheriff. They let it happen and did nothing to punish the men. The men who killed my uncle." Flip took a hard breath. "I never meant for him to die, but it was the general view that no one with that kind of nature should get to stay alive."

Eugene grunted. "So, on top of the trauma of abuse, you have guilt for causing someone's death?"

Flip didn't respond.

"I've seen it for myself, yes, sir," Eugene said as he rubbed his knees. "Spent days on a boat coming back from The Great War. Boys that had killed found difficulty in sleeping with their actions. Knowing you snuffed out a person is one thing, but these were all young boys fighting the like. They knew that to kill one person was to put an end to generations the deceased could have built. It could have been much greater a world if we brought forth their children and their children's children … But no, the shooter and the shot both came away from war differently." He released a breath. "The screams I heard on that ship coming home. The terrors those unhindered dreams bring. They pose as reality in such uncanny costumes that it seeks to devour the waking person who is bound within the unconscious world."

"Do you think they ever got over it?" Flip asked, his voice growing listless.

Eugene nodded in the dark. "Oh, yes. It's been nearly two decades since. Many have gone on to have families and become proper cogs of society. I can't speak for the scars of which only their families would be aware, but they seem well suited on the face of it."

Flip closed his book and shuffled on the mattress, springs creaking. "I hope to have kids one day. I need to be cured of this affliction first. Undressing is a part of it."

"I think you'll make a fine father when you get to it," Eugene noted. "Don't let my experiences taint you. 'It's better to have loved and lost than to have never loved at all,' and all that."

Flip stretched. "You haven't spoken much about what you've lost."

"My wife died tragically. She flipped our truck on the way to a Memorial Day feast." Eugene had trouble finding the intended conclusion. He changed subjects but remained somber. "Opal Lee never seemed to fancy boys. In fact, her interests seemed to revolve around other females. It made me angry to think about it. The citizens of Gad would have lynched her the same way your community would perverts. I guess I never found out for certain if her preferences were such. She never told me, and I never felt the bravery to inquire."

"If you had known, you would have told someone you trusted, and they would have put her up a tree just as well. Trust me. You don't want that burden."

"No. Especially since her transgressions are against no one."

Despite the room's warmth, Flip wrapped himself tightly in a blanket and faced the wall. Eugene remained sitting on his cot and watched the young man drift off. Eugene would be awake most of the night now, and there was nothing to do in the enclosure but think or try to read materials by the dim town light.

He missed Opal Lee. He wished he'd said more to her, hadn't spent his time speaking about the ward boys and their priapic activities. He wished he hadn't returned to the ward at all and considered why he didn't continue downward and make an earnest attempt to exit the campus.

Was that a curative sign or a symptom of a greater madness? Eugene considered. It was probably neither. The madness was in the clock tower. There were signs of pure evil, and it was time to consider his vision at the funeral parlor. Perhaps it was time to declare this building the target of the president's ire. It was time to burn it down.

Eugene fought the thread notions with his last strands of sanity but found defeat when a light appeared at the closed door. He looked up to see a glowing woman; her features flushed by the white light.

"Any of you awake to see this?" Eugene asked his slumbering roommates in a whisper from the corner of his mouth. Neither budged. Unsure if the phantom was the soul-devouring kind, Eugene dared not move.

The apparition made weird gestures with its hands at chest-level before raising a small box to its head. A light flashed, and the room was dim again.

Eugene remained wide-eyed in the dark. He tried to process and rationalize what he perceived, but no calculation added to reason. Eschewing common sense, he concluded the most senseless measures were obligatory. "Yes, sir, Mister President, I need to burn this place down."

BRITTANY'S SECOND ATTEMPT

Saturday, June 26, 1999

The summer days were indiscernible from one another for someone without the rudder of a career to guide them through the week. It was the weekend, but Brittany could only tell because her parents slept in later. Bottles around the house remained corked longer, and someone else had the responsibility of opening the RadioShack.

Brittany had roused first. A tall glass of orange juice, a slathering of cucumber melon lotion, and a call to the Weston Police Department got her day started. It was easy to convince Officer S. K. Prince of her plan to reenter the Kirkbride, but she still required his help to get through the door. Brittany only needed to sweet talk the security guards at the hospital. Only one guard would suffice—the weakest one. The one who allowed law enforcement into the building on those paintball-powered Saturday nights.

The night brought luck. Officer Prince was working and offered to speak to the guards once they arrived. He even relented when she asked if they could stop at the convenience store. She needed a fresh disposable camera and wanted to tack on a SoBe Elixir and KitKat bar.

When Sticky Vicky entered the parking lot, Brittany saw Jennifer talking with three of their former classmates.

"Don't dawdle," Officer Prince said. He placed the car in park but didn't move as it idled.

After Brittany exited, Jennifer stared at her, dumbfounded. The three girls with her soon displayed different degrees of the same expression. Brittany replied with an enthusiastic wave before continuing into the quiet store. No doubt there was more action going on outside than in, such was the nature of summer nights.

Brittany made short work of gathering the items, muscle memory taking her to the right places. When she reached the register, she suddenly thought of what rumors could spawn from riding around with a male officer. The truth was insignificant when the rumor wolves smelled fresh meat. The pack circled.

There was another young woman years earlier who had a flair for men in uniform. She spent a lot of time in police vehicles on and off duty, or so the tales went. The girl garnered the nickname Siren from the shrill noises she made in the back seats of squad cars parked on quiet country roads. *It was juicy, but was it true?* Brittany didn't even know Siren's real name. She hoped the rumors were true, for the sake of fairness. *It would be a great injustice to her name, whatever it was, if it were all a nasty falsehood.*

What would they call Brittany? Handcuff? Radar? Night Stick? She shuddered to think. Additionally, ponderings about Siren led to a new theory about the origins of Sticky Vicky.

Brittany took another chill and returned to business. Paying for her items and exiting the store, she cut toward Jennifer.

"We'll catch up later! I'm investigating something," Brittany shouted toward the group of girls.

"That was Siren's excuse, too," another one of the girls replied in a cough.

"Dammit," Brittany cursed under her breath and returned to the cop car. She opted to sit in the back seat, separate from any implied canoodling.

"They're gonna start rumors about us," Officer Prince said right away. He stared through the windshield with a hand to his temple.

"Yeah … That's why I'm in the back now. If nothing else, I hope they give me a better nickname than Siren."

Prince put the car in reverse. "You know, she's married with a kid now. She married a state trooper who was around here a couple of years ago. I think they live in Martinsburg, or somewhere in the eastern panhandle."

"She finally settled for one?"

"Oh, she was only ever with the one trooper. Gossip in parts like these, you know. Rumors fill the night. They occupy the spaces the public cannot see."

"No doubt," Brittany replied, and let her eyes drift toward the streetlights lining the ancient part of town. They would turn onto Second Street soon, and there was one more thing that Brittany needed to know.

"So Sticky Vicky isn't sticky for … that reason? You know, the Siren reason?"

Officer Prince took a moment to decipher the coy phrasing. "What? Ew, no. I was giving some kids a ride home after hours a few months ago. One of them opened a Mountain Dew bottle they had dropped on the sidewalk. Sprayed everywhere. Hit me in the back of the head. No amount of soap and water has made it any better."

There was a long break until the officer turned onto the hospital road.

"Her name was Sally Peet, by the way. Siren. Bet you didn't know that."

Brittany chose not to respond.

"That's the thing about small towns," Officer Prince continued. "The rumors will brand you, and that's all people will think. Twenty years from now, Sally will still be called Siren here. Twenty years from now, the Weston Police Department will still be known as the cops who ruined the value of a historic building with paintballs."

The officer paused, waited for a response, and turned to look at Brittany when he did not receive one. He found her staring back at him. The officer became uncomfortable with the contact and glanced down at her convenience store items. "Don't open your SoBe back there." He turned. "I like their green tea."

Brittany made a disgusted noise. "Green tea is garbage. Tastes like grass clippings."

The officer did not reply, but Brittany was indifferent to a response. She needed to focus on what was ahead and remained quiet as they drove through the gate, past the fountain, and stopped in the loop by the front steps. She was in awe of her master plan coming to fruition.

"You know, they were looking at turning this place into a museum," Officer Prince said. He put the car in park but kept the motor running. "There were groups looking at fixing this place up and making it something new. We ruined it for them … for the state." He leaned into the passenger seat and looked up at the towering facade. "They'll raze this place now. I'm sure of it. Blow it up, burn it down, take a wrecking ball to it—I don't know. It'll be a hole in the ground regardless, and the WPD will be the ones responsible for digging the grave."

"Give me a chance to document the activity inside," Brittany reassured through feigned confidence. She was bullshitting, and Officer Prince knew it.

"You watch too many shows about kids saving old places from destruction. These are powers beyond your knowing. Proving it's haunted won't do much. If anything, you'll accelerate its demise."

A security guard was approaching, and Brittany recognized him as the man who had apprehended her that fateful Tuesday night.

The window on Officer Prince's door lowered as the stocky man bent to meet his eyes.

"Hi, Chad. This is Brittany Loughry," Officer Prince started, pointing into the shady back seat. "She's the one you caught in the building the other night. She wants to ghost hunt and isn't willing to sweep her incident under the rug as we'd like her to."

"Ghost hunt? That's crazy." Chad huffed and stood up straight. "Don't you all still arrest people for blackmail?"

"We're trying to keep our jobs here." Officer Prince reached into a folder next to him and removed a copy of the ghost picture. "You should know. You're at greater risk of getting canned than I am."

Chad shined his patrol light at the picture and grunted in a curious way.

"This was taken that night up on the wards," Prince explained as he extended the photo to the guard. "She'd like another opportunity to investigate the subject in that image."

Chad tilted both the photo and his head as he tried to make sense of the image. "Huh? And there was no one else up there?"

"No," Brittany chimed.

"Looks like a double exposure."

"It was a disposable camera. The film can't be exposed twice."

"The lab messed up?" Chad continued to rationalize.

"It's that way on the negative." Brittany sighed irritably. "Didn't you hear me screaming up there? This was the photo I took in that moment."

Chad scratched under his black hat. "I never would have known you were in there if not for the screaming."

"We'd like her to keep quiet about the incident, and we bet you would, too," Officer Prince pressed. "She says some time to explore would help her keep her mouth shut."

The security guard took a step back from the car and looked around as if his distant supervisor would materialize. "She's going to get us in trouble."

"We're already in trouble. It's just a matter of time before the investigation ends and the dice rolls on who gets to keep their jobs. Let's try and make some good from it for now."

The guard continued to deliberate until Brittany decided to help. She pressed her head to the screen divider. "Do you believe in ghosts?"

"As much as I want to say no, I don't dare step in that building after dark unless I absolutely must. Hell, it's creepy looking enough during the day."

Brittany gripped the screen with both hands. "I wanted to say no, too, but I saw something, and I can't stop thinking about it. I see that spirit in my sleep—when I close my eyes even. I have to see it again."

"And you'll keep quiet?"

"You have my word."

Chad began to bob his head. "Okay. Okay, I'll allow you in under one condition. You need to tell me how you got in the building the last time."

She did not want to give away that knowledge, but Brittany wanted inside the building now more than anything. "There's a door with loose hinges near the rescue squad building side."

"Oh. Well, okay then." Chad waved her forward. "The only other thing I ask is that you stay out of the rooms, particularly the upper floors on the northern end. The building has only been closed for five years, and it's already showing signs of falling to pieces."

Brittany didn't budge for a moment.

"What's a matter? Does that scare you?" Chad goaded.

"Um, no. I'm in the back seat of a cop car."

"Oops." Chad gulped and hurried to open the door from the outside.

Brittany stretched from the car and gave Chad an appreciative look. "Thank you so much."

"Just don't make it worse for us," Chad answered.

Brittany started toward the front door, feeling weird that it was so easy. Chad and Officer Prince started an indecipherable conversation that ceased when she returned to the two.

"My shift ends at one o'clock," Officer Prince said. "I'll swing back around twelve-thirty. If you're not out here within five minutes, you're on your own to walk home."

"That's fair," Brittany agreed. She turned her attention to Chad. "Are you going to fix that door in the back?"

Chad chuckled. "No, ma'am. I was just curious. I'm a lowly night watchman who is paid as such. Fixing stuff goes well above my pay grade."

*****

Brittany sat quietly for more than an hour in Room 668 in Ward C on the third floor of the Kirkbride building. She occupied the space with her disposable camera at the ready. While she remained silent, the building did not. The same guttural groans of pipes echoed from the long halls. Footsteps started on one end of the ward, dissipated, then resounded from the opposite end. Brittany could understand the guard's hesitation to traverse the darkness alone. It was clear something was alive within the walls. Alive in a sentient, functioning sense. What plane of reality the entity rattled was up for debate, but it was making its presence known within the Kirkbride.

She wished she had known the time of her last encounter. Brittany didn't believe it to be beyond midnight, but her watch displayed the truth.

Brittany felt she was wasting her time on a single room and elected to do a quick investigation of the northern wings. Since Chad mentioned the poor conditions of the upper floors on that end, she decided to gravitate there. It was a short trip from 668 to the center of the building. The auditorium on the western side of the center was already taped off from entry. There would be no more dances in that third floor space.

Crossing into the northern wing through a brown metal door, Brittany noticed a change in the air. It was thick, sludge-like. The specks of dust and streaks of floating cobwebs intensified in this section and beyond. It felt as if human life had not entered this realm for some time. In contrast to Ward C, its diametric neighbor was silent, yet awoken by her intrusion, and Brittany tried to keep it that way. She treaded through the white-walled corridor and cut into the next ward. It seemed like more of the same with one distinctive difference.

There was a noise.

A penetrating metal-on-metal sound squeaked from somewhere in the center of the hall. It reverberated like a metal chair scraping across an unfinished floor. It was unnerving, but Brittany paid it no fright. She had spent her fear on the first night. Her scream purged from her the trepidation of the building and the unknown things within. In the two hours she remained within, that fear never returned, never even considered reentering her psyche. The northern wards were trying to test her resolve, but she was not having it.

As she drew deeper into the corridor, the squeal transitioned into an electronic popping sound. Brittany could see something on the ground in the warm glow of the exit sign and shined her light near the center. Several colorful items lined the walls.

Toys.

The electronic sound was coming from a small toy piano centered around a rubber ball and a worn doll. Brittany lifted the piano to inspect it. It was battery-powered, and a faint red light indicated the power was almost drained. She tapped a key and received the same electronic pop she had been hearing.

The noise was a simple case of the battery going dead, but Brittany wanted to know for sure. She flipped the tiny piano but found the battery case held closed by a single screw. Brittany had to know if the scraping sound had been coming from the instrument and kept it with her as she continued. She began toward the exit to see if she could access the fourth floor from there, but as she departed further, a dim feeling came over her.

Brittany was being followed.

Not only was she being followed, but it also felt as if something was running down the hall after her, giving her a subconscious need to flee.

Brittany forced herself to stop and turned to look down the hallway. The red glow didn't illuminate enough to see the full hall, but the viewable area proved empty.

"Am I taking your piano?" Brittany found herself saying into the void. She didn't know who or what she was talking to, but the sense she had done wrong overwhelmed her.

"I'm sorry. I will put it back."

Brittany stepped down the hall and carefully placed the piano back between the ball and the doll. With the flashlight, she took a final look at the keys and realized the piano switch had been off all along.

"I returned your piano. Sorry."

Brittany resumed her trip to the door. As she did, the electronic popping returned, growing more frequent until the sounds of screeching metal began again.

Past the exit door, the stairwell ran through all four stories. It lacked the grandeur of the oak stairs in the center of the building. The steps were concrete and coated with layers of grime and dust. The barred doors that once kept patients on their respective floors remained open, too rusted to be functional. Brittany climbed past the corroded features and emerged onto the fourth floor.

The air remained as heavy as the third floor, suffocating and oppressive in its heat. It was more to do with the proximity to the sun and lack of air-conditioning. The heat of the day was bottled there. Brittany would have compared it to the trapped spirits within the building if not for a new surprise underneath her shoes.

The floor creaked, which was not something it had done anywhere else within the building. Hardwood padded the fourth floor, and the thudding of her footsteps was overwhelming in the vast quiet.

Brittany looked at her watch. She only had fifteen minutes before she needed to meet Officer Prince, and there wouldn't be much time to look around. She was near the end of the building and decided to check the handful of rooms remaining in the stretch.

First, checking the hall with the light, Brittany noted a single chair at the end of the passage and nothing else aside from the dark brown wooden floor.

She could understand why the rooms were unsafe on this floor. Wood deteriorates much faster than stone and concrete, and water was the only thing needed to start the process. Maintaining an acre of roofline couldn't be easy, and it was a matter of time and neglect before rain intruded on the Kirkbride.

Sweat pooled in the place between Brittany's lower chest and stomach and moistened her T-shirt. It cooled her body, but the stickiness made her more uncomfortable as she scanned the first room. There was an old bed, weathered and stained brown. Brittany shined the light upward to see rings drawn on the ceiling in a similar color. Past rains had already found their way indoors.

The next room she viewed looked to be more of the same, except for one startling difference. The figure of a man, cast in shadow, sat on one of the beds with arms holding his knees. He seemed to be staring at Brittany.

She had not cast a light toward it, but the reflection from her light on the hardwood was enough residual glow to illuminate the outline of the person.

He stared at her, and she at him, and Brittany waited to see if fear would visit her. It did not. She lifted her camera instead. Flipping a switch and turning a small dial on the device, Brittany primed the flash. The dial *click-clacked*, echoing through the hallway as loudly as her footsteps.

Once the camera was ready, Brittany took careful aim and pressed the button. The flash overpowered the room, briefly bathing it in light, before the dark encroached deeper than before. When Brittany focused her eyes again, she found the bed unoccupied.

14

NEIL'S SECOND HOME

SATURDAY, JUNE 4, 2067

When Neil quit his job with Benson Parks, his boss didn't seem surprised. "Did you ever get lamp thirty-five fixed?" the park manager first asked upon hearing of Neil's departure.

"I spent many days on a ladder, changing the bulb, the ballast. Never did figure out why it kept burning out."

Neil, Demetry, and Miguel returned to Minnesota the next Saturday as planned. Silkie's diary was a treasure trove of information. A decade of simple documentation interspersed with well-worded letters about the condition of where she was traveling in the South in the late nineteenth century. The account also alluded to the existence of a second diary. The earlier account was sealed in a trunk and buried on a farm in Arkansas. The entry included a crude map and geographical markers. Demetry believed he could pin down the location based on the inclusion and proximity of the Arkansas River.

With the book project still alive, Neil had the green light to return to Weston and await research tasks. He arrived two days later, and almost immediately found a trailer to rent north of the city. The abode was in a trailer court across from the State 4-H Camp, called Jackson's Mill. The location was famous for being the rearing grounds of Stonewall Jackson, an infamous Civil War General. The land was later sold by the Jacksons and passed around through various families until it landed in the hands of the state. West Virginia took the property, rehabilitated it, and honored it for its historic value.

The state did not have the same interest in the Trans-Allegheny Lunatic Asylum. There was early interest in rehabilitating after it closed in the mid-1990s. The tour guides told of local and state police holding paintball matches that decimated both the value and the interest West Virginia had in the building.

It pleased Neil to know a private party had intervened and purchased it at auction later, sparing it the wrecking ball. Still, it was acres of a building that would take several more decades to renovate and return to its original beauty. He would have especially loved to see the clock tower someday, but understood it was so dilapidated it was last on the renovation list.

"Maybe someday," he would later say as he stared up at the lumbering spire. "Maybe someday I'll get to see what makes you tick."

Saturday night was ghost hunting night, and Neil had already pre-registered for the tour. He tried to sleep, but the morning sun cast a wide beam in his bedroom. The air mattress he slept upon did not provide enough real estate to roll from its sizzling path.

Caffeination was the next goal. With nothing in his trailer but unpacked boxes and a temporary bed, Neil drove to town to find a coffee shop. The building looked to be a large, brick house lined with white-framed windows. The interior also screamed antique. An exterior hallway wrapped around the main area, indicating it had once been an addition. The red carpet appeared to be from an era long gone. It was dingy, stained, and worn thin, but also held a panache that worked for the space. Hardwood floors lined the interior rooms. The sound of people clopping about with their drink orders was distracting, but the mood was otherwise peaceful. The strum of light guitars accompanied a crooner mourning over his lost Peggy. Neil sat in a rocking chair and sipped a matcha-infused concoction. He would need another recharge later, but for now, this was all the amperage his heart could take.

"It's a nice place, isn't it?" A woman near his age looked up from a book titled *The Hunting Party*. She had a black pixie cut and wore oversized tortoiseshell glasses.

Neil offered a polite smile and realized he had been staring. "It is. This is my first time."

The woman smiled back and lowered the book, keeping the cover visible as if she wanted Neil to see it. "This used to be a funeral home. This building."

"Really?" Neil pursed his lips between phrases. "What happened? Did they run out of dead people?"

"It closed abruptly a few years ago. No reason for it that I ever heard."

"Well"—Neil raised his glass—"the drinks are to die for, at least."

It was a bad joke, but the woman allowed a smirk. "Are you new here? To town, I mean."

"Just arrived this week. I'm doing book research."

The woman sat up a little straighter. "Oh, you're writing a book?"

Neil cringed. "No, no. A friend is writing the book. I'm here as boots on the ground. He lives in Minneapolis, so it's hard for him to get out here to do his own research."

The woman tilted her head. "You don't like writing?"

Neil set down his cup so he could gesture with his hands and better articulate his case. "Writers are people who generally have experienced a great deal of pain in their lives. They then try to synthesize into a story with the hope their pain is entertaining enough to be purchased in vast quantities. I'm not interested in pandering out my trauma."

"Well, you're a good friend for, um, helping to pander your friend's trauma." The woman gave a genuine smile and adjusted her glasses. "I'm Melanie Roe."

"Neil. Neil Hutchence."

"So, Neil, what could your friend be writing a book about here?"

"The asylum," Neil answered, and watched Melanie's mood shift to something mournful.

"My mom was a nurse there," she lamented, attaching her gaze to a window. "She won't even drive past nowadays. Won't talk about why she won't. If you're looking for trauma, your friend found the perfect place to get material."

Neil could feel the lingering sadness in the asylum well before the excitement set in his heart. But the dominance of the rush overrode the empathy he would have felt for Melanie's mother. Instead of offering any kind of meaningful reply, he changed the topic.

"Is that a good book? If I remember, it's relatively new."

Melanie lifted it and turned to the cover as if she had forgotten what she was reading. "Yep. It's a mystery. A real page-turner with a few twists, turns, and dead ends. I love those."

The two shared another smile, and an attraction fluttered in Neil's heart. It was a neglected feeling, atrophied from disuse, but still thumping at a low decibel. The feeling was short, interrupted by thoughts of Caitlyn—the last flutter. He couldn't move on from her. He had never tried. His indifference to her was making a difference now in how he treated others, and Neil felt a certain safety in the fog of dissociation.

She was cute to him, had a clear intellect, and her disposition seemed on the friendlier spectrum than Caitlyn's. But it wasn't enough. The ex-wife loomed large. When he told her he was moving back to West Virginia, she could only fixate on how he didn't send a present for Meriwether's birthday. It was a fair issue to find rage in, but when Caitlyn's ire loomed, there was no room for anything else.

Neil felt a catch in his throat. It was something like panic, but also a heavy feeling on his chest. The caffeine was working, but there had to be more behind it.

"Enjoy your book," Neil finally said as he stood. He needed to leave but didn't want to seem abrupt. "I hope to see you again."

Neil trundled from the building and headed toward the city center, realizing he had left his half-empty matcha on an end table.

Why were thoughts of Caitlyn causing panic? he wondered. *Was she the trauma? Were things so terrible for so long little scars accumulated? The lacerations created a deep wound that would prove fatal if cut further? It had nearly been fatal before.*

Neil reached a gas station and stopped. The town bustled on a Saturday morning. For the first time, he was seeing the commuters, pedestrians, and people providing the mechanisms to keep a community thriving. Neil realized he was home. A new warmth developed in his heart, replacing the current tension, and bringing a resolution with it.

Caitlyn was not the trauma. Her meanness, her unbridled henpecking, was only half the problem. The whole of the marriage took two, and his inability to respond was the other irreconcilable problem.

Walled in by the shame of failure, Neil was unsure of how to move beyond it but knew the best way to breach a wall was to go up and over.

*****

"In society today, Bedlam is a term more geared to chaos and confusion, but the origin traces to mental facilities such as this one. The name originates from Bethlehem Royal Hospital in England, which opened in the fourteenth century. Over the years, the name Bethlehem became truncated into Bethlem, and later into the nickname Bedlam, which is the term people know today. Though all the terrible connotations about mental asylums originate from the treatment of patients there, the Bethlehem Royal Hospital is still in operation to this day."

The spiel was similar, but the tour guide was different. It made sense to Neil. History never changed. The only improvising a guide could do is off anecdotal stories visitors have shared during their time of employment. In this case, it was adding flourishes of history relevant to the tour. Neil was willing to play, so long as he could sneak into Room 668 once they reached the third level.

The main deviation was the background on the history of Bedlam, which included slight detours to discuss the injustices of mental health patients throughout history. The guide, Audrey, seemed empathetic to the plight of those who had resided in these rooms.

The Bedlam remarks occurred on a remodeled section of the first floor while daylight still blended into the night sky. The sound of Weston's curfew siren interrupted. It was a sound to which Neil was beginning to grow accustomed.

On a dilapidated ward on the second floor, the tour guide said, "The science of broken minds, unfortunately, took much longer to catch up to the science of broken bodies ..."

By the third floor, Neil had tuned Audrey out altogether. It was later than the last time, and the short brunette commanded the tour despite her low stature, poring over every detail as they lurked through the wards.

The glacial pace made Neil antsy, and he devised a plan to sneak back into the ward as soon as the group departed for the violent male section. The later explanations of history, events, and ghost sightings now seemed to land the same tune with only mild riffing on the notes. The metal door at the end of the hallway swung open, and the mass of people wedged through. Neil held the door for the last person to exit and let it close in front of him without anyone taking notice.

The door boomed over the silent corridor, pinging Neil with an unease which ceased once the silence returned. He backtracked to Room 668 and made easy work of entering the space.

Neil closed the door quietly. He did not want to reveal his position. According to policy, being found in a different place from the designated tour group was an instant expulsion from the property.

The room was cold, like it had been air-conditioned, but there was no electricity coursing through this part of the Kirkbride. Besides, the early summer sun spent one of its long revolutions baking the building's exterior.

No room along the exterior wall feels like this, he thought.

Neil waited in the chill, but he wasn't sure how long it would take if it were to happen at all. It may have been a fluke anyway, or maybe he caught the spirit at a lucky time, and it would reappear with patience. Maybe he would have to wait all night. For many minutes, the room, dim and slopped with faded paintball splatters, remained dark.

There was a peculiar scent in the room—cucumber and something else. There was danger in the fragrance of cucumber, but Neil couldn't remember if the association was with strokes or copperheads. A few minutes of pondering landed on copperheads with strokes being more akin to toast. A quick survey of the room confirmed it to be snake-free.

Neil sat on the floor and continued to wait. He could hear people passing in the hallway. One person rattled his door to see if they could get it to budge. The footsteps faded, but a faint "Hello?" resonated inside the room.

The voice was soft, cautious, but Neil sensed something otherworldly. He stood as the room illuminated. He shielded his eyes and turned to find the person whom he had been seeking.

HENRIETTA'S SECOND GUESS

SUNDAY, JUNE 25, 1905

Jansy Porter came to the asylum after the murder of her husband and subsequent negligence concerning the disposal of the body. After twenty years of living in the heart of coal country on a secluded mountain near Pikeville, the isolation took its toll on Jansy. Unprovoked, she shot Clive Porter as he was walking to the outhouse and then left him where he fell. After passing downwind of the property, a wayward party of hunters detected the stench days later. The odor wafting from the ridge was so intense that the hunters thought something with a large hide had died.

When asked about her motives later, Jansy simply told the authorities, "I got tired of his griping."

Operating in constant maleficence toward humanity, it seemed her only source of joy was bringing others misery. She did so constantly, even when tethered to the violent female section of the West Virginia Hospital for the Insane.

Seven years and a dozen roommates later, Jansy was finally paired with a woman she did not care to assault. Mary Tippeleti took on the appearance of a storybook witch. She had thinned gray hair and an angular face with the requisite crooked nose. Mary had become an invalid over the winter after the amputation of her right foot and two toes on the left. They had become black for no reason the hospital was willing to officially state. Internally, doctors knew she had acquired the affliction through frostbite during one of the January cold snaps.

It was normal to move invalid patients to the lower floors, but doctors were hesitant to pair Jansy with another roommate.

Most believed Mary was deaf and mute, but she only lacked hearing. She was unwilling to contribute noise to a world she could not enjoy. Mary remained quiet and only gave audio cues in grunts and unhinged laughter.

Henrietta didn't meet Mary until the very end of her time in the hospital. Despite her penchant for silence, Henrietta became aware of Mary's presence once Jansy saw her for the first time. Upon learning there was a Black woman next door, the two spent many hours of the day kicking the wall between them. Three rhythmic feet pounded like pumping pistons of a primitive motor. They often woke Wallace, who wailed from the disruption.

Henrietta continued to work on the hospital farm on Wednesdays and Fridays. The Black wards worked the garden every other day, rotating with the white residents of the main building. Henrietta enjoyed the outdoor atmosphere and listened to the others sing hymns and chants as they toiled.

Today was Sunday, a day of rest. There was no farmwork other than tending to the livestock, and Henrietta lamented the loss of a day to talk more with Silkie. She had used her sparse words to tell Henrietta about how she fled to Arkansas after gaining freedom. Orla O'Neil, a widow from Pine Bluff, took her in and raised her as family. Silkie helped with the daily chores on the O'Neil's small farm, along with Orla's son, Ignace. The young man was an accomplished blacksmith, though his real talent was in gunsmithing. Despite being a savant with respect to metalworks, Ignace was incompetent in every other aspect of life. She said little else about him other than he was colorblind, except for pink, yellow, and light blue. They sold the farm when Orla died in 1881. When asked what became of Ignace, Silkie changed the subject to a startling confession.

"I killed the men."

When asked whom she killed, she said, "No one special. Leeman Saint Cloud in Charleston, South Carolina." But after a beat, she added a long string of names along with the location of each's murder. She had memorized them and expelled each from her lips like she had been waiting a lifetime for the right person to hear the secrets.

The admission shook Henrietta. The perfect recitation by a woman who was careful and deliberate in using truncated sentences was unnerving. Henrietta felt safe in knowing no women were on the list and did not view her as a threat, even as she continued to describe the crimes.

She spoke about the gun used. It was custom-built and fitted with a spyglass to grant the ability to hit targets at long distances. She spoke in detail about how she was able to kill Leeman Saint Cloud by shooting from a hidden perch atop a water tower. He and his wife were boarding a ship. The shot hit its mark true, and Leeman collapsed into the harbor. Silkie seemed proud to add how he drowned before blood loss could take him.

The story of the murders contained no motive, and Henrietta assumed it was her madness. It was hard to tell with men and women of the Black ward, who weren't parted by the level of violence in their mania. There were two separations in the Black building, one for men and one for women.

Silkie was as terrifying as she was fascinating, and Henrietta felt a kinship forming, no matter how it settled with her. Silkie had the spunk of her mother and relative age, if she had still been alive. The only nagging thing that kept Henrietta uncomfortable was Silkie's insistence that she name Wallace's father. Henrietta suspected Silkie was either trying to get Felix Koenig in trouble or find a way to harm the doctor. Either way, Henrietta was unwilling to point to his paternity.

On Sunday, the doctor finally paid Henrietta a visit. His absence was conspicuous. In her calculation, she realized he had been gone since the night of the phantom paint attack. Even so, she was glad to see Doctor Koenig, and he seemed to be happy, too. He greeted Henrietta with a warm smile tucked below his blonde handlebars, though he avoided any meaningful eye contact.

"How are you today?" Felix asked, as he sat beside Henrietta on the bed. The doctor reached to help her upright.

"I'm fine," she replied, leaning into the force of the doctor's hand, which was heaving her forward.

He lifted Henrietta's loose-fitting gown and paused, admiring the bare body underneath. Then he focused on the aging stitches.

"I think it is time ve cut these out. Ah, it looks like you popped a thread on der left side. Vere you doing anything strenuous?"

The question felt like a trap. She did not want to admit to going into the field. If the doctor found out, he would stop the nurses who helped or levy harsh discipline on them. On the other hand, if he already knew the answer, her deceit could land her in trouble. In truth, she could not at present think of a worse punishment than her current plight.

"No. I didn't even notice it had broken," she answered, and watched Felix's face to gauge a nonverbal response.

She saw the quick bulge of his tongue rub against his inner cheek—what she understood as his deep contemplation.

"All das same," he finally said. "Die stitches were expertly sown by Doctor Pryor. He did die surgery as vell. Now, I did not vant to tell you this until ve knew it was safe, but your surgery vas still quite experimental. It seems to be a resounding success und ve vill certainly replicate it in the future if need be."

Still angered over the violation, Henrietta said nothing. She instead turned to another contentious issue. "Aren't you going to ask about your son?"

Doctor Felix turned his head to look at the slumbering infant. "He appears perfectly healthy. No question required."

The curtness in his voice was enough to trigger Henrietta into shooting off a comment she did not intend. "You tried to tell me he was dead the last time I saw you."

As soon as she spoke it, her stomach sank. The doctor was still under her gown, removing the stitches. There was nothing there to stop him from ramming the sharp sutures deep into her abdomen. But he did not. He responded with a mild jolt and continued to finish the task on the opposite side. He placed the errant threads onto a metal tray and laid the surgical appliances down before sitting in the chair next to the bed.

"Vat makes you believe I thought he vas dead?"

A lie would have been convenient at the time, but excuses eluded Henrietta. She decided to angle for a blurred version of the truth. "A nurse told me you considered telling me he was dead to avoid the embarrassment of being discovered as the father."

"Vat nurse?" Doctor Felix asked with a tightened jaw.

"I don't remember. It has been too long." In fact, she could not remember which of the several nurses assigned to her delivered the secret. Henrietta only remembered it stung like a hundred balls of lead striking her body at once.

The doctor's blue eyes made contact for the first time and pierced deep, searching for the truth without invoking conflict. Silence ricocheted throughout the room, broken in an instant when Jansy and Mary began their morning routine of kicking against the wall. The loud knocking disrupted the doctor's truth scan and halted completely when Wallace awoke and began to bawl.

The doctor scowled. "Do they know you're in here?"

Henrietta sighed. "Word got around."

"Die krankenschwestern sind müll," the doctor murmured. "Das kind ist zu leicht. Du bist unerträglich."

Henrietta shook her head. "What are you saying?"

The crescendo came with a duet of kicks and cries. The doctor had fumed enough, and his voice clamored like a triumphant cymbal crash.

"I never desired a relationship vith you. I told you things I never told anyone in der guise of a sexual eróberung. Conquest. Victory. You vere never meant to have a child und he vas especially not meant to remain so vite, so leicht, so proud to promote my downfall. You vere confined here to keep das secret from returning to der administrator. Krankenschwestern! These nurses speak as freely as die mentally enfeebled among them. I vill no longer stand for it!"

He slammed his hand on the surgical tray. The full contents of the table vaulted toward the offending wall. Message received. The neighboring thuds ceased, but Wallace wailed louder with the clamor.

Henrietta needed to stop the oncoming rampage, so she said the one thing that might quell the raging doctor.

"I lied."

The doctor's hands were in the air, ready to shout Deutsche profanities at the dust particles buoyed in the light. He froze with the new information and stopped to look at Henrietta with glimmering cobalt eyes. A smile almost formed. *Had it always been his plan to coax an admission of guilt?*

"Go on." He lowered his hands and returned to his base demeanor.

With an inhale, Henrietta released a partial truth. "I was out the other day. I needed to walk the fields. Watch the workers on the farm milk the cattle and pull the weeds. We're going to have an abundance of canned peas to eat this winter."

Doctor Felix performed another truth scan, staring far past where their eyes connected. Wallace continued to cry, but Henrietta held her position until the doctor finally released his gaze.

"I hear das cattle ruined the prospects of succotash. It is the only American concoction I have come to enjoy."

"The corn appeared decimated," Henrietta confirmed, then rushed to finish the fib. "But on the way back to my room, someone yanked the sheet off me. My neighbor noticed and has been kicking the wall with her roommate daily."

The doctor stroked his mustache. He seemed disappointed. "Unfortunate. I vill tell them ve moved you back to die Black vard so they vill leave you be."

"Couldn't I go back to the Black ward for real?" Henrietta asked, trying not to plead.

"Not vith dem boy that you need to tend to." Doctor Felix jabbed a finger of annoyance. "They see that boy und there vill be no doubt. Once he's veened, ve'll send him down to die laundry room for adoption und you can return to die Black population."

As he spoke, the repetition of "die" began to sound less like an innocuous German word, and more like its English spelling. It irked Henrietta, who felt as if he intended a double meaning. Her thoughts could not dwell on it for long as another concern pressed harder. "What's in the laundry room?"

"Oh. That is … Ve are carving out space there … for die kids of des hospital … can grow und be adopted, if appropriate."

Henrietta suppressed her shock. Felix had never expressed compassion for Wallace and saw him only as a burden, nothing more than a red letter to his name. A feeling of abhorrence began to spread through Henrietta's heart. It was a seething that would only intensify in the coming days when she further realized the doctor had been false in everything. A false friend, a false lover, and now, Doctor Felix Koenig had revealed his hand as a false father.

"So, my son—our son—could be bound to this hospital forever?"

"There is a good likelihood," the doctor stated without empathy. "It should not be all bad at first. You und I vill likely be here for a long time."

*****

THE weeds made up for lost time on Sunday, stretching toward the heavens as far as they could reach. Fresh from an extra day's rest and ready to pluck green interlopers with new vigor, the Monday morning workers made short work of them.

The staff allowed Henrietta into the garden, her half-truth seeming to appease the doctor's sniffer for lies. The nurses were also safe, only given the note to not allow Henrietta too much exposure to others.

Feeling her freedom was limited, Henrietta entered the garden early as the rest of the Black ward finished breakfast.

She watched as the group flooded into the field and bottlenecked at the garden gate. Silkie was near the back of the group, moving at a pace fitting for a person getting up in years.

"You is early," Silkie greeted.

"I came to hear one of your stories," Henrietta said, flashing an affectionate smile.

Silkie bobbed her head. "Don't want to tell you a story. I fear there will only be a few kinds of stories they tell about us. Slave story, escape story, injustice story, big victory for a small thing story. No happy stories. No big victories for big things."

"If I tell you the doctor's name, are you going to kill him?"

Silkie snorted. "You figured me."

"Correctly?"

Silkie looked around her and nodded. "Uh-huh."

Henrietta became paranoid, too, and checked her back. "So, the doctor …"

"Depends on the name."

"Felix Koenig."

Silkie hesitated, letting the name whirl in her mind. "Don't know that one."

"Is that a no?"

"No."

"I'd consider it one of those big victories for big things," Henrietta said, giving Silkie a look of determination. "I need to protect my child. He'll rot here forever if Felix has his way."

Silkie nodded and didn't stop. "I will take care of it. Lure him to the field. I'll find some paint. Ready my process."

In his harness, Wallace whined and shifted into a nursing position. Henrietta tended to him only for a moment, but it was long enough. When she lifted her head, Silkie had vanished.

A visual comb of the area located her along the tree line leading into the hills. Henrietta watched as Silkie turned, scanned the corners of the garden where the attendants were lax in their duties, and disappeared into the vegetation.

EUGENE'S SECOND TARGET

FRIDAY, JUNE 30, 1935

By Eugene's own account, he purposely botched his psychiatric evaluation so he could remain at the Weston State Hospital. A more truthful interpretation would note he did not need additional effort. Days earlier, his beloved photograph of Janet Gaynor had vanished from its makeshift shrine above Eugene's bed. Fearing it had become the subject of the neighboring teens' masturbatory rituals, Eugene rampaged through the youth room. He flipped every mattress and examined every cranny he could find in the dorm. Miss Gaynor remained absent, and Eugene's despair drove him into volleys of anger beyond his penchant for Shakespearean mimicry.

The mental evaluation came as a surprise, but the doctors were strung so thin on their obligations that they could only carry out lesser duties when time allowed. The Weston Hospital held more than fifteen hundred patients in a building originally intended for two hundred and fifty. To make matters worse, the staffing reflected the number intended to treat the original quantity. To meet the intended ratio, the hospital would need ten times as many doctors. It was the bare minimum required to administer wellness to the entire asylum population.

A nurse retrieved Eugene. As she walked the corridor, whoops and hollers followed the nurse from various affection-starved inmates. The nurse had worked the floors enough to tune out the catcalls and kept a focus on the hall door as they passed out of the ward and down to the first floor.

The doctor receiving Eugene this time was half the age of Doctor Timmons, perhaps quite younger. He went by the name of Norsk Znewski. His Scandinavian genetics were apparent in the lush locks of golden-brown hair threatening to erupt into a full lion's mane. He had a plump, baby face only aged by dark stubble that remained noticeable against such a fair complexion.

"N-O-R-S-K Z-N-E-W-S-K-I," the doctor spelled upon Eugene's request.

"Doc, I believe both your names have a few letters that do not belong together," Eugene concluded after rubbing the letters together in his mind. "I don't partake so much in reading myself, but my feeble education informed me enough to see the compatibility of letters in a word."

"My father was from Norway," Doctor Znewski remarked. "The rules for words are slightly different there."

"And your mother?"

"Ah. From Indiana."

Eugene's eyes widened. "Yes, sir, I suspect there is a fascinating story behind your conception."

The doctor jogged his papers on the table. "You bet there is, but we're here for *your* story. You don't seem as uneducated as you let on."

"My wife was a reading fanatic, and God bless her, an even greater enthusiast of reading aloud. I collected a good many words from her."

"Sounds like a good wife."

Eugene changed subjects. "I previously gave my story to the codger who keeled over a few weeks ago. Did he bequeath my registers to you?"

The doctor's icy blue eyes darted between the papers and the man sitting before him. "I have the police report here." He flipped through the documents. "Yah. It says here that you were inebriated at your wife's funeral and urinated on the parlor floor. And told a patron that you wanted to 'burn the place down.' When asked why, you said, 'The president told me to.'"

"I got that impression based on his ghastly aura," Eugene clarified. "The only thing he actually said to me was 'Those damn trees get in the way sometimes.' You don't forget the words spoken by otherworldly officials."

"Yah," Doctor Znewski dismissed while he read through the last papers in the stack. "It would seem Doctor Timmons concluded that you were highly inebriated, possibly drugged to the point of hallucination. It is understandable, you would want to abate the grief by chemical means while at your wife's funeral."

"I never took much fancy to drink, Doc," Eugene defended. "Alcohol had always been an oily mark upon my family."

"It's understandable if you wanted to drink in this situation, though. Doctor Timmons's greater purpose in keeping you here was to ensure you dried out. He also made a note to evaluate you on your level of grief."

Eugene swallowed hard on the notion. "I shouldn't need such a study, Doc. Yes, sir, mister, my grief is one of outright avoidance of the subject."

"But that is not healthy for a sound mind," Doctor Znewski said. "It is better to address those troubles as a means of putting them behind you. Avoidance can only cause the psyche to fester and corrode. What I am saying is that you don't belong here, but the continued evasion of your troubles will build until a psychological breakdown is unavoidable."

Eugene huffed. "So, your prescription is to squirrel me away in your nuthouse ahead of schedule? Why not leave me to my freedom while I'm of sound mind and then ferry me back here once the breakdown occurs? It seems this establishment is doing an awful lot more to protract my trauma."

The doctor, tired of tit-for-tats with Eugene, cut straight to his evaluation. "How did your wife die?"

"Er?" Eugene He spat out several unintelligible half-sounds before arriving at a complete sentence. "She was killed in an automobile accident."

"Oof. What caused the accident?"

"A hillside."

"Oh?"

"She put the truck over a bank, was ejected, and crushed as the vehicle kept rolling."

Doctor Znewski observed his tone. Though Eugene could describe the event without emotion, he did so at a faster cadence, which seemed to outpace any such feelings.

The doctor continued questioning. "Were you there?"

Eugene gave a firm "No. Don't you have the report?"

"I've not seen it. Where were you that day?"

"Back on the farm. I had a few ewes that hadn't birthed yet—wanted to keep an eye on 'em. She was insistent on going to a Memorial Day dinner in Summersville, and I allowed her to set out on a solo excursion …"

The doctor was reading and didn't notice that despair was the cause of Eugene's pause.

"And you have a daughter?"

"Aye," he said.

"Where was she then?"

Eugene sighed. "Unsure. She was in Pittsburgh … or New York. She ran off Christmas Eve four years earlier, and I hadn't seen her since." He chose not to mention her sudden appearance at the hospital earlier that month. It was an interaction Eugene was beginning to believe never happened in the first place. It wasn't worth complicating the interview.

"What is her name?" The doctor picked up a sharpened yellow pencil. "Perhaps I can arrange a meeting for the two of you to reconcile."

"Opal Lee Spangold."

Doctor Znewski hummed. "Lovely name."

Eugene ignored the compliment. "You're going to leave me here until you find her?"

"It really depends on the difficulty of finding her. If we can get word to her in New York, and she leaves immediately, then maybe it would be worth your time to stick around."

"Nothing in this place is worth my time, Doc," Eugene spat.

The doctor lowered his head. "Yes, I know we are currently overpopulated and understaffed, and conditions are deteriorating by the day. Just bear with us a little longer, and you bet we will discharge you soon. Maybe for good."

Eugene's mind had grazed against the memories of Ethel's tragedy once again, as well as the questions surrounding Opal's disappearance, brief reappearance, and the questions posed once she had exited again. With the confluence of the two traumas and the bonus stressor of remaining at the asylum longer, Eugene's thoughts drifted back to his search for the missing Janet Gaynor.

"Doc, someone stole my photograph of Janet Gaynor. She is an actress I am quite fond of, and the photo was all I had to commemorate her goodness in my life. Yes, sir, it was my one joy here, and it is now gone. I don't believe I could reside without her another day, knowing she's tucked among the smutty literature of some of the more immature rascals. Yes, sir, mister, I sincerely request you form a party with your scarce resources to help conjure up my missing property."

"Did you check if your roommates had seen it?" the doctor asked.

"The boy, Flip—he denied seeing it depart. I trust him at his word, Doc. In fact, I would petition that he's the least deserving soul bound here. He's bright, and his plight isn't one egregious against greater humanity. The fanatic, Archie, also made such a denial. He's a wolf in sheep's clothing, who is unaware of said canine heritage. He spouts wickedness, believing it wholesome, so his assurances are less dependable. Yes, sir, Mister President, I suspect the photograph disappeared amongst the dormitory of the other youngsters of the ward. Their deprivation of hormonal mating activities will fashion them into the ravagers of tomorrow if they're given leave and found unfulfilled in their genital faculties."

The doctor was listening, scrawling new notes on the back of a paper. "We'll see what we can do. If we can find your missing photograph."

But the ranting continued and went down familiar lanes first traversed by Doctor Timmons. Eugene spoke again about the movies of Miss Gaynor, his hope she would visit, and how he had considered naming Opal as Eleanor instead. He even returned to the occurrence at the funeral home and recapped his conversation with the President of the United

States in vision. It was when he began describing the urge to burn down the funeral home that he stopped. He almost mentioned his new scheme to burn down the hospital. It was then Eugene realized he needed to remain at the hospital to carry out his new intentions.

"Those damnable ruffians make me so mad," he concluded before standing. Eugene kicked the wooden chair he had been sitting in. It made a percussive *thud* after tipping and bounced once on the hardwood before the room fell silent. The blast of noise interrupted the rant enough to bring Eugene back to reality. When he turned back to the doctor, he found him monitoring for further aggression.

Pacified, Eugene held up his arms with wrists together as if he were about to be handcuffed. "Take me back to my cell, Doc. Yes, sir, I wish to remain among my ward chums."

*****

THE hospital cafeteria was in a separate building behind the Kirkbride, connected to the main building by three catwalks on the second floor. A walkway was at the beginning of each wing, and a shorter one attached to the center hall.

The bell for breakfast, lunch, and dinner would usher the able-bodied patients into the hall for meals. Most wards sat together, and keeping the genders segregated was unenforceable but encouraged. Hormones ran wild among both wings, and daily dinner dates were the only thing that could stave off more primal urges until the monthly dance. Lust didn't often wait for opportunities, and the exits and hidden corners of the cavernous room were often monitored.

The young boys of Ward T especially intermingled with the younger women of the northern wing. There weren't as many girls of equal age, but the boys had little qualm in denying older women their wiles.

Flip Clevenger didn't join in on those teenage games, instead remaining in fellowship with his roommates for breakfast. The three sat on the far end of a row of tables and chewed scrambled eggs and ham while observing the intermingling of the other wards. The chatter between all the inmates was at a deafening level, even at the early breakfast hour. Many had already fallen into their mania and were shouting obscurities and obscenities. For all its volume, Eugene had converted the cacophony into white noise.

"I thought you weren't going to be here after the other day," Archibald griped. He reached into the corner of his mouth to retrieve a gristle of ham. "Why haven't you left yet?"

"My understanding is they are ranging the countryside for my sweet Opal Lee," Eugene said. He prodded a runny portion of his scramble and smeared it across the plate. "I suspect their difficulty equates to what I have experienced in my own years of scouring for her."

"Didn't you say she was here a few weeks ago?" Flip noted. He had eaten fast and was observing the other two men.

"Ah." Eugene returned his attention to the eggs. "Yes. She was, but I didn't disclose that information to my Norwegian host."

"Why not?" Flip pressed.

Eugene gritted his teeth. "Why are you imposing court on me, boy?"

"If you want her found, I just reckon you'd want to give them all the clues. That's all."

"To be honest, I think she may have been a hallucination." Eugene found surprise with his reply, and he paused to set down his fork. "I think she was a calculation of my mind to manifest a conversation with her that would bring me peace."

"But that didn't bring you peace," Flip noted. "You've been aggravated about it ever since."

Eugene gave a frustrated shrug. "Perhaps she was a phantasm then. A ghost come to torment me with unresolved questions."

"But that would mean she was dead."

"You need to speak more positively," Archibald interjected. "There is power in words."

Eugene choked out a laugh. "That way of thinking gives credence to the conman, Archie. If they're the ones who have power over you, I can see why you have landed upon such dire consequences."

Archibald huffed and tapped his fork against his plate. "If ghosts can visit us here, where has your wife been?"

Eugene's eyes narrowed as he aligned them with Archibald. "She's likely mingling with your congregation. How often do they pay *you* a visit?"

"I like to think they can hear me when I pray," Archibald gave in smug reply.

"They cannot. Yes, sir, you are alone until you can form a confederacy with like-minded zealots."

Archibald doubled down. "They can hear me. The Lord works in mysterious ways."

"There is no mystery regarding idiocy," Eugene retorted and bent forward.

Undeterred, Archibald pressed back. "The Lord says, 'Lean not on your own understanding.'"

"I tell ya, that is not the endorsement for ignorance you believe it to be," Eugene shot back. "Listen, you pull a lot of big phrases from your big book, but that Bible of yours has been poked and prodded and edited and translated and censored and censured and heedlessly amended. I tell ya, if you could read the unsullied account of what the meaning of love and caring and selflessness of that volume is actually about, well, the truth would shrivel your pious pecker clean to nothing."

The rant peppered Archibald with enough anger to react. He stood and pointed down at Eugene. "You're not even supposed to be here!"

Eugene opened his arms. "Yet here I am. It's nothing short of a miracle. Your mistranslated tome tell you that?"

"I destroyed that picture you had been looking for. I won't have smut plaguing my eyes. I should not want to have to pluck out my own eye."

Eugene bolted upward. "You self-righteous charlatan. I ought to whip you into next Wednesday!"

"Cast the first stone, old man."

Archibald took an immediate knuckle to the lip.

Eugene dove across the table. Attendants and orderlies rushed in to separate the men, but not before Eugene delivered three good punches. The third punch rendered Archibald motionless, but he may have fainted from the stress. Workers were quick to pin Eugene. Consciousness soon returned to Archibald as orderlies carted both away by their arms.

*****

Solitary confinement did not consist of the padded walls of legend. Glazed adobe-tinted tile lined the walls to a height above Eugene's head before returning to its normal plaster motif.

The straitjacket was not a legend. It fit Eugene's frame with a merciless snugness that felt like the unbending hug of a close friend. It did not feel friendly, and Eugene wondered if this was what it would take to despise human contact as much as Flip did. Being harnessed to the wall further diminished the notion of comfort, but he managed to find a sitting position that could help him rest.

The breakfast altercation had driven his punishment well past lunch. Eugene wasn't sure what floor he had landed on or even what wing of the hospital. All he could estimate was the time, three o'clock, based on the light beaming through the western-facing window.

The confinement area attendant turned the key to his door in the late afternoon.

"Mr. Spangold, you have a visitor," the attendant announced. Before Eugene could respond, the man was gone. In his place was another man dressed in a trim suit and tie.

"Eugene JD Spangold, it's good to see you again," the man declared.

Eugene pushed himself upward in the restrictive position and adjusted his eyes to the change in light. "Administrator Crane. Is that what they call you these days?"

A woman appeared in the doorway then. Eugene reckoned it to be Mrs. Stapleton, the matron.

"Feel free to start the investigation on Ward C without me. I shouldn't be long here," Willard Crane said to the middle-aged Stapleton. She nodded and disappeared. Willard returned his attention to Eugene. "How long has it been? 1918? What's that, seventeen years?"

Eugene grunted. "I headed back to the farm, and you saddled up for medical school. I notice you don't have a D R period in front of your name."

Willard smirked and rubbed his collar. "It turns out, being a doctor isn't required to be an administrator in the field of mental health. All you need are connections and charm."

"So, how did you get by with none of that?"

Willard laughed away the insults. "Such a huckster. What brings you into my fold of fellow simpletons?"

For the first time since coming to the Weston Hospital, words from his internal dictionary failed to materialize. "I expect you know the answer already."

Willard laughed again. It was a sharp bellow, which intensified in pitch the longer it persisted. "Something urine. Something fire. You may have gotten out of here before I noticed, but your file was misplaced for a few weeks after the untimely demise of Doctor Timmons. No, I'm here to investigate your altercation in the cafeteria this morning. I take time from my busy schedule to investigate all matters of violence that, too often, take place in this institution. It is what a good administrator does."

Willard was toying with Eugene, but Eugene could not understand how or in what way.

"Can we conclude this?" Eugene questioned. He decided it best to stall Willard from achieving his hidden objective. "Did you ever marry?"

Willard stopped smiling. "No. Once the Bloom family ran out of eligible debutantes, I ceased any meaningful pursuit."

Eugene's sister-in-law, Mildred, had become something of an item with Willard after the war. Mildred, being more sociable than her sisters, aligned herself to be the most eligible female in Weston society. Their courtship would have better positioned Willard as an heir to the Bloom family's glass fortune. His dreams of achieving such status died when Mildred did. The 1918 pandemic brought influenza to the area, and Mildred became an early victim.

"I do lament not being your relative by marriage," Eugene stated, though not as sarcastic as he meant. "Your rumbustious ways would have made a good pairing with the elder Bloom."

Willard paused to process the juxtaposition between comments and decided the sincerity of the first statement was false. "Are you speaking poorly of me?"

Eugene snickered. "No, I'm speaking generally of you. The fact it appears poor is more a testament to your value."

Willard huffed. "Well, maybe I'll wait and conduct this interview on another day. Perhaps sometime next week."

Cringing, Eugene tried to move forward, but the harness did its job. "Ah, wouldn't it be in your best interest to treat your patients with tender loving care?"

The administrator had started for the door but stopped. He pivoted toward Eugene as he opened his jacket to reach into an inner pocket.

"There was some discrepancy with the statements you had been giving to the doctors concerning the funeral home. You're not telling the whole story."

Eugene scrunched his unshaven face. "In what way?"

"You should know." Willard shrugged, raising both arms high. "I wasn't there; you were."

"My statement was the gospel of it."

Back in his coat pocket, Willard dug for an item. "Well, I would tell you what part of your story is wrong, but that would set you on a path to healing. We wouldn't want that happening so soon."

Eugene slumped against the wall. "What a wretched vendetta you wield. Edgar Bloom would be quite proud of his almost-son."

Willard smiled, beaming with pride. "He certainly would have favored me more, but that would have required little effort." He finally removed a red business card from his pocket and laid it on the floor near Eugene. "I can only keep you here for another year. After which it will be the next administrator's decision." Willard straightened his jacket and turned for the exit. "I'll check back with you in a week."

Eugene slumped to the ground as the lonely door eased closed and latched.

"Can I at least get some lunch?" he shouted, remembering his hunger pains too late.

Alone again, Eugene groaned and put off looking at the red card for as long as possible. He had days to ignore it, but the lack of anything substantial forced him to glance early. Bold and italic words, both serif and sans serif, adorned the face in heavy black ink. Eugene was not a strong reader, but what few words were there were not hard to decipher.

VOTE WILLARD C. CRANE
A REPUBLICAN FOR WEST VIRGINIA GOVERNOR

That rat is hoisting himself up on the backs of the mentally disadvantaged, Eugene thought to himself. *People in any mental form are not meant to be rungs of a ladder.*

The following days swirled with hunger and isolation. Eugene was eventually fed, but not at every meal. Bathroom breaks were scarce, and Eugene soiled himself on more than one occasion when the interval outlasted his bladder. The orderlies—repulsed but not surprised by the filth—would take him to a shower stall, strip him naked, and spray Eugene raw with a powerful jet. The army had prepared him for similar moments, but Eugene still felt like an old boar prepped for market.

He thought about how much greater Flip would have despised the method. *The boy's mental state was sure to worsen from the hosing. Flip would have found no cure if he had been subjected to similar treatment.*

With nothing else to occupy his mind, Eugene turned his focus to the fire. The dark spirits were in the building in more ways than one. He was unsure of whose presidency he had to save, but he knew now there was a governorship to save as well. An all-consuming fire on Willard C. Crane's watch was sure to end any such campaign for gubernatorial office. He began to scheme, and as he did, a delicious plan to suit his mission came together.

After the second shower, Eugene sat in his cell in only a white hospital gown. It was the third day, but the perpetual dullness made time difficult to mark. The orderlies decided he had been on good enough behavior to remove his restraints and left him to shuffle about the compartment all he desired. He chose to remain seated against the wall and could now lean forward and tuck his head between his legs.

Eugene could also touch his hands again. The restraining jacket had prevented it on prior days, but he could now rub his hands together, as he often did when fighting boredom.

His right fingers stroked across his left ring finger, and he gasped upon realizing the wedding ring was no longer present. The rise in pulse was brief when he remembered the ring was already gone. He placed it in Ethel's casket during her viewing at the funeral parlor.

It would have been easy to forget, given the other events of that evening, he thought. Despite the length of time the ring had been gone, he could still feel its presence haunting his hand. The skin where the token was still callused and displaced—an impression of better days.

He allowed himself to think about Ethel and allowed himself to miss her, mourn her, though he still couldn't bear the weight of her departure. Though the accident crushed her body, it remained undamaged in appearance. The Floyds did a fantastic job of presenting her for her final appearance on the Weston social scene.

She read to him every night. Eugene could understand enough to pick out library books based on their jacket descriptions, but he always chose a complex work. He enjoyed big words and learning about their meanings, but he always felt more at home in the way the vocabulary rolled from Ethel's tongue.

Sobs came, but holding back tears felt unnecessary in solitude. He let them drop to the tile, counting each one upon splatter. Thirty-two in all. After the fit, Eugene decided to tuck his mourning on the back shelf of his mind from where it was first retrieved.

On the fourth day of isolation, Eugene received a visit from Doctor Znewski, whom he had not seen since the botched interview.

"What brings your busybody to my avenue of hell?" Eugene asked.

The doctor seemed nervous at the display of attitude. "Ah, yah. I told you I would get back to you with word on your daughter, and it seems we have located her."

"Yes! Is she coming to visit? Please tell me."

"Yah, a-about that. Un-unfortunately, it would seem. Um …"

"Out with it!"

Doctor Znewski winced. "As it turns out, we had trouble quickly locating her. It is because she is institutionalized as well. Here."

Eugene's voice softened. "Come again?"

Doctor Znewski slid his blonde locks behind his ears. "Opal Lee Spangold is a patient here, too."

PART II

THE HAUNTED

BETHLEHEM

BRITTANY, TUESDAY, JUNE 29, 1999

In four days, John Rocco Loughry would be killed by a drunk driver. Only around the Independence Day holiday would he dust off his father's 1967 Velocette Thruxton motorcycle and take it on short trips around Weston. He would have survived the accident had he taken the indestructible gray Dodge minivan often used for commutes. Insurance would have given him more money than the vehicle was worth. The accident would have rattled John Rocco. For a few days he would have had bruises and soreness, but would have recovered and returned to normal. Instead, he lay in the intersection of Route 33 with unidentified parts damaged beyond repair. With no other option, John Rocco drifted into endless slumber as he stared at the last light of day.

Early in the morning, four days earlier, Jennifer invited Brittany to her house near the convenience store. Whispers were beginning to cycle back to Brittany about her sultry trysts with a town police officer, and she had called Jennifer to try and insert clarification into the rumor mill.

"This is still about the hospital?" Jennifer croaked as Brittany explained the situation. She contained her excitement, but Brittany could see it under the surface. "Is it such a big deal to you that you would blackmail an officer of the law?"

"Honestly, he seems as curious as I am," Brittany noted. "It's pretty touch and go, but I'm getting what I want for now."

"What do you want?"

"To explore."

Jennifer laughed half-heartedly. "Had you really not been in that place before? Even when it was open?"

"No," Brittany replied after a quick delve into her memory. The school field trips to the hospital stopped decades earlier when conditions became too ruinous to guarantee safety.

"My mom worked there back in the '80s," Jennifer whispered, as if it were a dramatic revelation. "The stories she told were horrendous. People were stabbed, people hanged themselves from the vents, a nurse was murdered and found tucked under a flight of stairs a week later … I snuck in after it closed just once—a year after it closed. It felt as terrible as my mom had described."

"Once? How did you know the back door would work?" Brittany wondered.

"There was never a budget to fix things. Anything broken four years ago ain't going to be fixed today."

"I guess the paintball damage will still be there in decades, too," Brittany seethed. "You should have seen it."

"Oh!" Jennifer perked up like she had remembered something. "Word has it the newspaper is publishing photos of the damage today."

"I'll be sure to pick up a copy."

"Can you bring me a copy when you come? I assume you're going to the GoMart."

"Ah, yeah."

"If you really want a Weston Hospital education, there's someone else at my house I'd like for you to meet. My grandpa is staying with us for a few days. He got kicked out of the nursing home for punching a CNA.

Admitted to us yesterday that he didn't like the confinement because it reminded him of the time he spent in the Weston State Hospital."

"He was a patient?"

"Reckon so," Jennifer said in a raspy grunt. "None of us ever knew it, including my dad. You especially would have thought he'd mention it during the time my mom worked there."

"How long?"

"Huh?"

"How long ago was he a patient?" Brittany amended.

There was a lull. "Dunno. You can ask him about it yourself when you bring my newspaper?" Jennifer finally answered. "Oh. You said the other week you owed me some smokes, too. Well, I'm ready to cash that in."

Brittany had to borrow the money from her mom, who remained glued to the morning praise show on TBN. She had been sulking over the loss of her favorite stemware. The school reunion glass had crashed to the floor days earlier, sending the tiny translucent shards in all directions of the kitchen. More than a day later, pieces continued to reveal themselves in the right projection of daylight. Defeated, Glenda resorted to taking her morning vino from a repurposed jelly jar.

"Going to town for a bit," Brittany stated as she removed $10 from Glenda's purse.

Mom lifted a weak hand to wave her daughter off but remained glued to the teary, pink-haired woman on the television screen.

"You're walking?" Glenda finally asked after Brittany had already left the room. Brittany chose not to double back for such a simple answer and made her way toward town on foot.

*****

THE headline at the top of *The Weston Democrat*'s Section E read PAINT BALL BLASTS LEAVE WESTON HOSPITAL INTERIOR ONE MESSY PLACE. Eight color photos of the carnage followed, presented for the first time against broad daylight and flashbulb.

Brittany stood at the gas station counter and purchased two of the newspapers, along with a pack of Camels and a SoBe Elixer.

The editions were hot off the press and delivered with a post date of June 30, 1999—a dateline intended for mailbox deliveries the next day.

In the afternoon sunlight, Brittany could take in the pictures in all their brilliance. She knelt on the curb and opened the paper to section E. Casting aside the remaining segments of the paper, Brittany placed her full SoBe drink, a pink concoction, on the stack to prevent the remaining news from being windswept.

The newspaper reminded Brittany it was Tuesday. The day of the week in which she had her first otherworldly encounter. Except for the dark spirit in the southern ward, she had not had much luck with ghostly visitation. Plenty of noises and tricks of the eye kept the visits interesting, but she wanted to see the light spirit again.

She began to think she was spending too much time on the subject. There were miles of Kirkbride to explore, and the expeditions unfolded on borrowed time anyway. The admittance into the building was only allowed because conditions were perfect to manipulate the gatekeepers. Her fortune could change at any moment for a plethora of reasons.

Satisfied with the newspaper's account of the damage, she tucked the section back into the greater weekly and backtracked three buildings to reach Jennifer's home. The two-story bungalow was shingled top to bottom with a reddish-brown tile. Brittany stepped onto the front porch and immediately caught sight of an older man gently rocking on a porch swing.

"Mornin'," the man greeted with a warm smile that retreated into a resting scowl.

Brittany returned a smile of her own and nodded. "Hello."

He pointed to the papers in her hand. "Jen said you were bringing a *Democrat*."

"Oh, yes," Brittany said. She extracted the unruffled copy and handed it to the man. "I'm guessing you're Jennifer's grandfather?"

"Vernon, though 'Pops' is what she calls me. Come to think of it, I never really went by Vernon to begin with."

He unfolded the paper by flicking it. The additional sections and a grocery store insert plopped onto his lap.

Brittany turned to see a green metal chair near the door. Vernon caught her looking and waved a hand. "Oh, please, have a seat."

Once situated, Brittany observed the man reading through the pages. He wore the typical grandfather garb: Khaki trousers with a light blue button-up shirt adorned with a World War II Veteran hat.

"The vandalism pictures are in the E section," Brittany told him. Vernon was taking little time to scan the headlines of the front sections but held longer once he arrived at the classifieds.

"I don't suppose I'll keel over before I get there," Vernon grunted.

Something about studying the paper's contents had diminished the warm persona Brittany had first encountered. She waited, and Jennifer soon emerged from behind a screen door.

"Sorry if Pops is being antagonistic. He's been salty all morning. I didn't know you'd be here this early." Jennifer stopped to spin the flint of the lighter several times. The stubborn flame finally appeared on the fifth strike. She placed flame to tobacco and sucked at the cigarette until it came alight.

Brittany handed Jennifer the new cigarette pack she had purchased at the store, but Jennifer motioned for her to set them on the railing. Grandfather Vernon transitioned to the next section and noticed the girls' exchange.

"You shouldn't smoke that shit," Vernon called from behind the next section. "It'll make you infertile."

"Don't worry about that, Pops," Jennifer dismissed sharply. "You have eight other grandbabies that can advance your legacy. My eggs shouldn't be any of your concern."

Jennifer pointed the cigarette toward Brittany before her line of sight followed. "Do you hear his language? Very unbecoming of a Methodist preacher."

"Retired Methodist pastor," Vernon grumbled.

"I'm starting to think you got fired for losing your way," Jennifer snapped back in a teasing way. Brittany would come to realize they displayed their love through harsh banter, which appeared cruel to the unknowing ear. The lighthearted catches of amusement tucked within the sentences were the key to knowing the difference.

Regardless, Vernon was growing tired of the exchange. He snorted and turned a page. "Your friend wants to ask about the hospital?"

Brittany and Jennifer locked eyes for a moment before Jennifer turned to her grandfather. "Ah, yeah. She's been doing a bunch of research about it. She's kinda obsessed with it."

"They should put a wrecking ball clean through it. Those police officers did us a favor by ruining any future plans to reform that hellhole."

"It's a fascinating structure," Brittany defended with an innocent voice.

Vernon lowered the section and folded it. "You've been in there?"

"Yes."

"What did you see?"

Brittany inhaled deep. "The wallpaper is peeling badly, the paint—"

"No." Vernon's deep-set eyes grew dark. "What did you see, as in, *who* did you see?"

"A light spirit on the third floor and a dark spirit on the fourth floor," Brittany blurted without considering the ramifications. She looked at Jennifer, but her demeanor had turned demure. She furrowed her brow at the new information. "You saw ghosts? You didn't tell me that."

"That place is haunted," Vernon agreed, then retrieved the next paper segment. "And I am someone who is skeptic about the existence of ghosts."

"Dark spirits and light spirits?" Jennifer questioned between drags. Her voice remained as disaffected as ever, but Brittany could tell she was very interested. "What do you think the difference is?"

"Good and evil," Vernon answered with matter-of-fact certainty. "Doesn't black always represent evil, and white represent good?"

"Maybe in cowboy movies," Brittany said. Her back went rigid against the chair. "Is there really anything outside of movies or art that tells you otherwise?"

Vernon huffed. "God's first act of creation was to cast light into the universe. Light is inherently good because it was the first thing God created."

"You said black and white, Pops," Jennifer noted. "What you mean is darkness and light."

"What's the difference?"

"When you say black and white, you just sound racist." The teasing undertone didn't exist in Jennifer's comment, and Vernon retreated from the conversation. He finally removed section E of *The Weston Democrat* and began to canvas the photo essay.

Though hesitant, Brittany continued. "Just because light is good does not mean dark is bad. Not every opposite has to be compared the same. Apples and oranges, you know?"

Vernon gyrated his jaw in a chewing motion as he looked down at the photo spread without moving the paper or his head. His eyes widened. "You don't believe those spirits are good and evil?"

"No," Brittany said.

The section dropped to Vernon's lap. "I'd like to hear your theory, then."

Brittany felt her chest compress. Her thoughts on the subject had been internalized until then. Bringing them out felt like part of her heart was exiting with the message. "Light is living. Dark is dead."

Vernon remained motionless as he blinked. His mouth drooped in the moment before his brow lines sharpened.

"Living ghosts?" he said in a higher pitch.

"Future ghosts," Brittany clarified. The theory—born into the world only moments ago—was already rendering her a great discomfort in existing.

"Back sixty years ago, when I spent some time at the hospital, my older roommate told us he saw a bright light apparition of a person in our doorway one night while we slept. Are you telling me what he saw was someone from the future?"

"Correct," Brittany said and bit her lip. A weird silence persisted until she added, "It could have been me for all we know."

"I don't know about all that. There's a certain way I learned about darkness and light. And at my age, I find it difficult to see any other way."

Jennifer, who had been dead silent during the exchange, ground the remaining cigarette filter into a nearby ceramic dish. "Is there anything you want to say about your time in the hospital, Pops? Is that roommate of yours still alive?"

"No. No. When I say older, I mean by several decades. Tuberculosis got him in the 1950s."

Vernon leaned back in the swing and tilted his head to the porch ceiling to reminisce. "That fella was an interesting sort. Spoke with a unique vocabulary for a backwater farmer. Yet, he was a schemer of the highest order. Had a plan to burn down the hospital, which he carried out successfully, if you know any history about the place. His daughter was a patient there, too. He helped her escape on the day of the blaze, though he claimed the two things weren't connected."

"There was a fire at the hospital?" Brittany asked. She cared nothing for the roommate's story. It was the history of the Kirkbride that she craved.

"Oh, yeah. The upper floors of the southern wing collapsed. Not the stone, mind you, but everything within. It singed some of the clock tower's innards, too. Of course, this was during the Great Depression. The building wasn't insured, so they had to rely on funds from the feds to repair the damage. They kept it cheap. There used to be ornate cupolas on either end of the building. The southern tower collapsed in the fire, but rather than rebuild it, they tore down the cupola on the northern side. The fourth floor, where I had spent time, got wood flooring instead of tile. The thick walls remained the same as they always had."

Brittany bounced. "I was on the fourth floor the last time I was inside. That was where I saw the dark ghost."

Vernon hummed as he sorted the spent pages in his lap. "Based on your theory, I guess whoever you saw was already dead."

*****

Dew dampened all things by the time midnight approached. To Brittany's favor, both Officer Prince and Security Guard Chad had drawn short straws for the night shift. The young officer went to an automobile accident and was not able to retrieve Brittany until midnight. The tardiness did not affect Brittany as it would have before. She only needed to visit one room, Room 668, prove her theory right or wrong, and then leave happy or sad.

"June is always the worst month for car crashes," Officer Prince said as he ferried Brittany across town. "The folks tonight got off easy, but that isn't always the case."

Brittany would remember those words days later, when it was her father who ran upon hard luck.

The moisture in the air saturated the front lawn of the hospital with mist and returned to the air as a cloud. The gloom filtered the streetlights from Weston, casting a glow against the Kirkbride megastructure. The scene captured the atmosphere of Gothic horror and twisted a nerve in the pit of Brittany's stomach. Despite the vibe, she knew conditions were too perfect to abandon the mission now.

The black JanSport backpack clopped against her back as she rounded flights up the oak stairwell to the third floor. It was a short trip from there. Three doors to the right, past the paintball mess, and past the desecrated wallpaper patterns.

668. The room, dark and slopped with dried paint splatters, remained dark.

Brittany stood in the center, waiting for something to happen. She didn't know how to trigger an encounter, so she began with the one thing everyone seemed to try.

"Hello?"

Her voice, though not particularly loud, echoed down the hallways before fading. The sound spooked her more than anything. Not the moment later when the room illuminated. Not the moment after when a full-body apparition appeared. Not the moment where it began to reach out a hand for her from the opposite end of the room.

She watched the bright hand extend and tried hard to focus on colors beyond the glow with no luck. It was a male, the same one as before. The Apple device still clung to a clip on his ethereal belt. Brittany finally looked at its face and could see with so much detail she could discern a smile.

The friendliness of the apparition compelled her to extend her hand in reply. Both bodies reached, cautious, and connected with the pads of their fingers.

The light passed into Brittany's hand. As it did, it created a sensation of static electricity, like placing a hand on a television screen. Still, there was a coldness to the feeling, like coming into an air-conditioned home on a sweltering day. It was a simultaneous shock and a chill, but another sensation tingled in her ears. As if tuned to a new frequency, Brittany could now hear breathing, a heartbeat, and the sound of a commotion outside that had not been there before.

"Hello?" a male voice returned. "She could see the apparition's mouth move, but the sound arrived through the resonance in her fingers.

"Wow," Brittany replied. "I can hear you."

"Wow, indeed," the male voice replied.

An unprecedented contact made, Brittany racked her brain for questions to ask the supposed ghost. *What year is it? What's your name? Why are you in this building? Were you a patient?* Before Brittany could land on a single introductory query, the ghost posed the first question in a gentle, calm manner.

"How did you die?"

BETHLEM

NEIL, SUNDAY, JUNE 30, 2019

"How did you live?"

A female voice returned the question, sarcastic from what Neil could tell. He choked with befuddlement. He was happy, a little scared, and fully confused. It was a bottleneck of all emotions at once and was unsure of what the expression on his face was conveying. Finally, Neil composed himself. "I mean. I'm not dead yet."

"Neither am I" the ghost said.

Neil thought back to stories about how ghosts often do not realize they are dead and expected the theory now proved true.

"What is your name? What year do you think this is?"

The apparition had sharpened in visual soundness enough that Neil thought he detected an eyeroll along with a head tilt.

"My name is Brittany Loughry. I am speaking to you from the year 1999. Am I glowing? Am I a white light?"

"Oh. Twenty years ago," Neil calculated. "You are glowing."

"I knew it! You're from the future!" Ghost Brittany's voice remained the same volume across the veil. "I took a picture of you the first time I saw you. You have an Apple product on your belt I don't recognize. It hasn't been invented yet in 1999. So, 2019?"

"Yes," Neil replied with awe. "June twenty-ninth, or rather June thirtieth since it's after midnight now."

"It's after midnight on June thirtieth here, too," Brittany replied with wide eyes. "Amazing! We must have been in the exact same place at the same time. That's how we were able to synchronize!"

"I don't understand any of this." The sudden rush of ethereal elements was exhausting Neil's weakened mentality. "When I saw you last time, I knew I needed to see you again. I felt something, like a … a sense of common destiny between us."

Neil removed his hand from Brittany and the static and sound of her vanished. He replaced it fast. It was a strange sensation of electricity and cold. Holding a cold living hand felt the most unnatural of any of the occurrence. More than being able to pass through her hand if he pressed too far.

"Sorry. We must have to remain in contact to hear and speak to each other."

Brittany stared at the connection. "It does seem that way."

"Can we sit? This will get exhausting after a while." Before he could finish asking, Brittany was already bound for the floor.

They stared at one another, in awe of the impossibility. Distance and time were the only things that could keep people apart, but there they were. There was no distance between them, but an unscalable mountain of time.

The questions from Brittany began, and they were eclectic and rapid-fire. She gasped as each came to her.

"Ooh! Who's the president?"

"Would you believe it's Donald Trump?"

"The real estate guy?"

"He'll be known for other things."

"Sounds ominous."

"It depends on your politics and TV-watching preferences. I guess he and Bill Clinton in your time aren't so different."

"How so?"

"I don't want to ruin it for you."

"What if I don't live that long?"

"Then you are blessed to never know."

"Ooh! Who won the Super Bowl?"

"Why? Are you going to place a sure bet?"

"Wouldn't anyone?"

"Ooh! What about Y2K? Do all the computers crash? People here think it will end the world."

"I had forgotten about Y2K." Neil laughed. "It doesn't do a thing."

"Ooh, how old are you?"

"I turned forty a few months ago."

"Hey! I'm eighteen. We're only like ... two years apart in age."

Neil laughed. "That's some weird math."

Brittany laughed. "Yeah, it is! Did you go to Lewis County High School?"

"No. I'm from Moundsville, up near the northern panhandle."

"Ooh! Where did you go to college?"

"West Virginia University."

"That's where I'm going in the fall. Maybe I'll run into you there."

"I don't ever recall meeting a Brittany Loughry."

"Ooh! What's the hospital like there? Did you have to sneak in to meet me?"

"It's a tourist attraction now. It has private owners, and they hold historical and paranormal tours. I'm on a ghost tour now but I snuck off so I could find you."

The more questions asked, the more concerned Neil felt about accidentally upsetting the course of history. In the back of his mind, he held the realization he had the power to prevent all the tragedies of the world. The terror attacks of September 11, 2001, hadn't happened yet, the November 9, 2007, Sears Tower bombing that killed his brother, or the Boston Marathon Bombing ... He could send Brittany to warn and possibly stop it all. She could be an agent of time, correcting all the things that go wrong in the twenty-first century. He would consider it, but for now, there was still plenty of time. If he could reestablish future connections with Brittany, Neil could sleep on that decision for now.

"I want to meet you again. Are you able to return here each week at this time?" Neil realized it was the first question he had asked since they sat.

Brittany appeared somber. "I do have to sneak in, but I have a police officer and a security guard who gave me cover. I only have about an hour each time, though, or I have to walk home. Ooh! In fact, I may have to if we talk much longer."

"If we were together, I would give you a ride home," Neil said. He realized it sounded a bit like a pickup line, but let it linger without correction.

Brittany stood, and Neil struggled to follow her hand and rise with her.

"Next Tuesday, then?"

"It's Saturday here."

"Oh, yeah. Leap years and stuff," Brittany said. "A week from today?"

Neil reached and placed his other hand against her shoulder. It felt present, even though it was only a projection, a film from years ago flickering its halogen against a tattered canvas.

"Yes," Neil said, and his heart accepted the joy of the moment. "I'll see you again in a week."

Brittany disconnected and turned but then abruptly jerked back and connected with his hand once again.

"Ooh! What is that Apple device on your hip?"

"It's a phone," Neil said. "They're very popular and have pretty much replaced regular landline phones. I couldn't live without it."

Brittany pumped a victory fist. "Good job, Apple. I'll have to tell my dad to invest."

Neil returned home from the asylum early. He had gotten what he sought. A chance to have a conversation few people ever had.

That night, he lay on his air mattress and stared at his peeling ceiling. He was restless again, but it was for a reason he had not felt for more than twenty years.

He was counting down the hours until he could see Brittany again.

*****

SATURDAY, JULY 6, 2019

To keep from having to steal away every Saturday, Neil made a special arrangement with the tour guides to conduct special experiments in Ward C, though he managed to keep the location of his pseudo séances secret. The asylum tours rarely had weekly repeat customers. This allowed Neil's high-roller status to grant him certain privileges not given to first timers.

The Brittany who appeared the following week was a much different version of the young lady he had met the week before. Her chipper demeanor was gone. Her excitement of their unique situation had evaporated into malaise, but the reason was just.

"My dad died," Brittany finally revealed through sobs. "He was killed by a drunk driver, Dustin Creedmore. If you run into him on the streets in the future, punch him in the face for me."

"I will," Neil said, though the opportunity was unlikely to arise. He reached around her and gave her the best hug he could, working with only shadow, light, and whatever passed for ectoplasm.

"You didn't have to come see me tonight," Neil said. Her feelings were infecting him from afar. "If you need to be with your family, you should."

"The funeral is tomorrow." Brittany sat cross-legged on the floor. "I do need to get some sleep. Doubt I will, though."

"Where is he being buried?" It was an odd question, but Neil was decades late to the funeral and wanted to pay his respects in some way.

Brittany did not answer the question. She looked up and stared beyond Neil.

"I need to know my mom will be okay. She has been drinking a lot lately, even before this happened. It took a maximum dose of Valium to get her through the funeral arrangements. I doubt she'll stop once the mourners go back to their lives." Brittany took Neil by both hands as best she could and stared at him in the eyes. "Can you check on her for me? Can you see if she is still alive in twenty years? If she's not, can you find out when and how she died?"

Already concerned about the ramifications, Neil felt it to be an unwise idea, but he liked Brittany, and wanted Brittany to like him. He masked his hesitations and gave a sincere nod. "I will."

Relief washed over Brittany's opaque face. She slumped but kept both hands touching Neil.

Fearful of losing the momentum of the connection he felt with her, he decided to share details of his own paternal figure. "My father left us when I was twelve. I saw Harry Hutchence once after that, at my older brother's graduation. He never came to mine. I'm not sure if he is still alive. My mom remarried and cut him off from access to us, or he never bothered to contact us again. I'm not sure."

In speaking it, Neil realized he was replicating the pattern with his own children. It also made him realize another detail about his current outlook in life, one he had avoided speaking about to anyone in his present realm.

"My brother died in a terrorist attack in Chicago in 2007. I spent a decade trying to forget what had happened, but with other failures in life, the trauma caught up with me. I lost the point in living. I lost sight of the meaning of life. Life felt so short and suddenly it seemed like there wasn't time to do anything. So, I did nothing, but that didn't stop the world. Society kept moving, my family kept moving, and before I knew, it all left me behind."

The sentiment seemed to impact Brittany in some way; her brow quivered as if tasked to press back additional tears. "Did it get better?"

Neil matched the sadness on her face. "It is now. That is, you've helped me see a pathway to wellness. Maybe, with luck, I can do the same for you."

Brittany smiled and clumsily patted one of Neil's hands.

"Maybe you can show me a pathway, too."

*****

SATURDAY, JULY 13, 2019

On Tuesday evening, Neil had called his children. He talked
to Madeline for only a few minutes. Even though they hadn't spoken
in months, the grade-schooler only had a few short answers to Neil's
questions before handing the phone back to Caitlyn. Meriwether was
chattier, though her words were incoherent toddler phrases.

More important, Neil apologized to Caitlyn for his negligence in
raising their family. He explained the underlying trauma involved in his
disassociation. Caitlyn would not usually be unforgiving to such attempts,
but she must have detected something different in his tone.

"Grief is like a cavity," Caitlyn began. She always relished in the
opportunity to speak in metaphors. "If you don't take good care of it right
away, it tends to rot from the inside out. I'm glad you're taking care of it
now."

Neil thanked her but did not ask for any kind of resolution to
their failed union. After more than a year of divorce, diplomacy was finally
established. There was no need to sully the shaky prospect of peace with
unnecessary gestures.

The next day, Neil visited the cemetery. It was the same memorial
garden he could see from the hotel they stayed at the first day in Weston.
Neil located the gravesite of John Rocco Loughry in a family plot sectioned
off with colorless paving stones. Eleven markers resided within the
perimeter, with room for at least three more family members inside. The
back row contained the older stones, the most ancient was Henry McNelly,
who died in 1984. Neil followed the trail of men and their respective
spouses until a marriage changed the surname to Loughry.

Rocco George Loughry and his partner, Susan, had the most ornate
of the markers. A sizable obelisk protruded from the ground, announcing
the couples' names along with the range in which they cast breath on the
Earth. Above Rocco's name was an engraving of what appeared to be an old

farm store, but Neil was uncertain how the illustration steered him to the conclusion.

Among the McNellys were two other Loughry stones on the plat. A George Oren Loughry died in his twenties, and John Rocco Loughry passed on July 3, 1999, at what Neil calculated to be forty-five years old.

Chiseled in the stone next to John Rocco's name was his spouse's name, Glenda Jean Davis Loughry. The stone listed her as being born September 4, 1955, but the date of death remained blank.

Neil wished he had checked the cemetery first. Going to McGary Avenue and meeting Glenda in person felt like a violation of some unwritten code of time ethics. The universe could hand down an indictment at any moment. Punishment for defying the laws governing spacetime could be proactively or retroactively applied. That was how it felt, at least, an unease echoing beyond the known sciences into a quantum level. The information he gathered from Glenda felt forbidden, and he tried as best he could to ignore or forget what he had learned.

Even when he visited Brittany, when they held cold hands of static and spoke at one another, Neil dreaded the question still to come.

When the question did come, it was from a young woman still broken and mourning but improving in mindset.

"What did you find out about my mom?"

Neil had to stare into the naivety of youth and do the only thing a sensible, responsible adult could do …

"The good news is I found your father's tombstone, and I paid my respects. I sat there and stared for many minutes. It was overcast today, and a cool breeze swept through the valley. It was peaceful, and I think your dad is still at peace, too. But while I sat there, I couldn't help but notice your mom's name is on the tombstone. There's a birth date, but there is no death date."

"Are you saying there's bad news?" Brittany asked, her face sinking. "Did you go up to McGary Avenue?"

Neil nodded. "I did. I did. I couldn't find the address. As far as I could tell, 723 is nothing but an empty lot." He bit the inside of his cheek, mad at how well he sold the lie.

BEDLAM

Henrietta, July 4, 1905

Fireworks crackled and popped from a northwestern ridge on the outskirts of Weston. Red, white, blue, and an assortment of other shades illuminated against the leafy trees and front lawn. The light was made more vibrant by a Weston still shrouded in pure darkness. Lampposts remained unlit for such occasions so residents could line the streets and yards to observe the spectacle.

Following the display, a public dance began in the hospital auditorium. It was the only venue in town using electric bulbs, though the air circulation was as bad as any. The heat of the day pooled in the upper floors of the hospital, and Henrietta expected the social event to be a sweltering affair.

Henrietta only discovered the dance because she could hear a cacophony of cheery voices filing into the auditorium. The assembly hall was close; three doors and a short walk to the center of the building. The commotion was not deafening, but still difficult to ignore.

The night nurse confirmed her suspicion when she made a final stop to deliver a glass of water and retrieve her dinner plate.

The nurse noted the only remaining food item on the platter. "You're not going to eat your tomato?"

"Don't much care for tomatoes. Devil's fruit, I call it."

"Oh. Strange." The nurse winced.

"Seems noisy out there," Henrietta pointed out.

"It's been quite a night." The nurse gave a gleeful smile. "The fireworks were fabulous. Did you see them?"

Henrietta sat on the floor and tightened the bolts on a partly assembled autoclave. "I'm on the wrong side of the building for it."

"Ah. That's a shame." The nurse was much more animated than usual. "ER Bloom Glassware Company sponsors the fireworks event every year. They spare no expense in procuring the explosives for the show. If you're here next year, you'll surely get to see it."

The thought brought a pang of unease in Henrietta's chest. She lowered the wrench and debated how to respond, ultimately neglecting to answer altogether.

"How is that coming along?" The nurse gestured at the autoclave.

"A little longer tonight, and I should have it ready to go by morning."

The nurse sighed and settled into a more lackadaisical attitude. "Nurse Hatfield must be awful trusting to let you handle heavy tools. We count the silverware after meals to make sure no one fashions a spoon into a deadly weapon, but she gives you access to actual sharp instruments."

"I'm not crazy." Henrietta returned to her work. "I'm being kept here against my will."

Snickering, the nurse retreated to the door. "They all say that."

"Don't anger the lady with access to sharp instruments," Henrietta joked, waving the wrench. The nurse whipped her head around, but Henrietta winked to confirm the levity. The nurse breathed a sigh of relief but was still quick to exit the room.

Since Silkie vanished, Henrietta could not stop thinking about her own possibility of escaping. Eloping, as the staff termed it. She couldn't understand the reasoning for calling it such. Eloping was often meant to be a romantic gesture for lovers who could not wait for formalities to become bound together for life. She could not run away with Strickland, but she would flee with Wallace. Eloping was the only chance she would have to make a normal life for the child. And if he remained light-skinned, he would have a greater opportunity in the world. It was a sad matter-of-fact, but one she could not deny, given her status as a de facto prisoner.

There was no one out there. Her father, perhaps. He knew she was in the hospital. He was outside the courthouse the day the judge declared her mentally unsound. In the year since, he made no known movements to retrieve her, prove her stability, or even visit. He was surely embarrassed by her commitment and couldn't afford to take a hit to his station among the elders of his hamlet.

She would follow the river north. The West Fork River would merge into the Monongahela, and that mighty waterway would lead her to the only home she knew before Strickland.

But she needed Silkie if she were to consider carrying out any kind of plan. The aging woman was a methodical killer somehow never associated with her crimes. She seemed willing enough to admit to it. But by Silkie's account, it was her masochistic nature which landed her in sanatoriums. Henrietta could neither understand the joy of pain, nor how the infliction was anyone's business.

Regardless, Silkie dipped into the overgrowth at the edge of the property, never to reappear. Four returns to the garden acknowledged her continued absence. Others from the ward confirmed Silkie was gone, but it was never clear if anyone on the staff had even noticed. They did not appear to do a headcount. Even at bedtime, there was no effort made to ensure the numbers.

The next day bucked the trend, even as Henrietta lost hope. Silkie appeared in the field, entering with the rest of the ward like it had been any other morning on field detail.

Henrietta placed a hand over her heart. "I'm happy to see you. I wasn't sure you were coming back."

Silkie rolled her eyes like the concern was ridiculous. "Needed to prepare. Ready now." Silkie shook a small sack and many little things swished about. "In the meantime, we're plantin' broccoli."

"What was it?" Henrietta was curious about what important item could have taken days to procure. "What did you need to get?"

Silkie grinned and leaned close. Her remaining teeth showed, which was atypical for her average smile. "War paint."

"War paint?"

"Small bottle. Hid it in my mattress. Bright light blue." Silkie was proud, but Henrietta could not gauge why.

Silkie continued. "Folks in the South call it Haint Blue. They paint 'em big porches with it. Is 'spose to scare off evil spirits, but it ain't never scared off me."

Baffled, Henrietta closed her eyes. "I don't understand the connection between the paint and your murders."

"Child, I told you a lotta secrets. Still would like to keep one or two for me." She paused to place a hand on her hip and eyed the pathetic-looking mother and child. "Tell you what. When it's all over, I'll leave a letter about the rest."

"Why are you doing this? Why are you doing all of this for me?" Henrietta asked the question with sincere gratitude tucked in her tone. This woman—a generation removed from her—acted as a great friend with little time to form lasting bonds. To Silkie, that was the point.

"You don't belong here. If us Black folk are ever gonna rise, we need to stop being captives of the system."

Silkie pulled open the small cloth bag and peeked inside. "Seeds are fascinating. It starts small, grows into a leafy thing that adds more and more branches. All those leaves and branches add up to a single moment when they're most important. The fruit. Families are like that, too."

Like many other times when she said something profound, Silkie grew ashamed and tried to shrug it off.

"You know you don't belong here either." Henrietta was quick to stop the process, though in truth, she knew her history, her secrets. Perhaps it wasn't true.

Silkie rolled her eyes much like earlier. "You right. I belong someplace much worse."

"That's not what I—"

"Doctor Felix Koenig. What's he look like?"

"Tall, skinny, blonde, blonde mustache. It's a long curly mustache," Henrietta replied. "Blonde."

Silkie bobbed her head as she thought. "Shouldn't be hard to spot. Get him out here on a garden day and I'll do the rest."

*****

THE protocol to reenter the Kirkbride was always the same. *Return to the kitchen in the back corner of the first floor, knock three times on the back door, and ask for the kitchen manager, Mrs. Kneely. Ask Mrs. Kneely for Nurse Showalter, then head to the back door, but do not stand directly in front of it. Meander. Pretend you're watering flowers. Can't find a watering can? Just pretend. Plenty of patients pantomime it anyway. Once inside, get covered by a white sheet and let two nurses lead me up the emergency stairs to Ward C.*

The nurses often forwent the instruction about the stairs, opting to take the much shorter route through the main oak staircase. It was the breaking of protocols that exposed Henrietta to the ward originally. The nurses had learned nothing from the error, and Henrietta was again about to be penalized for their mistake.

Counting flights as they climbed, Henrietta noticed the escorts stopped on the third flight, halfway between the second and third floors. There was a silence in the stairwell, and only the distant clamor of patient shouts and banging seeped into the background static. After a long moment, footsteps began to descend, slow and deliberate. They halted again when Wallace began to coo and squeal.

"Vat is Henrietta doing out of her room?" a voice asked.

Henrietta knew one of the nurses was Chokio but did not recognize the other. *Was she familiarized with Henrietta's secret outings?*

"She was out in the garden pulling weeds," the unidentified nurse's nasally voice announced without a care.

"She is not to be out of her room beyond health und sanitary needs," Doctor Koenig said in a dim tone.

"I thought she had been doing this for weeks," the nurse added with squeaky confusion. "That's what Nurse Showalter said, at least."

Nurse Chokio kept quiet. She dared not correct the other nurse, avoiding her own implication.

"How long have you been vith us, Nurse Vilkins?" Doctor Koenig asked.

"Oh, I've been here for more than a year, but I was moved from Ward One last week."

The doctor hummed. "Expect a promotion soon. Please take Miss Cedric to her room und leave her for die night."

The nurses remained mute as they completed the journey to the third floor and placed Henrietta in her room. Replacing their voices were several muttering female patient voices and one screaming, "There's that negro ghost!"

Following the shriek was the sound of metal clanking, hit Henrietta, then a mild commotion. The nurses hurried Henrietta to her quarters before subduing the attacker.

In the safety of her room, Henrietta sat on the bed and nursed a happy Wallace. He slurped the milk until he achieved a state of infantile drunkenness and sullied off to sleep.

All the while Henrietta waited for Felix to barge through the door, bang and slam, and do everything but violate the parts of the Hippocratic Oath he still respected. He did not come for the night. No one did, including dinner, which was usually delivered at six o'clock sharp.

Hunger woke her in the morning, but it would still be another two hours before eggs and toast came to the room. She fed herself, fed Wallace, and waited some more. Henrietta stared out the window, an activity she rarely partook in despite her captivity. The lawn was lush and kept shorn. The trees were fully engulfed in their summer coat, and the vibrance of the green hues reflected against the sandstone walls of the exterior.

Henrietta tired of it all. She always had been, but now her body, mind, and soul were all screaming in unison, asking why she didn't arrive at the conclusion sooner. She had to escape. Maybe because escape felt impossible before. Maybe because a person's body decides to pace itself when moving through a bad life position. Whatever the case, the internal regulators informing her tolerance were now gone. There was nothing left to do but run when there was an opening. Those triggers should have alerted her before each violation. The violation of her body by an unethical doctor. The violation when a surgeon excised her reproductive organs. The pain was still there in the scar tissue. Henrietta tried to channel agony into resolve. She certainly wasn't finding pleasure.

The door opened. Doctor Felix Koenig stood in the precipice, his arms folded and prim against his waist. He looked serious, but not angry, and held a stone position as he looked at Henrietta standing at the window.

"A voman is on her vay from Elkins. She vill likely arrive on Saturday. She lost twins in childbirth. Very sad. As you might expect, it took quite a toll on her psyche. She is ripe vith grief."

"Yes, I could imagine," Henrietta said as she rounded the bed.

Felix closed his eyes and gestured with his head before proceeding. "It has been decided that ven she arrives, Vallace vill be staying with her, und if she can overcome her acute mania, she vill be allowed an option to adopt him."

"Do I have a say in the matter?" Henrietta asked, clutching every molecule of her remaining composure.

The doctor gave a biting sneer. "You have no rights here."

"The story would be different if he had my skin, wouldn't it?" Grit was coarse in Henrietta's words. "You took my heart, but I see now all you were taking was advantage. You wanted my body, but not any kind of responsibility for your actions. You wanted to tuck me away, but not even your most loyal nurses found that fair. You take my Wallace away, and I'm telling everyone about our affair."

"Der garden knows nothing of it?" Felix asked, hopeful, seemingly ignoring the content of the statement that preceded it.

"I have told no one, and Wallace was wrapped tightly under my gown. Not a single person has seen him any time I've been out there." She knew it was a flimsy lie, but the doctor seemed to have taken to a new thought he did not share.

He sighed and eased his posture. "I vill consider the contents of your threat. Time is short, so a verdict vill be given soon."

The doctor took a step back and closed the door, leaving Henrietta alone once more. She returned to the window and stared at the trees once again. Hidden beneath the heft oaks and pines was a young poplar, which had yet to rise to its full potential. Henrietta gazed at it with a spark of unexpected optimism and tried to imagine it in another time and place.

Maybe in fifty years when all its branches have expanded, when it has reached its full potential, the fireworks will bounce their colors off its plumage for someone unable to see the light show.

She sighed, realizing the metaphor Silkie provided about trees had fallen short. *Not all bear fruit.*

BEDLAND

Two weeks out of solitary confinement found Eugene back on Ward T. In the week and day he spent inside the tiny cell, Eugene lost his place among Flip and Archibald. The administration gave the spot to an elderly man by the name of Reginald Bratt. Reggie, as he preferred, had been the victim of a stroke. The man's face drooped on one side as if half the man had already died. He spoke rarely, but when he did the words were often unintelligible and slurred beyond comprehension. Sly, the gentleman with the clef palette, managed to speak with greater eloquence.

Eugene had not a nice thing to say about Reggie. It wasn't the man's fault he took the space. The overcrowding had elevated Eugene's bed to prime real estate, and it took little time to draft someone else. Reggie should have been in the geriatric section two floors down. Eugene knew they had the specific housing but had heard it was much more occupied than their top-floor suites. In the elder ward, beds—sometimes only the mattresses—remained in the hallway, where invalids were often kept for ease of changing bed clothes and pans.

The seething Eugene resumed his daily habits of his early days. He dressed early, though his street clothes had disappeared in his absence. His fatigues now consisted of a hospital-issued pullover gown and loose-fitting socks. He was at least offered fresh garb every day. After situating in the costume, he would share the platform with the radiator and stare through the tiny half window at the ER Bloom Glassware Company building. The view was different from his old angle, but not by much. Eugene's new quarters were on the opposite end of the hallway, not far from the feces-throwing Peter. His episodes had resided since his insulin treatment, but his mannerisms spoke more to fear of further discipline.

Charlie Geon and Hector Tompkins were Eugene's new roommates. Though he did not have anything particularly harsh to say about them, he found them difficult to engage with and their presence unentertaining.

The demure Charlie's upbringing was from Korean grandparents who immigrated to the eastern edge of Appalachia. His guardians gave him an Americanized first name in hopes of better integration into their new society. They felt his birth name, Shi-woo, didn't have quite the same potential for new-world opportunity. A mean streak kept Charlie from enjoying the benefits his grandparents tried to provide. Now pushing thirty, Charlie was a man who deserved to be on the fourth floor as a means of preventing escape. Three years earlier, he successfully robbed a Charleston jewelry store. The heist had been successful, but enough clues led police to Charlie's home north of the city.

Fearing discovery, Charlie prepared several gasoline bombs. The first combustible cocktails popped against the hard hoods of the police vehicles and ignited. As Charlie threw the third bottle, it tipped back too far, spilling gas and flame onto Charlie's face and chest. Three years on, the resulting burns remained prominent on his face, chapping almost every centimeter of skin below his eyes. His lips had healed into his skin, making them invisible against his reddened complexion. The shriveled mass of his nose protruded weakly from his face. What parts had healed did tautly, giving his complexion a waxy appearance.

The justice system seemed sympathetic to his self-inflicted circumstance. The judge sentenced him to Weston Hospital rather than hard time at the Moundsville State Prison.

The only thing about his new appearance considered fortunate by some was his face no longer registered Asian features. It spared him from being housed in the minority ward—the section of the hospital where conditions were most dire. Eugene never knew the reason why it was so bad. He decided either because conditions were a horror beyond speaking, or because the less racially tolerant of the hospital staff decided it was the worst by ignorance. Either way, rumors spread as such, and there was no way to separate them from truth, fiction, and madness.

Eugene was intolerant of racism. He saw a lot of it in the army and in the way Black troops remained segregated from their lighter counterparts. Though he didn't see too many Black individuals in his Nicholas County hollows, he spent a day with a platoon in the French countryside during The Great War and found them to be the same as anyone else. They laughed the same, feared the same and dreamed the same, and the blood they shed for the country was the same color as anyone's. From then on, for every racist comment Eugene consumed, two insults would counter the speaker's ignorance.

"People are who people are, and that's all they can be," he would often declare once the spat ended. However, for a long time, he harbored the belief homosexuality and gender identity were products of choice. The former eased by his wife's insight toward a greater love for all humanity.

Though Eugene had reason to cross the first two from his list of intolerances, he had reason to add inbreeding to his list. Hector Tompkins was such a product, and his simple nature kept him stowed among the halls of the hospital. One of five children to parents who were half siblings, Hector was born and raised in the isolated woods of central West Virginia. The mountainside on which his family resided was many miles from a civilized center. The families who lived in the deep woods spent years intermingling genetics until a single family formed and remained. It was a problem among the hills for a time, eventually resolved by modernized infrastructure. It was too late for Hector, who possessed a toddler-like view of the world even though he was approaching midlife. He had a crooked smile, which was almost constantly turned upward in increasing variables of joy. He laughed at almost every comment directed at him, pleased more at social interaction than the weight of any subject, pleasant or dire. His laugh was guttural and full of abandon. His happiness measured against his lot in life was envious.

Hector's existence saddened Eugene. His parents—much like the teens of the ward—were victims of the combination of arousal and limited options. It was a choice that affected the souls of the next generation. There was an unfairness to it. People are who people are, after all. But Hector didn't have to be who he was. That was his parent's choice.

Hector kept to himself. He usually remained in the room and played with wooden blocks with the corners filed smooth.

In contrast, Charlie spent his time outside as much as possible. Though he was a criminal sentenced to an unspecified amount of time at Weston, he had gained the trust of the hospital staff. The trust was regularly tested by Charlie's habit of spending any free moment near the edge of the wrought iron fence. He flaunted the minimum-security nature of the facility but never breached the boundaries outright. He would, however, return often with a carton of cigarettes tucked under his shirt.

"Where are you acquiring this contraband?" Eugene finally asked.

Charlie thought of the shortest way to answer the question. "A friend stole crates. Provides weekly."

"What do you do with them all?" Eugene asked. The plan he had for burning down the building was now in place, but he needed funding to implement it in a way that kept him distant from blame.

"Sell them in Bedland."

"What? Bedland?"

Charlie acted as if he wanted to clarify further but stopped himself and nodded.

Eugene perked and patted Charlie on the shoulder. Charlie winced and Eugene drew back. He realized he had no idea how extensive Charlie's burns were under his gown.

"Hey, listen," Eugene started. "I am in critical need to raise funds for a project, and I wonder if I can deal in on your enterprise."

Charlie grunted and limped to his bed. "What do I get?"

"Depends. How high do you price this illicit mercantile?"

"A penny each."

Eugene sat on his new bed and whistled to himself. "Do you think you can increase it to a dime?"

Charlie grunted again, this time with a heavy mix of irritation.

"The way I reckon it," Eugene said, "the only folks in this establishment who have any coin on them either find it, are given it by generous relatives, or are short-timers who bring their own change. In those first two scenarios, it won't matter to them how much a smoke costs. They either possess it, or they don't."

Another grunt came from Charlie, and he closed his eyes and caressed his chest.

Thinking he was still not convinced, Eugene moved to close the deal. "We'll split that in half between us. I'm only looking to raise ten dollars, so as soon as I fulfill my funding, you can either go back to selling penny smokes or keep the price at a dime and collect the full gross."

The final groan sounded more like a sigh. Charlie opened his eyes and nodded. "A dime."

Eugene lit up with excitement. "You agree?"

Charlie nodded again.

"Fantastic! How long does it take you to sell a carton?"

"Weeks." Charlie stuck out his thumb and motioned to the opposite edge of his bed.

Eugene made a confused face. "Weeks? Where are you housing them if they're not moving quick?"

Charlie leaned in the direction he faced and reached into the space between his mattress and the wall. He removed a full, unopened carton and held it above his head. "Help sell these fast, and I'll be happy."

*****

THE time between things happening at the Weston Hospital seemed to crawl at a sluggish speed. It had been weeks from the time of Eugene's admittance to the time he received his second evaluation from a doctor. It had now been two weeks since he found out Opal Lee was at the hospital, but in that time the doctors had yet to produce her for a meeting.

Eugene grew frustrated at the lag and went as far as venturing beyond the ward in hopes he could see her. Opal Lee had never made an appearance in the cafeteria during meal hours, but the dining hall could not sustain the entire asylum population, so meals were staggered. A floor at a time consisting of four wards each, though the first floor had the superfluous wards known as Bedland.

Bedland sounded like Bedlam to Eugene, which came from the name Bethlehem. *Not the birthplace of Jesus Christ*, Eugene hoped. He could not look at the inner workings of the hospital and see salvation. *It was certainly a place that could use the Lord's touch. Jesus himself was the only one ever to cure mental health by removing the demons from one's body and placing them into swine. Hogs so unnerved by the affliction found it best to run into a river and drown.*

Whatever festered within these captive souls was not so easily removed. Those tending to the ill already took the practice of tending hogs. *Perhaps that is why the gates were so easily passable. Access to the West Fork River made drowning an easy option.* Though, as it related to suicide, hanging remained the popular choice.

It was Peter who strung himself up by bedsheets on Ward T. After his bout with bad eggs and the altercation that followed, the gangly man became convinced the asylum food was being poisoned. He refused to eat and his weight plummeted. The tallest man in the ward went from pencil-thin to as frail and brittle as a graphite core. It became such a concern of the attendants that the orderlies strapped him to a chair and force-fed him butter. Convinced the substance was a poison, Peter saw no resolution but death. He waited until his roommates slept and tied a bedsheet around the vent grating above the door.

When the attendants discovered Peter the next morning, they ushered the Ward T population to the front lawn. Many still watched as orderlies carried Peter's covered body down the oak stairs en route to the morgue.

Eugene had made the occasional visit to the grounds in search of Opal Lee with no luck. Ward T was the only section on the lawn now, making a search for his daughter unnecessary. He would spend the morning focusing on his plan to burn down the hospital.

Though he spent plenty of time speaking with Flip on the floor, Eugene was very careful not to mention his plan in front of orbiting ears. Outside, the elements gave coverage to a conversation that needed to happen in private.

Flip stood by the empty fountain near the main entrance of the Kirkbride. Groundskeepers drained the basin a week earlier after someone slipped detergent into the cycling water. The ensuing foam expanded high and wide, spilling onto the nearby walkway and lawn. Grass unfortunate enough to be near the flow was discolored by the powerful lye, burning a brown circle around the masonry. Flip inspected the border where green grass met brown and kicked the darker grass to test for liveliness.

"Watching the grass grow?" Eugene asked. "It must be another exciting day on the nut farm."

Flip remained fixated on the varying greenery.

"I commend whichever lady or gentlemen of the gown played such a worthy prank on our dear administrator," Eugene gushed. "I expect Willard C. Crane was red in the face at such a display of chicanery."

"What do you have against Mr. Crane anyways?" Flip asked much in the same way he asked about Archibald weeks earlier. "You seem to curse his name quite a bit without resolution."

"Oh, I seek to resolve it. Yes, sir, we'll get to that in a moment. To answer your question, let's cast aside Willard's poor military leadership that needlessly ended the lives of current and future generation West Virginians. Mr. Willard and I were almost brothers-in-law."

Flip looked from the grass. "Oh, yeah? In what way?"

"He was betrothed to Ethel's sister as a way for advancing his position among Weston's elite," Eugene explained. "The dowery ended when she died of influenza. Her fate matched the other viable daughters of the Bloom clan. Seeing as how I was already married to the remaining local daughter; a deep jealousy seeded within Willard. It has come to bud with my incarceration in his facility. Yes, sir, mister. To elevate matters, my dear Opal Lee is now also a member of the socially discarded."

"You had mentioned that before," Flip said. "Did you ever locate her?"

Eugene shook his head. "If she is here, they have tucked her somewhere within the acreage that I cannot view. My doctor has not paid me a visit since the revelation as well. Only that she was here and had been for some time. He agreed to arrange a gathering, but no word has come back from that golden Northerner. Surely the Scandinavian thinks me a cod—salty, slippery and full of lies. Yes, sir, President—"

Flip cut off the continuing rant. "I'm sure you'll see her soon."

Eugene detected a downtrodden nature to Flip and changed the subject. "Hey, you ever finish reading that book? The one about the bridge?"

"*The Bridge of San Luis Rey?* Yeah. It is a sad book."

"Oh? What is it about?"

"In short, it's about why bad things happen to good people."

Eugene scratched his beard. "Does it provide an answer?"

"No." Flip was glum in his answer. "At least not in a way that I found."

"I could give you that answer. The reason bad things happen to good people is there are no good people. Yes, sir, there is only a good presentation."

"Can I provide a different answer?" the voice of Archibald offered from their backs. Flip and Eugene turned to see the man standing with a humble posture, straightened in a way that felt disciplined and non-threatening.

Though Eugene's time in solitary was because of his tumble with Archibald, Eugene felt an uncommon peace pass between them. There was also something to be said for how two people duking it out could ease tensions. Whatever the case, Eugene felt happy to see his old roommate.

Eugene bowed his head. "You may proceed with your answer."

"Bad things happen to good people because God does not judge us while we are still alive. There would otherwise be no point of an afterlife judgment."

After a moment of considering the answer, Eugene hummed to himself and nodded. "The logic is sound in your testament."

Archibald took the agreement as an invitation to approach. "I want to apologize. My beliefs on life and death were wrong and now I am questioning everything I knew. Before my church drank the poison, our leader told us our deaths would not matter because the world was ending on July third of this year. A prediction based on his interpretation and an angel who confirmed his belief in a vision."

"He told me this last week," Flip added.

Archibald sighed. "The only thing in this world that can negate a stubborn lie is the indisputable truth. When July third came and left, I knew for sure the stories I was told all those years were all a jumble of deceit. So many people died who didn't need to."

Eugene offered a smile. "It seems my path has always run diametric of yours. I remained clear of churchgoing to stave off the judgmental gaze of a small community. My grandfather of Gad was well-known as one of the more unsavory types. Sunday worship was one of the few places where everyone gathered in a congregation, and it became clear to my mother that she was the subject of the parishioners' whispered tongues. She avoided church like the plague from then on, and so did I for much the same reason." Turning to Flip, Eugene added, "I will also point out the Bloom daughters were church frequenters who likely caught their bout of influenza in the sanctuary. Yes, sir. So, when I say avoid it like the plague, I mean not as a turn of phrase."

"I would like to start over—my life, that is," Archibald said. He looked to the rising clouds in the morning sky. Maybe go as far as changing my name. Uh … Could we maybe forge a new path forward together? You've had too little religion, and I've had too much. We can look to strike a balance?"

"If the two of us escape this place, I'd be agreeable to it," Eugene responded with a snort. "There's no place to do so beforehand. Trying to gain religion while already in hell is surely moot."

The bell rang for breakfast and the attendant called from the main steps.

"Ah, Flip, hold here a minute," Eugene requested while Archibald and the others shuffled toward the Kirkbride to the dining building. Eugene waited and looked around to make sure no one was within earshot.

"I'm looking to raze this mental fortress with a hellfire so intense, they'd never think to build on this spot again. Now, what are your thoughts on that?"

Flip's eyes seemed to dart outward. "Well. Are you going to do that with people inside?"

"Ideally, no, but doing so may be perceived as more humane."

Flip sighed and coughed and spit in almost the same outward burst of air. "Why are you telling me this?"

"I would prefer one of your pyromaniac friends do the deed. They already have the will, what they lack is the financial backing and encouragement from an endeavoring adult."

Groaning, Flip pressed his thumb against a closed eye and rubbed. "I'm not going to tell them that."

"Nor should you. Yes, sir, you are a good kid who is a mere victim of circumstance. I imagine you will leave here, and life will treat you well. All I ask is you identify the adolescent fire starters and arrange a meeting with me. I will tell you no more of my plan if it makes you feel more at ease."

Another barrage of windy noises came from Flip. "All right."

"Wonderful. Let's go reunite with Archibald. If he's changing names, I have a few suggestions."

The two began walking toward the Kirkbride, passing straight through the main hallways and through the back door to the cafeteria.

"You know, Archibald spent a couple of days in solitary confinement, too," Flip revealed when they reached the front door to the Kirkbride.

"Huh," Eugene mused. "I'd say he got the better attitude adjustment. Wouldn't you?"

"I'd say you came out in opposite directions, which makes the truce between you all the more baffling."

*****

234

I**f** Bedland were Bethlehem, there likewise would have been no room for a newborn Christ. A manger would have already had an occupant if one had been in the ward.

The other striking thing Eugene noticed about Bedland was the lack of attendants or orderlies. They remained at a station in the perpendicular hallway. There wasn't room for them inside. Just as it was described, the beds were side by side, so tightly packed patients had to crawl over the foot bar to lay down. The concrete floor was only visible for a three-foot width before a new row of beds began. Three rows in all ran the length of the corridor, which did not appear to be the same length as a regular ward. The two Bedland wards ran west from the buildings and only consisted of a single floor. It was one of the oldest parts of the building, which was evident in the exposed stonework near the top of the wall. It looked like river stones were directly plucked from the West Fork and hammered into their respective grooves.

With a carton of cigarettes cradled under his arm and an open pack grasped in hand, Eugene shuffled through the cramped space.

"Cigarettes, just a dime!" At first, he was concerned about an official hearing the solicitation, but the deafening volume of the room prevented discernible words from escaping.

"Cigarettes, just a dime!"

A man came forward with a nickel. "Could you split one in half?"

Eugene huffed. "No, but find another companion with a nickel and you can split it yourself."

Eugene had told his Ward T attendant he was going to try at arts and crafts. It was paper mâché day, and the vast majority of those attending were looking forward to making dolls from wet newspaper. The cover story would only hold as long as no one noticed his absence in the arts and crafts room.

"Lucky Strikes, ten cents each!" Eugene called out. "Finest snipes available on the market today. Yes, sir, you'll feel ten feet high when you puff one of these."

A hopeful man approached with a copper coin in his flat palm. Eugene regarded it with disappointment. "I'm afraid you cannot sew a wheat penny with what I am offering. These smokes are priced at a premium. Take it from me, good sir, the funds will be well utilized."

The man lowered his hand in a fist and hissed before bounding back into the sea of people.

Eugene tiptoed around men curled on the path, men who sat cross-legged playing cards, and men who sat with legs stretched, singing garbled songs to themselves. They paid little attention to Eugene and his attempts to render transactions against a penniless population.

For the first time, he began to feel uneasy in a room with the mentally ill. Eugene chalked it up to the overcrowding. The pressure of the room squeezed on his temples and rang a minor headache in the space above his sinuses. The volume of the chatter, wails, and cries did not help matters. Even disregarding those aggravations, there was a note of sadness whistling at such a high pitch he could not detect the note until now. It struck a deafening tone on Eugene's soul. He looked around the room, into as many eyes as he could, and slumped in defeat. For many, their stowage within hospital walls would be a lifelong commitment. He was beginning to feel unsure of his own mental aptitude, but he did not actualize it yet. For now, Eugene had hope his grand arson would set them all free. All he had to do was keep pressing forward.

"Cigarettes! Get your cigarettes here!" Eugene called as he returned to the beginning of the room. "Each purchase is an investment in your liberation from this madhouse."

After splitting the profit with Charlie, he would only need to sell four-hundred cigarettes to raise his intended funds. It sounded like a daunting task, but that many cigarettes only amounted to two cartons, and he had already made twenty cents off the first Bedland ward.

The second ward came up empty, leaving Eugene to only part with two cigarettes in total. Dejected, he exited the ward and began back to the oak stairwell. He considered smoking a cigarette himself, but doing so would require reimbursement. He did not want to cut his daily profit in half.

"Deed," he said in defeat. He placed a cigarette on the corner of his lip with no intent to smoke it. He just wanted to have the sensation of doing so for a moment.

"Are you lost?" a woman in a white nurse's outfit called to him from a hallway door.

"No, I am not," he answered and tucked the cigarette back in the pack. "Yes, sir, Mister President, I am in no hurry to get where I am going."

TO LOVE

John Rocco's computer workshop was nearly empty. Only a dozen boxy monitors remained, arranged by screen size along the room's back wall. The sanitation service frowned upon disposing the screens, but were required to take them away, regardless. To ease the garbage man's disdain, Glenda and Brittany would periodically sneak a screen into a black garbage bag with lighter materials.

Glenda's outlook on life seemed to improve after the initial month of grieving. Her wine consumption decreased, and she began to go on regular walks to contemplate her new era of widowhood. Her viewership of cable church programming continued, but she no longer spoke about the end of the world. The apocalypse had already come for Glenda, and she withstood it in a way she did not expect. It had to be God who saw her through, and all praise continued to flow to him and his broadcast partners.

An empty lot? Brittany could not fathom what would cause their house to vanish in the next twenty years, but she made sure it would not fall under her watch. Brittany made regular checks of all the areas where a fire could ignite. She even persuaded Glenda to hire an electrician to confirm the wiring was still to code. Once fireproofed, Brittany assumed a blaze could only raze the house in the event of human error. She eyed every lit candle and made sure the baseboard heaters were clear of stray debris that could combust when used in the late fall.

Given the tragedy of her father's death, Brittany chose not to go to college for the fall semester, out of concern for her mother's wellbeing. She would consider a winter start or hold off until the following year. Glenda was growing more self-sufficient every day. A sign that told Brittany West Virginia University would not have to wait long for her arrival.

Sam Beck became the temporary manager of RadioShack. For a moment, it seemed as if he would not have a college career as well. His parents insisted against it, as they had already paid a semester's tuition out of pocket, along with a year's lease on a house near campus. With no choice, the regional manager brought back an unlikeable fellow named Doug, whom John Rocco had demoted as assistant manager before Doug quit outright.

Jennifer also had her departure to college thrown into doubt. Grandfather Vernon suffered a stroke in early August. With the new, addled state of his mind came a revelation. He was not Vernon Sampson. Embarrassed by his time in the Weston Hospital, he changed his name in the late 1930s. Whether it was brain damage or sixty years of disuse, Vernon could not recollect his real name. The records had to be floating around, but even the oldest items he possessed only listed the name Vernon. He thought it might be Eugene, James, Archie, Frank, Larry. He seemed to even recall the name of a Lieutenant Rust. No answer was had before Vernon died a week later. The family's scouring of court records in the days following services revealed his birth name to be Archibald Jonah Clump. Given their patriarch's desire to change the name and keep it hidden forever, the family made no reference to it on the gravestone or obituary.

Sam and Jennifer overcame their hurdles to start higher education careers, and Brittany's barrier was almost cleared. Her only hesitation now was that she did not want to leave Neil.

The pair would meet every Tuesday, speak for an hour, and hold one another in the most awkward of ways. Brittany refrained from asking questions about the future, at Neil's insistence. He held concerns about the consequences of knowing too much about the things to come. He did consider the notion of telling her about national tragedies so she could see about preventing them. The idea was terrifying to Brittany, but she was up for it if it would change the world for the better.

Their Tuesday meetings would become difficult when she went to college, and Neil's Saturdays were the only nights he could be available. Even if they could resolve that issue, there was still a problem with getting into the building. Officer Prince was fine with continuing to deliver Brittany to the Weston Hospital on the nights when he was on-duty. For the nights he was not, Brittany began driving John Rocco's minivan and parking near the hospital grounds. Once there, the security officer, Chad Witschky, continued to allow her into the Kirkbride without question. She suspected his leniency was also why he permitted the police officers into the building during their paintball escapades.

If she was ever busted by a higher authority, Brittany could at least pose the same defense the officers had. *It is not trespassing if you were allowed into the building. Officer Chad would have to be thrown under the bus once again.*

It had been two weeks since she had spoken with Officer Prince, and tonight would be no different. On their last trip, he admitted to her that he and the town officers involved in the paintball exercise were now under investigation by the West Virginia State Police superintendent-colonel. The state police officers also involved in the incident were on administrative leave. If the state investigators decided to come down on them, there would be no one to stand up for them in the chain of command.

With another Tuesday upon them, and Officer Prince taking an earlier patrol, Brittany drove the minivan to the town office and parked it in the lot. From there, it was only a block of walking to get to the main gate of the hospital compound.

"There you are again," Chad commented after shining a light on Brittany. "How goes the spook hunt?"

241

"I think I'm going to get 'em this time," Brittany replied with false enthusiasm. She held up a cassette recorder. "I'm going to see if I can catch a voice on tape tonight."

The security guard swung his arm toward the door. "Go right ahead. If you get anything weird, please share."

"Will do."

Brittany and Neil tried to understand the logic behind how they were able to communicate. They spoke at length, but it was more about throwing half-cocked ideas and seeing if they could land a eureka moment between them.

"I had a dream about you," Neil would say when he and Brittany first made contact on September seventh. "Well, it was kind of about you."

"Please tell me," Brittany pushed.

"We were in a massive room. Like, an endless auditorium. Walls, benches, and seats were all white, like the light was drowning out all the color. The people sitting in rows were of all races and nationalities. Everyone was there, and everyone was singing in their native tongues. I've never been a good singer. I can't carry a tune in a bucket, but still, I joined in song, and as the notes came out, they perfectly fell into tune with the chorus. The languages I couldn't understand all fell into place; the accents I couldn't discern all aligned with their part of the chorus. The message I understood was that we all play a part in the choir. No matter how we sound, it all fits into place as an ensemble. The loss of any of us would cause the song to fall flat."

"Kinda about me?" Brittany wasn't sure what her part in the dream was until the two sat on the cold floor.

"At the end of the dream, as I was singing, I caught an ear of your voice, your piece in the song. I scanned the row for you, but couldn't make out your image. The light was drowning everything out. It wasn't until you heard my voice and looked back at me that we connected. You smiled this beautiful smile as everything else faded away, and your glowing face was all I could see."

Brittany was glowing from hearing the story, though Neil would not know. She was always glowing with whatever spectral illumination lit his presence.

Brittany hoped the sentiment she had brought would compare. The tape Brittany had in her recorder was not for capturing purposes. It was a mixtape she had compiled for Neil.

The sounds around them seemed to travel over their connection, and Brittany did not have to play music very loud for Neil to hear on his end. Because of this, Brittany was all too eager to share her music tastes with someone.

Neil's musical preference of the late 1990s had been pop and rap, and he now regretted sleeping on the post-grunge era. It was a problem to which she had a remedy. However, there were ulterior motives to Brittany's music selection. She kept her plan hidden on the third song.

"'Raspberry,' by I Mother Earth. It's a Canadian group I discovered through a satellite channel called *Much Music*." She played the song, which clocked in at more than five minutes. Neil seemed to enjoy it, bobbing his head at the parts that rocked the most. He leaned back while sitting and propped himself up with both hands, leaving Brittany to keep connection by holding his knee. There was something about grasping any part of him that wasn't a hand that felt some new level of awakening inside her. There was no way to act on it until a romantic interest physically materialized.

The entire length of the song played before Brittany announced the next recording. "This one is a West Virginia band called Distorted Penguins." She pressed down on the play button.

A few seconds in, Neil interrupted her. "Oh, this isn't alternative rock. It's, um, whatcha call it? Jive? Jump, jive, and wail?"

"Ska," Brittany corrected.

"Yeah, Ska. This isn't really my thing. I was looking for some harder music."

Brittany felt nervous about playing the third track now, but she fast-forwarded the tape and landed a few seconds before Tonic's "Lemon Parade" began.

"Can we dance?"

Neil pushed his body forward, but Brittany disconnected and stood. She reached down for his hand like she had the power to lift him. He mimed a firm grasp with hers but then pushed himself upward with the hand still behind him.

Neil was a couple of inches taller than Brittany, and he looked down at her with a caring expression. She returned a look of captivation as they swayed in place, and Neil seemed to take note. He had seen the look before at some prom or homecoming dance ages ago, when a closed loop of infatuation could be achieved with hands around the hips and hands around the shoulders.

"I can always smell something when you are near," Neil said as his face drifted close to her neck. "It's the smell of cucumber and something else."

"It's cucumber melon," Brittany answered without delay. "It's a lotion I use."

Neil made an appetizing sound. "Cucumber melon, I will have to remember."

She couldn't look past the fact he was older, which gave her some discomfort, but the age was only relevant to their era. Somewhere in her world, there was an age-appropriate Neil, doing keg stands and chomping on cheap pizza at some covered-porch ramshackle off the main college campus. She wanted so bad to go there and find him. In their conversations over the last two months, he had already given her all the clues she needed. He lived on Grant Avenue in Morgantown, where the wild parties happened, in a blue, two-story house near the only dorm on the street.

"Whatever feelings we may be having, for us to be fully together is impossible right now. I know that," Neil said. The comment snapped Brittany from her pining. Her want for him must have been bleeding across the ages.

"Any time you miss me," he continued, "I want you to look to the moon. I want you to know I am looking at the same moon, and the *when* doesn't matter. The moon does not take measure by the same longevity of our lives. It looks back upon us with merely a single frame, a photograph of our existence in the stillness of time. When you look to the moon, the moon will look back, and so will I."

Brittany had been feeling more like a comet lodged from his orbit and drifting helpless and lonely across the cosmos. For now, it was about finding comfort, and his words soothed the soreness of her situation.

"Can we meet?" Neil asked, and asked with a measured tone that felt different, serious.

"If you would know me, I would run to WVU right now and see you," Brittany answered with eagerness. "I don't want to have to wait twenty years to meet you for real the first time."

"I know, but there is no other way," Neil said, and caressed what he could sense was the back of her head. She felt it, though her hair did not move with the action.

"I don't want to wait." Brittany turned her head and leaned it toward his chest. "I love you now."

"How about Halloween in 2019?" Neil did not respond or reciprocate her declaration of affection. "What better time for two ghosts to meet?"

"Yeah." Brittany thought she had lost connection with him then, and he did not hear the comment. She wasn't ready to try again.

She looked up into his eyes. "How about in the graveyard? That would be the most appropriate, wouldn't it?"

"I love the idea. Six o'clock?"

Brittany nodded and felt her lips pinch together. "Six sounds good."

"Write it down somewhere." The song ended and Neil stepped back from her while still touching her hand. "I don't want you to forget in twenty years."

Brittany looked at him with doe eyes as the song ended. "Oh, Neil. How could I forget?"

22

TO FORGET

It had been late June since Demetry last checked in with Neil. Despite his lack of communication, a check for two thousand dollars would arrive in the early part of each month. Neil would cash it, pay his meager rent, and head to the asylum to book a month's worth of ghost tours, paying the admission in advance. He budgeted the remaining money for food, gas, cell service, and other research expenses, as loosely defined.

"How is the book going?" Neil asked once he heard Demetry's voice on the other side of the call.

"It's moving along, but there are still a lot of hurdles to clear," Demetry said in a gruff voice. "Do you have time to look into some things for me?"

Neil scoffed. "Uh, yeah. Absolutely. This is the first assignment I've gotten since you left. Was starting to feel like I wasn't earning my keep. I got my check yesterday, by the way. I'm headed into Weston to cash it shortly."

"If you can keep me from hitting this dead end, you'll be worth every penny," Demetry assured. "Get something to take notes."

Pen and paper were absent in Neil's trailer. He had no need to write until this occasion. Thinking fast, Neil opened a text app on his phone and moved Demetry to the speaker.

"Ready," Neil announced, thumbs poised at the keys.

Demetry cleared his throat. "The final entry of Silkie's journal, dated New Year's Day in 1906. '*I have written many letters to my dear Henrietta, but she has not returned. Perhaps the letters are not finding their mark. I had no address to go by, but I sent them to her last known town in hopes the postmaster would direct them to her door. Time has grown short, and the pain calls me. I have placed a curse upon the stone of Jasper Wyatt and anyone who disturbs him. Eight hundred and fifty-one steps from the clock arrow will tell you more.*'"

Demetry concluded his reading. "And that's it—the diary ends there. Silkie hanged herself from a transom five days later, and her diary found its way into the public record of the hospital. Then, into legend."

"It's strange no one has investigated this until now," Neil commented as he finished typing. "Do you need me to walk 851 steps from the clock tower?"

A groan came from the phone. "That doesn't make sense. The clock still works, doesn't it?"

"Sorta," Neil answered. "And you're right, it doesn't make sense. Plus, there are three different clocks up there."

There was a brief silence before Neil continued. "Want me to check the cemetery for Jasper Wyatt?"

Demetry scoffed. "I doubt you'll find it. Stay out of there. But to your point on the lack of investigation, there were a lot of strange deaths back in those days. Primitive forensics hadn't yet expanded to bullet analysis. Even if it did, they never found her gun. I would consider that my holy grail on this quest. We could unlock so much more if we had that one item."

An idea lit up in Neil's mind. "That reminds me. I have a friend at the hospital who gives tours. He said there is an abandoned tunnel in the basement that contains a mountain of unclaimed items—decades worth. Maybe her gun is hidden in there?"

"I don't know, man," Demetry said. "What are the odds of it being down there for one hundred and fourteen years?"

"I reckon it depends on when the tunnel was abandoned," Neil replied before exiting his trailer.

"I reckon?" Demetry repeated. "Sounds like your Appalachian dialect has returned."

"I like 'I reckon,'" Neil defended as the neighborhood tabby brushed his ankle. "It's a term that says, 'I very much agree,' but with the suppression of any kind of enthusiasm."

Demetry hooted. "Whatever, man."

Neil ignored him. "If there is a chance the gun is still inside the asylum, that is the most likely place it is going to be. You gave me a job, now let me do it."

Neil bent to scratch the cat's back, which arched its body in approval. Rainclouds were fat on the horizon, and the stray feline seemed to forego the day's hunt for a position close to shelter.

"Do your job then, Neil," Demetry said. "You'll not hear me complain about money well-spent. Besides, I will absolutely jump at the chance to visit a room no one has seen for several decades."

The friend was a tour guide named Brady, who had split time between overnight paranormal tours and daytime tours devoted to the criminally insane. By chance, Neil encountered Brady between bank errands as Neil entered into the Kirkbride to book a new set of night tours.

"You're not working today?" Neil asked Brady as they passed.

Brady held up an envelope. "I was just coming to get my paycheck."

"Do you think you have time to show me the basement tunnel today?" Neil asked in haste. "I was conscripted into asking as part of my research work."

The question planted Brady on the ledge of the stairs, and he scratched his dark stubble. Guests and another employee milled past, and Brady waited for them to clear them before continuing. "We're not really allowed down there. We'll need to be sneaky about it."

"That's fine. As long as I can get down there to verify some things, it'll at least ensure I get my next paycheck."

Digging into his pocket, Brady retrieved his phone and checked the time. "How about I meet you back here in a half hour? I want to get my check in the bank and pick up Audrey. Do you know her?"

Neil nodded. "Yeah, she's been my guide a couple of times."

"We're dating," Brady said, as if embarrassed. "She has a key to the side door near the basement entrance and has also wanted to see what's down there. She's big on patient rights and has wanted to see the contents of the luggage for some time. For letters, or memorabilia that can be returned to surviving family members."

Neil snorted with derision. "How would you even go about doing that?"

"There are plenty of genealogy resources out there." Brady started to step away. "You'll have to ask Audrey about it. She will give you an earful."

*****

A passage near Second Street allowed the trio to enter a back way. The whitewashed door was rotten and appeared as if it could be yanked from the frame with ease. Despite the door's sorry condition, the handle was brand-new, and Audrey had one of the few existing keys.

The entrance led them down a hallway of murals that once made up the arts and crafts section. Plastered along the hallway was an illustrated cliffside lighthouse overlooking the ocean, and a painting of a rainbow arching over a green field into a pot of gold. The faux frescos were not *The Last Supper*, but they, too, endured long after their creators.

The stairwell past the section was covered in grime and decay from the building. Rust and plaster had snowed from the ceiling and accumulated on the cement steps. Paint peeled in wide ribbons and hung like loose bark from the walls.

"It's creepier down here than anywhere else," Neil remarked as he affixed a headlamp to his ballcap.

"I expect the basement is worse," Audrey commented, sidestepping loose boards lying across the landing.

Beyond the pile was an unpainted metal door. It looked as if it had not seen use in ages, but Audrey assured him a maintenance worker slipped through weeks earlier. The door squealed open as Brady loosened it with a forceful push of his shoulder.

"Careful," Audrey chided. "The door may be supporting the wall more than you realize."

Even so, the door only widened enough for one body to slip through at a time. Neil squeezed through the narrow opening. The echoes of his noises indicated a cavernous space in front of him. He activated his headlamp and looked deep into the room, finding no end with the power of his bulbs. The light added by Brady and Audrey's heavy-duty flashlights still did not reveal a terminus, but an end was not what they were seeking.

Dirt and muck coated the surface and carried a few inches up the wall. The sublevel appeared to have flooded at least once in recent history. Archways girded the passage walls every fifty feet and looked as ornate as the main hallway in the Kirkbride. But this area was not meant for public eyes and had hosted none for many decades.

Brady pointed to the floor. "There may have been a railway system here, from what I understand. It would ferry items from one side of the hospital to the other. They think it was to deliver food. At one time, the kitchen was clear on the southern side of the building. I imagine dinner would be cold by the time it was walked to the northernmost ward."

"That must have been later though," Audrey said, trudging down the tunnel. "Originally, this area was used to pump heat into the building from the boilers in another building." She stopped at a wide opening a quarter way down the corridor and shined her light into the crannies. After some investigating, she turned and pointed into the maw. "One of the shafts collapsed further down, but this one looks to be where the abandoned baggage is."

Neil approached and glanced into the squared ventilation shaft. The new tunnel extended deep into the backyard and disappeared into shadow. But before the dark could swallow it, stacks of bags and trunks lined the channel. Forgotten and tangled with cobwebs, the luggage was so caked in dust their true colors were unrecognizable.

The opening was tall enough for Neil to stand upright without scraping his head against the stone. He walked along the wall of items and made careful work of examining the size of each one.

"What my author friend is looking for is a large, long case—at least the size of a rifle."

Audrey cut to the obvious. "Is your guy looking for a rifle?"

"Yes," Neil replied. "It's probably a long shot, no pun intended. Every inch of this building is worth a search."

About halfway down the row, Neil found a stack of four large trunks, amassed evenly for being a similar shape and size. "Here." Neil pulled the top two trunks by their handles, but the grip of one snapped and crashed on the floor. The echo was tremendous and all three cringed at the sound. Neil left it where it fell and grabbed the third one.

"Let's take a quick glance at these and see if we can at least find what era we're in."

Brady opened his case first. It was a brown leather-lined case that had severe water damage on its top. The lid creaked with disuse and fell open with a defeated *thud*.

Brady shuffled through a stack of white and blue cloth. "There are some clothing items here, nothing interesting otherwise."

Neil went to work on his case and found the clasps so rusted they snapped off when he tried to open them.

"Try not to destroy these," Audrey warned. "These belonged to somebody once."

"They're destroyed either way." Neil groaned as he removed one of many silver cans from the steamer. "US ARMY FIELD RATION C," he read aloud from the side of the can. "There are at least eight of these inside."

"Likely World War II era," Brady noted.

Neil sighed. "I'll need to go at least forty more years back."

Brady held the light to his face. "Let's finish these out to see if they're in chronological order, then we'll move on to another stack. I'm sure there are more tunnels with these down the way."

Audrey opened her case as Neil pushed aside his first dud to focus on the trunk on the bottom of the stack. It was black with silver buckles, almost identical to the one Audrey was opening. The only discernible difference was Audrey's had a scuffed Toronto travel sticker affixed to the lid.

"A typewriter …" Neil noticed right away and lifted a silky material next to it. "Women's underwear, I think." He peered deeper. "Blank paper, some round items like little film tins. Some beauty items I don't recognize. I think this might have been lipstick?"

"A letter!"

Neil looked to see Audrey raising a brittle piece of paper as high above her head as the ceiling would allow.

Brady peered into the case. "Looks like you hit the jackpot there."

"I did," she answered, excited, and matched his gaze back to the case. "It looks like there is an empty picture frame, a stained picture of some woman, and a pair or two of suspenders."

Audrey shoved her flashlight into Brady's empty hand and quelled as she delicately opened the note.

"What's it say?" Brady asked with an eager whisper.

She scanned the first line and began to read:

OCTOBER 1, 1935

A brief account of Eugene James David Spangold

I willfully submitted to the Weston Hospital after committing transgressions against the Floyd Funeral Home. It consisted of property damage through bladder alleviation and drunkenness beyond my character and that of a basic civilized man. My issue with alcohol began with my daughter's estrangement, that, of this moment, has not yet found resolve.

My daughter, Opal Lee, struck out on her own after an argument with her mother on Christmas Eve of 1931. I was near the barn, chopping wood and only witnessed her departure at a distance. My wife, Ethel LeeAnn, stated Opal Lee had intended to see friends rather than spend the holiday with us, and that was a sin too great against our family in Ethel's eyes.

As a father, I tried to avoid the hooch, as both my grandfathers were wholly consumed. But having felt unemployed as a parental worker, I saw no need to evade the family curse. And so, I consumed alcohol, and the alcohol consumed me. For four years I let the haze drift me through melancholy days until I set anchor at this sullen port. This hospital where souls set alight with madness are put aside to let their candles rend to unusable nubs. What maddens me? Even in this confessional, there are things I am not willing to consider because the regrets have pressured me in ways that cannot be released without a forceful explosion against my frame. We won't speak to that mania, though the spirits play a role.

It was otherwise the round nature of the universe that has most disturbed me. The years, the circling bodies churning in perpetual unison. The wheel spins, history plays along, and we return to start. Repeat. The repetition is as maddening as the realization the cycle is eternal. Time is a sound that echoes in distant halls and reprises into oblivion. Long past my demise will my spoken words fade to silence within the reverb? Or will they be noted and scrawled in some clerk's fat tome for the remainder of recorded history? Would my legacy support that? Would my imprint on Earth even be worth the ink in the obituaries to come? When my mortal motor seizes, the soul driving this jalopy body will not sit patient. My spirit will exit the heap, pat away the dust of mortality, and amble onward. I will lap this world until the resolution I crave is found. A ghost chases the horizon when its desires remain beyond sight. Another unending loop is all I expect to find, though each revolution should bring me past a better season. Something to look forward to along the circuit. When you catch my name spoken in the spiraling light of day or some midnight hour, what emotion will it evoke? There must be more to my tale than what is inscribed here. To whoever reads this letter: Don't allow me to be a fading echo. Tell my full story if you can find it among the heap of broken tales. It will still be here, somewhere.

Yours in life,
EJD SPANGOLD

Someone was speaking to Neil from the past. Brittany had always done so, but her plight was not one of captivity. This man from eighty-four years prior was speaking from his soul directly into Neil's. It was the only way the man could communicate now. Neil preferred the memory of a person to the actual person because sympathy was not required. It was an assault on the fortifications that held his regard for other people in check. He closed his empathy off years ago, for fear it would grow too great—that all grief would consume him. It began when his brother died. The pain felt so great. Neil abandoned much of his feelings for others. He would rather feel nothing at all than feel such sorrow again. The barrier was now cleft, the breach sent forward the emotions he had been holding back and was bound to let something enter the vacuum.

"These were real people." Neil closed the trunk and sat on it. It slumped under his weight.

Audrey furrowed her brow and motioned at the endless wall of luggage. "Each one of these was a person. Not only that, but these had to be people who never left. Or they decided the things they brought were no longer important to their freedom."

"We're only looking at one row," Brady added. "There are probably more in the other tunnels."

Neil sobbed. He tried to laugh to mask the emotion, but it only distracted his facial muscles blocking the tear ducts. The weight of the revelation pressed his being, and briny secretions emerged from his eyes. He tried to hold back, but it was dark enough, and his friends had the courtesy to aim away their lights.

"We had such fun on the night tours," Neil said after a long breath. "It is so easy to not consider the actual persons who suffered through it. Physically, mentally, and emotionally—every piece of their being was butchered and left to rot. They broke everything. How can this place operate like it was okay?"

"We don't!" Audrey took offense to the comment. "This was never something to be sanitized. We educate all the same. If you came on more of the historical tours, you would know. That's not to say there aren't good folks on the night tours, but our drunken frat boy crowd is exclusive to the night. Ghost hunting seems like fun and games until you realize there was human misery attached to the other end."

Lifting his head, Neil thought again of Brittany and the mild deceptions he had put her through. He had feelings for her, but there was too much time between them. He could not go back, and she had too far forward to travel.

"What can I do to help these people?" Neil looked at Audrey. "What can I do to put these broken minds, bodies, and souls to rest?"

Audrey sighed in a determined way. "Find out who they were, who their families were, and tell their story. I can give you the resources to get started. There are a lot of bare family trees out there. We can add back some of the missing branches and leaves."

Resolute, Neil stood and nodded. "Show me how."

"Okay … but I'll have to warn you: the work is not easy and there are a lot of dead ends."

"Just like life," Neil summarized. "And try as I might, life was something I couldn't bring myself to hate."

TO HATE

HENRIETTA, FRIDAY, JULY 7, 1905

Wallace began to cry in the night. This and persisted long enough to arouse Mary in the other room. She beat a fist on the wall. Doing so only intensified the baby's sour mood. Rocking, singing, and nursing were unsuccessful. The babe only quelled when his cloth diaper filled with diarrhea. The room contained the means for Henrietta to clean the mess, but there was nowhere to extinguish the smell.

Exhaustion finally overtook Henrietta, and she slumbered well past sunrise. The daylight warming her face told her it was around ten o'clock. Now that she was able, Henrietta shifted onto her side to block the light.

The sounds of her bed creaking made a peculiar sound. The noise did not carry like normal. The discrepancy was enough for Henrietta to pry an eye open and scan the room. She could not see anything from the poor vantage, and she cleared her throat to make a new noise. The echoes seemed longer and fuller. It was a little detail of Henrietta's life, but little details were all she had for months. She knew they could add fast into bigger things.

Henrietta shifted to her back and immediately took sight with what was awry. The door was open. She looked to the bassinet to see Wallace still stationary and sleeping soundly. A twinge of the brow told Henrietta all was well with him.

She considered whether this was her moment to run. She rose, trying to limit her sounds. Everything about the opportunity signaled a trap, but Henrietta could not gauge how or why until it was too late.

The ward was completely silent. Breakfast had long passed, and it was not quite time for lunch. Henrietta inched her head through the door and peeked to the center of the building. No one. She looked down the hall, to the greater end of the ward, when something caught her around the neck.

"Gotcha!" an aggressive female voice shrieked.

Once the fabric was around Henrietta's neck, the woman pulled her to the ground and tightened the cloth before Henrietta could react. She could see Jansy Porter standing over her with an elated look detached from reality. She held a bedsheet with one end flattened and attached to Henrietta. She tried to scream, but Jansy already had the makeshift noose tight enough to obstruct the volume.

"I got you!" Jansy continued, elated, as she hauled Henrietta into the room next door, lacing slurs between heavy breaths. "Doc told me he'd lure you out with a fire drill, and you could be the thing we light up. We don't have the means to burn you, but we can give you a proper lynching like you deserve!"

Jansy pulled Henrietta into the center of hers and Mary's room and threw the opposite end of the bedsheet over a low pipe crossing their ceiling. Henrietta tried to take the split moment of release to get up and run, but Jansy retrieved the end as it came down from the pipe. Jansy yanked. Henrietta fell but caught her balance before the sheet could snap tight. Because her hands were still free, Henrietta grabbed the sheet above her head to take the pressure off her neck.

"Now you stop that!" Jansy kicked at Henrietta's shins, the only part she could reach. "You die like a good slave girl should."

Off the ground, Henrietta could see Mary was still in the room, too. She leaned forward in her bed and mindlessly cackled. She enjoyed the hateful spectacle as much as Jansy enjoyed executing it.

After a minute, Henrietta's arm muscles grew tired, but the older Jansy seemed spry and willing to hold tight for as long as the job took. To ebb the process along, Jansy would try to swing the sheet back and forth so the other end would mimic the movement and jostle Henrietta's grip.

"Come on, we don't have time for you to be stubborn," Jansy squawked.

Henrietta let one arm rest, but the tightness became too much around her neck, and she tried to pull herself back into position, to no avail. As she struggled, someone from the ward returned. Henrietta did not see or know who it was, but a very concerned voice called from the corridor.

"Jansy, what are you doing?"

"Mind your own!"

"No! I'm going to tell an attendant!" the woman replied and clopped down the hall.

Jansy let go of the sheet. Henrietta plopped to the floor, gasping.

"Stay there! I'll be back," Jansy threatened before dashing off to follow the witness.

Henrietta continued to choke and grapple for air while Mary laughed and pointed. Henrietta felt a dormant rage erupt, and she lunged at Mary, punching her in the face, which sent the old woman backward in the bed. Henrietta unbound the sheet from her neck and tied it around Mary's, leaving more length to guarantee a secure noose. She threw the sheet over the pipe, as Jansy had, and tugged as hard as she could. Mary was a smaller woman and much lighter than Henrietta.

She released a garbled sound before losing the use of her windpipe. With adrenaline pulsing, Henrietta managed to pull Mary high enough to tie the sheet to the end of the bedframe. Mary's writhing ceased by the time Henrietta exited the room.

Wallace remained sleeping when Henrietta returned to retrieve him. She struggled with the decision of whether to run or close her unlocked door and escape later. Henrietta chose to leave, even though doing so would imply guilt toward the person she rightly murdered. But if she stayed, they may find her guilty anyway. Then, her incarceration under Doctor Koenig would be permanent. Whereas escaping would allow her the chance of incarceration in a proper prison. Above all, running would benefit Wallace. He had the opportunity to live the good life he deserved.

Henrietta moved to the emergency exit leading to the side stairs. The fire drill crowd likely exited the building that way, but would not have come back, especially with the nurses' apparent disdain for the route.

After entering the stairwell, Henrietta left the door ajar with a nearby woodblock so she could hear the results of her actions.

"I was not trying to kill someone," Jansy said to whomever returned with the tattletale patient. "Just look and see!"

"Jansy, what have you done?" the attendant cried out. "You killed Mary!"

"I did not. It was that Black woman next door. The darky ghost!"

"Everyone is still out on the fire drill."

The witness was also there and chimed in with "This is what I saw. She was hanging someone!"

Jansy became belligerent "No. The doctor told me … No … Listen! It wasn't me; it was the nigg—"

Henrietta pulled the door closed and started down the stairs. She had heard enough.

At the bottom of the stairwell was a door leading to the rear courtyard of the hospital near the Black wards. It was Friday and the crew would already be working the garden.

The light blinded Henrietta for a moment, but her pupils adjusted enough to see a line of people shuffling into the back door of the Kirkbride.

"Hey, all of you!" Henrietta shouted to the row waiting to go inside. Many of them turned. Henrietta held up Wallace. "This is my baby! I had him with Doctor Felix Koenig! Tell all your friends!"

"All right!" one voice cheered back with an overabundance of vigor as others mumbled.

Henrietta began marching toward the field when she heard her name called from the rear door. She turned to see Felix.

"Vat are you doing?" he shouted across the yard. She was looking back at him from beyond the Black ward and felt confident she could beat him to the garden should it come down to a foot chase.

"You were trying to murder me?" Henrietta called back so all could hear. "You ordered this fire drill? That old dingbat you sent couldn't get it right. Murdered her roommate instead! You'll have to try it for yourself."

Doctor Koenig began marching at a brisk pace. Henrietta, concerned it could erupt into a sprint at any moment, began a brisk jog. It was several hundred yards before she would even be able to see the garden, but every time she looked back, Doctor Koenig appeared to be at the same distance.

"Silkie!" Henrietta called when she felt she was in earshot. "Silkie, it's time!"

She could see several individuals rise from the vegetation and stare, but could not detect if any among them was Silkie.

When she reached the fence line, Henrietta turned to realize Doctor Koenig had accelerated his pace and was gaining ground. Henrietta tried to maneuver, to evade and cut through the gate into the field. As she did, Felix lunged at her. He caught an ankle, causing Henrietta to fall. She twisted to give Wallace a soft landing and let him remain in the grass while she dealt with the father.

"Silkie!" she called out again and rose to glance back at the tree line. She thought she had spotted Silkie in that area, but there was no one.

"Silkie, help me!" Henrietta screamed again as the doctor regained his footing and lunged once more. He knocked her off balance, and as she fell, Felix's fingers caught her necklace. The pressure severed the strand. An explosion of bronze links glimmered in the light before they disappeared in the matted grass. The action threw Felix off balance, and he fell on top of Henrietta.

"Ich wurde wegen dir gefeuert!" Felix struck her across the chin. "Du wirst diesen Ort nie verlassen! I vill make sure you leave through das morgue!"

Felix hit Henrietta again. A burst of the light followed the blow to her temple; the impact briefly blurred her vision. The doctor got on his feet and had retrieved a hoe. He had not even raised it yet when Henrietta rose forward and grabbed the blade. He kicked at her but missed. He tried jerking the tool away from her, finding the first try unsuccessful. He tensed to heave again when something caught his eye. Silkie appeared from above Henrietta and struck Felix across the face.

Silkie looked at Henrietta. She had three streaks of bright blue across her face, painted on with her fingers. One line ran across her brow, and the other two ran over her cheeks below her eyes, skipping her nose.

"You need to run, now," Silkie commanded. Felix tried to rise again, but Silkie pressed him down with a foot and bent to slap him across the cheek, light blue paint exploding across his face as she did.

It was the last thing Henrietta saw at close range. She gathered Wallace and fled the garden, scooting as fast as she could to the opposite hillside. She touched a place where pain radiated from her neck and found the necklace had broken skin where it snapped. Her Indian Head Penny necklace was gone, lost somewhere in the field where there was no returning.

The thought of returning was further discouraged by the crack of a gun. The sound exploded across the small valley as the sound ricocheting in all directions. Henrietta dropped to the ground, uncertain if she had been the target. She secured Wallace's head and landed prone, leaving enough gap between her and the ground to avoid crushing his body.

A few seconds had passed. Henrietta detected no wound and glanced back to see all the members of the garden fleeing in every direction. Felix, or whom she presumed to be the doctor, lay by the entrance to the garden, writhing on the ground. He had been the target, but nothing else was clear.

Silkie did not appear armed before, and she now seemed to be absent from the garden altogether. Silkie had always operated with the scarcity of a phantom, and Henrietta had to leave it at that. Whatever the case, Henrietta knew Silkie made a sacrifice so Henrietta could have a chance at freedom. Now was the time to take it.

Henrietta got back on her feet and continued to the property line. Still thinking about the penny her mother had given her, she made a mental note of where they had scuffled. If she were ever to pass through Weston again, it was something she would need to remember.

TO REMEMBER

"Black flag up, boys. Today I have a grand bargain at no cost to your person but will garner you funds in the amount of a single sawbuck." Eugene held a crisp ten-dollar bill over his head with both hands. The boys marveled.

Charlie's associate had provided the bill in exchange for a weighty sack of dimes, nickels, and pennies Charlie begrudgingly delivered to their meeting point on the edge of campus. The three teens that stood beneath him oohed and jeered at the display of currency.

With cash now on hand, Eugene was meeting with as many teens as he could fit into his busy schedule of window-gawking. Reggie, the replacement in his old room, had died of a stroke in mid-September. The death gave vacancy to a space Eugene still coveted. He returned to his original perch behind the radiator and remotely coached the high school football team that practiced on the lawn. His afternoons were set aside for business affairs with the adolescents.

Flip had facilitated most of the meetings, but the three on the first day of October would be the last the young roommate could gather. The doctors and Administrator Crane granted him leave of their care, with September thirtieth being his last official day as a patient.

Eugene sighed at the thought, which staggered the rhythm of his spiel to the youths.

"Yes, sir, Mister President, like I stated, boys, the ripe sum of ten dollars in pure minted American legal tender can be yours simply for executing a deed in my stead. No, sir, this is no depression scrip. It is bona fide paper money and can be yours. All you need to do is put your God-given talents of pyromania to work. Hoist your dark flag of chicanery and set this structure ablaze. Mister President, set a spark as close to the clock tower that you can get and let that light accumulate the wealth for you." Eugene pinched the bill and rubbed his thumb and forefinger across both sides. "I tell ya, only one of you will be able to claim this prize, so act with haste. You are the last clutch of boys I've informed of this offer. The others have the advantage. Best get to scheming, gentlemen."

The boys shot from the floor and scattered from the room. Eugene watched the last depart, only to lock eyes with Archibald at the door.

Archibald chuckled to himself and sat on the edge of his mattress. "What wicked deed are you having these boys carry out?"

Eugene knew Archibald had asked the question in jest but elected to give the blunt answer. "I've tasked them with razing this fortress of frailty with hellfire so that we can purge demons from this place and return to the outside world. The kind of business that your late cult fellowship would endorse."

The smile left Archibald's face. "Are you making fun of me?"

"Huh?" Eugene grunted and then thought a second while he sat. "I suppose that does sound like some religious malarkey loose with your brand, but this is my own configuration of the world. Mister President. This palace of neglect must burn."

"Wait. You are serious?" Archibald's eyes widened and his breath grew short.

"Yes, sir. President of the United States told me to do it. Orders from the executive branch."

The ballooned eyes of Archibald darted around for a beat and a new smile grew, but it was one of blatant insincerity. "Is that what this president business is about? The one you often mention between sentences?"

"I do no such thing."

"You've been doing it for a while. Mixed with 'yes, sirs' and 'misters.' It's gotten worse since you were last in this room. Has no one mentioned it to you before?"

"It's the natural cadence of how I speak. No one gets uptight about it." Eugene leaned forward. "Don't sidestep the topic at hand. Now that I've told you my secret purpose, be a gem and do well not to share. You wouldn't want to be the Judas of my tale."

Archibald groaned and his mixed expression wilted into glumness. "That would be of concern if you were any kind of Jesus."

Eugene laughed, leaning back in his bed. "That's fair. Quite fair."

Before the levity could end, Flip returned to the room and gazed at both his former roommates. "Have they given my bed away yet?"

"Flip!" Eugene said with excitement. "We haven't been formally notified, but I expect reassignment is imminent."

Flip sighed. "My Aunt Eunice was supposed to pick me up this morning, but I haven't seen her yet. I'm afraid I'm going to spend my first day of freedom sleeping on the streets."

"Oh, dear," Archibald said.

"I tell you what"—Eugene stood—"you can take my bed if yours comes under contract. I need to make a focused effort to locate my daughter among these cavernous slums. With my prime directive nearly complete, I can finally focus on personal agendas."

"I appreciate that," Flip said of the bed.

"I mean, don't hang out about these grounds," Eugene insisted. "Come back before lockdown. If you're free, please do us the pleasure of gallivanting about the municipality. Do the things we aren't given access to. In fact, if you go now, I would like for you to procure some paper and a writing utensil from the nearest dealer of such mercantile."

"You can get that from the arts and crafts area now," Archibald noted.

Eugene pointed to him. "That's true! And on the government's coin no less."

*****

STARING from the window, Eugene dictated his letter while he watched the low sun cast brilliant beams over the autumn vegetation. The leaves had died their seasonal death, and their orange and red hues intensified as their journey back to the earth began. He considered the seasons while he spoke to the cycles of life.

"To whoever reads this letter." He paused to consider more about punctuation than what he knew. "Put a colon there, I think."

"Uh-huh," Flip confirmed while he scrawled. "Is it 'whoever' or 'whomever'?"

"I couldn't tell you."

Flip grumbled, and Eugene allowed the intermission before continuing.

"To whoever reads this letter, don't allow me to be a fading echo. Tell my full story if you can find it among the heap of broken tales. It will still be here, somewhere. Yours in life, EJD Spangold."

Eugene turned and his eyes adjusted to the room. "I reckon that will do. I wanted an account of my existence, should no other offering come available."

Flip sat his pencil down, along with the book he had used for a hard surface. Eugene extended a hand to retrieve the note. "I feel better," he concluded while he folded the letter into a quarter of its size.

"Good," Flip said. "You said your other project is finished? The one with the fire starters? Are they going to do it?"

"Time will tell," Eugene said with tepid optimism. "I expect one will devise a creative solution. The attendant is sometimes sloppy with supervision of the matches. It would only require a dab of luck to lift one from the box while he's helping light the daily drags."

Eugene laid on his bed and shifted so the box springs groaned and bobbled. He laid in the last light of day and picked at his fingers. It was a burgeoning habit he hadn't acknowledged until he noticed the skin around his thumbnails was raw.

"Mr. Spangold," a woman's voice called from the doorway. Eugene shifted to his far sight to catch Matron Stapleton. Shouldering her were two orderlies who looked as if they spent their free hours hoisting boulders.

"Present." Eugene shifted into a sitting position and gave a wide grin.

The display seemed to disturb the matron, and her jowls tightened. Eugene took pleasure in the achievement of bringing discomfort to a mastered nurse who had seen every displeasure the wards offered.

"Administrator Crane would like to speak with you about some pressing matters," she finally said. The matron took a step back into the corridor and allowed the strapping assistants to move through the door.

"I'll come willfully." Eugene lifted his hands and the grin vanished. "No need for brute force."

Eugene followed Matron Stapleton, clenching the folded note tight in his palm. For good measure, each of the orderlies took a hand under an armpit to prevent any sudden break for the exits. Upon leaving the room, Eugene spotted Archibald hugging himself on the opposite wall.

"Hey!" Eugene yelped to gain Archibald's attention. "Just as Judas betrayed Jesus, you have betrayed me. I'm not well read on the religious classics, but I know a Judas when I see one."

"No. It wasn't me," Archibald said, panic in his voice. "I did not squeal on you!"

"I brand thee Judas!" Eugene had to turn to point at Archibald, which forced the orderlies to take Eugene by the arms and drag him.

Archibald slumped further. Eugene cackled maniacally as the muscular men removed him from the ward.

*****

Doctor Znewski tapped his fingers against the surface of the long table he sat at. The chamber sat next to the administrator's quarters, which made Eugene guess Willard would emerge straight from his bed to hand-deliver Eugene's next round of torture. He found that much of the answer satisfying when Willard entered from a room containing a bed.

"How's my old acquaintance?" Willard C. Crane questioned as he entered and poured a drink from a crystal decanter by the door.

"I would rather be forgotten," Eugene spat. "Is it your mission to torment those who you did not manage to put down with enemy fire?"

Willard snorted and swirled a half-full glass. "I regretted my decision to send my men on that charge—the one I think you're speaking of. The soldiers who survived their injuries forgave me. Why can't you? Is it because you weren't injured?"

The two orderlies let go of Eugene, and Willard motioned for him to have a seat on a chair with yellow velvet padding.

"It's because your intent in life is not to care for other lives under your purview. You see human bodies as step stools to loftier stations. I am not fooled by the ruse."

Willard stepped close and leaned toward Eugene. "Which one of us is in here because of our mania?"

"I would argue both," Eugene delivered with confidence, sparking a gasp from the matron. "But my delusions are not that of grandeur. We both fumbled our way into the Bloom family. The difference is that I was aware it was outside the boundary of what I deserved."

Willard straightened his posture and placed his free hand behind his back. "Yet you are the one who is actually confined here because of your mania. Does your self-awareness inform you of your actual madness?"

"I detect nothing wrong with my mental fortitude."

Crane snorted. "Well, I can tell you that you are actually mad."

"So sings the common chorus," Eugene dismissed.

The room fell silent until Willard took a sip from his glass. He made a pouty face that only Eugene could see before starting to the table where Doctor Znewski sat.

"He had this letter on him," Matron Stapleton said, handing Willard the folded note. The administrator dismissed it at first, letting it flop on the table in front of him. It started to unfold of its own accord, which prompted Willard to hold and see how far it would unfurl itself.

It stopped shortly after, and Willard turned to his left and waved an arm. "Doctor."

The cue prompted Doctor Znewski to open a folder and pull out a handwritten rule paper.

"Several boys in your ward have signed a letter to the administrator, claiming you offered them money to set fire to the building. Is there any truth to that?"

Eugene's stomach knotted. Archibald was not the betrayer. He had counted on it. He had planned to be questioned and detained while the boys carried out the deed, allowing him plausible deniability. The boys' treachery was unexpected. Eugene realized his name would now be all over the crime, if it were carried out at all.

"You have a history of planning to start fires, so this is of some concern to us," Znewski continued. "You said the President of the United States told you to burn down Floyd Funeral Home. Is this the same for Weston State Hospital?"

"Doc, I am operating on the same set of orders. I have yet to carry out my mission in any way whatsoever." Eugene leaned back in his chair. "Yes, sir, Mister President, as a bonus, any embarrassment I can inflict on your grand administrator would do good to salve my soul. To see his face contort like the grotesques adorning the rear of this facility would do me a lifetime of pleasure."

"Instead, I am going to appear as a hero," Willard boasted. "I am someone who paid attention and foiled a plan to destroy hundreds of thousands of dollars in state taxpayer-funded property. Do you know how good that will look as I go about campaigning next year?"

There was truth to the statement. Eugene had not only failed his mission, but he made Willard C. Crane look all the better for it. His mood darkened.

"We've brought you here this evening not as punishment, but to cure you of your delusions," Willard said after taking a larger swig of his drink. "Floyd Funeral Home. You tried to burn it down during a wake?"

"I spoke of it, yes," Eugene admitted.

"Whose body was in the parlor that night?"

Eugene emitted a long sigh through his nostrils.

In the lull, Willard stood again and approached his prey. He repeated the query, stretching his words until it almost sounded melodic. "Who was it?"

"My wife."

"State her name for the record."

It was not a trial. No one was keeping record, but Eugene bit. "My wife, Ethel LeeAnn Bloom Spangold."

"Yes!" Willard clapped a hand against his glass; the ring on his finger clanged against it, making a metal chirp. "You say it was your wife, Ethel LeeAnn Bloom Spangold, but I have a revelation here you're going to enjoy."

Willard's energy came to life. He turned and pointed. "Doctor Znewski. On what date did Eugene's funeral home incident take place?"

"May 28, 1935," the doctor read from a sheet of paper in the bottom of the folder.

"Four months ago," Willard noted. He sat down his drink and knelt in front of Eugene. The move prompted the orderlies to flank him once again.

"Here is the question I have been struggling with. If Ethel Lee Spangold's wake was on May 28, 1935, why did it take four years for you to bury her?"

Eugene began to snort rhythmically, the tempo increasing as the data forced its way past the internal walls of repression.

Willard smirked. "Ah. For someone so versed at bumping gums, you have nothing to say now?"

"Mister President, n-no. What?"

"That was precisely what I said when I read your file." Willard hoisted himself upright. "As someone who has great admiration for the Bloom family, I knew for certain Ethel died in a vehicle accident in the late spring of 1931."

"No. No! This cannot be. How could all that time have passed? Mister President! Whose funeral was I at if not hers?"

"Alice Candler was her name," Doctor Znewski announced from across the room. "She was a homemaker from Jane Lew. We know nothing about her otherwise."

Willard polished his remaining drink and sat it down so he could place both hands behind his back. "You see, the real tragedy here is the story of Ethel Bloom. Plucked from high society and replanted on a backwoods farm in Gad. There was no way to grow quite as brilliant, or as beautiful. It was selfish for you to want that life for her, and it wouldn't have ended in Nicholas County. She would have lived lavishly in anticipation of her father's fortune and not bared any mind to paupers and dirt farmers." Returning to the table, Willard remembered the folded note and made little effort in unraveling it. "So, let's see what this is. A confessional?"

The sight of Willard reading the letter enraged Eugene. From the depths of his soul, he dredged a truth he even refused to admit to himself.

"I killed her!" Eugene blurted out.

Gasps filled the chamber.

He placed both palms into his eyes and sobbed. "I was the pilot of our vehicle on that fateful day. Even then I was trapped in a boozy cycle, and I don't remember much of the event. I dodged the automobile as it tumbled down the hillside, but Ethel could not escape. Fearful, I ran back to our house and pretended to not be the architect of my dear wife's passing."

"I'm sure the police in Nicholas County would like to know," Matron Stapleton stated.

Eugene cried. The wall of lies he had built as a levy to retain his guilt was felled by truth and sobriety. Emotion poured from him, drowning all other thoughts, feelings, and words.

Willard lowered the letter from his eyeline. "This is not a surprise. You stripped her of everything. Why not life, too? She could have borne great wealth and children of much higher stock."

"Please, let him be," Doctor Znewski chided. "There are a lot of suppressed memories he has coming forward."

"Very well." Willard handed the letter to the matron. "Place this back in his personal effects. It's nothing worth adding to his file."

Children. The word Willard uttered reminded Eugene of the daughter he and Ethel had produced together. She was still lost somewhere within the mental health system. "And what of my sweet Opal Lee?" He

271

suppressed tears to ask. "Are you keeping her here because she is not the stock of Bloom you would prefer?"

"No," Willard answered, contemplating. "She is here for her own reasons. She has been for a while. In fact, she predates my time as administrator. My understanding is that she has been in solitary confinement for the past two months because of a two-day elopement."

"Elopement?" Eugene exclaimed.

"Escape," Matron Stapleton clarified.

"She's been a naughty girl, that one. Just like her father," Willard concluded. "I expect she'll spend the rest of her life in this building."

"No!" Eugene screamed, standing, jutting forward to dodge the reach of the orderlies while grabbing the ornate top of the chair. He swung it toward one orderly while the chair leg hit the other in the back of the knee. The maneuver put both to the ground long enough for Eugene to dart toward the door. He hoped for a locking mechanism that could slow their pursuit, but found none.

Outside the chamber was a short hallway that opened into the center hall. He found the oak staircase and began his descent to the first floor. He stomped down the flight until he reached the bottom. Rather than turn for the exits, Eugene crossed the hall and started up the staircase's twin on the opposite side. After rounding the corner, he walked quieter, and listened for the cacophony of feet spilling down the opposite stairs. The sound of the steps was so jumbled that he couldn't make out the number, but felt certain everyone who could had given chase.

Eugene climbed the flight to the second floor and glanced around to see if any of the party in the chamber remained nearby. The way seemed clear, and he resumed his climb upward.

Five steps up, he heard a woman's voice call from behind him. "Excuse me!"

Turning, he caught enough of Matron Stapleton in his periphery to know the ruse was up. He hurried up the stairs as fast as he could while shouts from the matron were all that followed.

"Hey! He's up here! Eugene is going upstairs!"

The calls faded as Eugene reached the fourth floor. He sped through the halls until arriving at his door in Ward T. It was nearing time for lockdown, but the doors were not yet closed when Eugene entered his room and slammed the door.

Flip had already claimed Eugene's bed and was leaning against the wall with a book propped on bent knees.

"Get your pencil and paper ready, Flip," Eugene said between pants. "I have one more letter to dictate and a different mission. Nothing is downtrodden about this correspondence. In fact, it is a task you are going to love."

THE PARADOXICAL DOOR

25

Brittany, Wednesday, September 15, 1999

A clumsy hand slid along the curve of Brittany's side as she lay on the floor of Room 668. Neil did his best to treat her body like a solid surface, but the cold static penetrated her skin on several occasions. The sensation was electric, arousing hair follicles into prominent goosebumps.

Despite what Neil might have thought of Brittany, he avoided expressing love aloud. He instead displayed a tender affection. He acted interested in her, but the impossibility of their relationship stood in the way of true romance. *At least, without breaking some rules,* she thought. *And weren't the rules of spacetime already broken here?*

Neil mentioned his divorce, that he had met his wife in college, and that everything after had been intermittent levels of unpleasant. *Why wouldn't he want to erase that?* She suspected there was more Neil wasn't saying. Things he did not wish to compromise about his life. She needed to know. She needed to press the issue.

"Neil?" Brittany whispered as a hovering hand rested on her hipbone.

"Yes?"

"I want to meet you," she uttered with longing. "Why can't we start now? Erase the last two decades of disappointments you've had."

The notion came too soon for Neil. "I … don't want to talk about it." He gripped her tighter, his static enveloping her.

"You're hiding something," Brittany said, which came off more biting than intended.

"I have the whole future to tell you about. There is more than the Sears Tower bombing. I still need to tell you more about September eleven, the Boston Marathon …"

"You're keeping things about yourself, too, aren't you?" Brittany tore free from Neil, not that he could stop her. She moved to her knees. Neil seemed surprised by the detachment and remained where he lay.

"I do not want to wait twenty years," Brittany repeated. "I can't shake the feeling that you're hiding something. That there is something in your future you don't want to give up."

Neil moved to his feet and placed hands on his own hips. "You have to consider … You must consider that my future isn't the only thing you'll be changing. You'll be changing your future, too."

The notion should have felt considerate to Brittany, but her frustration toward their distance overwhelmed her. "My future isn't written yet."

"It is where I am." Neil cringed like it was a blow he didn't intend to deliver.

Brittany gasped and moved to her feet. "You know about me, then? Have you already met me?"

"No! I haven't." Neil motioned a palm downward. "I swear."

"Do you know where I am? Do you know my future?"

Neil wouldn't answer. He pulled away, severing their communication, and rubbed his hands through his hair before slapping his hands back to his thighs.

Brittany touched his chest to reestablish contact. She furrowed her brow. "I'm going to meet you."

Brittany exited the room as Neil reached for her, but his hand passed through her and stoved against the door, still closed in his time.

Brittany crossed to the opposite hall, turned to see Neil rush toward her like a flying banshee. The sight startled her, and she froze.

Neil grabbed her wrist. "Brittany, please!"

"Don't try to stop me!" Brittany shouted, but she yanked away mid-sentence, preventing Neil from hearing it all.

He grabbed her wrist again and scoffed. "How are you going to find me? You have no idea what I was doing in September of 1999. I don't even know."

"You may be lying to me about my future, but I won't lie about your past. You've given me all the clues! You were at WVU on Grant Avenue in the blue house just past the only dormitory on the street. It was the party block, so you have no reason to be anywhere else on a Saturday night."

Neil paused, as if he were skimming his memories for any other possibility. "You can't ..." He stopped. "I remember now!"

Brittany gave a smile teeming with malice. "You can't stop me."

"I have two daughters," Neil blurted in a desperate move to change her mind.

Brittany clinched her fists. "What?"

"I didn't see a reason to bring them up, so I didn't. I've not been a good father to them, but even after all the shitty things that have happened in my life, I don't want to risk snuffing them from existence."

Brittany ground her teeth and stared at the transparent figure who appeared to be projecting a sincere expression.

"Please wait. We'll meet on October 31, 2019, at the asylum cemetery."

"What happens then? You meet me there and stop visiting me here? You meet future Brittany, and then what? Act like I don't exist here? Are you going to date both versions of us?"

Neil's body jerked. He hadn't considered the complications of dating across time. It wasn't a concept he could have prepared for.

"Exactly." Brittany took his body language as an answer. She leaned closer to him and pointed an accusatory finger. "You were going to abandon me in the past the second my future form arrived. I have news for you. What you do to me in the past will hold its resentment in the future."

Neil took a step toward the door, but Brittany grabbed its edge to block him from moving further.

"Please. Halloween, 2019." Neil had only her right pinky finger left to hang onto. "Can we talk?"

Brittany slapped it away, and somehow his body responded to it. He staggered back.

"No!" Brittany shouted a final time before flinging the door as hard as she could. The door swung sharply and landed in the frame with an explosion of sound, as if all the doors in the ward had slammed at once.

A white light blasted through the hall and temporarily blinded Brittany. She stumbled backward and struck the opposite wall. Paint and plaster crackled behind her as she landed and slid to sit on the floor.

It took a minute for the interior to return to its midnight dimness. It felt unwelcome for the first time, and Brittany felt a need to leave as fast as possible.

*****

Neil, Sunday, September 15, 2019

Neil staggered backward. *Had Brittany pushed me?* It felt so real that he reacted. *Was it real?*

With an enormous thunderclap, the door swung shut and Brittany disappeared all in one violent eruption of sound and fury.

What followed was a long, dark, corridor. Neil could only hear his breathing for a few moments. Following was the creak of a heavy door on the far end of the hall. A flashlight rounded the corner and shined toward Neil.

"Did you hear something?" one of the guides asked. It was a new employee Neil did not know. *Brett,* he thought his name was.

"Yeah, it was a shout and a door slam," Neil played coy. He looked at Room 668. "I think it came from this door."

Brett shined a light at the sealed door but came no further. "Is that the door that never opens?"

"Yeah," Neil answered.

278

Brett lowered his light. "One of the senior guides had a theory it makes a slamming noise around this time every September fourteenth or fifteenth, whichever day it is now. He wanted me to listen for it, but I forgot."

Neil tugged on the handle, but it would no longer budge for him. "You can tell your coworker his theory has merit."

The guide nodded and turned. "We'll be moving on to the fourth floor soon."

"Oh, I believe I'm done for the night," Neil replied, though not loud enough for the guide to acknowledge it.

Neil had heard something, from before, and his mind only now latched onto it again.

Brittany shouted *"No." She said it and I heard it, though our connection had already been severed.*

Neil jerked on the door some more. He shined a light on the door plate and found the latch embedded into the door jamb. It was unwilling to budge, no matter how hard he yanked and twisted.

Neil admitted defeat. He backed away from the barrier. He stared at the stain-marked door surrounded by peeling pink plaster. The smell of cucumber melon lingered for a second more, then vanished. It was time for Neil to vanish, too.

Neil returned to his trailer a half hour later. He lay on his air mattress but remained awake throughout the night, replaying the events. A recap of the months followed, and then the years. He wasn't sure if he did the right thing with Brittany. His actions were a continuous series of little wrongs adding up to another catastrophic showing in his life's journey. But his actions and sacrifices were just, or so he prayed.

He wanted to calm himself. The only aide he had available was a bottle of cucumber melon lotion that he had found in a mall near Clarksburg, the next city to the north. The scent typically gave him enough comfort to ward off insomnia, but that was not the effect he was looking for tonight. He remained awake, waiting for daybreak. When the clock marked eight in the morning, seven Central Standard Time, Neil placed a call to his ex-wife.

"Hello," a groggy Caitlyn answered.

"Hey," Neil replied. He was groggy in the other direction. "Are the girls awake?"

"Yeah. They are having breakfast," Caitlyn answered, confusion coloring her tone. "You … want to talk to them?"

"Yes. I just want to hear their voices."

"Okay." There was a shuffle, a rattle, and muffled voices on the line before a toddler's voice returned to the receiver.

"Hi, Dada," Meriwether said.

A breath caught in Neil's throat, and he choked on the congestion. "Hey, Meri. How are you?"

"I'm 'kay!" the young girl answered happily. It was clear she would be a morning person. "How are you, Dada?"

The warm feeling in his windpipe only intensified. Neil recognized the precursor to tears, but couldn't find a reasonable way to evade them. He sucked in, hoping to bar them a little longer. "I'm okay, too, baby."

THE THREATENED TIMELINE

26

The interstate was fog-laden and bustling, which would not have shaken Brittany, except it was her first drive alone on I-79. Cars buzzed past her like she was stationary. She wasn't used to the seventy-mile-per-hour posted speed and kept a firm foot on the gas pedal. Even with the extra effort, vehicles still blew by her with ease.

It was close to eleven o'clock at night, but Brittany was barreling toward the exit into Morgantown.

Brittany wasn't exactly sure where Grant Avenue was among the various arteries of the city. The entire area was essentially the campus of West Virginia University. Being close to a dorm meant nothing. Arriving at the first major intersection by the punchbowl-looking basketball arena, the road formed a half-mile straight line leading to the hospital, football stadium, and a cluster of dormitories.

With no luck, and not wanting to stray too far from landmarks, Brittany backtracked to the basketball coliseum. She began driving further down the original road. There was no one she could call for directions. Neil didn't know she was coming, didn't know her for that matter. Glenda was home, asleep and unaware of her daughter's sojourn.

Then she remembered Sam. Sam Beck had given her the address to his house. Brittany pulled over at an auto parts store at the bottom of a hill. She reached into the middle seat to retrieve her pouch of pictures from the first ghost hunt. The slip with Sam's address on it was still tucked inside: 424 GRANT AVENUE. There was no phone number, so Brittany would have to muddle ahead in the worn-down minivan.

Another mile down the road brought her to a stoplight that turned onto University Avenue. Brittany decided to try her luck on that inclined road. The steep grade further taxed the van's power. Brittany released the pedal halfway up the incline when she spotted a green GRANT AVENUE sign to her left. The muffler thundered as Brittany returned to the gas and pushed the vehicle as hard as it could go. As it lifted onto the new street, a new detail caught Brittany's eye. A black and white ONE-WAY sign alerted her to an error. She pumped the brakes, looking for a place to turn around on the tight road.

Before she could go much further, the minivan sputtered and seized. Brittany cursed and let the dead vehicle drift into a dirt lot where it would not block traffic.

The movement through the city had been slow and was nearing midnight. Brittany found the time of night the appropriate occasion for her first in-person meeting with Neil. She was nervous but pressed forward. The five-story dorm building was to her left. It made the houses situated around it appear puny in comparison.

She was close, and the loud clamor of music and shouting told her the party was not too far beyond the tower.

The closest blue house was a turquoise structure two lots adjacent to the dorm. There was a concrete landing wide enough to park a single vehicle, but it was already occupied by partygoers milling about. Between songs, the *tap-tap* of ping-pong balls clattered across a table on the porch, knocking about plastic cups with various levels and types of alcohol. The speakers, perched in the porch window, began to play "Genie in a Bottle" by Christina Aguilera, which prompted a cheer from the crowd. A beachball knocked about the porch, tumbled down the stairs, and into the yard. Those attentive enough to acknowledge it picked the ball up and struck it back to the porch. One young woman was very enthusiastic about retrieving the ball. She would shout profanities at anyone who kicked it away before she could get there first.

Brittany paid the scene no mind as she stood on the concrete slab to scan for Neil. He would be much younger, but his ghostly iteration never gave away the full detail of his looks. She wasn't sure of what color his hair was. She believed it to be a dusty-brown, but even that could have changed with time.

After a few minutes of looking, one of the guys doing a few rounds of beer pong stopped to take a breather and sat on the ledge of the steps. His hair was lighter, altered by peroxide or some type of cheap dye. The bridge of his nose and his deep-set eyes matched what she knew of Neil's later appearance. All she had to do was walk up to him and ask the question "Are you Neil?" A harmless query no matter the answer.

Brittany took a step forward, eyes locked on the man. He had a cigarette in his mouth and was trying to drunkenly extract a single strike from a matchbook. Neil never said he smoked. *It could have been some college experimentation that never took hold.* With the match free, he started to brush it against the exterior red strip with no success.

The beachball obstructed Brittany's viewing. It struck the tip of her shoe and bounced away from her before rolling back to her feet.

"Knock it over here!" a frat boy called from the nearside of the porch.

Brittany seethed at the delay. She lifted the lightweight ball and volleyed it back with a hard smack. The speed slowed with the drag of the air, and it fell short of the porch, striking the rails and rolling into the next yard.

"That was my ball!" a voice shouted behind Brittany.

Brittany realized she shouldn't have interacted with the scene and refused to acknowledge the perturbed woman. She started forward again.

"I'm talking to you!" the woman continued, and Brittany felt a firm hand grab her shoulder. It pulled on her, causing Brittany to spin around.

The night had been hard. Getting to Morgantown, getting to Grant Avenue, getting to the party—every level of it had been full of obstacles and frustrations. Brittany arrived at the final obstruction. Her vexation boiled over, and a very cross Brittany screamed back at the woman. "I don't care if you're talking to me!"

"An ignorant bitch, aren't you?" The blonde ponytailed woman took offense and leaned in for a shove, but Brittany stepped back, and the woman lost her balance, falling to the ground.

"Fight?" someone near them asked with building enthusiasm.

"No," Brittany said, and retreated a few feet. She didn't want this to be the first thing Neil saw of her.

The woman stood, shouted belligerent curses, and rushed Brittany. Now fearing for her safety, Brittany evaded but only made it as far as the concrete slab before the woman tackled her.

"Fight! Fight! Fight!" a drunken chorus shouted.

The woman put a knee in the small of Brittany's back and punched her in the back of the head. Brittany managed to roll to her back and knee the woman in the groin, but Brittany took two more punches to the face for her efforts.

The woman placed both her hands around Brittany's neck, which left her defenseless enough for Brittany to deliver a hook to the woman's face. The blow landed hard, and the woman rolled off Brittany, giving her a chance to get up and run. The woman did not want to cede defeat so easily and grabbed Brittany's pants leg, and they both went back to the ground.

Striking her in the face again, the woman's hand returned a final time with blood on her knuckles. Whose blood it had been was never in question. Brittany could feel liquid running across her lip, and she transferred some of it to her fingers when she shielded the subsequent strike. The block was enough for Brittany to reach with the other hand and grab the woman's hair, yanking locks free from the ponytail. The woman screamed and flipped end-over-end when she found Brittany would not free her. They tumbled and rolled in a tangle further down the sidewalk.

"That's enough," another woman's voice shouted. The assailant seemed to recognize the voice and stood, towering over Brittany as she remained face down on the sidewalk. Brittany cringed and waited for another assault, but nothing more came.

Brittany turned her head to see the woman confidently return to the party. She shook her hair loose as she strutted like a peacock to the porch. Who she assumed to be Neil remained where he had been and seemed enamored by the victor. He said something to her in passing. She squeezed his shoulder and continued toward the door.

"Good one, Caitlyn," one of the partygoers complimented as the woman disappeared inside.

Now unpresentable in both body and spirit, Brittany stood and started to run down the sidewalk. Pain radiated from her ankle. Brittany only now realized it got twisted in the scuffle. She slowed her pace and hobbled into the night.

Even though it was after midnight, a quick answer came when Brittany rang the doorbell on 424 Grant Avenue. The brown two-story house would have had tenants, fortunately Sam Beck was the one who answered.

Horrified at her bloody appearance, Sam could only stare. "Oh, gee, Brittany, what happened to you?"

"Got in a fight down the street," Brittany seethed. "It's not been a good night."

Sam stood back and opened the door wider. "Do you need to call the cops?"

Brittany crept through the entrance. "It wouldn't make a difference. It was at a party, so I suspect the cops will be there soon, anyway. Or maybe they don't care enough to begin with."

"Let's get you cleaned up." Sam motioned to an open door that led to the basement. "I was just up here on the PlayStation. Saturday is the only night my roommates aren't on it. Let me go turn it off. There's a bathroom downstairs to the left. You can clean up in there."

"Thank you." Brittany limped down the carpeted stairs.

The bathroom was small. The shower, toilet, sink, and mirror were all styled with a yellow, sickly porcelain. Black stubble littered every surface. Brittany didn't mind it. She looked much more grotesque. Blood had stopped leaking from her nose, but it left a red stain on her lips and chin. Purple was already beginning to emerge from under her left eye, and a small gash on her forehead that had already began to clot.

"What brings you to Morgantown?" Sam asked once he reached the bottom of the stairs. "I thought you were taking this semester off?"

"I … I was looking for someone. A guy I met."

Sam removed cotton balls, adhesive strips, and antibiotic ointment from under the sink. "Oh. Well, did you find him?"

"No. And I don't think I should keep looking." Brittany took one of the rounds of cotton and ran it under running water. "Something tells me I never should have been looking to begin with."

Sam watched as Brittany washed the stain from her face as best it would clean without soap. She put a cotton ball between her lips and pressed them together to clear the blood. Lastly, Brittany took the ointment and applied a dab to her forehead.

"Let me get a Band-Aid for you," Sam insisted. He fumbled through a box of assorted adhesive strips until he found one to suit her. He took care to remove the paper and plastic backing. Brittany turned toward him and studied his expression as he gently applied the bandage. She had never watched his face as close before. There was a great deal of care in the curl of his lip, the way his eyebrows puckered as he insured the workmanship on his curative contribution.

"Thank you," Brittany said again, more sincere.

Sam lowered his arms and nodded. "Anything for a friend."

Brittany took the comment to heart, and advantage, immediately returning with "My van broke down. I'm going to need a place to stay for the night."

Without hesitation, Sam pointed to the room next to the bathroom. "You can take my bed for the night. I can sleep upstairs on the couch."

Brittany stepped into the room and scanned. It was a typical college setup. Shoddy furniture surrounded a spring-suspended bed. The posters decorating the walls were a mix of popular movies from decades ago and recent, obscure films. Tan carpet thinned in places and stained in others.

"Where did your van break down?"

Brittany pointed in an obscure direction. "Back at the entrance to Grant, toward campus."

"It will probably get towed. It doesn't take much to get towed on this street."

Sitting on the bed, Brittany looked to Sam, who was still standing in the doorway. "Can you stay here for a little bit?"

"Sure, I can hang out." Sam sprung into the room but chose to sit along the far wall, holding his knees as he pressed his back to the wood paneling.

"It is hard to get to know someone." Brittany stared catatonically into the distance, still facing away from Sam. "All you get are windows into a person's heart and mind. Even then, there are plenty of clouded windows. Distorted glass that blurs the image on the other side … I'm tired of looking through windows, Sam. I want through a door."

Sam didn't know what Brittany was talking about. She was resigning herself to never knowing Neil. She couldn't suspend her life for his happiness, not for the length required.

After some pontificating, Sam leaned his head back and smirked. "I like to think of us as pieces to a puzzle that we'll never see completed. Because the puzzle expands faster than we can place the pieces. There's always more to come."

Brittany hummed, amused at Sam's attempt to make sense of the senseless. "I don't think that guy was right for me," Brittany said, now turning to Sam. "It was a bad situation. I'm not sure why I ever bothered to make it work."

Sam shrugged. "Sometimes being told something is bad is what sets us on the search for the goodness in it."

She admired Sam's efforts to sooth her. It was working. For a moment she forgot the pain and smiled, even though it caused her lip to crack and seep blood. She ignored it and kept eye contact as she dabbed the leak with a fresh cotton ball. "You're a good friend, Sam. I can't begin to tell you how thankful I am that you exist."

The comment prompted Sam to shimmy. "You've always been one of my favorite people. I am honored to know you and was honored to know your dad. I'm still sorry he is gone."

It was the first mention of her dad since his death that didn't invoke a mournful reaction. Instead of frowning, she smiled more.

"Sam," she said with a happy huff. "I had some sense knocked into me tonight."

27

THE ABANDONED COOP

Thirty years from now, Henrietta would return to Weston in a yellow pickup truck she had spent years saving to buy. There was a break in her work schedule, she was near Weston, and Wallace was on her mind. She wanted to retrace the steps of her elopement as much as the roads would allow. The hurried rush North was a blur, and three eventful decades further wore the memory down to a few streaks of long-term recollection.

From the hospital grounds Henrietta started her exodus in what was Polk Creek, the first new detail that she would recognize in thirty years. She knew then that the waterway was small and spilled into a larger body. Whether it had been the West Fork or not, Henrietta decided that the river was flowing north, and that was enough.

She knew the Monongahela River well and this lesser body was likely the western fork. It was near her home north of Morgantown, and close to her matrimonial home of Monongah. The West Fork River merged with the Tygarts River in nearby Fairmont to form the mightier body. From Fairmont, it flowed 130 miles, across the Mason-Dixon Line, to Pittsburgh.

From there, she was in the true north, above the arbitrary parallel and into the echo of Appalachia. Henrietta believed she could travel anywhere without prejudice. To New York, Chicago, Boston, someplace where none would notice her for her tint, the tint of her son, and their incompatible tones as a package.

Henrietta did not have time to secure Wallace, and in the scurry to leave, she neglected to retrieve the fabric used for swaddling. She instead held his body tight as she kept balance along the uneven banks.

Sometimes rocky, sometimes thick with bramble and hidden trip hazards, Henrietta made slow work of the journey to keep a sure footing. She slowed further once she was beyond Weston and concealed by a shag of summer trees.

Two hours into the journey, Henrietta slowed her pace before stopping at a fork in the river. West Fork continued north, but another creek flowed from further west. She would have to ford the smaller waterway to continue progressing, and began, unsure of the water's depth.

Henrietta dipped waist-deep at the center of the creek before beginning to rise again. She cradled Wallace with both hands, pressing him tight against her chest. He seemed unbothered by the splashing. The sounds of water seemed to soothe him more than anything.

Henrietta had become so preoccupied with the depth she neglected to check her surroundings along the bank. Two-thirds through the creek, she noticed a grist mill rising from the knoll at the top of the incline. She would need to be more cautious while passing.

Her return to stealth lasted only a moment when she scanned the lower portion of the bank and spotted a young boy watching her from the tall grass. The towheaded lad sat along at the mouth of the creek, slapping a birch switch in the river. He ceased once Henrietta's presence became known. The boy stood statuesque and observed her further, unsure of how to proceed with the visitant.

"Howdy," he said once she reached the creek line.

Henrietta examined the area for anyone else. "Good day. Are your parents around?"

"Only my father now," the boy said. "Mother died right after we bought this farm. Childbirth."

"Well, I'm sorry to hear that," Henrietta replied. She put a free hand to her mouth. "Childbirth can be difficult."

The boy noticed Wallace. It was the baby that seemed to assure him that Henrietta was not a criminal.

"You look a mess. Would you like one of my mother's dresses? Father piled them up in the old blacksmith shop. He has no use for dresses, or blacksmithin.'"

Henrietta looked down to acknowledge her half-soaked gown, caked with silt and mud. The boy led her up the steep bank, while she struggled to balance Wallace and keep her own footing.

"Father ran to town for some provisions." The boy had already crested the hill and was swatting at dandelion puffs with his switch. He watched a cloud of them catch the wind and paused to admire his swordsmanship. "Father tries once a month to bake bread. It never comes out right. Not like mother's anyways. Sometimes I think that's what he misses more from her."

"Sometimes it takes something simple like the smell of bread to recreate a memory of happy times," Henrietta explained, trying to appear as a wise sage passing through. "Your father cannot bring back your mom, but if he brings back her bread, that's a little bit of something. That's a little piece of your mother back in the world."

The boy stopped and smiled at Henrietta, squinting deep in the light of the day before brushing aside his golden bangs.

"Would you like something to eat?" He trotted along a large pond to a small stone building near the grist mill. The latch and hinges groaned as the boy made efforts to open the door.

"Don't have any bread, of course, but we have some early harvest apples. Golden ones. Pretty sweet this time of year. We also have several tomato plants that can be harvested. The tiny ones that pop in your mouth."

Henrietta politely declined the tomatoes but agreed to take a sack of apples. The boy, who identified himself as John, led her into the blacksmith shop where a stack of ten casual dresses were strewn over an anvil near the center of the room. Not wanting to take advantage of such generosity, Henrietta chose the dress on the top of the stack. It was a plain cream-colored number that fit loose once on. She let John hold Wallace outside while she shimmied out of her hospital gown and put proper attire on for the first time in months.

"How come your baby ain't Black?" John asked while bouncing Wallace. The baby was wide awake and beginning to fuss.

"His father is white," Henrietta answered, feeling empowered to admit it for the first time in the outside world.

"Don't know nothing about how that works. Not sure how a baby gets its looks from the father just by kissin.'"

"There's more to it than that," Henrietta admitted with a smile. "You'll figure it out one of these days."

John smirked in return. "Yeah. I reckon I will."

The two sat along the pond and ate apples while Henrietta nursed Wallace. John seemed to enjoy her company, but she also noticed him stealing peaks at the suckling child.

"You can see I'm good to Black folk," John said, unprompted. "Before we bought this farm, it used to be owned by the Jacksons. Boy was raised here named Thomas Jackson. He went on to be a Civil War general they called Stonewall. He fought the United States to keep you as slaves. I don't want to be like that. You seem nice."

Henrietta said nothing and focused on chewing the apple flesh. She knew about Stonewall from *The Weston Democrat* papers the nurses let her read. She did not realize the hospital had been this close to his ancestral home.

John continued to speak around a mouthful of cherry tomatoes, which Henrietta chose not to lay eyes upon. "Them guys were so bad they shot Stonewall, their own general—amputated his arm and let him die of pneumonia. I don't want any kind of trouble like that, so I'm being extra good to everyone. This farm needs to be known for something good."

Henrietta smiled. "I think you'll amount to more than he ever did."

John looked at Henrietta and grinned while he absorbed the flattery. Tomato juice ran down the sides of his chin. Henrietta recoiled with knee-jerk disgust but concealed the reaction with a snicker, which the boy shared.

Wallace detached, and Henrietta tucked her breast away, using a blanket found in the blacksmith shop to swaddle him. With some contorting, she was able to secure Wallace and a small, burlap bag of golden apples against her body.

"You have been of great help, John, and I will never forget it."

John stood and dusted off his canvas overalls. "Father says you hafta do your best to right the wrongs of the world. 'Cause if you don't do it, no one else will, and things will stay bad."

"That's a good way to put it." Henrietta had secured her load and resolved to continue the journey north, taking a final moment to think on John's outlook. "You're right." She bit her lip. "We don't want things to stay bad."

*****

Sunlight rimmed the horizon when Henrietta reached Clarksburg. By then, she had put eight hours of foot travel between her and Weston. Feeling safe for the evening, she moved from her low position on the riverbank to more exposed footing on the town level. A bridge by her exit point declared the position as Pike Street, off the main stretch. The road was a brick construction, with all the macadamized lesser roads flowing into it.

With the heart of the city so close, Henrietta chose not to go any further. Night was coming and there were many unseen pitfalls of hiding in plain sight. The building closest to her happened to be a station of the Clarksburg Fire Department, an older detachment by the condition of the structure. Hand-hewn logs held it together by gravity and a heavy chinking and was in a late stage of deterioration.

A derelict cart sat isolated in the back of the station. Several spokes were absent from one rear wheel, and the other was missing a section of the ring, proving immobility. Within the small walls of the cart were two large wood crates. One looked sealed tight, but the other was missing its lid. Someone had removed the straw inside and what remained was strewn around the cart's surface.

293

Henrietta gathered as much of the straw as possible to make a bed for Wallace. He had grown fussy in the final hour. Being unbound from his mother and left to extend his tiny legs seemed to pacify him into a neutral state.

Climbing onto the cart, Henrietta did not lay down immediately. The day had been a marathon, and she required a moment to cool down. Her mind could not move as fast as her body, and it needed time to catch up and review the events of the day.

What happened to the doctor? Felix? He had been such a good friend, good lover, an ally she trusted with her care, her body, her soul, and her heart. But it was all for him, and what he gifted in return was only the illusion of compassion. The isolation she endured was not for her safety, but for the safety of his reputation and credibility. It was always obvious, but how little Henrietta had gotten out of the transaction was only clear from her view now on the outside.

I killed someone today, she reflected. *No, I murdered someone. And not even the person or persons who had deserved it most. I strung up an invalid. Someone who was unable to walk or talk. Whose only crime was having a wicked roommate.*

As Henrietta sat, her mind began restocking the odds of her outcome remaining positive. The hospital would do an investigation to prove Jansy's guilt. If found innocent, Jansy would undoubtedly cast blame in the correct place. A manhunt would lead to her recapture, judgment, and assignment of a proper slot among the pantheon of violent females in the ward.

Wallace would return, too, stuck in the laundry-adjacent orphanage and adoption center. He would remain until his uncaring state overseer releases him at the exact second of adulthood. Wallace would wander about the world, bitter, with no skills and a bleak future. He would earn his transience and return to the hospital as an official member rather than a byproduct.

The realization brought tears, and she slid into a fetal position and tucked the now sleeping Wallace into her bosom. She wept harder and began to worry someone inside the fire hall would hear her. It was now dark enough that no one else would otherwise detect them among the night.

Henrietta decided to leave him there. The fire department would move him to a proper orphanage—one free of hazardous lye and detergents, one that would care for him at least until some childless couple subjected themselves to his care.

It would be the best outcome, she told herself. *Really, it would be the only good outcome.* If she carried him all the way to Morgantown and abandoned him with her father, he may not accept Wallace. The bastard spawn of his mentally ill daughter seemed to check too many boxes on his list of embarrassments. Even if her father would accept him, Wallace would be a lone white boy in a Black community. She wondered if that would be much better than being the only Black woman in a ward of violent white women. Henrietta shook off that thought. *Of course, that situation would be better. Humanity wasn't so monstrous as to cast away an abandoned child because of his color. A baby was a baby, and maternal or paternal instinct would trump the prejudice.*

But the opportunity was dwindling. It was still another day's hike to Morgantown, and Henrietta decided to do the one thing that seemed unthinkable. In the morning, she would leave Wallace and return to Weston to face her crimes.

After a fitful sleep, Henrietta arose as the sun reappeared on the opposite horizon. Henrietta nursed Wallace for a final time. She gathered the loose strands of straw from the crate, placed him on top, and swaddled him in a burlap sack, leaving a single arm free. When Wallace decided he was hungry again, he would erupt and alert anyone within earshot. He did not scream in deep fits often, but when he did, he was sure to let the whole world know about it.

Henrietta stood on the cart, locking eyes with her son in one more moment of admiration. When she decided to let go for the last time, her sight drifted to the open crate. Inside, underneath the sparse layer of packing straw, was a bundle of wooden handles. She reached down to remove one, finding the object heavier than expected.

The opposite end revealed the items to be custom-made fire axes. The red metal head had an engraving of the Maltese Cross on the side. Branded on the handle was lettering spelling out CLARKSBURG.

A fire began burning in Henrietta's heart, and she realized Doctor Felix Koenig could still be alive after Silkie's attack. She needed to know, too, what had become of Silkie. But first, she would need to deal with the doctor if she were to have any further peace in her remaining days.

28

THE DISTILLED SPIRITS

EUGENE, THURSDAY, OCTOBER 3, 1935

Eugene's outburst didn't result in solitary confinement this time. Because he admitted to being an alcoholic, Doctor Znewski recommended a day of hydrotherapy to flush out what chemicals remained in Eugene's system. It had been four months since his last drink, so Eugene questioned what more there was to flush. His protest went unanswered, and orderlies placed him naked in a cold tub of water. They strapped a heavy tarp over the rim, leaving only a space for his head to emerge.

Full-body shivers rippled the water for the first several minutes, but Eugene seemed to adjust to where he found solace within the chill.

Eugene had been willing to admit to himself that he had started drinking. It began not long after Opal Lee's departure from his life. His despair turned to the bottle and the genetic need to satisfy the craving became overwhelming.

It was the trip to Marvin Levy's Memorial Day party that changed everything for the worse. Ethel never felt apt to driving an automobile and left the task to her husband, even when he operated in a state of

297

inebriation. Muscle memory was always enough to get Eugene from point A to point B around Gad. He always bragged he could make any familiar journey in his sleep, and may have done so a few times.

Eugene didn't see Ethel's body get crushed, but she lay lifeless in a bed of bramble. The vehicle lay on its side yards below her, coming to rest against an elm bordering the forest below. Eugene checked for a pulse, checked for breathing, and checked the distance to home.

The lost days brought more booze and less sleep. Insomnia reigned over Eugene's consciousness, cured only by drinking enough to pass out. It was a task that became harder and harder as his tolerance to alcohol grew.

Police came and interviewed Eugene on his whereabouts during the accident. His drunken state allowed him to cry with sincerity and establish the false narrative that he had not been at the scene. The lie came easy from how effortlessly Eugene accepted it as the truth.

The funeral was at the Floyd parlor, but Eugene entered the building in a blackout state. He could recall the warmth of hugs, his father-in-law's accusing eye, and the continued absence of Opal Lee. To his knowledge, any alleviation of his bladder that night was in the correct receptacle.

The Spangold farm fell into disrepair and the flock began to dissipate by various means all pointing to neglect. Eugene could only stand at his dining room window and stare into the pasture. The lost days replayed so verbatim that none felt different from the other.

Four years passed without permission. In May of 1935, the sheriff seized the farm to pay property taxes. Rather than pay the dues, Eugene packed up his black steamer trunk, with silver buckles and Toronto sticker, to adopt a life of vagrancy.

It was a three-day hike from Gad to Weston, but only because it was not Eugene's destination. He gravitated north, stopping at every general store along the way. He bought up the cheapest spirits and continuing onward while he dictated his picaresque tale—a memoir no one would read. He stumbled into Weston in late May, close enough to the anniversary of Ethel's death that he believed he was experiencing it again in real time. The circular nature of the years confounded Eugene to the point where he stopped believing in its advancement. But the spinning wheel had brought him back to start. To the place where his life had crumbled to ruin. The ghastly vision of presidents past, present, or future were a byproduct of the delusions. His desire to light fire to evil spirits was a feeble effort to excise his own demons.

When orderlies released Eugene from the bath the next day, he found that the crude method had worked. At least to the extent that he had come to terms with the truths he long denied.

Because time in the water had cost Eugene his land legs, the orderlies gave him a ride in a rudimentary wheelchair. The shoddy contraption consisted of wheels and wooden planks bolted together to form an uncomfortable mode of transportation.

To avoid lugging him up to the fourth floor, the orderly placed him in a room on the center of the first floor, adjacent from the room where Doctor Timmons first admitted him. It was as plain as the admitting room, but contained temporary tables stacked with the luggage of those committed to the hospital.

Not willing to stand, Eugene panned his head around the wall of baggage, trying to spot his trunk among the collection. After a moment, the door swung open, and another wheelchair-bound woman entered, followed by a nurse and an orderly.

"Opal Lee?" Eugene called as the woman came to a stop in front of him. She was now dressed in a similar gown, and her head was drooping against her left shoulder. Her hair was longer, but disheveled and damp.

"What's wrong with her?" Eugene growled.

"She completed a similar treatment and had been sleeping when we removed her," the nurse answered and pointed to Eugene's chair, a cue for the following orderly to place Eugene's hands in leather binds.

"You're both prone to escape. We don't want you taking flight if you find the sudden power to walk," the nurse said as the orderly completed the task. "Administrator Crane will be down to speak with you shortly."

The two employees disappeared back into the hospital, leaving the Spangolds to their words.

"Opal Lee, can you hear me?" Eugene asked as he made a nudging motion with his head. "Are you okay?"

Opal's eyes opened and she caught a blurry glimpse of her father. "Dad?"

"Yes, I'm here." Eugene smiled and tears formed in his eyes.

"I'm a patient here," she admitted. "I'm sorry I didn't say so when I saw you last."

"We have a lot of things we misrepresented. Both of us," Eugene said, and looked at the luggage again. "How long have you been here?"

"Five years, thereabout," she calculated. Liveliness seemed to be returning as she further woke.

"Five years? Criminy, that's been just about as long as I saw you last."

"I've been here since Christmas of 1930," Opal revealed. Strands of hair dangled in front of her face. She tried to brush them aside but remembered her strapped hands.

"Why? Weren't you going back to Pittsburgh? New York? Why did they do this to you?"

There was a long pause, and the soggy father and daughter stared at one another from mirrored sides. A look of shame cleared Opal's face and her eyes broke contact when she finally spoke.

"I have a desire for women. Women … as opposed to men."

"Oh," Eugene uttered. It was the kind of tone as if to say, "Is that all?"

"I told Mom Christmas Eve and indicated my desire to inform you as well. She felt it was a terrible idea to tell you, and we had an argument."

"She never told me what it was about," Eugene admitted.

"There's more. I had a lady friend. A romantic partner I wanted to bring to Christmas dinner. Her name was Frances Indra. We were living together and were making plans to move to New York after the New Year. Frances had gotten a position as a writer for *Life Magazine*. I was finally going to pursue my dream as a book editor at a large publication."

Eugene's heart sank, puzzling out the logic of what had to happen next.

Opal's eyes reconnected with Eugene's for the first time during the tale. "After the fight with Mom, I drove back to Morgantown and met with Frances. I told her it would be better if I had dinner with you and Mom alone. She understood, we kissed, and she departed back for Pittsburgh. I didn't realize that a police officer was watching us. He arrested me for indecency, and the legal system recommended I be placed in this hospital indefinitely. Homosexuality is something they have yet to find an effective cure for."

Eugene didn't speak. He wasn't sure where to start. The past five years, the drunkenness, the accident, were all a misunderstanding he was unable to piece together until now, a half decade later.

"Are you mad at me?" Opal looked on the verge of tears.

"No," Eugene answered so quickly Opal barely had time to finish the question. "No! How could I be angry about love? How could love of any kind be indecent, especially when mutual? Who's to say what my answer could have been in that bygone time. Parenting is prone to snap miscalculation. There would have been shock, I'm sure, but acceptance is never far down the way when there's love in the argument."

Opal sagged in her chair. "I should have tried to contact you. Shame kept me from it. Part of me felt I belong here. Still do, in some ways."

"No. Do not blame yourself for the intolerance of others. Besides, the justice system should have been the one to contact me. It is clear there was no justice in it to start."

A confused face appeared on Opal, and she shifted to nuzzle her chin against her right shoulder. "I was most afraid of *your* intolerance."

Eugene closed his eyes and sighed. He spoke slowly to address her concern. "You would have been right at a time. Being a parent allows intuitiveness toward your child that cannot be fully hidden. We could see your desires for a feminine companion long before you did. I held a lot of animosity toward the potential. One day, I said something to your mother, and she came back with something that changed my outlook."

Opal straightened her head in anticipation of the answer.

"She asked 'would you love her any different if it were true?' I thought about it for a moment and decided no. I would not love you differently. That seed grew into a philosophy I apply to everyone now. If those differences are not outwardly harmful to someone else, then they are worth respecting. And so, I respect you for your feelings and desires, and I will not bring an obstacle into the way of love. I wish I had let your mother know as much."

With tears trailing down her damp face, Opal stared at her father with new appreciation. She had sought his approval for longer than she could remember and never imagined the ease with which it was received. A lifetime of pent-up tension released all at once. "I love you, Daddy."

"I love you, too, sweet Opal Lee," Eugene's said. "You are all Ethel and I have to send beyond our days. You are the hopes and dreams and wishes unfulfilled, though your existence already fulfilled much. I will touch the grass of the future through your hands. I will breathe the air of the future with your lungs. You will take us much further than we can go ourselves. And if you send no one beyond yourself, that is all well and good. When you go, we go back to the earth together."

The two stared at each other with a mutual appreciation deferred for far too long. The accumulated interest could never be repaid, but they made an unspoken agreement that this moment was payment enough.

"Now what?" Opal finally asked.

"Yeah. Ethel is gone, and we're both mental patients," Eugene said with a calm he didn't usually reserve for uttering his wife's name. "I've laid a plan to get you out of here. All we can do is wait for it to hatch."

"I tried escaping before," Opal said. "I tried to get to Granddaddy Bloom's, but I was recaptured by the time I reached the edge of town."

Eugene chuckled. "This won't be an escape. When you leave here, it will be bona fide freedom."

"How will you manage that?"

Eugene winked. Opal recognized it as a sign from youth that meant "You're just going to have to wait and see."

"Just do one thing for me," Eugene said.

"What?"

"Run. Get out of West Virginia. Go to New York. Find Frances if you still feel a way about her, but otherwise, move on from all this. Be the strong, independent bookworm you were always meant to be."

Opal frowned. "What about you?"

Eugene was unsure of his fate, but it didn't matter. His daughter was denied years of happiness, and she needed to reclaim the lost moments in double time.

"Don't you worry. You went this long without seeing me. What's a lifetime more? My job was to rear you to adulthood. The task is complete. I have nothing more to offer in happiness, wisdom, or otherwise. Go be Opal Lee Spangold."

Opal went to respond when the door opened.

"How is the family reunion going?" Willard C. Crane asked. He entered with a single orderly and stood near the door. The orderly continued inward and began removing Opal's restraints.

"I got your letter." Willard held up a sheet of paper. "That is to say, I received a carbon copy of it by your father-in-law."

Willard shifted the paper so that he could focus on the words.

To Edgar Robert Bloom, Jr.,

I am writing to inform you that your granddaughter, Opal Lee Spangold, has been captive within the walls of the Weston Hospital for an undefined period. The administrator, Willard C. Crane, is refusing to grant her release. I feel this is done in the spirit of cruelty due to his animosity toward her father, one Eugene JD Spangold. Given your closeness with Mr. Crane, I suspect you are a major contributor to his impending campaign for West Virginia Governor. I request you withhold any further financing until this matter is resolved, and your granddaughter is released. I know we have had our differences in the past, but you will take pleasure in knowing that I am now also a member of the Weston State Hospital menagerie and will remain here as a permanent fixture in exchange for Opal's freedom.
Yours in fellowship,

EUGENE JD SPANGOLD

Eugene winked again at Opal, but she did not seem amused.

Willard lowered the paper so fast the note made a crumpling sound. "Mr. Bloom has indeed threatened to cut off all funding to my campaign, including convincing other financiers to cease their contributions. It would seem I miscalculated how much he valued his granddaughter."

"Blood is thicker than bullshit, Willard." Eugene laughed. "Besides, weren't you digesting those words? I get to be your pincushion for years to come."

Willard huffed. Staying at the hospital was not in his plans for much longer, but he declined to say so with the orderly listening. He gestured for the underling to leave.

Now free, Opal stood and rubbed her wrists as she looked around for what to do next.

"It doesn't matter." Willard scoffed when the door closed again. "When I'm governor, I will have more resources in which to sanction your family. In the meantime, there are a lot of sinister devices we can use to punish you here."

He stomped toward Eugene, smiling wide in the way a person broken inside would. "I will not hesitate …"

Opal swung at Willard, connecting with his cheekbone. The man yelped and staggered back. "You!" He shouted, but lost the next word. He placed his palm over the hurt area and glared at Opal.

"Should have kept your minions here, Crane," Eugene said, laughing.

Willard pointed to retort, but a shriek came from outside the door. "Fire!"

Willard stopped and turned to face the screams.

Another nurse's voice. "Fire on the fourth floor! It's spreading fast."

A whimper came from Willard, and he turned back to Eugene. "How? We sequestered all your conspirators."

"Where's the administrator?" someone yelled in the hall. "Can someone find him?"

Willard howled again and began to breathe in panicked gasps. "I don't know what to do." He squeaked before tearing from the room.

The orderly entered at the same time, but Willard pushed him aside. The orderly bumped against the jamb, hesitated, but followed his boss through the crowd swarming in the corridor.

Opal watched the chaotic scene unfold and turned to Eugene to gauge his reaction.

He remained calm and stared into Opal's eyes. "You're free. It's time to run."

Not accepting his advice, Opal approached her father and removed the leather belts from his wrists. "I'm certainly not going to let you burn to death."

"That's a good girl." Eugene massaged his wrists and started for the door.

The front entrance to the Kirkbride was wide open, with patients and staff fleeing in droves, none paying regard to one another. Eugene and Opal glanced at each other and followed.

Emerging into the light, Eugene caught sight of a swell of people standing together, staring at the southern side of the clock tower. Eugene and Opal walked far enough into the yard they could turn and see the ensuing carnage as well. Flames shot skyward from windows near the clock tower, followed by more fiery tendrils that spread away from the spire and spread toward Ward T.

"This is terrible!" Opal blurted as she watched the fire bead into black puffs of smoke.

"I'll say." Eugene watched as ash debris began too snow around them. "It looks as if I owe someone ten dollars."

A LETTER OF ADMITTANCE

The door would not budge, not even for Brittany. She did not feel the force she exerted to close it could have been enough to permanently lodge the door. She slammed it in anger, and all the jaded spirits that never left the Kirkbride were holding it in place. The handle would rotate, but no amount of tugging would purge its position.

Neil was able to enter the room in the future, but he had remarked that no one else could enter but him. Brittany was unsure now if he would still be able to enter, but she knew for sure that she could not. There had always been an impenetrable wall of time between them, but now there was a literal door in the way, too.

A groan uttered from deep within the Kirkbride. It had been active in the night's journey to Ward C, like it was trying to deliver a message in a form of communication unknown to her. An explanation to her about the door? *A warning that she was no longer welcome? Instructions on where or how to best access her unrequited love?* Not that the latter was especially important to her now.

Between the unrelenting heat of the day, and the soothing cool of sleepless nights, Brittany had resolved to let Neil go. There was nothing left to do but deliver a message and facilitate a final goodbye.

The Dodge minivan was still dead. The head gasket had blown and wasn't worth the time or money to hoist back to Weston. It was sold for salvage and sent to be cubed. Brittany, in her resentment, declined to remove the few personal items still inside. Several empty SoBe bottles and candy wrappers lined the passenger floorboard. A ketchup-stained tank top balled in the hatch. A photo sleeve in the back seat containing pictures of the thing that haunted her most.

Officer Prince, Brittany's ride for the night, inquired about the black eye.

"Got my clock cleaned at a party in Morgantown. Drunk, angry, blonde bitch. I ripped her ponytail clean out and got a few licks in at least." As soon as she said it, Brittany remembered she was talking to an on-duty police officer. "Oops. I …"

"Relax, Morgantown is well outside my jurisdiction," Prince assured.

Brittany wished then that she had sat up front. She now felt like a criminal in the back, made more uncomfortable by Sticky Vicky's increased adherence from the daytime heat. The tar-like viscosity remained when she returned to the Crown Victoria later, mindlessly entering the back seat and realizing her error once she closed the latchless door.

"That really was a short trip." Officer Prince turned and noticed a despondent Brittany through the divider.

"Something wrong?"

Brittany sighed. "I didn't mean to sit back here, and doors I can't open seem to be taunting me tonight."

Exiting the vehicle without speaking, the officer opened the door to allow Brittany a chance to take the passenger seat.

"I've got one more trip in me—to this place," Brittany said after she closed the door. She craned her neck and stared up at the unlit clock tower.

"Did you ever find anything?" Officer Prince had seen the pictures, presumably still had the copies in his possession, but never posed the question about Brittany's hunts until now.

Brittany wanted to tell him the whole story, but hearing it practiced in her mind came across as madness. She feared Prince would have her committed to the new psychiatric hospital; her madness acquired via osmosis from the old facility. She could only imagine his reaction when she revealed she had found her ghost. *It was a future ghost, on whom she developed an infatuation, but was now brokenhearted, bordering on jaded. No, not on the border—deep within jade country, a sovereign member expatriated from any feelings of affection.* But even that wasn't true. She simply needed the feeling's power to move beyond Neil and the Kirkbride.

"I saw a lot of strange things," she ultimately answered. "I heard a lot of strange things. I felt a lot of strange feelings. The madness in there is contagious. If a person didn't come in there with it, they were sure to catch it before they left."

Officer Prince scratched his shorn, black hair. "I never want to go in there again. The things we saw during paintball … I still lose sleep over it. I won't keep my service pistol in the bedroom now because I almost shot off my toes one night before realizing it was their shadow. I've been shot at, tackled murderers, saw bodies mangled in horrible traffic accidents. I haven't lost sleep over any of that. Two weekends playing in that hospital and I could feel the horrors inflicted on the people who were there when it was open. People were lobotomized, electrocuted, drugged, and none of it did a lick of good in the end. All that's left in that place is resentment and a faceless entity trying to manifest into some kind of vengeance."

"Did you see more than you told me?" Brittany wondered. Sticky Vicky was approaching McGary Avenue.

"No. There was just a feeling of dread that came over me that never left. If I look at the building from any distance, a churning in my gut starts. Like a thousand screaming voices are rattling my insides to mush."

"They are looking for justice," Brittany said with a glum tone. "But they're looking for something they won't find."

In front of the Loughry residence, Brittany exited the car but stood with the door still open.

"I'm definitely going to school in January. When I'm gone, can you keep watch on my mom? Maybe make an extra trip down this road on your patrols?"

Prince made a motion like he was tipping an invisible cap. "You got it, ma'am."

It was a promise the police officer couldn't keep.

Three days later, Stuart Prince arrived in plainclothes on Brittany's doorstep. The investigation into the illegal paintball game had concluded, and he was being removed from the Weston police force.

"Where will you go?" Brittany's heart sunk for him even as she tried to avoid attachment.

"Private security most likely—that's where most failed police cadets end up. Same for disgraced officers, I suppose. I have family down in the Beckley area and they're always looking for people to watch over the coal equipment."

Brittany subdued the urge to give Stuart a sympathy hug. She had not seen him out of uniform before, and his chiseled form was clear under a tight black shirt. Brittany felt any embrace would be a selfish one, so she remained with arms at her sides in the threshold.

"I'm sorry. Did you think this would happen?"

"Not really. Punishing officers is inconsistent, and we were optimistic we would get off. And some did, but I'm not important enough, I guess."

Brittany wanted to say it was because the transgression was against state property rather than someone's liberty. That seemed to be the difference to her, and it as a harsh opinion regardless.

"Anyway," Mr. Prince concluded, "I'm going out of town to visit my parents, and I may not see you again before your final hospital trip. Think you can make it on your own?"

"Oh, yeah. It wouldn't be my first time."

*****

TUESDAY, SEPTEMBER 28, 1999

THE departed sun took the heat with it as daylight retracted and tipped to colder days. The forest-carpeted mountains presented their bouquet of colors, early in the window between beauty and death.

310

It was beyond the blackened hour that Brittany Loughry came down from her hillside home on McGary Avenue and into the municipal blocks of Weston.

Traveling from point A to point B in West Virginia was never a straight line, but there were fewer distractions than in the summer. School was back in session, and the town's youth remained indoors after hours. The glass-pack pickups that rattled windows as they bellowed down tight streets had either moved on to another town or reserved their disruptions for the weekend. The cicadas were gone for another seventeen years, their mating days done. It was up to the next generation to start the cycle anew.

The chilly air carried the aroma of fresh wood smoke from chimney tops and the decay of vegetation from forest bottoms. The orchestra of olfactory delights achieved a crescendo in Brittany's nose. Autumn smells long carried the nostalgia of season's past, but that couldn't be her focus tonight. She had a letter to deliver.

Past the convenience store where no kids loitered, and the curfew siren blared in vain. There was no one around to give it consideration, no one to usher home. Even if there had been, the police department was now tremendously understaffed.

Beyond the historic district, across the bridge, past the town offices, Brittany found herself on the last leg of the journey when she stopped at the front gate of Weston Hospital. There was a new security guard whom she did not recognize.

"Is Chad Witschky working tonight?" Brittany asked a much taller watchman. He had such a long torso his tucked white shirt seemed to pucker like stretch marks.

"Mr. Witschky is no longer employed by the state," the guard said with a firm voice. "You can try him at home."

Brittany stared at the Kirkbride before returning her focus to the guard. "Um. Thank you."

She pivoted and returned to Second Street, unwilling to let her trek be for nothing. In her jeans pocket a capped Exacto knife jabbed her thigh with every step, reminding her of the agony it took to reach this point. She had one more task to accomplish before putting the hospital behind her for good.

Past the Kirkbride and turning at the EMS building, Brittany tucked out of sight between the perpendicular wards, to the faulty door. *Turn the latch, pull upward, and voila!* The key to the back door still worked.

Brittany took a breath and tilted her head upward. She didn't expect the moon to be in view, but there it was, knuckling through clouds on its way to the western sky. A waxing gibbous, she recalled. A cycle within a cycle, like a clock, like a mating cicada, like time itself. Yet, as she stared deep into the craters of the incomplete face, she saw no one staring back. Neil was not there, John Rocco was not there, Sam Beck was not there. Brittany became awash with nihilism and embraced the angst of the moment. *I would have made a fine subject for a rock song.*

She entered building and made short work of finding the fire exit stairs to the third floor. Brittany knew the way so well now that a flashlight was not required.

In ward C, she tried to enter Room 668. The knob turned, but the door did not give. Brittany uncapped the knife and went to work digging into the door's damaged lacquer. If Neil came around again, he would see the note, etched above the escutcheon housing the knob and keyhole. Maybe Neil had always seen it but never knew the meaning. Or maybe it would not appear until it became relevant to their association. Brittany was ignorant to the paradox. Either way, she took a step back and shined a small light on her handiwork.

BL NOTE IN CLOCK TOWER FOR NH

Now she had vandalized the Kirkbride as well, with her initials no less. There would be no law enforcement to blackmail this time. Breaking and entering, trespassing on government property, defacing government property would be the charges levied by the state. The town could not save her.

It wouldn't matter. She only had one last thing to accomplish.

TO NEIL HUTCHENCE
SEPTEMBER 25, 1999

*I hope you find this letter, and I hope this letter finds you well.
Over our time speaking, I had developed strong feelings for you. I know you had
feelings, too, and I wished there had been some way we could have made our
relationship official without inconveniencing either of our lives. This couldn't be
the case, and now life seems to be pulling us in separate directions for good …*

On the fourth floor, Brittany located the entrance to the clock
tower. It was the standard metal door found at the end of every ward in the
building, but this one had an extra lap of rust.

A padlock kept the door secure, but the latch was so deteriorated
the screws sat askew in their sockets and were all removed with a simple
pluck.

Brittany found the door led to another flight of oak stairs, a
continuation of, the staircase linking all floors. The steps appeared damaged
by water and felt more brittle with every step. Brittany held to the edge,
grasping the rail in case the wood gave way.

Beyond the landing was a small floor patched with metal plates.
The floor had become so damaged by water on this level, the cheap fix
appeared to be placing metal sheets over it and praying the whole level
didn't give at once.

*… I did go to see you in Morgantown, and I believe I even found you, but a
woman stopped me and beat me into a pulp. I still have a black eye from the
fight. I view her as time correcting itself. I was trying to change the course of
your life, but the keepers of time sent an agent to stop me.*

The ladder to the clock tower presented a new challenge. It did not
appear water damaged, but rungs were charred, like a fire had once lapped
at the hardwood. Brittany inspected the floor again and realized that it
was not water damaged at all beyond the steps. Between the metal panels,
ash and cindered chips of wood pushed upward, marking obsidian stains
against the metal.

Brittany trod carefully, first testing the ladder's integrity by
standing on the bottom rung and bouncing. The blackened bar held better
than most of the floor leading to it. Deciding to trust the climb, Brittany

placed the flashlight in her mouth and ascended to the clockwork. Brittany kept to the edge of the ladder to shift weight away from the center of the rungs, worried she would happen upon an especially weak step. A few near the center of the ladder fit the description, and Brittany was thankful she had planned her path.

At the top, levers and pulleys created a simple network, with each clock mechanism independent of the other. Now, it made sense why each kept different accounts of time. Brittany focused on the front-facing clock. From the gears, a shaft reached out to the clock face, which turned the hands. Brittany put the light on the apparatus. She inspected it, but didn't understand how it all worked.

The clock face's glass was frosted white, obscuring any hopes of seeing Weston from a unique vantage. Brittany huffed in disappointment and returned her light beam to the central array of gears. She placed the folded note on a flat surface above a crank, further securing it in a gap where the surface met the frame holding the gearbox together. So long as water and wind did not penetrate the chamber, it would be secure for the required decades.

I want to thank you for those times in the Kirkbride. I can't stop wondering how we were able to make such a meaningful connection. It's not a thing you hear about in ghost stories. I'll never forget it. Finding you when I did helped me cope with the loss of my father and helped me to see my mother in a new light. I hope the fire didn't kill her. I hope you had been lying to me all along …

Starting down the ladder, it became difficult for Brittany to locate her footing with the flashlight still orally held. The lack of visibility caused her to drift to the center rungs without realizing it. She only recognized the error when the last bar she had put her weight on snapped. With only a loose grip on the sturdier rungs, Brittany slipped from the ladder and fell. She landed foot-first on the metal panels, which managed to hold against the impact.

An automatic shriek left her body as something in her left leg gave way. The flashlight tumbled across the level and came to rest along the stone wall.

*I want to meet with you a final time to say goodbye. On October 5 of our years.
You can tell me all the other bad things that will happen in the next century,
and I will do my best to stop them.*

Brittany rose and tried to dust the ash off her hands, only smearing
it further and staining her jeans in the process.

She put weight on her ankle. It hurt, but not in an excruciating way.
Pitching it forward or backward further increased the pain, but Brittany
decided she could at least get off the hospital property with the injury. She
would have to move slowly down the water-damaged stairs either way,
but her pace did not improve once she reached the fourth floor. Brittany
started to the northern wing. As she passed beyond the midsection of the
Kirkbride, she thought she heard Neil's voice cry out in agony. Following
the noise was the scuffing of shoes across the gritty floor.

Staring back toward the section, Brittany could not see the source
of the activity. She waited for the tumultuous sounds to cease, then went
about her way.

An emergency exit at the end of the last ward would bring her
outside. She was ready to be free of it. Even in colder weather, the stale air
of the hospital felt smothering. She was eager for a fresh breath. She was
eager to receive everything fresh.

Brittany Loughry never went inside the Kirkbride again.
Sometimes, when she caught a whiff of early spring grass clippings or the
first wood smoke of fall, a certain nostalgia would fill her. If Brittany found
herself in Weston, she would take her scuffed black JanSport backpack and
go down to a park bench along the West Fork River. She sat and stared at
the Kirkbride as the seasons changed, thinking about her ghost. Brittany
wondered how much different the future could have been if she had
managed to change it.

*Twenty years from now, you may try to seek me out. I would like to humbly
request that you don't. Don't look for me. I will do my best to move on and have
a life without you. If I find, on Halloween of 2019, that I am alone, depressed,
or looking to reclaim some lost glory of my youth, I will meet you in the*

cemetery. It won't even be any kind of a wait for you. If I don't show, it means I've moved on, and I want you treat me like I was always a ghost.

A PLEA OF INSANITY

A long groan churned from the curfew siren as Neil exited the closing coffee shop. A live folk band kept the establishment open beyond normal hours of operation, and Neil took the occasion to snag the rare late-night matcha. The green tea concoction would give him the boost needed to get through the ghost hunt. He hoped to spend extra time mending hardships with Brittany.

In truth, he was desperate for reconciliation but wouldn't allow himself the reality. He had bruised their distant relationship, and there was no other way for them to communicate the issue in a timely way. He cared for her, and there were truths he needed to dispense for them to have any kind of future together, friendship or otherwise.

More than anything, he needed to make sure she would be safe and healthy in 2019. Doing so would be a delicate balancing act.

The guides for the night were familiar: Brady, Audrey, Manager Greg, Jason, Lauren, and Dustin. Craig was the lone employee unacquainted with Neil. Craig was a creature who appeared to revel in the lore of the unknown. Middle-aged but with a youthful energy, his mix of long blonde and gray hair caught the air as he pivoted about in excitement. He sectioned off groups with the fervor of a true bird of the night. The guide offered to lend out advanced tools of the paranormal investigator: dowsing rods, PKE meters, and spirit boxes. Neil had needed no such implements to speak to the other side. All he needed was access to Room 668. Neil did have some time to kill, so he decided to stick out the first part of his group's tour before paying Brittany a visit.

The tour started in reverse order, with Greg taking the reins of Neil's group. It began with the hardwood-clad north wing of the fourth floor and transitioned to the much creepier southern side. A single circular fan at the end of the hall spun with the outside breeze, flapping the peeling green plaster sagging along the upper walls. The outline of asbestos tiles left white tracings of the positions where they had once been set.

Neil yawned at the stories. The floor had once been doctor's quarters before overcrowding forced the administration to repurpose the space into a long-term drunk tank. Neil once saw a man take ill on the ward, complaining of the overpowering aroma of spiced rum. The story about alcoholic patients had just concluded, and Neil assumed much of the man's distress tied to the power of suggestion.

The third floor tour also started in reverse order, with the violent male ward beginning first. Bedpost murder, Big Gus, random scratches, it was all the same as usual. Neil made a cursory pass through the area most resembling a prison. It was a tight-quartered hall with barred doors that had been once kept under lock and key. The brown tile lining the passage was only seen elsewhere in the electroshock rooms.

Neil's revelations about the real people behind these stories had cast the dark halls in a different light. He strode through the area with more respect for those that had been there, even the ones who had acted out of violence due to their mental afflictions.

In the violent female ward, the stories rang similar. It was the most dangerous ward, with the now-removed engraving of LOVE in the tile. Flower art on plaster masqueraded as wallpaper. Seclusion rooms where the sizzle from electroshock therapy could still be here. A peculiar door that slammed and would never open again.

Room 668 was the finale this time. Neil fidgeted as the story concluded, and the group began to cross the center of the Kirkbride to the southern wards of the third floor.

Neil slowed to the back of the group and disappeared into the first open door of Ward C, waiting for the group to slam the heavy door on the other side. With the area clear, he could now enter the room undetected.

But the door to 668 still would not open. Like a childproofed exit, the door had no give. The knob gave the impression that it was turning, but the latch did not receive the message.

Neil tugged harder, growing more frantic. "No. No. No!" No amount of shimmying, tugging, jerking, or pushing was even loosening the door's position. "Fuck!" Neil resigned himself and slid to his knees. He thought he could reverse engineer the mechanism to work again. Flashing his phone light at the gap between plate and jamb revealed the space was so tight that only a sliver of the metal latch plate was visible.

As the inspection continued, Neil noticed something he had not seen above the doorknob housing: an etching. Small and hard to read with the peel of the varnish, it read *"BL NOTE IN CLOCK TOWER FOR NH."*

The clock tower … The one place where no one had access. It was also the place unspoiled by humanity in the intervening decades. Neil didn't weigh the pros and cons for long before rushing to the center hallway. He climbed the final flights of stairs to the top floor. Craig, the manager, had been standing in the entryway to the auditorium and saw a blur of a person race up the stairs.

"Hey!" Craig called, but Neil didn't slow, too tunnel-visioned on his destination to fool with the living.

At the top of the step was the access door to the clock tower. The door was recently replaced with a sturdier steel barrier that stymied Neil the same as door 668. The padlock further reinforced the security.

Frothing with his desire to reach the clock tower, Neil placed what fingertips would fit between the door and hinge and pried. With all his might, grunting, and groaning with the effort until the tips of his fingernails bent. He swallowed the pain and doubled his effort.

Craig reached the level and immediately spotted Neil. "You need to stop, brother. That is a restricted area."

"I can't. There is a letter for me up there!"

"No one has been up there for years." Craig took a walkie-talkie from his belt. "I have a situation at the top of the fourth floor. Anyone who is available, please come assist."

"I didn't give her details about 9/11!" Neil raged as he continued, staring at the ceiling as if he expected someone to come down and open the door from the inside.

"I didn't get to tell her about the Boston Marathon. I didn't get to tell her about Oklahoma City. Pearl Harbor! The cancer! Mister President!"

Craig placed a firm hand on Neil's shoulder, and the sudden feeling jerked Neil into fighting mode. He swung around and struck Craig across the temple. The guide's long locks whipped across his face as he spun and dropped to the ground. At the same moment, three guides reached the floor from two entry points and swarmed Neil.

Undeterred, Neil returned to the door and started pawing at it in vain. "Don't take me away! This is my last chance to talk to her!" The force of men laid a squirming Neil on his chest and pressed his arms against his back.

"There's a note for me up there. Brady! Tell them I need to get up there!"

Out of the corner of his eye, Neil could see his friend.

"I don't know what you're talking about." *A swift betrayal.*

"There are more items to uncover up there. She's waiting for me! I need to know!"

"You can't go up there," an unidentified voice said. "It's not safe."

Another said, "Fire and water damage messed up the floors."

"I don't need a history lesson. I need to save her!"

"Someone call the Weston Police," Craig ordered. "Ping the sheriff if no one is available."

The four men lifted Neil by the arms and legs and carried him to the nearby projector room overlooking the auditorium. He could be better monitored and guarded in the smaller space.

"No!" Neil screamed and whimpered as he watched the door to the clock tower shrink from him. There could be no reconciliation now.

321

A CHRONIC AFFLICTION

Henrietta, Saturday, July 8, 1905

What was the life that Henrietta wanted? For many years she thought marriage, education, and justice were enough. But spouses die, and education uncoupled from opportunity is a solitary pleasure. She had education and a marriage, plus a child and happiness, but those slipped away in one mishap after another. Still, her horrors inside the hospital were trivial compared to the pain and madness that swirled around her. Injustice was everywhere. It was a stationary hurricane where she remained in the center, catching minor gales from the true maelstrom raging beyond the eye.

Henrietta arrived back at the West Virginia Hospital for the Insane in the early afternoon. There was one injustice she knew she could solve and only needed the responsible party to show a final time.

The wrought iron gate felt more welcoming from the outside, but Henrietta hesitated to pass through again. She only opted to do so when a carriage at the front door unloaded a wailing woman. Believing it to be the individual who had lost the twins, Henrietta moved forward fifty feet onto the property and shouted at the entrance.

"Hey, doctor!"

A shorter man in a suit and bowler hat took notice and gave an uncertain wave. He turned to another man who appeared to be an attendant and said a few words before starting his approach.

Henrietta, knowing it wasn't Doctor Koenig, placed the fire axe inside her dress and held it secure to her waist with her left hand. The approaching man didn't seem to notice any of this, but he kept distance regardless, holding position about ten feet from the disheveled woman.

"Can I help you, miss?" the man asked. He was a clean-shaven doctor in his midthirties who looked as if he were just arriving at the hospital himself. "Are you a patient here?"

"I am here to see Doctor Koenig. Is he available?"

The man shook his head. "No. I arrived only a few hours ago from the Spencer Hospital. My name is Doctor Samuel Timmons."

Henrietta eased her grip on the axe. "Good to meet you, Doctor Timmons."

"Could I … help you with something?" Doctor Timmons offered. He took notice of the placement of her left hand.

Henrietta wasn't sure how to proceed, so she cobbled together a patchwork of facts and mistruths. "I was a patient under his care, and I wanted to thank him for his time in healing me. Maybe catch up a bit. Could I inquire as to where he has gone?"

"I'm sorry, what is your name?"

She tightened the axe handle again. "Henrietta. Henrietta Tidewater, or I suppose Henrietta Cedric was the name given here." She answered with truth because no other name came to mind, and hesitation on such a simple question would register suspicion.

Doctor Timmons's chin tightened. "Ah. I have actually heard your name. Could you come and speak with our administrator? He certainly has some things to say to you."

"This is all the more comfortable I am about entering the property again. I'm sure you'll understand once you spend any kind of time inside."

"Oh, trust me. Are you familiar with Spencer State Hospital? It is this asylum's twin, except it takes in many more unwanted children. The place was not pleasant." The doctor shuddered. "At least this place has fewer children."

Henrietta's mind trailed to Wallace. "I'm sorry. I have to leave."

"Please! Please speak with the administrator," Doctor Timmons pleaded. "I can assure you that you are not in trouble. Quite the opposite."

The statement tickled a hopeful place in Henrietta's heart. "Okay. But send him out here. I will wait, but not long."

Doctor Timmons pursed his lips and agreed. "Okay. I would tell you myself, but I am not permitted to do so. Just a moment. He's not usually here on Saturdays, but you caught us in the right moment."

The doctor trotted back to the Kirkbride. Once he was out of sight, Henrietta removed the fire axe and tucked it under a bush to the left of the front gate. She made short work of covering it with fresh topsoil. At least she had a hidden weapon within the grounds in case she ended up incarcerated again.

After a few minutes, another suited man emerged from the Kirkbride. He descended the stone stairs, passed the fountain, and proceeded toward her. He clutched a small leather bag with both hands.

"Miss Cedric," the man greeted, stopping in the same place Doctor Timmons had.

"I prefer Miss Tidewater."

"Very well, Miss Tidewater. I am this facility's administrator, Doctor Reginald Pifer. I understand you were a patient until recently."

The man was stocky with a mustache that only extended as far as his lips. It was black and did not curl. There was warmth in his voice, but Henrietta had felt heat blow from a cold-hearted mouth before. She chose to approach the conversation with blunt honesty.

"I was a patient until yesterday."

"Your doctor was Felix Koenig?"

"Yes."

"And you had a child, too. Where is your child?"

"At a fire station in Clarksburg."

"Who is the father of your child?"

"Doctor Felix Koenig."

The administrator paused to nod, lick his lips, and offer an appreciative smile. "I value your honesty."

Henrietta sighed. She pressed her hands together and bowed in thanks.

"Were you aware of the doctor's other affairs?"

The question caught Henrietta breathless. "What?"

"Yeah … He fathered several illegitimate children besides yours. We have been investigating him for weeks. It wasn't until he tried to fire his nursing staff that they admitted to me the depths of his ethical abandonment. We fired him yesterday morning during the fire drill."

"Wasn't he shot yesterday morning?" Henrietta felt like the event had happened days ago.

Administrator Pifer scratched his head. "I know nothing about that. There were gunshots reported in the garden yesterday, but I was never told about a shooting."

"Curious," Henrietta said. She tried to reconstruct the series of events, but what the administrator said next interrupted her thoughts.

"It seems we owe you an apology. We tried to review your records but could not find them. It appears Doctor Koenig kept them on his person. It did not take us long to deduce that he was holding you without appropriate treatment. All considerations indicate the Doctor Koenig should have discharged you from our care a month after you first arrived. Had your affair started then?"

A heavy sigh came from Henrietta. "It had."

Administrator Pifer released a disappointed grunt. "That cad. Well, he is gone. Relieved of duties. I expect he'll be heading overseas, back to Germany. He left everything behind except his medical bag."

"Good riddance," Henrietta felt energy course through her as she said it. "This last year has been a nightmare."

"Again, you have my sincerest apologies." Administrator Pifer released a hand from the bag and made a motion like he was brushing away the past. "This bag contains your personal effects from your first day. We will also give you a ride to your destination of choice."

Henrietta finally felt comfortable in moving deeper onto the hospital grounds. She accepted the bag from Administrator Pifer and was quick to name her destination.

*****

Changing clothes in the lavatory in the main Kirkbride hallway, Henrietta finally began to feel like herself for the first time in more than a year. The feeling lasted until it became clear her clothes were not washed since she entered the asylum. The musty smell of old sweat lingered in the air during the carriage ride from Weston to Clarksburg. It was a journey that contained many hairpin roads, but the way was level, and the trip took half the time with horsepower.

Henrietta exited the cart with the leather bag and what few tokens remained inside. The carriage rested in front of the fire department while Henrietta rounded the building to first check if Wallace was still in the cart. He was not in the place she had left him, though it had been more than twelve hours since they had parted.

She rattled the back door of the fire hall after finding the front door locked.

"Hello!" she called. "Is anyone in there?"

A man unlatched the door. He was a tall man with black, greasy hair, and not dressed like someone on a fire brigade. "Yes. Can I help you?" he said with some urgency.

"I left a child in the cart here this morning for adoption but have changed my mind. Do you have him?"

The man furrowed his brow and clicked his tongue. "No." He thought a beat more before disappearing into the hall.

"Hey, Paul! Did you see a kid out back this morning?"

"No!" Paul answered, followed by something muffled.

"No, I mean a baby."

"Oh!" Paul responded, but Henrietta could not hear a reply.

The first firefighter returned to the threshold. "Me and Paul have been here since this morning, and we never saw a child."

Acid bubbled into the back of Henrietta's throat. "Has anyone else been here?"

The man shook his head. "We've been the only ones here today, and I've not seen anyone. Hey, Paul …"

Henrietta did not stay to listen. She jogged down to the water's edge to see if Wallace somehow rolled from the cart into the river. The bank seemed clear and the water calm and meandering. The mud showed no disturbance downhill from the cart.

The firefighter exited the building and met Henrietta at the top of the bank. "Neither of us have seen anyone around today. Are you sure you're in the right place?"

Henrietta tried to stay calm, but something had gone awry if Wallace had vanished. Anyone could have passed and abducted him. And since he was already abandoned at a fire department, it wasn't like a kidnapping. He was up for grabs in the most literal sense.

"Maybe I'm wrong," Henrietta conceded, even though she knew it wasn't true.

The firefighter nodded. "Well, let me know if you can't find him. We can get the sheriff on the case if he's still missing."

"Thank you," Henrietta said while climbing to the top of the bank. The firefighter nodded and returned indoors.

Henrietta checked the cart more closely, hoping for a nook or cranny he had wedged inside. The crates were tightly placed, but it was worth a final look.

On closer inspection, Henrietta noticed something she couldn't see from a distance. In the place on the cart where Wallace had been resting was a small token. An Indian Head Penny, which wouldn't have looked unusual except for the hole drilled into the top. The chain that had been thread through it now missing. Her heirloom had returned to her, but at what cost?

She pocketed it and every fiber of her existence raged. Doctor Koenig had not been mortally wounded. It was clear now he rebounded quick enough to pursue her along the West Fork, staying at distance enough to stalk his prey. He could have pounced while she slept, but he waited for some greater opportunity to wound her. Abandoning Wallace was the moment.

Henrietta's emotions frothed to the surface, and she released a raucous scream before charging to the front of the firehouse. The hospital's carriage had already departed, leaving Henrietta stranded.

Felix had a twelve-hour lead to abscond to whatever part of the world he wished. It was unlikely he would bring Wallace along. As a doctor, he knew how to heal, but also knew the most efficient way to kill. There was no reason to believe he would show the baby mercy. Wallace had been his burden and his downfall. If revenge was the doctor's desire, it was already too late to act.

*****

Henrietta Tidewater died on the doorstep of the Civil Rights Movement. She was in Washington DC on May 15, 1954, awaiting the Supreme Court decision on Brown v. the Board of Education of Topeka.

She spent the evening at the home of Macie Slyke, an acquaintance from their time lobbying for a woman's right to vote during the suffrage movement.

She passed in her sleep. Even in her 70s, she continued to fight for the American Creed. *Liberty and Justice for All*, though she never saw the battle won. Henrietta did leave knowing progress was moving in the right direction, and that was enough. It had to be.

She never located Wallace. She would check the local orphanages in the hopes the doctor abandoned him someplace safe, but the canvass never yielded a result. In the end, Henrietta decided Wallace had been either reclaimed by the Appalachian Mountains or taken to be a citizen of parts unknown under the tutelage of his father. She gave up searching after a year and decided mourning would be more productive. Often, in the years that followed, she would see an age-appropriate child smile, think it could be him, but have no way to say or ask. The occurrence happened often, and there could only be one Wallace in the world. She would need to go by more than looks alone.

Henrietta attempted to return to her father's home, but he had disowned her. A family member who had spent a year in a mental hospital was too great of a wound to inflict on the Tidewater name. He would not accept her again. When he died two years later, she was living homeless on the streets of Wheeling, in West Virginia's northern panhandle.

Henrietta's sisters sold their family house and hired an investigator to track down Henrietta. The man found her after a month. Days later, a courier from Western Union delivered her share of the inheritance. Henrietta's sisters never had the desire to visit themselves, but they cared enough to not cut her out of the family fortune. It was a lesser sum than her sisters got, Henrietta suspected, but any money was better than what she had.

She used the funds to rent an apartment in Wheeling, which she furnished with a bed, a couch, and a houseplant. Henrietta also bought a bicycle that had to be assembled from a diagram.

Finally on her feet, Henrietta found work at a laundromat. The regular work irritated her incision scars over time. She saved a few months' wages and sought a doctor to inspect. She wanted a female doctor, and it happened that Wheeling boasted the first licensed female physician in West Virginia.

Her name was Doctor Harriet B. Jones. Besides being a female doctor, she also shared a connection to the West Virginia Hospital for the Insane. In the late 1880s, Doctor Jones had been the hospital's assistant administrator.

Henrietta discovered this during casual conversation following her first appointment. The story poured from Henrietta. She told the doctor of her affair, captivity, and escape. Doctor Jones felt for her story, and the two formed a close bond.

Doctor Jones gave Henrietta a job as an office clerk but assigned her a special task unrelated to her duties. Doctor Jones was also a leader in the state's suffragette movement. She tasked Henrietta with producing literature for their campaigns to allow women to vote.

Doctor Jones compensated Henrietta well, and years of saving allowed her to trade her bicycle for a used Everitt 30. It was a clunker, but

Henrietta endured until she could replace it with a new yellow Ford pickup truck. No assembly required.

Doctor Jones eventually closed her practice and began traveling around West Virginia, giving lectures on women's hygiene. She also advocated the right for women to attend colleges and hold elected office. Jones herself became an elected official in 1924, four years after West Virginia ratified a woman's right to vote.

It was the final push for women's voting rights in 1920 that galvanized Henrietta's resolve to fight for equal rights for all. She arrived at the West Virginia Capitol in Charleston to watch the vote. She entered the Capitol Building, but an officer stopped her from entering the Senate chambers. Henrietta was denied because of the color of her skin.

With the battle won for a woman's right to vote, it became clear the war remained. Equal rights for each color and creed would come next. Despite every inch gained toward bringing equality to the world, Henrietta was still a long way from justice.

A CURATIVE EFFECT

There were many competing stories on who had the idea to sound the dinner bell after the fire erupted on the fourth floor of the Weston State Hospital. The most popular tale claimed it was the Weston Fire Chief Gary Marsh. However, the fire spread so fast he would not have arrived on scene soon enough to save anyone. Some say it was a fast-thinking nurse, some say a patient ran down from the fourth floor with the idea—what all the legends agree on is whoever was responsible for sounding the dinner bell saved every life in the hospital that day. The patients—most unaware of the blaze—calmly filed into the dining hall expecting a meal. The staff ushered patients from the overstuffed cafeteria to the front lawn once they had accounted for everyone.

"There goes a tower!" someone yelled near Eugene. He looked to see one of the minor cupolas collapse into the building. Wails reverberated across the yard as a slow boom thundered from the southern wing.

It had been an hour and four more fire companies joined the fight. Eugene wasn't close enough to the action to read the names, but he guessed every nearby town had their firefighting unit sent to quell the inferno.

Opal stood with her father for several minutes and watched the fire spread. Eugene insisted she depart for greener pastures. In the mayhem of the scene, she had managed to find civilian clothing and change in the center of campus. So much commotion transpired, not a single person noticed the woman stripping to nothing. It was not unusual as other evacuees were also in various stages of undress.

Once she was ready, they exchanged a final embrace before Opal Lee Spangold disappeared into the world. First to her Grandfather Bloom's home, then to New York City with whatever provisions and money the elder Bloom was willing to provide.

The Clarksburg Fire Department arrived around noon with the largest detachment of men yet. Their combined efforts with the other volunteer departments extinguished the fire by midafternoon.

Eugene watched the dark plumes brush across the sky as he stood on the campus of Weston State Hospital. He felt proud of it. A vagrant from drunkard stock committed a deed men and women came from all around to witness. Many more traveled from great distances to observe the spectacle. Black clouds signaled to them that something had died out here. The demons within died and were being purged from the building, purged from Weston, and purged from the world. The patients were being freed. It was now their opportunity to run if they chose to do so. Some took the chance, most did not, but it was enough, it had to be.

Flip emerged from the crowd and stood next to Eugene as the last of the flames were being dealt with. He appeared timid, disconnected from the scene.

"Your kin neglected to show again?" Eugene asked.

Flip shook his head. "No. I expect they're around here somewhere now though. If not, I'll just go off on my own. It seems I won't have a room here to go back to tonight."

"Same for me, lad. I was on the first floor at the time. Do you know who ignited the blaze?"

"I've been asking around. It wasn't a Ward T boy. Heard it was a boy by the name of Forrest. He was probably one of the guys from Ward V. Some of them go trading stories with our guys."

Eugene grunted. "Just as well. That sawbuck was still in the room when the blaze started. The fire redeemed it, rather than the fire starter."

"I hear they're going to move people from the upper wards to the 4-H Camp at Jackson's Mill," Flip said. He had been in downtown Weston when he saw the dark clouds of smoke and doubled back to do his own investigation.

As the havoc concluded, Eugene smiled wide at the scene. "It's been a good day, Flip. I reconciled with my daughter and managed to secure her release. Many thanks again for delivering the letter to my father-in-law. It did the trick."

Flip nodded with gratification.

Eugene grunted before continuing. "My plan to burn down the hospital was successful. Those demons we purged from our lives will make the president happy."

"What president?" Flip asked. "You've been mentioning this president you need to help, but it doesn't make sense. Roosevelt never contacted you."

"It wasn't Roosevelt. I told you, boy, it was a crippled fellow I did not recognize. A younger fellow. It was a garbled message, but he identified himself as such through the mental link we had. Yes, sir, I don't know what more you want me to say on the matter."

Flip was not interested in hearing it anyway. "Listen, I'm going to take off. If they don't have their paperwork handy, the nurses are going to think I still belong here and rope me inside. Listen, I will be fine. Don't worry about me."

Eugene smiled at the boy. "You feel pretty good?"

Flip returned the smile and stuck out his hand. "Yeah. I'd say I feel great."

Eugene reciprocated, and the two shook hands.

"Attaboy," Eugene congratulated.

Flip nodded and backed into the shuffling mass of people.

Eugene never saw Flip again. At age sixteen, Vernon Philip Clevenger died by hanging near his uncle's old home. An apple tree at the edge of a grove overlooked the homestead. Flip decided the way the sun cast twilight in orange was the perfect final thing to witness. Eugene never received the news. Archibald Jonah Clump learned of Flip's death shortly after being discharged from the rebuilt wing of the hospital. The news so distraught Archibald, he honored the boy by choosing Vernon Jonah Sampson as his new name when he kept his resolve to start life fresh. The former cult follower fell back on the core of his faith and became a Methodist pastor. He acted as a chaplain during World War II and later started his own church. He kept a respectable congregation until retirement.

As the fire was being extinguished, staff not watching the patients went to work recruiting drivers. Firemen managing the influx of town traffic drafted onlookers and passersby into service. Three hundred patients needed to take temporary residence at the State 4-H Camp. The camp sat five miles north of Weston at the childhood home of Confederate General Stonewall Jackson.

The coordination of the impromptu fleet happened without the authorization or help of Administrator Willard C. Crane. Upon seeing the breadth of the fire, he fled the scene, never to return. Willard wanted to show that he could be fiscally responsible with managing the hospital, as it would translate to a campaign talking point when his bid for governor began in earnest. In making cuts to the hospital's funding, eliminating insurance to the building appeared to be the simplest way to save. With the building aflame, Willard C. Crane knew the revelations to come would tank any advancement of his political career. His campaign for governor never came to fruition, and his name altogether vanished from the hospital's history. Willard C. Crane reappeared months later as a bank manager in rural Virginia, gradually moving further south until he retired to Miami in 1955. A heart attack felled him in 1958. Despite his exile, his body returned to Lewis County. Family buried him in a Weston cemetery among the stones of the city elite.

A convoy of passenger vehicles entered the skinny path that extended from the front gate to the front door. As they formed rows on the lawn, Eugene scouted out a pickup truck in which he could travel in the bed. He wanted the sensation of the wind blowing across his face as they traveled. After some time observing, he spotted a yellow Ford pickup passing through the wrought iron gate. Eugene made a quick wave to the woman driving and climbed over the side. He sat and smiled, tapping his knees while he watched patients make similar maneuvers. Nurses had to course correct the loading to extract patients not meant to go to the camp.

"What ward were you in?" a nurse asked Eugene, placing a palm on his shoulder to get his attention.

"Ward T."

She tapped him in approval. "Excellent. You're good to go."

Two more men entered the bed soon after staff cleared them. A third, Sergeant Rust, sat in the cabin with the patient woman as she waited in the idling truck.

With no insurance and funding nonexistent in the depression era, President Franklin Delano Roosevelt released funding in the amount of $150,000 to rebuild the damaged portions of the hospital.

What president? Eugene snorted, echoing Flip's last words. He smiled, but asking the question to himself now begged an answer.

There was no president confined to a wheelchair. What did I see? What did I hear to make me think I was speaking to some unknown president? Everything Eugene experienced had to be the cocktail of booze and insomnia that expedited into mania by the stress of homelessness. The vision was so vivid and had felt so much like real orders, Eugene never bothered to quiz himself on whether it was real or not.

The bright yellow truck shifted into gear and began rolling along the path. It made a loop around the fountain before crawling toward the front gate. Eugene's back was to the smoldering hospital now and he could feel its gravity pull away from him.

When the truck reached the edge of the property, Eugene felt his mania vanish. *The deal with the president didn't exist because there was no young, crippled president. The man in question couldn't have been older than thirty, well below the age restriction for a US President. No, I had the hospital burned down because that's what I wanted. I only needed to invent a reason to do so.*

The reason was gone now, and the sudden sensation stunned Eugene. It was gone and his smile faded.

What have I done? He didn't know then if everyone had escaped. *How many did I kill with my objective? How many could I have killed? Was this the same recklessness that killed Ethel LeeAnn?* The mania inside Eugene was gone and the vacuum filled with grief and regret. His wife was dead, his daughter was gone, and his ancestral home was seized and resold to a better steward.

He had failed to defeat the demons because he neglected to realize he operated as a demon himself. In the decompression, Eugene began to weep, and the aggressive breeze of the pickup's movement chilled the tears on his face.

Eugene James David Spangold remained at the Weston Hospital the rest of his life. He could prove his delusional manias had gone away but considered his grief and regrets a different kind of mania. When he was finally considered well enough to leave, Eugene chose to stay. The ward had become his family, and it was now the only kinship that persisted.

Tuberculosis took him while he was asleep on March 15, 1951, at age sixty-four. With no family around to claim him, Eugene's burial was in the Weston Hospital Cemetery located on the back edge of the property. A small stone cube noted his location and included chiseled documentation of his name, birth, and death. When the cemetery became too full, workers stacked a plot mate a foot above Eugene's casket.

When the hospital closed, state crews found it easier to mow the fields if they removed the cemetery markers. Many of the tombstones became lost, tucked away in state storage, or recycled into do-it-yourself projects around the greater Weston area. Eugene's marker found its way into the masonry of a retaining wall on McGary Avenue.

Caskets in the cemetery contained a bottle with the deceased's name, birth date, and death date, but only exhumations could confirm their true location.

No one would ever know Eugene's exact resting place. Like all the other members of the field, officials and historians could only grimace and say it's a mystery—certain only in the knowledge Eugene is still out there, somewhere.

PART III

THE MOMENTS

33

CYGNUS CANTUS

Brittany was physically impaired, Neil mentally. Neither made the October fifth meeting that Brittany commissioned in her letter. Brittany left the hospital with a hairline fracture in her femur. By the time she stumbled back to the convenience store, her leg became too aggravated to continue. A phone call to a slumbering Glenda brought her the rest of the way home. In the morning, she went to a different hospital. At Stonewall Jackson Memorial, Brittany's leg was set in a cast, along with wrapping for a mild ankle sprain. It mended over several weeks, but Brittany would carry a limp with her for the rest of her life.

Neil left the asylum in handcuffs by the Lewis County Sheriff's Department, who had responded in place of the overburdened city police. The sheriff himself took Neil's unhinged statement and, in the morning, sent him for evaluation at a different hospital. At William R. Sharpe, Jr. Psychiatric Hospital, sibling to the Trans-Allegheny Lunatic Asylum, Staff kept close watch on Neil's behavior. The doctors cleared him after a week, but Neil earned a ban from the Trans-Allegheny Lunatic Asylum for the rest of his life.

He felt the sheriff had gone easy on him. He would likely face assault charges later, but the sheriff could have pursued so much more. When Neil told the unfiltered story of ghost love and loss to Sheriff Prince, the officer presented body language and facial cues like he somehow believed the story. There was a particular quiver in the Sheriff's brow when he mentioned Brittany Loughry by name. Whatever the motivation, Sheriff Stuart Prince never revealed what he thought under the surface, only sharing, "This place has a way of confusing the mind."

As Neil spent time at Sharpe, his mind quieted, and the therapists who visited were years overdue. Neil did not speak of the paranormal. Taking the fifth in preference over taking the first. He knew better. When asked, he only responded to the events in the asylum by parroting the Sheriff's comment of "That place has a way of confusing the mind."

What Neil did speak on was his brother's death. The sudden loss in a 2016 car accident spiraled him into an unacknowledged depression, and numbed his interest in all things, including wife and daughters. His divorce became another topic altogether. Speaking the words, sending them into the bright universe to sparkle, fade, and evaporate under the ultraviolet, released Neil from their curse. By the third day at the psychiatric facility, Neil felt for the first time in years that he could truly move forward with his life.

The rooms were simple and only lacked posters and static-laden televisions to resemble an old dorm room. Dull edges cornered everything in the room, and most furniture comprised of hard plastics. Neil passed the time there lying on the bed, thinking about the path that brought him to this destination. A divorce, a statue of Jesus, a kind offer from a friend, and shoddy light pole thirty-five at the park in Benson, Minnesota.

That damn light kept cropping up in his mind. It was a thousand miles away, but never too distant from his idle thoughts. *Why did a lifetime-guaranteed light keep burning out? There had to be a loose connection further down the pole causing a short.* It was the only thing he never tried before leaving the time zone.

On the final day in the hospital, Neil received a surprise visit from Demetry, who first peeked his head through the door, followed by a full strut.

"Hutch, you're taking your job a little too seriously."

An automatic smile crossed Neil's face but soon retreated. He sat up in his bed and shifted against the wall so he could lay upright.

"I would argue I wasn't taking it seriously enough. I got banned from the asylum."

"You were chasing ghosts a little too hard." Demetry retrieved a chair and sat near the bed.

Neil sighed. "That's a pretty accurate description of what happened. I'm sorry."

Demetry clasped his hands and stared at the floor for a long beat. "Remember Eddie Swan? The missing person we used to hunt for in rural Minnesota?"

Neil nodded.

Demetry took a long swallow before speaking. "They found his remains. It was a couple of weeks ago."

Neil's mouth opened to ask what and how, but Demetry had already pressed forward with the answer.

"It appears he was swallowed by a sinkhole at the edge of marshland. A farmer carving a new irrigation channel pulled up his remains with an excavator."

Neil felt a sudden sadness. Searching for Eddie Swan used to be an activity he and his Minnesota friends would do for fun. *For sport.*

"My point is, sometimes when you go chasing ghosts, you catch them," Demetry concluded. "Then what?"

There was no happy end to the game, Neil realized. *Cheap thrills were all the excursions had to offer—a disrespectful display in the end. If we had uncovered a body, it would have been traumatizing for everyone involved.*

Quiet permeated the room. Neil tapped the concrete wall with a knuckle to test his ears.

"What about Silkie's body?" Neil wondered. "The ghost we were chasing here?"

Demetry huffed. "We'll never find her. There are too many bodies in that field, and not enough markers."

Neil shifted forward. "I'm planning to go out there next month. I'll have to sneak in, but that's fine. I can check it out for you if you want."

Demetry dismissed with a chuckle. "You don't want to go out there."

"Seriously, what has you so shook about that cemetery?" Neil was beginning to feel annoyance at the secrecy. Whether he was being coy or cryptic was beyond the point.

Another laugh came from Demetry, but this one felt directed at himself, like a joke only he knew and delighted at the punchline. "If you're really going to go to that cemetery, I'll let you see for yourself. I don't want to spoil the surprise."

"Or you could just tell me. Isn't this still part of the research?"

"It's not. I think I have everything I need here anyway. Miguel went to Alabama and found a treasure trove of information. One of the victims, Henry Keyes, still has family trying to solve his murder. They have been collecting evidence for the better part of a century and are allowing us to access their resources. They believed the shooter to be a white man, though, so it may end up debunking our work after it is all said and done."

"Or you could end up debunking theirs," Neil countered.

Demetry slapped the bed. "Like all murder investigations, it would help immensely if we could find the murder weapon. Did you have any more luck in your search before your incident?"

The half hour in the basement was the closest Neil had come to finding the weapon. He had already reported that account to Demetry, with Neil noting the impossibility of searching every piece of luggage. Especially since they were items Neil didn't have official permission to canvass. What Neil didn't say was that he felt uncomfortable rummaging through the personal belongings of people stripped of everything.

"I don't think it's there." Neil masked his true feelings. "If Silkie had been transferred from other mental hospitals, it was likely confiscated at one of those. Plus, the other two hospitals are still in operation. They may have a better account of patient inventory."

In truth, Neil had already considered the possibility, but his reason for withholding the information at the time was to avoid giving up his weekly ritual in Weston.

"Miguel had already been to Milledgeville. No dice there," Demetry said. "Plus, he's getting off the project. He met a lady in the cities and wants to quit running long-distance errands."

"I can pick up the slack," Neil offered with subdued enthusiasm. "I think I'm ready to move on from here. Mentally, at least."

"Are you going to come back to Minnesota?"

Smacking his lips, Neil looked to the shaded window, to the light trying to seep between the blinds. He was only just starting to think with clarity about the future.

"No. Not yet. I think I'm going to stay in Weston. But now I can do other things, visit other places. Weston can be my … homebase."

Demetry nodded. "Very good." He started for the door, but one more item was troubling Neil and he needed someone to talk to about it.

"Let me ask you something?"

Demetry paused. "Uh, sure. Anything."

"Sorry. It's a weird hypothetical."

"Out with it. You have piqued my interest." Demetry laughed.

"Let's say you had the opportunity to change the past and you didn't. Would you feel guilty about it?"

The question took Demetry by surprise. He grunted but then went to work gnawing on the answer. He pursed his lips and stared at the ceiling for a long time.

"I think if one were to alter the course of history from the future, we would never know whether we succeeded. The things we changed would cease to exist, and you'd cease to remember they existed. It's all … paradoxical."

"Sure." Neil didn't find satisfaction in the idea and slumped.

In contrast, Demetry felt wholly satisfied with his explanation and expanded further. "It's like the baby Hitler paradox. Would you kill baby Hitler knowing it would prevent the Holocaust? World War II? You would save millions of lives by killing that precious baby, but could you do it?"

Neil shrugged. "I guess if you're right and I wouldn't remember it later anyway."

"Exactly!" Demetry walked to the door and placed his hand on the knob. "It's best not to think about the baby Hitler you didn't kill. You may have killed dozens of baby Hitlers, but you would never know if you did. And you know what? That's good enough." He laughed. "For the sake of your mental wellbeing, it has to be."

Did I change anything at all? Neil wondered, wishing he could pose the question to Demetry. He would decide in the coming days that it doesn't matter. *Every day is new. Every day will proceed the same. I have no reason to look at it any differently than anyone else.*

34

OCCULTUM NOTA

There were many ways to get into the Trans-Allegheny Lunatic Asylum's back acres. Forests encircled the vast field, further fortified by the soft grade of Appalachian hills. Neil considered an access point from the back of Sharpe Hospital, which shared proximity to the old hospital grounds. To keep his bearings, he instead chose to trespass near the EMS building situated behind the Kirkbride and keep along the tree line to avoid detection.

If it had been any other Thursday, Neil's forbidden expedition would not have registered on anyone's radar. Since it was Halloween, the potential for shenanigans put law enforcement on high alert.

The date didn't seem ill-chosen at the time, though a certain degree of trespassing was always required for either party. Visitors weren't allowed into this parcel without express permission, and someone banned from the compound altogether was especially unwelcome.

As Neil moved beyond the rolling hills where anyone could spot him at a distance, he finally arrived at a large stone sign. Below an engraving of praying hands was a marker announcing the cemetery.

DEDICATED TO THE MEMORY OF PATIENTS OF WESTON STATE HOSPITAL WHO DIED AND WERE BURIED HERE DURING THE YEARS OF 1901 TO 1938. DEDICATED OCTOBER 1999

The sign would have been recently erected in Brittany's time, twenty years prior.

Demetry wouldn't speak on the horrors of the cemetery, first ignoring the topic, then playful in denying Neil the truth. Neil decided it was unimportant if Demetry was withholding the information for sport. The truth was now in front of him, and at first, didn't seem all bad. The realization sunk further as Neil looked around at the empty field. In a cemetery of tens of thousands, only a handful of stone markers remained. Seven gray, rectangular stones protruded from long stalks of grass browning with the season. There were few who were identifiable. Silkie Le Margaux was still out there somewhere, Eugene JD Spangold was likely out there, too. There was no way to know or relabel their final resting places without exhuming the thousands.

Neil took respite on a hillside. He removed a folded newspaper clipping before sitting on what could have been a grave. He stared in the direction of the retreating sun and considered weeping as he did in the basement of the asylum. The desecration and abandonment of the graves felt like a war crime. The old keepers may as well have dug a trench and kept note of every individual cast into the crevasse. Instead, a city of dead resided beneath the soil, with acknowledgments for an infinitesimal few.

He rubbed the folded newspaper between his thumb and forefinger, felt the grain of the paper and grease of the ink, and considered the news within. Neil didn't want to unfold it again, but it was the reason he snuck into the cemetery. He had to face the reality.

Brittany wasn't coming. It was an impossibility now that he clasped her obituary, clipped from *The Weston Democrat* three weeks earlier. With

no other way to stall, Neil unfolded the clipping and brought himself to
read it once more.

*Brittany Jean (Loughry) Beck of Hundred departed this life on Oct. 3, 2019,
surrounded by family and friends at her home.
She was born June 10, 1981, in Weston and was the daughter of Glenda
(Davis) Loughry of Weston, and the late John Rocco Loughry.
She was a 1999 graduate of Lewis County High School and a
2004 graduate of West Virginia University. She worked as an office manager
for Brightbar Insurance in Hundred for the past seven years. She loved music
from the 1990s and was an amateur historian, collecting what information she
could about centennial buildings around the Wetzel County countryside.
On Sept. 10, 2008, Brittany married Samuel Beck, who survives.
Brittany is also survived by a daughter, Cora Kellen Beck and a son,
Joel Samuel Beck, both of Hundred.
Visitation and funeral services were held on Oct. 6 at Tennant Funeral Home
in Hundred with the Rev. Michael Wilcox officiating. Burial was at the family
plot at the Weston Masonic Cemetery in Weston.*

It was ovarian cancer. Neil had known about it for months, first
revealed in his inaugural visit with Glenda. It looked treatable at the time,
but by late mid-August the disease had spread and metastasized, leaving
little hope for recovery.

A thin shard of moon stabbed the evening sky. Neil remembered
what he had told Brittany about the moon, about its indifference to the
passage of time. He looked to it as one way to see her again, but the
gesture was as empty as when he'd said it. The moon had seen them both
at different times of their life but did not care to introduce them. In the
end, Neil was never able to see her living, but she had lived, and that was
enough. It had to be.

Neil did visit her in death. He went to her visitation, followed by
the funeral the next day. He offered condolences to her husband, Sam, and
greeted their young children, too distraught to notice the world around
them.

Once the pleasantries concluded, Neil took a moment to speak
with Brittany's empty shell.

"I'm sorry. I could never decide if I should be meddling within the fabric of your life." Neil glanced over his shoulder at her children. "If we had acted too soon, it would have been their lives. But I acted too late, and it was yours."

He placed his hand on hers. It was cold. It was always cold, but now the static had gone from her, and the scent of cucumber melon was his. She was less of a ghost now than she had been in life.

A gust rushed through the cemetery hills, and Neil let the news clipping slip from his fingers. It tumbled in the breeze until a draft sent it upward and blended with the distance before vanishing.

Guilt filled him again. The feeling he had too much control over the knowledge critical to Brittany's life. He gave her what she needed to be happy, what she needed for her kids to exist, but used the rest so he could feel loved. Small wonder that it all unraveled. His selfish deeds were slim to go unpunished, and this time there was a victim to suffer the consequences.

Wood smoke wafted in from somewhere. It would have had to travel a great distance for it to reach Neil's nostrils in the middle of the asylum cemetery grounds.

Forlorn and feeling aimless, Neil left the plots assigned to patients of the early twentieth century and moved to another empty field. The area was part of the cemetery also, but there were even fewer stones. In fact, only a single marble stone stood out among the country weeds.

The death year was 1887. Neil rubbed his eyes to adjust his pupils to the fading day and began to orate the name.

"JASPER WYATT. FIRST ... SERGEANT. COMPANY E. JUNE 7, 1822. NOVEMBER 2, 1887."

Neil had heard that name before. *But where?* He had never laid eyes on this stone before.

Stone? Stone!

Neil retrieved his phone and pulled up his notes that he had taken from Demetry the month before.

A curse upon the stone of Jasper Wyatt. 851 steps from the arrow will tell you more.

Silkie was still in the cemetery somewhere, but her last act in life was to ensure her presence was still felt among the living. The Haint had one last score to settle and placed a curse upon the veteran's marker. The warning frightened the staff with superstition, ensuring the gravestone would go untouched so future generations could solve her puzzle.

Rubbing his hands over the marker and searching for an indentation that could give him the next step, he finally arrived at a groove on the top of the stone. Straining his eyes to make visual confirmation of the weathered mark revealed a small arrow pointing south.

"Eight hundred and fifty-one steps." Neil hastily counted out his numbers. The sun had disappeared, and twilight would only hold the night at bay for a short window. At step 720, Neil reached the edge of the cemetery. 798 sent him up a steep bank. Finally, at 851, a rock ledge formed a wall, but several small boulders lined its base.

The bottom stone was quick to pry loose. Neil gave it a hard push so it would roll to the bottom of the incline. The lodestone gave way to the others, and four more clomped and thudded to the forest floor below. Behind the small boulders was a natural limestone enclosure. Inside was moss, the skeletal remains of a small rodent, and a large leather case.

Though the nook seemed damp, it appeared as if it was never touched by rain. The case, though peppered with moss and organic particles, still managed to keep its durability against the long wait to discovery.

Sliding the vessel toward him, Neil inspected it, marveled at its existence, and was careful as he loosened the buckles. They cracked like the luggage in the Kirkbride basement, but with much more resistance in the hinges.

Inside was a rifle with an octagonal barrel, a modified spyglass with a custom attachment, an ink bottle with contents hardened and dry, a quill, several sheets of parchment. The last of the contents removed was a two-page letter folded and tucked inside a leather sleeve.

Neil replaced the items, shut the case, and latched it as best he could. One buckle refused to return to its closed position, but it was snug enough. He cradled the case under his arms and slid down the grade on his butt, kicking the displaced boulders as he reached level ground.

The light was almost gone, but Neil no longer cared. He was confident he could find his way out of the field. The light from Weston, and the curfew horn that blew at ten o'clock, would guide his way home.

*****

WHEN the school year after Brittany's passing ended, Sam Beck relocated back to Weston so his parents could assist in rearing their children. Eight years later, Sam remarried.

Jennifer Aldridge—the former Jennifer Sampson—had also lost her spouse. The small-town dating pool was only so big for widows and widowers at midlife, but the pair found compatibility through their commiseration.

Two years back in his hometown, Sam became the superintendent for Lewis County Schools. The first hires under his tenure were for a math teacher, two school bus drivers, and a maintenance technician. Neil Hutchence was a perfect fit for the latter position. Refreshed in his career, Neil went five years without missing a single day. He always kept the automatic doors in working order and never came across a light fixture malfunction he couldn't diagnose.

At age fourteen, Meriwether Hutchence could not stand to live with her mother any longer. Emboldened by adolescence, she demanded a transfer to her father's home in West Virginia.

The high school freshman caught the eye of an older boy, and the two began dating in the fall of 2031. On their one month anniversary, Meri invited the boy to meet her father, though Neil was already well-known to the students.

It was then Neil was formally introduced to Joel Samuel Beck.

"My father is the superintendent," he proclaimed, hoping his pedigree would be enough to grant Meri's father's approval.

"I know who he is, and believe it or not, I know who you are," Neil said, while in a trance of reminiscing.

"Is that good or bad?" the boy asked.

Looking down at Joel and holding his unwavering smile, Neil suppressed tears as he answered the boy. "Let's just say that I approve."

The relationship held through high school, and the real tests came in college, but the couple overcame the obstacles and married in the summer of 2040. After a decade of fertility roadblocks, they had their first child, Joel Samuel Beck, Jr. He was followed two years later by a daughter, Darrah.

At age forty-nine, Neil also remarried. Colleen Kimball was a kinder, gentler alternative to Caitlyn's gruff approach to kinship. He did not meet her at a party following a fistfight. They met by chance in a church basement while standing in line at a Fat Tuesday pancake supper.

Their marriage extended into their sixties, but cancer waged its perpetual villainy and invaded Colleen's pancreas at age sixty-two.

The nest was empty once more. Retirement came. Meri married and started a life with Joel in Morgantown. Solitude, once so peaceful to Neil, now screamed. There was no remedy to it now. In the calls, where Neil expected to hear the despair of knowing the end of life was far closer than the beginning, Neil instead heard other voices. The genealogical work he had been doing in his spare time, which had become the only time he had, was calling. Those unnamed thousands underground were calling. The time finally came to answer.

From the confession note of Silkie Le Margaux. Republished in "The Haint: Chasing the Vengeful Ghost of a Dixieland Serial Killer" by Demetry Oswald, published by Lohr Books.

My dearest Henrietta,
I hope you are able to find this note. It requires you to find my diary first. Then, the tombstone that would lead you to my weapon case. I chose Jasper Wyatt because he was the only tombstone I found who I knew to be a Union officer. Paper is scarce, so onto my confession. Leeman Saint Cloud was my one and only kill. The other murders were carried out with this weapon, but not by me. My adoptive brother, Ignace O'Neil, my beloved, whom I simply refer to as "I," carried out the killings. My role was to operate as his spotter. I would go into the area and mark three vertical blue lines so he would know where to look. If the situation involved crowds, I would paint blue marks on my face to better coordinate with him in the ground. Remember I told you he was weak on seeing color? Light blue he could spot at a great distance. Leeman was difficult for him because of the nearness of the ocean and the surrounding blue buildings. I took the shot for him. I never lied about his role, but I let the language mask the truth. Regardless, I would accept the crime for my brother every time.
He does not appreciate pain like I do.
For every hospital I visited, Ignace would follow. He would camp in the forested area around the hospital grounds, of which all the hospitals seem to have. Two times before he found his way into killing doctors or inmates who gave me trouble. Fearing I had something to do with the deaths but not proving it, the doctors would move me elsewhere. On this last occasion, we used the gun and decided to run. No one was watching the field closely that morning. We made it a town over and began walking along the main road when a carriage struck Ignace in a blind turn. My beloved Ignace was trampled by one horse and then crushed under the wheels of the carriage. I fled back into the forest as Ignace remained lifeless. Lost and heartbroken, I chose to return to the hospital. I will hide the gun in this rock wall in hopes you will find it and these answers. I will leave clues in hopes you find these as a free woman. If your days are young, and you wish to use this weapon to free me, I would consider it an adequate repayment. We can be free together. I shall despair until I see you again.

YOURS,
SILKIE

35

MEMENTO VIVERE

Ten days before Neil Joel Hutchence died of a stroke, his heart made the first grand attempt. The attack landed Neil in the hospital, striking a blow to his body, but leaving his spirit and resolve intact.

At age ninety-one, he took his progression to the finish line in stride. There was no other direction to go, and he was not resistant to the destination. Arrangements were already settled through the Griffith Funeral Home—a newer mortuary reclaimed the building that had once been Floyd Funeral Home. The coffee establishment, whose matcha Neil fancied, relocated a half-century ago. The businesses that followed were a revolving door. It had been a thrift shop, a dentist's office, the Lewis County Republican Headquarters in 2056, and a second coffee shop before it returned as a mortuary.

Though he had reclaimed his life as a West Virginian, his burial location remained Murdock, Minnesota. The statue of Christ he was so enthralled by could watch over his remains. His ghost could walk from there, hopefully meeting the real guy on the other side of eternity.

Thinking back to his grim days in rural Minnesota, he knew fifty-one years of borrowed time was plenty. It was a debt he could neither pay back, nor pay forward, but he wanted to pay something with the time. The answer came from the place which excised him from his darkest days. The Trans-Allegheny Lunatic Asylum saved him. He may have been the last living person to achieve wellness within the wrought iron gates.

He owed it something now. He felt an obligation to those who came before that did not find a cure. By his number, more than twenty-thousand people had died there during its century and a half of operation, but the cemeteries had only markers remaining for fewer than ten individuals.

Upon his retirement, Neil began researching the genealogy of the individuals buried there. Tracing back as far as he could, and forward, if applicable. The family trees often told tragic accounts, incestuous tales, or no stories at all. If he could trace a family into the present day, he would attempt to contact the living kin. Most found the phone call strange, or off-putting. The revelation you had a family member in a mental asylum still held the same stigma as it did then. He found as many elated by the news, who expressed appreciation of Neil's efforts.

In fifty years, Neil had traced the family trees of almost three thousand patients who died there. It was an entire forest of kinship, but there was still one tree he could not find.

Henrietta was the woman whom Silkie had addressed in her letters and allusions to her escaping by Silkie and Ignace's hand. But who was she? There was no record of a Henrietta ever being a patient at the asylum during the period Silkie had been there. The mystery confounded him, and he fell in and out of obsession with the hunt for decades.

The week prior brought a new lead, and Neil made a special trip to Morgantown to pore over historic Monongalia County court records. Among the weathered slips, he discovered a file for 1904 public health concerns. Among the names was a Henrietta Cedric, ordered to the then-named West Virginia Hospital for the Insane in April of 1904. She was to be examined for a period of one month, according to the document.

It was still not the time frame, but it was close. No other Henrietta had presented herself over the years, which made it, by default the best lead Neil had uncovered. Before leaving the courthouse, Neil cross-referenced the data with historical marriage records. He discovered Cedric was a married name. Her maiden name, Tidewater, contained more substance, and more data presented itself in online searches.

Henrietta died in 1954. Her obituary listed her parents as Henry and Malkia, and sisters Pauline and Jules. It was a clue from Jules that had led him to Morgantown in the first place. A 1905 article in Virginia Beach's *Ledger Star* quoted teacher of the year, Jules Kinny, as saying her only regret was that "baby sister, Henrietta, had been committed to a West Virginia crazy house." The unabridged quote added how she felt responsible for her sister's predicament.

From the discovery, the mystery began to unravel. Detail after detail poured out about this mystery woman until his heart became too stressed by the revelations, and gave pause.

In the hospital two days later, Neil would fill in the final puzzle piece—one that would make all his years of research worthwhile. It was like the lost souls he reconnected all at once leaped from their desecrated graves, thanked him, embraced him, and handed him the reward for his decades of labor.

The next day, he called for his family. Daughter, Madeline, came from Minneapolis. She never reconciled with her father in any meaningful way but did not hesitate to visit, rending him a long goodbye just in case it was the last. Madeline's three children and two grandchildren never knew him and did not feel the need to start at the end. She came and went before his younger daughter's family had a chance to breach the doors of the medical center.

Meriwether Beck arrived with her husband Joel and teen daughter, Darrah. The three embraced before Neil addressed the absence.

"Where is JJ?"

Joel Samuel Beck, Jr. was an adventurous sort who possessed a keen intellect. Always on the move, always chatting unceasingly with every person he met. He oozed charisma, an anomaly within the family genetics.

But every introverted family needed the royal extrovert to speak for them, and he was more than welcome to do so on their behalf.

"He's downstairs with his girlfriend, Vivian," Meri said, pronouncing Vivian with derision. "He broke his leg in a ski accident last week. Getting around hasn't been easy."

"Oh, my," Neil said. "How does he get up those steps at WVU?"

"There are other ways to get around, PawPaw," Darrah grumped without looking up from her watch.

"Be respectful," Meri snapped. "Your PawPaw brought us here so we could hear his last words."

"Not last words, per se," Neil corrected. "Perhaps last words with any kind of significance. I found what I have been looking for all these years."

"Henrietta?" Meri asked. She said it like the answer was obvious.

Soon after, the door squealed open, and a young woman wheeled in a man of similar age.

"PawPaw, how are you?" JJ asked immediately.

"Better than you by the looks of it," Neil quipped.

JJ presented his typical heavy smile. "You know how it is with skiing. Those damn trees get in the way sometimes."

The infectious smile reminded Neil of Demetry. His award-winning friend went on to write four more books. His successes followed him for all his days, and he left the world in peace at the age of eighty-three. Neil missed everything about his friend, but it was the glowing smile he pined for the most. He was sad the smile had gone from the world, but it warmed him to know many more were taking its place.

He remembered their last conversation. The good friend had begun teaching himself Latin for a new book he was writing about the rebirth of dead tongues. Demetry ribbed Neil for his halfhearted attempts at learning Latin in his younger years and spoke correction to a phrase he had remembered Neil mention.

"'Memento mori.' You were all morose in talking about 'remember you die,' but did you know that's not the whole phrase? It's 'memento mori, memento vivere.'"

In a reversal, Neil became inspired when he heard the full translation. *Remember you die, so remember to live.*

"I'm glad you're all right, PawPaw," JJ said as Vivian parked him in a free corner of the room. "I'd be bummed if I could no longer see your smiling face."

Neil scoffed. "Enjoy it while you can. Time does all the work and only asks for you to thrive, then depreciate. I've never really did either in the correct order, but time must have forgiven me if I got this far. But my days of thriving are done. Being this old is kinda like being shot in the heart with an arrow. You know your end is near, and you can remove the arrow and let it kill you faster or keep it in place and die a slower death. A slow death allows for goodbyes, and that's my choice. Not just yet, though."

Neil retrieved a folder he had squirreled along the edge of the hospital bed. He removed the scribblings of his most recent research and placed them on his lap. "For Henrietta."

Meriwether perked. "You've been chasing her for some time."

Neil tapped his nose. "And I caught her."

Sharing her father's passion, Meri pulled a chair close to Neil and read over his shoulder.

"Henrietta is Henrietta Tidewater. She was born in 1885 near Morgantown. Died in Washington, DC, sixty-nine years later. For whatever reason, she never had a record at the asylum, but I managed to link her to a doctor there. Doctor Felix Koenig. This fella was a scoundrel. He fathered several children at the asylum, of which Henrietta's son was one."

Neil sat down a sheet containing a photocopy of Henrietta's obituary and his notes, illegible to anyone else. He retrieved two more photocopied papers from the pile.

"Her obituary mentions a son, a long-lost Wallace, whose fate is unclear. I uncovered a birth record for a Wallace Tidewater by mother, Henrietta. If I had found this paper first, it would have saved me decades of grief, but it was filed under Wallace's name, and I wasn't aware of the Tidewater name at the time. No father was listed on the certificate, but "—he shuffled papers—"included with a warrant for Koenig's arrest was an extensive complaint laying out his breach of ethics. Wallace Tidewater is listed as one of his illegitimate children, although this appears to be based on witness accounts rather than Henrietta's own statements. It is unclear where she is during this period. Regardless, Felix Koenig fled the country, and the warrant was never served."

Neil retrieved another paper. "I tracked him to England, where he became a spy shortly after World War I began. German soldiers shot him on August 24, 1916, while he was trying to cross into the country from France. Medics took him back to England, where he died from gangrene two weeks later." Neil lowered his stack. "He left behind a diary, which is a practice I wish still occurred. Such rich information comes from these accounts."

"Do you want to rest, Dad?" Meri asked.

"No, no. We're getting to the good stuff."

Neil grabbed a yellow note. "I didn't think I would get it this fast, but an archivist at the Imperial War Museum sent me scans of the contents. They had the whole diary digitized and on file. According to Felix's account, Henrietta fled the asylum with Wallace and abandoned him at a fire station in Clarksburg. The doctor had followed her and recovered the boy. He planned to take him to England, but the baby cried nonstop, and he was suffering from a gunshot wound to the shoulder. How he got shot is not entirely clear. I hope our friend, The Haint, had something to do with it, but I digress. The doctor left Wallace on a random doorstep with a note listing the baby's name as Henry King."

Neil switched to handwritten information scrawled on notebook paper. "Now this is where the doctor's account leaves us. It's unclear how long the boy stayed at this home, or if the resident passed him to someone else right away, but a year later, the Henry King name turns up in adoption records at a Morgantown orphanage. Fredrick and Estella McNelly adopt him and raise him in Bridgeport, not too terribly far away from where he was originally abandoned."

"Who were the McNellys?" Meri asked. The rest of the room also seemed lost.

Neil chuckled. "You should know. You married into them. Henry McNelly married Margaret Mason, and they had four children. Among them was Susan McNelly, who married a young man by the name of Rocco Loughry."

The room was beginning to make the connection, and a collective lightbulb illuminated.

Neil lowered his remaining papers and rushed to a conclusion. "They had three children, among them was John Rocco Loughry, who married Glenda Davis."

Neil looked to Meri's husband, Joel Sr., who always remained silent in rooms at capacity. Neil's eyes became wet as he looked at his son-in-law.

"They had a single daughter, Brittany Jean Loughry. Your mother."

The room fell silent in awe of the detective work and the revelation that the basis for their family was a woman, a child of slaves, barely overcoming the odds of psychiatric captivity 166 years earlier.

"Henrietta Tidewater," JJ repeated the name. "We should do something to honor her."

"Absolutely," Joel, Sr. agreed with several nods around him. "She is the whole base for one pillar of our family. She should never have been forgotten."

It pleased Neil to hear their response, and he tucked the papers back into his folder. "Now that I know her full name, I've been finding out more and more about her. Her work in the suffragette movement and her early work in civil rights. She did it all out of Wheeling."

Putting his head back against the hospital pillow, Neil remembered what Demetry said about the plight of the Black population and his prediction for their future. Henrietta was a microcosm of his idea. First in bondage, then fighting to escape, then fighting to survive, then struggling to overcome the prejudices of an unfriendly world. Now, with those battles done, a bunch of white folks stood around and agreed she had been a valuable part of society all along. *Just like he said.*

Neil felt an air of relief blow over him. "I'm glad I could be a part of this. Your family. My family. There were many days when I didn't think I wanted this, but looking at you all here today, it makes me feel like it was worth it. Not just for me, but all the connected individuals that are part of our circle."

Neil wished Brittany could have been there to see the family they produced from two different sides of time. He wished he could have warned Brittany about her illness. She could have gotten her ovaries removed before the cancer metastasized. But if he had, and she had followed through too early, Joel and Cora would not have existed. There would have been no family to see, and a different paradox to consider.

"You had the greatest role in this," JJ assured. "Without you, we would be fragments in perpetual disassembly. We needed you to complete the picture. How could we have been here at all without you?"

"Bah," Neil dismissed. "Right now? Right now, I feel like I've done a great service to humanity. Before that? I felt like less than nothing. Not worth the ink in my obituary. Not worth the epilogue in my conclusion." He took another longing look at his assembled family, and they returned the warm expression. "Some days, I simply felt like I was just the guy from the end."

THE KIRKBRIDE TRIED

IT WAS 2071

Henrietta, Eugene, Brittany, and Neil's time in the world had passed. The things they loved and the things they hated encircled their living days. But beginnings and ends were crucial only for setting the boundary of their life and understanding everything within the circle. Now, in the great thereafter, my wish was for them to finally understand the moments where they contributed most to humanity's cause.

Regarding the mechanisms behind my sentience, there was more to the science than what could be seen or understood. The cipher sat beyond sight. The key needed to decode the puzzle and reveal its secret schematic could lay the groundwork for a new scientific field. Novel science was an imperfect build with shaky walls and leaky roof; however, new details were often introduced to ensure the soundness and patch the holes. Eventually, science became steadfast and remained for all of history. Still, as solidly built as truths could be, a stray detail could crack the foundations of what we had come to know.

My clock tower was the key to how I could think and store memories. Moments bottled themselves within the limestone of the building and fermented into something more potent when later consumed by the senses of the visitor. Even dormant, the maladjusted clockwork remained the active mechanism in allowing the replays to flow unhindered. No one ever suspected it. Now, in 2071, an unintentional remedy had come.

The timekeepers went to work once the clock tower renovations were complete. After a deep cleaning, replacing the stressed timbers of the clock tower's frame, and repairing the flooring damaged by moisture and ancient fire, the moving parts were next. The machinists calibrated the gears so the three faces of the tower all finally displayed the correct hour. New instruments made sure the clocks continued to spin indefinitely and with atomic precision.

There was nothing I could do now. I would begin to lose the secret of what made me special. Perhaps it was due. The paradox between Henrietta, Eugene, Brittany, and Neil had been resolved. The relay was complete; the circuit was closed. Neil's death weeks earlier would have completed the loop. I had not heard the news of Neil officially, but something in the aether echoed regrets about not repairing light pole thirty-five.

Brittany's letter to Neil remained in the clock tower until its discovery in a heap of dust during the clock's final adjustments. The crewman opened it, read it, found it incoherent without context, and knew matching the name to a living person would be impossible. It was cast into a pile of miscellaneous debris.

Had Neil received the note late in life, I know he would have left it unread all the same. It was an item fit for Pandora; no box required.

It was not the ghosts that haunted, but the moments. I hope Neil, Brittany, Henrietta and Eugene find peace in the realm beyond my knowing. I hope they can speak directly, embrace, trade stories, and unlock the mysteries barred to them in life. It could be an everlasting reunion for the four who never knew how much they required each other. Only just discovering the tsunami that rose from the ripple of their days.

Neil's family fulfilled his burial wishes, laying him to rest in Murdock, Minnesota. It was a long trek across the country for most of the family. In fact, only one member ever visited beyond interment.

Neil and Brittany's shared grandson, Joel Samuel "JJ" Beck, Jr., would pay a visit in the summer of 2104. His stop was brief but meaningful. A gaggle of reporters flocked around him, snapped pictures, and shouted questions while he honored his grandfather. JJ ignored them. He stood in contemplation for as long as it was palpable before it was time to move to the next campaign stop.

He had a vivid memory of his grandfather's funeral. Getting around the parlor was difficult during the brief time when he was wheelchair dependent. More memorable was what happened as JJ spun the usual yarn about his ski accident. In his periphery, he swore he saw the faint apparition of a middle-aged man urinating on the floor.

These events are becoming less clear to me. My foresight to peer deep into the days was diminishing. Still, I calculated the outcome based on my knowledge of people, events, and the moments bounding them and bounding me. I choose to accept what I estimate as truth. As an entity about to lose its sentience, that was good enough. *It had to be. It must be. It will be.*

In some distant future, my clock tower may become neglected again. The rods could slip, the power could falter, or a chipped gear could throw off the account once more. When those days come, the hauntings will begin anew.

In the meantime, I rested.

REFERENCES

Gleason, E. (2015) *Lunatic: The Rise and Fall of an American Asylum*

Brake, S. (2014) *The Haunted History of the Trans-Allegheny Lunatic Asylum*

Rose, J. (2015) *Trans-Allegheny Lunatic Asylum: A Short Story*

Segrest, M. (2020) *Administrations of Lunacy: Racism and the Hauntings of American Psychiatry at the Milledgeville Asylum.* The New Press

Martin, B. (2014) *The Matteawan Asylum.* St. Lepay Publishing

Lash, C. (1999, June 20). A town sees red over police vandalism: Site of planned museum trashed beyond belief in paintball games. *Pittsburgh Post-Gazette.*

Whelan, G. & Harris, G. (1999, June 30). Paint Ball Blasts Leave Weston Hospital Interior One Messy Place. *The Weston Democrat,* E1

Izzo, Will et. al. "Jackson's Mill." *Clio: Your Guide to History. March 11, 2017.* https://theclio.com/entry/25780

B. Adler on behalf of City of Weston and Anna Cardelli. "*West Virginia & Pittsburgh Railroad Depot.*" *Clio: Your Guide to History. July 13, 2021.* https://theclio.com/tour/1774/2

MORE FROM THE AUTHOR

Heartspark
(2018) Cressen Books, LLC

Fairchance
(2019) Cressen Books, LLC

In the Country Dark
(2020) Cressen Books, LLC

Burning Without Knowing
(2022) Cressen Books, LLC

In the Morning Hour
(2024) Cressen Books, LLC

For more information on these books, visit MLMallow.com or CressenBooks.com

SPECIAL THANKS

EDITORIAL SUPPORT
Jeni Conrad
Tara Wine-Queen
Ashley Earley
JP Nutt
Joel Brigham
Derek Krissoff

CONSULTANT SUPPORT
Martha Williams
Laura Moyers Fears
Kelsea Reeves
Brad Cook

BETA & OTHER SUPPORT
Jason Smith
Sharon Martin
Jean Flanagan
John Connor
Michelle Connor